To The reunion of Love

Ariel Oliver Comparán

DEDICATION

To my son Ariel, for always being there, supporting me, emotionally and in every way, in my crazy ideas.

To my daughter Anahí, for always being that special love that embraces me every time she sees me, for also being there for me, supporting me.

To my parents, Rogelio Oliver Hernández and Ma. Elena Comparán Jaramillo, for being my example and teachers in the art of love, much of what I know, I learned from you, thank you, I love you.

To my father, God, the creative mind, to whom I owe everything, my unconditional love for you, daddy.

CAPÍTULOS

I A question of energies

He's a bastard! How could he do this to me? Ellen, a beautiful blonde with a statuesque body that didn't show her age, wiped her tears with the purple cloth napkin. Karla and Erika, her friends since childhood, listened to her attentively, Erika took her hand to comfort her.

-He's a bastard, I've given him the best years of my life and now... -the crying couldn't be contained, she sobbed and covered her face in shame, she didn't want to be seen by the other diners, the glasses with water reflected the light of the candle in the center of the table and created a romantic atmosphere, the diners at the tables around turned to look at them and commented something in low voices among themselves. A feeling of true pain was felt suspended in the air.

-But Ellen, what happened? -Karla questioned.

The crying did not allow her to speak, an enormous pain came from within her, feelings of inferiority, of not being enough, of not being attractive anymore because of her pregnancies, had her soul in their hands, and her pain was intense and true.

-She is younger than me -she said sobbing- and he has fallen in love with her, he has told me that he is in love!

-Damn it -Erika asserted- all men are the same -her comment did not relieve her friend, but it reminded her of her own experiences- you see, Carlos left without warning, only to find out later that he was already with someone younger, fortunately we did not have children, so well... -Karla made a gesture with her face, telling her to concentrate on Ellen.

-Come on friend -Karla rubbed her back trying to comfort her- this must be fixed, you two have been together for how many years?

-Seventeen, seventeen years thrown away, thrown away, as if nothing mattered, as if your children or I were not important.

-When did you find out? Do you think it can be fixed? You are a beautiful couple, surely this is temporary, -Karla tried to ease her friend's pain and give her hope.

-It may be temporary -Erika pointed out- but the man who did that to you once will do it to you again, and that cannot be forgiven.

The afternoon was cool, the summer sun was beginning to set and Ellen entered a coffee shop, stood at the counter and ordered:

-A cappuccino with lactose-free milk, please.

-Wow, a woman who knows how to take care of herself.

A man's voice took her by surprise and she turned to see the person behind her, a tall, thin and attractive young man, smiling at her with a row of very bright teeth. She felt embarrassed and just smiled, turning to the young cashier who at that moment was handing her a glass with her order prepared.

-Excuse my comment, I hope I haven't bothered you, -he said in a pleasant voice.

-No, you don't really bother me, -she replied taking her glass and turning around to face him, smiling openly, as if they both recognized each other, when in reality it was the first time they had seen each other.

-What would you like to order? -the young cashier took him out of the spell of Ellen's eyes.

- Sure - she hesitated - an American coffee, please.

Ellen had walked to a table at the corner of the place, the sight of the cars driving down the street, showed her a pleasant view, pedestrians on the sidewalk, walking without hurry, helped her to enjoy the moment.

- Excuse me - the gentleman's voice brought her out of her thoughts - I don't want to be inconvenient, but are you alone or are you waiting for someone?

- Actually, I'm alone.

- Allow me to accompany you, I'm alone too.

- Sure, sit down. - she said without hesitation.

The glances and smiles were present, the conversation flowed without stopping, they laughed about past adventures that they told each other, she charmed him with her smile, it was so natural, without posing, without trying to look good, in an impulsive movement, while she laughed, she stretched out her hand and caressed his arm, he felt an electric current run through his body and lost his smile a little, feeling disturbed, a second later, his face showed her a smile that she loved, both remained silent and stopped laughing, they could not stop looking at each other, she put the straw of her drink in her mouth and took a sip, smiling mischievously while she watched him. He told her the joke about the lame horse, and she burst out laughing that made him spit out his coffee.

-Ha, ha, ha, ha, sorry, it's what, ha, ha, ha, - she took a napkin and approached to clean his shirt.

-Don't worry, nothing is wrong -as he did so, he put his hand on hers to stop her, he felt her warm skin and her thin fingers, this caress made him feel a beautiful energy that automatically brought out a beautiful smile and his eyes searched for hers; she felt his hand on hers, and an energy ignited in such a way that it ran down her arm and reached her nipples, which began to erect, she looked at him, and their eyes met and smiled.

-Sorry, it's just that you took me by surprise and that story is great.

A year later they got married, from that summer afternoon in the cafeteria, they never separated, the desire to be together was uncontrollable and six months later he asked her to be his wife.

-I can't believe it, where did I fail? What didn't I give him? I thought everything was fine between us.

-To be honest, this also surprises us, you two looked so in love. -But my friend, it's not your fault, it's the men's thing, they just see a nice ass and they're already getting hard, they don't think, they're like animals in heat. -Erika continued expressing her pain for her past experiences.

-I'm sure that this is something temporary my friend, it will pass and he will come back to you -said Karla.

-Thank you, my friend, -she said patting her hand- it's true that Richard and I don't have as much sex as before, but I take care of myself, I exercise, I try to look good...

-But of course, you look good my friend -Erika intervened- I wish I had that little body -she ran her hands over her slightly wide hips- I tell you that it's more because they are stupid, they don't know how to appreciate what they have by their side.

-No Ellen, don't hurt yourself, it's not your fault, what Erika says is true, all men look for something more sooner or later, but it's not because of you, you've given the best you could.

-What am I going to do, I love him!

-Talk to him, give each other a second chance, but you have to be willing to truly forgive, to recognize that it was just

an adventure and that he loves you.

-Yes, but he told me that he is in love.

-Well, remember Esthela, the same thing happened to her and her husband

he left home and after six months he came back very sorry, because his relationship with that woman was over, he swore that he was very much in love and in the end, he returned home, so who knows, you have to talk to your husband and be clear. But you have to be willing to forgive. You know, Ellen, Erika, last week I met a very interesting man, and he explained things to me that I really liked. Why don't we go see him. Who knows, maybe what he tells us will help you heal your relationship.

Ellen was calmer, she had let off steam and was sitting in the chair, devastated, not wanting to fight and not knowing how to resolve this. Her mother's messages echoed in her mind: An unfaithful man will be forever, so don't get the idea that they can change, vote for him and move on.

-Well, I don't know, friend, right now I think I need all the help I can get, I don't know how to solve this.

-Let's not talk anymore - Karla looked at the waiter and when she saw him she said - young man, bring me the bill please - she took out her cell phone and dialed a number - ready friends, he's waiting for us.

Erika continued to hold her friend's hand, but she didn't say anything, the silence helped a little to heal her aching soul.

The friends left the store and got into Karla's car, they arrived at a one-lane street, with cars parked on both sides, the houses were mostly two stories, and one or two buildings up to five stories.

-This is it, let me find a parking lot.

-There, friend, there you fit - said Erika pointing to an empty space between two cars.

They got out of the vehicle and walked to a modern and luxurious building.

-Let me see the apartment number - she took her phone out of her bag, looked for the address, she was standing in front of the intercom buttons, she pressed the number 504, a bell rang, and seconds later a man's voice greeted her.

-Hello, who is it?

-Karla, Alberto, I'm Karla.

-Come in, welcome - A bell rang and the door opened.

The building was quite elegant, white ceramic floors with gray veins, they were guided to an elevator, the door opened and they got in.

-You'll see, friend, I think he can help us, I met him at a dinner, he's very nice.

The doors opened again and they went out into the hallway, apartment 504 was open and an older man was standing welcoming them. Despite his age, he was very jovial, his gray hair on the sides and black on top, gave him an interesting air, he was thin, he had a beautiful smile.

-Hello Karla, nice to see you again - She approached and gave him a kiss on the cheek.

-I want to introduce you to my friends, this is Ellen, the reason why we are here - she said this while hugging her affectionately, he stretched out his hand and shook it.

-This is Erika - he did the same and invited them in.

The apartment was quite elegant, and very bright, it was noticeable that there was a certain wealth in that house. The living room was very large, the windows showed the trees in the park, they sat in one of the armchairs, and Karla on an individual sofa. He sat on the other.

-Shall I offer you something to drink?

When everyone was with their glasses or cups in front of him, he asked.

-Did you know that sexual relations are actually the meeting of our energies?

The question took them by surprise, they did not expect that. -Well, Alberto, it's just that...

-He turned to look at Ellen and said- did you know, Ellen, that when you meet someone and you feel attracted to that person, it's actually because your body energies like each other and want to get to know each other, in order to merge? -This took her by surprise, it was as if he guessed the type of problem she was going through.

The friends turned to look at each other strangely.

-Excuse me, girls, excuse me, I'm very hasty, tell me, to what do I owe the honor of your visit?

-Alberto, it's just that... -Ellen interrupted Karla and spoke up- my husband is in love with another woman -her eyes filled with tears and they began to run down the side of her eyes.

He stood up, walked to a small table in the hallway and took a box of tissues, he passed them to Karla, she brought them to Ellen and she took one.

-I'm sorry Ellen, hearing this is difficult, how do you feel?

-Disappointed, I feel betrayed, we have been married for seventeen years, we have two children, and I never imagined something like this, I thought we had a good relationship.

-That definitely makes it hurt even more.

-Why are all men the same? -asked Erika- you are a man, can you give us an answer, right?

He thought a little about his answer and said

-Actually, these things happen because it is part of the energies.

-What do energies mean? What do energies have to do with this?

-How curious, I just started talking to you about this without knowing that you had a problem with it.

-Are you referring to the question you asked us about body energies or something like that?, said Erika.

-Yes, I was asking you if you knew that when two people meet and are attracted to each other, it's because their energies like each other and they want to get to know each other and merge.

-No - answered Ellen- I don't really know anything about that.

-Alberto explained that to us at the dinner where we met, that's why I wanted you to come and meet him.

-Thank you Karla, for coming and for bringing your friends.

Karla gave her a knowing smile.

-Getting back to our topic, let me explain a little, you have time, because this is not a simple matter and it will take time.

-No problem, my children are with my mother, so I have no problem.

-Excellent, well, our body has the ability to perceive the outside world thanks to power centers that are located along the spine, the famous chakras.

-Yes, I know that -said Erika- I practice yoga.

-How nice, that is a beautiful activity. Well, these energy centers perceive the energies of the environment and tell us if something is good or not, they warn us, they make us feel comfortable, happy, joyful, sad, excited, angry, etc. What did you feel when you entered my house?

-Oh no -answered Ellen- your house is beautiful, and it feels like a very pleasant atmosphere, very... I don't know how to say it.

-Spiritual -said Karla- it feels very spiritual.

-I felt like I was in the house of someone I had known for a long time ago -added Erika

-Excellent, how good that you felt that way, if you notice those are sensations caused by the energies in this environment. If you arrive at a friend's house and she had been fighting and arguing with her husband a few minutes before, isn't it true that you can feel the energies in the environment?

-Yes, you definitely feel that - Ellen affirmed, everyone confirmed it.

-Also, if you arrive at a certain place where there is a very negative and thick energy, your back even starts to hurt and you want to leave there, right?

-Yes, that happens to me a lot in certain places, I am very sensitive, - Karla said - and I can't stand being in those places, or in the company of those people.

-Yes, the environment has the ability to reflect certain energies, as well as people, some are loaded with very thick energies, so that we end up saying: Oh, this person has a very thick or heavy vibe! Or there are people who have a very positive vibe and they always seem nice to you, you even like being in their company.

-Yes, definitely yes, we can feel that.

-Well, what you feel from the environment or from people

are energies, and these are captured by our chakras, so everything we experience is allowed to be felt by us thanks to the chakras. If we didn't have these energetic power centers, we wouldn't perceive the world or its sensations.

-I had never thought about it -said Erika- I didn't know anything about this.

-Well, it turns out that when two people meet, our chakras perceive the energies of the other and we know if we like them or not, that, on the one hand, and on the other, because we also have an energetic body, this body is the one that is charged with negative or positive energies, depending on the type of thoughts we have, if the dominant thoughts are of love, respect, desires for well-being, harmony, etc., our energy will be very light and positive, if the dominant thoughts are of anger, sadness, resentment, negativity, annoyance, etc., our energies will be negative, and when we meet someone, their energetic body is seen by our energetic body and is accepted or rejected depending on their energy. Our environment also impregnates our energetic body with its vibrations. If you live in a dirty place, lacking harmony and love, the energies in this place impregnate your energetic body, and, on the contrary, if you live in a clean space, full of love and harmony, this environment also impregnates your body.

energetic.

-So, if you go to a house, you can perceive its vibes and feel comfortable or not in that space?

-And you also perceive when someone is flirting with you when they approach you, right?

-That's right Erika, that's right Karla, our energetic body

perceives the environment, so when you meet someone you really like, it's because you really like their energetic body, it's not so much their physical appearance, it's more their energy. When you feel that someone is flirting with you, it's because their energetic body flies towards you and gets too close, if their vibe is not pleasant to you, your energetic body immediately rejects it and becomes defensive. I confess that before I knew this I was very, well I don't know what the term is to define myself, but as soon as I saw a woman I liked, I felt how my energy went towards her, and they immediately rejected me or became defensive, when I understood it, I began to control my energetic body and not let it loose, now I can see a beautiful woman like the three of you, because the three of you are very beautiful -she gave them a smile, and they accepted it tilting their heads a little- and you no longer feel my... -she thought a little looking for the right word- harassment, yes, that is what it feels like, energetically you feel like you are harassed.

-True, yes, that is how I feel when I go out on the street and men, it seems like they never see a beautiful woman.

-It's true Ellen, unfortunately, men are not taught this about energetic bodies and they are always on the loose looking for an attractive woman, if we learned to control our energetic bodies, we could see them and admire them, without making them feel harassed.

-Oh, Alberto -said Karla- I wish they could really teach them this, many problems for women would end.

-And for men, because the same thing happens to them too, not to all of them, of course, they don't pay attention to me, ha, ha, ha. On the other hand, how many times have you met a man that you really liked physically, but when you are with him, even if it's just talking, you feel that you don't want to be with him anymore, not that you don't like him, but that in reality you don't want to be with him anymore, you even thought when you met him that you could have sex with him, because he was very physically attractive to you, but then you realized that no, that sexually you didn't want anything with him.

-Yes, that has happened to me - Ellen indicated.

-Me too - Karla confirmed - I often thought that because he was good I could want everything with him, but no, there was no chemistry.

-Exactly, that's what we all say, there was no chemistry. But in reality, it's not a question of chemistry, but of energy, it turned out that his energy was not compatible with yours. Do you realize?

-Well Alberto, in reality they had never explained this to me, I knew about chakras, but I didn't know what they were for, or anything about energies.

-Unfortunately, Ellen, nobody teaches us

this, if they taught us in schools, from a young age, we would be more careful of our energies and our emotions, can you imagine how we would be as a society if they taught us this?

-No, well - Karla affirmed - we would be a society with less anger and fights, because we would take better care of our energies.

-We would also be more careful with our houses… -Erika, he was thinking and remembering that she never made her bed, and she only swept on weekends, and not every weekend, her apartment would accumulate dirty dishes all the time, she would wash them until she had no more clean cutlery or glasses to use.

-Erika, I'm home! -Carlos was returning from work, he was tired, the firm was growing and he felt overwhelmed and very stressed. When he met Erika he was very attracted to her way of being, she was very carefree about many things, she was very cheerful and always affectionate, he loved coming to her house to visit, because it made him feel at peace, but after living together for some time, her carelessness about things reached the extreme of not taking care of the simple things in the house, the dirty dishes were piled up in the sink, full of leftover food from the week.

-Erika, why don't you wash the dishes every time we finish eating, then you wouldn't struggle having to wash so many.

-I don't like washing dishes, because it's better if you don't wash them.

-Because I have to work hard to give you the things you like, don't you like me to support you?

-Yes, although I don't need it, but I also don't like washing dishes.

-No, I don't like making the bed or sweeping either, you don't like that at all.

-Well, that's just the way I am - she always justified herself that way and he was tired of arguing.

-Erika, Erika, are you okay? We're talking to you and you left.

Karla was standing, passing her hand in front of her eyes.

-Sorry, yes, I just got distracted thinking about something.

Karla raised an eyebrow and sat back down.

-But then Alberto - Ellen asked - are you telling us that the attraction between two people will depend on their energy, and that if they reject us or we reject them, it's because of our energy?

-Yes, that's right, attraction is initially physical, they say that love enters through the eyes, right?

-Yes, of course, because if I don't like him very much I don't pay attention to him, said Erika.

-Oh, my friend, don't pretend, do you remember Raul? Don't tell me

that he was very handsome, he was really ugly, he was fat, short and had that mustache. Oh no, don't tell me that you liked him a lot, even you told us...

-Well, yes -he interrupted her- he wasn't an Adonis, but he kissed really well -she said, sensually running her tongue over his lips.

-Oh Erika -said Ellen smiling, everyone laughed at her comment.

-What happened there is that physically at first you didn't think he was handsome or nice, but you did have his energy - Alberto assured.

-No, well -Karla agreed- he was very nice and made us laugh

a lot, he was very light, but that always ends up running them off.

-But let's see, then, if I reject someone it's because I don't like their vibes, but what happens if I do like their vibes, but after two weeks I don't want to be with them anymore, what happened there?

-Personal relationships, whether romantic or not, have the objective of learning something or solving something related to our past lives.

-Do you believe in reincarnation? Because I don't - Erika assured.

-Of course, I do - said Alberto smiling.

-Me too - Ellen raised her hand - I have always thought that this is not my first life.

-The other day - said Karla - my mother shared with me a video of a boy who said that in his past life, he had lived on an island and even remembered the name of his mother and father in that life, the truth is that it was very interesting.

-The advantage of the Internet is that now we can see many stories and real cases of reincarnation.

-Well yes, I have seen those videos, but I don't think they are true, you know, you shouldn't believe everything you see on the Internet - said Erika raising her eyebrows and shaking her head.

-Yes, you shouldn't believe everything you see, but never close yourself off to the possibility. Instead of saying: I don't believe in this, say: Well, it may be possible. That will allow you to be more open to receiving more information.

Otherwise, your mind will close and you will become a skeptic of everything, one of those who deny even when they are presented with evidence and say: Well, what if you fabricated that evidence to convince me?

-Yes, friend, because we have always told you not to be so negative about things, open yourself up to possibilities.

-Well, yes, okay, I admit it, I'm going to be less skeptical.

-Excellent, then, when you meet someone whose energy clicks with you, Alberto snapped the fingers of his right hand as he said this word, your energetic body, or spiritual body, wants to establish greater contact. When he or she touches your skin, his or her energy begins to be received by your energetic centers in a greater way, and the desire to have greater contact increases. Remember when you met your partner. Isn't it true that when you looked into his eyes you felt like you already knew him, or maybe something special caught your attention?

-Yes, when I met Richard, it was in a coffee shop and when I looked into his eyes I loved him, then, when I touched his arm I felt something very special, we were sitting having a coffee and he told me a joke, I laughed so hard that he made me spit the coffee on his shirt, it was very embarrassing, I took a napkin and wanted to clean his shirt, but he took my hand and when I did, wow, no well, it's just that yes, we definitely clicked, here between us, I think I even got excited, she said a little blushing - remembering all this her eyes clouded over again.

-Oh friend, that's why I'm telling you that you can fix this, - Karla took his hand.

Alberto waited a little, she dried her eyes and said: -Oh no, I don't want to cry - she made a great effort to contain herself - come on Alberto, continue, don't make me remember anymore.

-These things hurt Ellen, but once you understand you will see that everything has a solution. So let's continue, what happened to you that day is that his energy and yours were very happy with each other, and they wanted to join together to merge, that's why the chemistry was so strong between you. Surely that day, when you went home, you couldn't stop thinking about him, right?

-Yes, of course, I think I even missed him and I was just waiting for him to call me.

-That happened, because your energy took part of

his energy, and he took part of yours, that's why he couldn't stop thinking about you either. How was your second meeting?

The cell phone on the nightstand began to vibrate, he ran to grab it before it fell to the floor.

-Say hello.

-Hello gorgeous.

-Who's speaking?

-Excuse me, are you Ellen?

-Yes, who's looking for you?

-Hi Ellen, I'm Richard, we met a couple of days ago.

-Yeah, of course I remember, the one about the lame horse, ha, ha, ha, I haven't been able to forget that joke, I fell asleep imagining the horse.

-No, and the rider, poor guy, ha, ha, ha.

They both laughed out loud.

-I love your laugh Ellen.

He remained silent waiting for the answer.

-Thanks, I like yours too.

-I'm not inopportune, aren't you busy?

-No, actually, I finished dinner.

-How, so early?

-Early, but it's almost nine o'clock at night.

-Sorry, I thought it would be around seven thirty, I think I'm falling in love and that affects my time.

-Oh, yes, and who is the lucky one?

-A girl with a nice smile, I'll introduce her to you.

She knew he didn't have any commitments, so she didn't worry and even felt flattered.

-I was thinking Ellen, would you like to go have a coffee with me?

-Right now, don't you think it's too late?

-You live alone, right? That's what you told me.

-Yes, but Claudia doesn't let me go out late with gentlemen, and even less if they're very handsome.

-Claudia?

-My kitten, ha, ha.

-True, I had forgotten, look at you giving a kitten a human name.

-Yes, I'm a little weird.

-And I love that! But well, then I'll pick you up in, let's say... five minutes or less.

The intercom bell rang

-Wait, someone is knocking at the door.

She ran to the kitchen, picked up the receiver and the small screen of the device was activated, there he was, standing, looking at her face to face with his

beautiful smile.

-Hello, beautiful, -he said when the light of the intercom came on.

-But... oh no, Richard, I'm not ready.

-Surprise... come on, darling, I'll wait for you down here.

-Well -she said smiling- it's okay, wait for me.

She hung up both phones and ran to her bedroom, sat on the edge of the bed and began to put on her tennis shoes. Claudia, in one jump, climbed onto the bed and purring with her tail raised, rubbed her body against Ellen's back, she seemed to sense the energies of her owner, and with her purr she told her that he was good for her.

-Yes, beautiful, now that you meet him, you will see that yes, you will like him a lot. She stood up, took a very tight sweater out of the closet, which allowed her to show off her beautiful bust, and put it on. She ran to the mirror, fixed her hair a little and put on a discreet lipstick. She saw herself beautiful and said, looking into her eyes: Come on, darling, finish him off!

He was standing, leaning against the wall, admiring the street, when he heard the door behind him open. He turned around and there she was, with her beautiful smile and those pink lips that he had wanted, ever since he saw them in detail while they hugged the straw of the cappuccino and painted it red.

-Wow - he said admiring her - you look beautiful.

-You, sir, look very good tonight too.

-Just tonight? - she said jokingly.

-Well, no, the other day too, you looked good too... - she fell silent and smiled, thinking to herself: Very good, in fact, you looked very good.

As she remained silent, he perceived her message unconsciously.

-You too, Ellen, you looked very, very good that day.

They both approached to give each other a kiss on the cheek, and when they felt each other, their energies came closer dancing around each other, barely touching.

-Come on, I know a place nearby, we don't need the car.

They began to chat, at times, and accidentally brushed their hands in the back and forth of the walk, both smiled and the conversation flowed without restrictions. The cafeteria was almost empty because it was already after nine.

-Good evening, welcome -said the waitress, come in please.

They chose a table near the window, the street was still very busy, pedestrians and vehicles passed near them, but because of their joy the outside disappeared, they returned to reality when the waitress approached.

-What are we going to serve you?

-I want a cappuccino with lactose-free milk.

-I'll have an American coffee, please.

-With pleasure, we also have carrot cake or apple pie.

-Yes, please, -he said- do you want any? -He turned to look at her and continued without waiting for her answer- what's more, if you allow me, miss, bring us both, we'll try them and share them.

-Okay, let's try them, but I'm not sure I want to share the one I choose with you - she said jokingly.

-It doesn't matter - she said, leaning both elbows on the table, and holding her face to admire it - they will all be for you alone.

She gave him her beautiful smile.

While they were talking, both of them placed their hands as if by accident near the other's, until he took them and began to caress her slender fingers.

-You know Ellen, you have beautiful fingers, they look like the hands of a pianist, I'm sure you don't know how to play the piano?

-Absolutely sure you don't.

-Well, I'm sure those beautiful hands caress and awaken many sensations.

She felt self-conscious and retracted her hands, she was starting to get excited and tried to avoid it, the Kundalini energy was starting to accumulate in the root chakra and that's why the excitement arose.

Time passed quickly, between laughter and anecdotes.

-Excuse me, we're going to close, it's eleven at night, I'll leave you your bill.

They paid and left the premises, the street was empty, the night was cool, but very pleasant, they reached the door of the building, she wanted to invite him to go up, he wanted her to invite him to go up, but neither of them wanted to rush things

-Well Ellen, it's late and tomorrow you have to work, I had an incredible time.

-Me too Richard, thanks for coming, I had a lot of fun, it's been a while since I had such a good time, thanks.

-Well, beautiful, I'm leaving - he approached her, hugged her, and gave her a tender and long kiss on the cheek, both of them embraced each other feeling their bodies, their energetic bodies embraced each other as well, raising their energy in the root chakra, and, therefore, their excitement, so they separated, so as not to provoke more.

-Tomorrow I'll look for you, would you like to eat together?

-Sure, I'd love to, but tomorrow I can't, it will have to be the day after tomorrow.

-You're punishing me, but it's okay, then until the day after tomorrow, rest.

He turned around, she watched him walk, and then went inside.

-Well, what I do remember is that I really wanted to see him again.

-But not only that Ellen, your body began to want to be with him sexually, right, every time he touched you by mistake or on purpose, your energies caressed each other and increased the desire to want to be together.

-Yes, that happens to me a lot, said Erika, when I meet someone I click with - she snapped her fingers and smiled mischievously - my little thing... - she pointed to her crotch - goes crazy and just wants to be satisfied.

-Ha, ha, ha, ha, everyone laughed.

-I love your freshness - Alberto smiled at her.

Erika was a woman of almost forty years old, she had a very pretty face, but in recent years, she had gained some weight and it was already noticeable, but her beauty was still there, her carefree personality of many things, had led her to not worry about herself.

-So, the excitement of your little thing, is caused by the increase of energy in the root chakra, and it happens when the other's energy is very attractive to us.

-Wow Alberto, I've never known this. -So our arousal is energetic.

-Yes, and then it's biochemical, because the body forms hormones and special substances that make our thing wet, sorry for the specificity, and in the case of men, to have an erection.

-Ok, keep going, this is getting good - said Karla squeezing her legs without anyone noticing.

-When we finally have an intimate sexual encounter, through caresses the energies increase, the kisses and the caresses of our erogenous zones lead us to the desire for orgasm, we want to have an orgasm, if the orgasm is very long, the energy remains longer in our body, normally you stay lying down waiting to recover, you close your eyes and you stay still, because your energy is settling into your physical and energetic body; When sex has not been with someone special, but only to satisfy sexual desire, the orgasm is shorter, less explosive, and the energy produced lasts less in our body, you do not need to stay still, sometimes you just want to get out of there and never see that person again, right? I'm sure it has happened to you.

They all turned to look at each other.

-Well yes, said Erika, that has happened to me and the truth is that it is not so satisfying, but I have also had some encounters that wow, that Carlos, yes, wow... those were orgasms.

Ha, ha, ha, ha, they laughed.

-Yes, I have felt that too - said Karla.

-Definitely yes, with my husband I felt those orgasms for the first time, I had had many experiences, but none like with him, that's why I fell in love like a fool. But now... - she was going to start crying, but Alberto interrupted her.

-No -she shouted and raised her hand, this action took her out of her moment and she stood still, he smiled at her- no, stay in your mind with those beautiful moments between you and him, stop thinking about what is happening now, you will solve it, but it is not by hurting yourself or thinking about the bad, but by focusing on the good and beautiful that you have, you will understand why I tell you.

-Yes friend, said Karla, you have something very beautiful, let's keep talking and we will solve it.

-You are right, remembering all those moments has taken me to that beautiful time, and well, continue.

-Do you want more coffee, or something else, a free cuba, or something like that?

-Yes, please, would you give me a free cuba with rum and mineral water, it's just that soda makes you fat and one must take care of oneself, ha, ha, ha.

-No Erika, soda does not make you fat.

-Of course, it does, it has a lot of calories.

-It makes you fat, ha, ha, ha, everyone laughed.

-I'd like a whiskey on the rocks, please, for Karla that drink reminded her of a beautiful love story in her life.

-I'd just have mineral water, please - said Ellen.

After everyone was served again, they sat down and continued the conversation.

-The truth is, I would never have imagined that an orgasm was an explosion of energy, said Karla.

-But it is, we are beings of energy, when a person dies, the body cools down, because the energy leaves it, have you ever touched a corpse?

-Oh no, not even joking - said Ellen

-Well, as soon as a person dies, it doesn't even take ten minutes before they get cold, it's a special sensation, but that's how it is, this happens because the energy is no longer in the body, that shows that we are energy, don't you think?

-Yes, I hadn't thought about it, but if we register everything with our chakras, and they only register energies, then yes, we are definitely energy.

-A caress is the record of an energy, there is a big difference between a caress from a friend and one with sexual desire, right?

-Yes, it's true, that is perceived.

-I hadn't thought about it -added Erika- but yes, it is definitely felt, when your boyfriend touches you just to caress you and when he does it because he wants something more.

-Well, then -continued Alberto- we said that the environment has the capacity to impregnate our energetic bodies with its energy. Also the energetic body of our partners and our own energetic body have the capacity to impregnate themselves and impregnate the other's or the environment. But we are like a cup or a glass, we can only receive a certain amount of energy, so if you want to put more water in the glass, it will be thrown away, because it can't hold any more. In the same way, our energetic body can only receive a certain amount of energy for a certain time, after that,

He starts to reject it because he can no longer receive it. When your partner has been transmitting his energy to you for a long time, and you to him, your body reaches a point where it can no longer receive it and we begin to reject each other. Isn't it true, girls, that after a while with the same partner, sexual relations are no longer as frequent as they were at the beginning?

-Of course, when Richard and I started having sex, no, well, there wasn't a day when we didn't do it, but then, well, we started to cool off.

-How was it, my love?

Richard was coming back from work, it was eleven at night, and he was taking off his tie.

-It's been a very hard day and then Roger decides to start together at eight at night, because of the new corporate building project in the center, it's a very important project and you'll know how it affects us.

-The children are sleeping, come sit down.

-Wait, I want to take a bath - he approached her and gave her a passionate kiss, playing with their tongues.

-And that kiss? - she smiled flirtatiously.

-Well, I want to pamper you tonight, I'm going to take a bath and I'll come out.

He went to the bathroom, returning twenty minutes later wrapped in the towel, which showed his well-defined belly, with almost no accumulated fat, and the hair on his lower belly gave him a sensual air, he was a thin but strong man, who liked to take care of himself. The light in the bedroom was off and only the lamp on the nightstand on the side where he slept was on.

-Ellen, are you asleep?

Ellen snored almost quietly, the tiredness of the day, her work and the children, had exhausted her, it was almost midnight and sleep overcame her.

-Damn it -he said angrily- it's been a while since we had sex and... - he didn't want to be annoyed anymore, he went to bed, turned off the lamp and fell asleep.

At six in the morning, he woke up, put on his sports clothes, took the suit bag with the clothes he was going to wear that day and left the house without saying goodbye, after the gym he would go to work and come back late.

Ellen was still sleeping, her routine didn't start until seven, getting the kids up and getting ready, the maid would prepare breakfast, she would go to the gym after the kids had left on the school bus, and then go to her office, she was a sales agent at a real estate brokerage.

-In relationships -Alberto continued- because these relationships are energetic, and because our energetic bodies are the ones that give and receive energy, and because they have a saturation point, where they can no longer receive more energy, there comes a time when sex, being an act of energy transmission, is no longer so desired and so necessary, do you understand?

-Wow -exclaimed Ellen- I would never have understood it, I thought that our husbands simply no longer love us, or that we are ugly and that is why they were looking for someone better. Wow Alberto, you are clearing my mind.

-See friend, I was right, we have to come back to see this man.

-Yes, I do, said Erika.

-Have you seen the time?

-Oh no, but it is already after two in the morning, how quickly time has passed, let's go. But then Alberto, it's not that my husband doesn't love me or I him, but that our energetic bodies can no longer receive so much energy from each other, that's why we distance ourselves sexually.

-That's right Ellen, in reality all couples who at some point decide to get married, it's because they have a very beautiful love, but they get divorced, because they don't understand or don't know this about energies, if we knew, well, it would be another story.

Everyone stood up.

-Ellen, let me suggest something to you, don't make decisions yet, wait until we finish talking about this, go on, if you want to invite Richard, I would love to meet him, it's more like if we have a couples meeting, next Saturday, I'm free, come and we'll have dinner, if you have a boyfriend bring him, or come alone, as you wish.

-Count on me, but I don't know if he'll be willing.

-Talk to him and tell him all this, I know you will have doubts, but tell him, that will help you understand more, and do not make drastic decisions, let's continue analyzing this topic.

-I'm coming -said Karla- and I'll come with someone.

-Me too -confirmed Erika- I'll see if I come alone.

-Excellent girls, I loved meeting you.

Ellen arrived home, opened the main door and entered, the atmosphere felt warm, just entering brought her back to the difficult moment she was living and she felt devastated. She went up the stairs, entered her son's bedroom, approached the bed, bent down and gave him a kiss on the cheek, he felt the kiss, but he just turned around and continued sleeping. She closed the door and went to the room across the street, her daughter was sleeping, when she felt her mother's presence, she woke up.

-Hi mom, how did it go?

-Hi my love, fine my sweetheart, it's late, sleep.

-Are you okay mommy? -she sensed something.

-Yes, my love -she smiled forcefully- go to sleep, she leaned over and gave him a kiss.

She entered her room. Her husband was awake, but pretending to be asleep, lying on his side with his back to her. She went to the bedside table and turned on the lamp. The room was dimly lit. He remained motionless, with his eyes closed. She entered the bathroom, unbuttoned her white blouse and took it off, then put her hands on the clasp of her bra and it came free leaving her beautiful breasts exposed, her nipples erected and she rubbed them to relax the sensation, she took off her pants, which fell to the floor, she picked them up with one foot and folded them placing them on the little armchair next to the door, she took off her white lace panties, her body was very beautiful and sensual, she took the nightgown from the small closet in the bathroom and put it on, she stood in front of the mirror and began to remove her makeup, when she looked into her eyes she began to cry, she loved her husband and did not want to lose him, but she did not know how to solve it, the messages learned from her grandmother and her mother echoed in her mind: "Once the man cheats on you, it is because you no longer fill him, you no longer satisfy him and then he will look for another." She looked into his eyes, trying not to cry out loud, her tears were wetting the cotton with which she was removing her makeup.

-What didn't you give him? You see - she said to herself - this happens to you for having rejected him so many times, but why did you do it? Stop, Ellen - a voice in her mind stopped her self-punishment - remember the energy, stop, Alberto told you not to punish yourself, that everything is a matter of energy, don't hurt yourself anymore - She finished removing her makeup and left the bathroom, turned off the light and closed the door. She lay down, covered herself with the quilt and closed her eyes. It had been months since they had said anything to each other when they slept.

-Hello beautiful, how are you?

Ellen had picked up the phone and heard those words, she immediately recognized Richard's voice.

-Hello handsome, I'm fine, and you?

-I'm anxious to see you, the day of our meal has arrived, but I was thinking, don't you prefer it to be dinner? I have the whole afternoon free, so if we eat I have no problem, but I wanted to invite you to a drink after eating and if you have to go back to work, well, that wouldn't be possible, so I thought it would be better to have dinner and then a drink, what do you say?

-I don't know sir, your proposals are very tempting, wait, let me see my agenda..., you know what, I don't have anything later, so we can eat together, I don't have to go back to the office.

-Excellent, I'll pick you up, I know you have your car, so why don't I pick you up at your house and we'll go in one vehicle.

-I like the idea, I'll see you at my house at three thirty.

-Great, see you there, beautiful day, bye.

She didn't answer, she just hung up the phone.

The cell phone rang insistently, he read the name on the screen and answered.

-Yes, please tell me - he said in a solemn voice.

-Hello beautiful, oh, how serious, it scares me, ha, ha, I'm here, I'm downstairs, I'll wait for you.

-Give me a few minutes, I'll be down now.

He was standing, leaning on his vehicle, he was hugging a teddy bear, he was wearing work overalls and a sports cap, he had a beautiful smile.

She came out, she was wearing a wide-flared emerald green dress with a fitted neckline, her beautiful legs were adorned by sneakers high heels. He admired her, he couldn't believe her beauty.

-Wow Ellen, you look amazing.

She turned around, and her dress rose a little, revealing even more of her beautiful thighs above her knees.

-Do you like it?

-I don't like it, I love it.

He approached her and showed her the teddy bear.

-How beautiful -he said taking the teddy- how beautiful it is - she hugged it, pressing it to her beautiful breasts.

-I'm glad you like it, I didn't know if you would like it.

-It's gorgeous, thank you.

She approached him and gave him a kiss on the cheek, staying a few seconds feeling their faces. He hugged her affectionately and then squeezed her tightly, this hug excited her, her Kundalini energy had awakened.

-Shall we go? -he said letting go of her.

-Sure, let's go.

He opened the door of the vehicle, gave her his hand to enter, and in doing so he revealed even more of her beautiful legs.

-Thank you, sir.

He walked around the front of the vehicle while she watched him, opened her door and sat down.

-You look beautiful Ellen, you don't know how much I like you.

She watched him as he drove, his slightly aquiline nose made him look very attractive, his lips were thin, but she longed to taste them.

-Where are you taking me sir, you're not thinking of kidnapping me, are you? - she said mischievously.

-That will depend on how you behave at the meal, if you eat all your food, I might steal it from you, ha, ha, ha.

-Well, then we'll see, it will depend on how you behave at the meal, we'll see if I finish it all or not.

They arrived at the restaurant, he stopped his car and the valet parking man approached to open the door for her. He quickly got out of the vehicle and said:

-No young man, thank you, I'll take care of it.

She looked at him again as he walked around the car to open the door for her.

-Get out, beautiful lady, he said, extending his hand to her.

She got out, and was able to admire her charms again as she got out. She stood looking into his eyes, he approached her slowly, his lips moved towards hers, she closed her eyes, and at the last moment gave him a tender kiss between the corner of his lips and his cheek, she smiled.

-Shall we go in?

Ellen was a little confused, but she loved this game, it made her desire greater.

-Welcome - said the waitress once they were seated at the table - can I offer you something to drink before your meals?

They ordered their drinks and the conversation flowed as always, charming, sometimes deep and very happy, their energies dance hand in hand, spinning around them.

-You know Ellen, something is happening to me that won't leave me alone.

-What, is there something wrong with you?

-Yes, it's here inside - she pointed at his chest, her face was serious.

-Don't scare me Richard, do you have a heart condition?

-Come, feel it.

He took her hand and pulled it towards his chest, she put her palm on his shirt and felt his palpitations, his pulse was really racing.

-Do you feel that?

-Well yes, your heart feels very fast

-It's because of you Ellen -he said smiling- you're getting inside me very deep.

Taking advantage of the fact that he had her hand, he got up a little from the chair and leaned towards her, his lips finally tasted her delicious flavor, both gave each other a very beautiful kiss, a tender kiss, they rubbed the sensitive skin of one lip on the other.

The place had disappeared, finally he separated from her, and both smiled a little shyly, they felt like teenagers, giving their first kiss. He didn't take his eyes off her, she lowered her gaze arranging the napkin on her legs.

- Did it bother you? - he asked.

- No, it's just that it's been a long time since I felt this way and it's very... I don't know how to put it.

Her beautiful eyes stared at him.

- Well, if it's worth anything, I'm the same as you, it's been a long time since I felt this way for anyone, of course I've had girlfriends, but to be honest, it's been a long time since I felt something so strong for someone. Ellen, I know it's very soon, we've only known each other for a short time, but I want to ask you to give me the chance to be your boyfriend.

She opened her eyes in amazement.

- Does the idea bother you?

- It's not that, it's that, we certainly have very little time to get to know each other.

-I know, but what we feel is not normal, so why not try it, let's get to know each other better and see if we move forward or not, what do you say?

-Let me see how the food is, if I finish all my food then we'll see.

-Good, he smiled relieved, I hope you like it a lot.

-I like it a lot already.

-The food, I meant the food.

-Of course, I also meant the food -he gave her a mischievous smile.

The rest of the conversation flowed, like a river on a summer afternoon with a clear sky.

-Is everything okay with your service? -the captain approached to greet them- can I offer you anything else, a dessert, perhaps? We have chongos zamoranos or chocolate tiramisu.

-Yes, yes, sorry, beautiful, do you want something?

-I don't know, I was very satisfied, and you see, sir, I finished all my food - she said happily looking into his eyes.

He just smiled.

-Well yes, tiramisu, please.

-For me, chongos zamoranos, that's my favorite dessert.

-Look, I've already discovered something else that you like a lot.

-There are three things you can poison me with, mole enchiladas, chongos zamoranos, and with that beautiful little body - he said, looking at her breasts and face.

-Okay, I already know how to poison you when you make me angry, ha, ha, ha.

After finishing the dessert and looking at the clock, he said.

-We're leaving, I want to take you to a special place.

-Let's go - she confirmed, she left the napkin on the table and they went out, the valet parking, brought his vehicle, and wanted to go open the door for her, but he was already opening it.

-Come in, beautiful - he stepped aside so she could get in, she turned around, and surprisingly put her arms around his neck and kissed him, a soft kiss at first, but as they began to feel each other, she played a little with her tongue on his lips, with this kiss they ignited their energies, the sexual chakra began to spin more quickly, causing an incipient erection in him, he pressed himself tightly to her and their tongues made their appearance, caressing each other softly, after a long kiss they separated.

-Yes, Richard Cisneros, yes, I want you to be my boyfriend.

He kissed her again, softly and tenderly, his tongue

barely brushing her lips trying to prolong the sensations. She sighed deeply and he let go of her, holding her by her hands.

-You'll see, beautiful, you won't regret it.

-I'm sure you won't.

He got into the car and as he got in he showed off his beautiful thighs again. He closed the door, gave the young man a tip and went in.

-Okay, beautiful, let's go.

-Richard, it's almost seven, how about I invite you to a drink at my house - he said with that special smile of seduction.

-I love the idea, let's go.

While driving, he reached out his hand and caressed hers,

they intertwined their fingers and she began to caress his veins.

-You know, Richard, it had been a long time since she had a boyfriend.

-But why, if you're so beautiful?

-I've gone out with some gentlemen, but the truth is that no one could get to the point here inside - he pointed to his heart - and since we saw each other the first time in the cafeteria, it was as if when I saw you, I knew that you were that special guy.

-Oh my love, he said for the first time.

She turned to look at him, and smiled.

-That sounds nice.

-That's what I feel with you, and you should know that the same thing happened to me, I'm not lying to you, I've gone out with other women and with some I have come to feel something special and of course I have fallen in love, but when I saw you that day, something uncovered itself in me, it was also like the certainty that we should be together. After we said goodbye, I couldn't stop thinking about you, and when I did, my face only knew how to smile, my friends asked me what was wrong with me. Saul, my childhood friend, asked me: Brother, are you in love? Yes, I answered, yes I am. And who is she? Tell me. She's the prettiest girl you can imagine, she has beautiful eyes, and a body that you can't imagine. Oh no brother, introduce her to me, how about I'll take her down. That's why I'm not going to introduce her to you, I said. Of course we laughed a lot.

-So you've already been showing me off to your friends.

-Not with everyone, I just smile differently since I met you.

Their energies were together, embraced, they let go a little and touched each other again, they couldn't separate completely, one from the other, they were like two children discovering each other and playing at feeling each other.

They arrived at the building, parked and entered the apartment, it was very clean and organized, she was very careful with her things, nothing was out of place, the windows were open, so a fresh and pleasant current of air came through them.

-Wow Ellen, your house is really beautiful, did you decorate it?

-Yes, that's right, I've always had a knack for combining things.

-You're going to have to go to my apartment to give it a good hand, because well, I'm simpler, I live well and I'm very clean, but for decoration, well, I'm not that good, yes, I consider myself a man who has very good taste.

Saying this he approached her and they kissed, at first only their lips melted, but little by little she began to let his tongue caress her lips and he accepted it, savoring the sweetness she gave him. His Kundalini energy increased, while their tongues increased the game.

-Beautiful, are you sure you want this?

-Yes. Yes I do, come.

She took him by the hand and they walked to the bedroom. She began to unzip her dress.

-Wait, let me help you.

When they began to undress, their energies held hands and hugged each other, they turned and rose in a beautiful spiral, their root chakra and their navel chakra turned activated by the Kundalini energy; He stood behind her, hugged her waist, pressing his body against hers, feeling her beautiful buttocks, he kissed her neck, she caressed his hair, he separated and began to lower the zipper, when he reached the bottom, he raised his right hand sliding the back of his hand all the way down her back, a shiver ran through her, it was the energy that rose up her spine activating the other chakras a little; his hand reached her shoulder, placed both hands on them under the straps of the green dress and slid them towards her arms letting her dress fall to the floor, a light green lace bra, transparent

revealed her beautiful back, he kissed her neck again and hugged her waist, she turned around and their lips merged.

-Oh my love, you are so beautiful.

Looking at her from the front, her beautiful breasts were on display, the bra did not prevent his eyes from reaching their beautiful peaks, he put his hands behind her back and unhooked the bra. He caressed her hair in rapture, while she closed her eyes, he passed his open hand over her face, sliding his fingertips softly, up to her lips, he caressed them tenderly and kissed them, biting them softly, savoring their sweetness. Their energetic-spiritual bodies embraced each other, spinning in love, joyful, filling the whole room and going out, illuminating everything, the love that was being born was very special; They both reached orgasm at the same time, they embraced and kissed tenderly and passionately, while their energy exploded orgasmically in a mixture of beautiful colors, both energetic bodies losing their shapes as they merged, then, and little by little, they rejoined their physical bodies, recovering their original form, but not their colors, these had changed, her energy was now in his energetic body, and his was in her energetic body. They both lay embraced, he on top of her, giving time to recover, while their energies slowly reestablished themselves again.

-Oh my love - said Richard - you are so beautiful, that was incredible.

-Oh Richard...

-I like it when you call me my love, I feel very nice.

-Oh my love - she said tenderly caressing his face and giving him a long and passionate kiss, her tongue awakened again the energies that were still excited, his virility showed signs of coming back to life.

-Are you sure you want more?

She kissed him again, then pushed him away and turned him around, placing herself on top of him.

-Of course, I want more.

The love continued to grow, their energies were so pleased with each other that they were spiritually filled and satisfied.

II A sinking ship

The alarm clock brought her back to reality, he was putting on his sports clothes.

-Richard, can we talk?

-Not now, I have an early meeting and if I'm late I won't do what I have to do.

-Can we eat together? I'll pick you up at work, it's important.

-Okay, I'll confirm in a while, after the meeting, the project is complicated, if I have time I'll let you know.

-Ok, I understand.

He stood up, picked up the garment bag and walked to the door, before leaving, he turned to look at her, she was trying to hold back her tears, he turned around and left. His children were still sleeping, he hardly saw them, he was with them mainly on weekends, but for a few months, he had stopped being with the family. He got to his car, took his things through the back door and sat in the driver's seat, put both hands on the steering wheel and rested his head on them.

-What am I doing, do I really want this? I know Larisa is very beautiful and we get along very well, but do I really want this?

He tapped the steering wheel trying to get the answer. He started the vehicle and left the garage. His wife watched him from the window, she raised her right hand to say goodbye, but he didn't see her, so she just rested her palm on the cold glass. A cold that pierced her heart deeply.

-I don't want to lose him, I don't want to...!

-What's wrong Richard? You've been very serious lately.

The meeting room was still empty, there was only him and his boss, Roger, who was a very good friend.

He couldn't stand it any longer, the silence overwhelmed him and he couldn't find the answer, he had to talk to someone.

-I have problems at home with Ellen.

-It must be very serious, you've been very serious for days.

-It is, I told her that I'm in love with another woman.

-How? -The sixty-year-old man with gray hair opened his eyes in surprise.

-Good morning, gentlemen.

One of the clients accompanied by other people and other colleagues from the office were

present.

-Well Richard, we'll keep talking, he said, patting him on the back, change that face.

Richard forced himself to smile.

Months before.

-Richard, I want to introduce you to Mrs. Larisa Macedo, she is the client I told you about, she wants us to build her residence.

-Madam, it is a pleasure - he said, extending his hand to greet her.

She was very attractive, she was thirty-five years old, with dark skin, her long curly hair fell over her shoulders and framed very beautiful light brown eyes, her dress allowed one to see very sensual breasts, men had to make an effort not to look at them, and not to seem vulgar.

-This is Richard Cisneros, and he will be the Chief Architect of your project.

She smiled when she saw him, their eyes connected immediately and when she did she felt as if she already knew him, she remembered him from somewhere, she extended her hand.

-Architect, nice to meet you.

-Madam, it will be a pleasure to work with you.

-Well, what do you think if we talk about this sensational project - said her boss.

-Mrs. Larisa, first of all, I have a series of questions to ask you, to find out what your house would be like or what needs it has to satisfy, so I'm going to ask them to shorten time, okay?

-Sure, I'll be happy to ask you.

-Are you married?

-Madam, Richard, excuse me, I have to leave you, do you think you can work on this and then tell me, I have something to do and I had forgotten.

-Sure, no problem - they both said.

-I'm divorced - she said facing Richard on the other side of the table.

-Do you have children, and how old are they, do they live with you?

-Two children, the oldest is ten years old and the youngest is nine, they both live with me and spend the weekends with their father.

-Is there anyone else who lives with you or who you think will live with you in the future?

-Not really, just the servants.

She came from a wealthy family, her ex-husband also had a personal fortune, so money was not a limitation in her life.

The conversation and questions continued for a long time, he was very pleasant and she was delighted.

-Madam...

-Larisa, please call me Larisa, can I call you Richard?

-Sure, it will be a pleasure. Larisa, I think that's enough for now, we'll be in close contact, please tell me your phone number and register mine to stay in touch, this will really require a lot of communication between the two of us.

-I'll be delighted -she said flirtatiously.

He felt her energy approaching him, and he had to restrain himself from letting his own get the better of her, they had both been very attracted to each other.

-Richard, you have a call.

His secretary standing under the door frame, brought him out of his thoughts, she was sketching a residence, in a sketchbook, on her desk.

He picked up the phone that was on her desk.

-Hello.

-Hi love, sorry to bother you.

-Ellen, why are you calling me at this number.

-I called you on your cell phone, but it sent me to voicemail.

-Gosh, I forgot, we had a meeting and I always put it in airplane mode, I'm sorry, what's wrong? -he said in a serious tone.

-You agreed to call me for lunch and you haven't.

-What time is it?

-It's going to be three o'clock, I'm free, do you want me to pick you up?

He remained silent, he didn't know what to say to her, he didn't want to confront her, even though he knew he would have to.

-I'm not done, I don't think it will be possible.

-Come on Richard, let's give ourselves the opportunity to resolve this, I don't want to lose you.

For months their relationship had cooled down deadly, she began to stop wanting to have sex, she didn't know if it was because of the hormones or what was happening to her, but she wanted to have sex with him less and less and that was pushing them away. Her contempt had led him to resolve his need in another way, and he had fallen in love.

-No, not today, I already have a meeting later, so I'll be home tonight, don't wait up for me, he hung up the phone.

Ellen watched her wedding boat move away from the port and a tear ran down her cheek, she hung up the phone with her heart crushed.

The cell phone was vibrating next to the drawing board. She read the name on the screen, it was seven o'clock at night.

-Hello - she said reluctantly.

-Hello baby, how are you? I can hear you listlessly.

-Hello Larisa, I've had a very hard day.

-I want to see you baby, you haven't been to my house for a week, what's going on, is everything okay?

-Sorry, it's just that we have a lot of work and I don't have enough time, Roger brings me here on errands.

-I know, but you've always had a lot of work and, even so, we've given each other time.

-Precisely because of that, now the work has piled up and I don't have enough time, I'm sorry, I have to get these things done or the projects will be delayed, I'll call you during the week or on the weekend to see each other.

She hung up the phone, annoyed.

-Richard, let's go, I'll buy you a drink, I think you need it.

Roger was standing, holding on to the door frame.

-Boss, I have to get these assignments out - he replied, not wanting to leave.

-I know, but this is more important, come on - he slapped the door frame.

He had no other choice, he turned off the lamp on the drawing board and went to the coat rack to get his jacket. The office staff had already left, it was almost nine at night.

-I want a double whiskey - said Roger.

-I'll have a free cuba, please.

The bar was busy, they had found a table in the middle of the room, a pianist was decorating the atmosphere with his melodies.

-So, brother, what's going on? Tell me.

-Oh Roger, I think I made a big mistake, I fell in love like a kid.

-Who, why did you never tell me anything?

-Larisa.

-Our client?!

He nodded his head affirmatively.

-Wow bro…, I don't blame you, that woman is really hot, I tried to hit on her, but she turned me down and I didn't insist, business comes first. But that you fell in love with her, wow, that is great news, but don't tell me you told Ellen.

-Yes, you don't know how much I loved my wife, but we were…

-But of course I know Richard, we've known each other for seventeen years, I think you were just married when you started working with me. And I always admired your relationship, and also, let it be said with love and respect, your wife is very beautiful, he said this raising his eyebrows and bringing the glass to his lips.

-Yes, it is, but we haven't had sex for a few months and our relationship has cooled down, and now, well, she knows.

-What are you going to do? Do you want to get a divorce?

-I don't know, I have a lot of doubts in my head, I don't know how to solve it.

-But you love Larisa, right?

-That's what I thought, but since I told Ellen, my relationship with her has also been affected, I haven't seen her for a week, she calls me insistently to see each other.

-Well, thank goodness her residence is almost finished, otherwise she would have sent us out on the street.

-When did you start dating her?

-About four months ago. We clicked from the moment we met, but I always stayed away, we flirted, but I didn't take any further steps, I didn't want to affect my relationship and I didn't want to affect the project, so I stayed away, but when Ellen and I started to distance ourselves and stop having sex, you know...

-Oh yes, you become neurotic and you spend your time climbing the walls, that was my story when I was married, that's why we got divorced, but well, it's not about me.

-I was desperate, I complained to her about why she didn't want to have sex, but she only told me that she felt uncomfortable, she even said that I hurt her a little, when before that didn't happen, we had the most beautiful sex I'd ever had, if I think about it a little, not even with Larisa have I felt what I feel with my wife.

-I understand you -said Roger- it's true, now that I think about it a little, it was hard for me to find someone with whom I could feel what I felt with my first wife, until I met Rouse, she and I did connect, but you see, I'm still single, I didn't want to get married again and she finally left me, I think I'll live alone the rest of my old age. Cheers -he said raising his glass.

-Cheers, but now I don't know what to do Roger.

-Excuse me gentlemen.

An older, thin man with gray hair was standing next to them.

-Forgive my intrusion, I was at the bar listening to your conversation, I couldn't help it,

I apologize, would you allow me to invite you a drink, there is something I would like to share with you.

They both turned to look at each other, Roger sought permission from his friend.

-Sure, please sit down.

He pulled out the empty chair and sat down.

-My name is Alberto, it's a pleasure to meet you.

-Hi Alberto, I'm Roger and my friend is Richard.

-Nice to meet you, gentlemen. I suggest we call each other by your first name, to make this more friendly, do you agree?

-Of course, Alberto, I'm delighted, said Richard.

-I couldn't help but listen to your conversation and I wanted to

share with you something that I think can help you, if not now, then in the future. From what I heard, and I apologize again for my indiscretion, you've fallen in love with another woman. How many years have you been married?

-Seventeen years married and we only lasted six months as a couple.

-Wow, that was a short courtship, which means you were really in love.

-Definitely yes, you don't know how, she was so beautiful and her energy was so special, I couldn't get her out of my head just after meeting her. So yes, I got married extremely in love.

-I know, I met him when he was newly married and they were all honey everywhere, we would go to some meal with our families, and when they got up from their chairs, they would leave honey spread everywhere, ha, ha, ha, ha.

Everyone laughed at the joke.

-That's great, those kinds of loves are special, you know,

those kinds of loves are not common, there are many beautiful loves, but there are some that with just their presence, bless those who are by their side, and teach them about love, that energy is transmitted and it is something very beautiful, those couples become teachers for many others.

-Wait, what do you mean teachers, just because someone sees us?

-Think about it, if you see a couple that is showing their love, don't you learn that it is beautiful and you would like to have someone by your side to

show your love in that way?

-Well, seen like that it's true, I remember some older gentlemen who poured honey, he was extremely affectionate and attentive, a real gentleman, I saw him opening the car door for his wife and from that day on I did the same, women love that, well, some, you know, others are very self-sufficient and feel weakened if you show them attention, on one occasion, to a friend, whom I was trying to win over many years ago, I wanted to open the car door for her and she said: I can do it, it's not necessary. I do it not because you can't do it, but because I'm a gentleman, I answered. That little detail distanced me from her, I never saw her again.

-Well - Roger added - I had never thought about it, but it's true, watching others you learn how to treat a woman or how not, because there are all kinds - he said raising his eyebrows - Cheers to the masters of love.

Cheers said everyone.

-Sex -said Alberto- is a matter of energies and our energies mix with those of our partner -he joined his hands, interlacing his fingers and flexing his wrists simulating a twist- so that, when sexual intercourse ends, your energy takes part of hers and she takes part of yours, that is how we spiritually learn and grow, every time you have sex with a partner other than your wife, this new energy somehow enriches your energy and our spirit.

-Wow Alberto, let's see, repeat that for me, please.

-When you have sex with a partner, your energies join with hers and they mix -he made the gestures again- when sex ends, your energy takes part of hers and she takes part of yours. Through energies is the way in which our spirits are enriched. At this very moment, our three energies are getting to know each other, getting closer and liking each other, that doesn't mean that we are going to or need to have sex to enrich our energies, but at the end of our meeting my energy will take a bit of yours and yours a bit of mine, in that way our spirits are nourished and grow, everything is spiritual, life on this planet is spiritual. At the end of time, when you die, the body will stay on earth and your energy will live on, enriched by all your experiences, sexual or friendly.

-Wow, Alberto -said Roger- this blows my mind. Waiter, three equal drinks, please.

-So, our lives are actually spiritual -replied Richard- and our spirit is enriched by the energy of others.

-That's right, think about it, do you like going to a shopping mall when there are no people?

-Not really, we prefer a place with people, it makes it more fun.

-Not me, I don't like crowds, I prefer to go when there aren't so many people - Roger added.

-Yes, but you don't go when the place is empty, right?

-Well, yes of course, never actually.

-That's right, but in reality the reason is energetic and spiritual, when you walk through the hallways you pass by people, and your energies see and get to know some that are very nice to you, you touch them, and when there is someone that is very attractive to you, sexual or not, you approach her and you want to touch her, but you just look at her, it's not true that that happens to us.

-Well yes, if a hottie passes by me, but of course I feel how my energy goes to her, if I go alone it's better, because if I go with my partner, you know, it seems that they have a radar and they notice, and you be careful and turn to look at them, ha, ha, ha.

-It's all a matter of energies, Roger.

-How incredible, I would never have thought it was like that.

-But wait, it gets better, it turns out that our energetic or spiritual body only allows a certain amount of energy from another person, nobody can stand someone hugging them all the time, because we hate them and can't stand another hug, right?

-Yes of course, my cousin is like that, and I can't stand him anymore, he wants to hug us all the time.

-But you can't stand him, because energetically your spiritual body no longer allows his energy, and the same thing happens with sex with our partners.

-Oh, no, but then... is that the reason why our partners no longer want to have sex?

-Bless you Richard, are you getting the point?

Richard did not raise his glass, his eyes filled with tears, and he looked down.

-I have been very unfair, I didn't know anything about this...

His friend patted his hand.

-Don't worry brother, this is hitting me hard too. Now I understand why...

-That's right friends, unfortunately, no one teaches us about energies and spirituality, we think that spirituality only has to do with God, religion and all those things, but it is not like that, spirituality has to do with our spirits, they live and grow through the experiences that our physical bodies live, when they die, we continue to live energetically and spiritually, but that is something that I am not going to explain to you now.

-Are you talking about reincarnation when you say that we continue to live energetically and spiritually?

-Yes, that's right Roger, but we shouldn't talk about it now

-Oh Alberto, what you're telling me makes me understand why my Ellen didn't want to...

-That's right Richard, it's not that she didn't love you, it's that spiritually she couldn't receive so much of your energy anymore, her energetic body, just like ours, gets saturated, some sooner and others later, but everyone gets saturated, the problem is that we don't understand it and we just think that they don't want us anymore, or that they've stopped loving us. There are women whose husbands don't want to have sex with them anymore and it's for the same reason, they get saturated sooner.

-So, that's the reason for so many divorces, we think that our partners don't love us anymore, and that they have someone else, because we don't satisfy them anymore, but in reality, it's a question of energy saturation.

-And agreements, but that's another story -said Alberto.

-Agreements? -Roger asked.

-Yes, but I'll tell you about that later. The most important thing, Richard, is that you love Ellen. What you've had with the other woman has only been the need to satisfy the spiritual desire to meet another energy to enrich yourself and physically satisfy your need, because men, if we don't get rid of the Kundalini energy that accumulates in our root chakra, we all go crazy.

-Yes - said Roger - I say that we go around scratching the walls and we become like, well, if I'm not sexually satisfied, I can't even work, I can't concentrate and everything distracts me, I just go looking for someone to help me.

-That's right, Kundalini energy is very powerful, and in some people, men or women alike, it's stronger. Those business men

or women are more sexually active than people who are a little less risky. So, if a woman is married to

a man who owns a business, or with a high level of activity, she will need to satisfy that man more, or vice versa, the powerful woman needs more sex than her husband, who will surely be a little more passive, let's put it that way.

-But that is a problem in our society, how do we do it if our partners can no longer receive our energies and we have needs?

-Well Richard, that's where love comes in, but true love, honest love.

-What is that?

-In our society Roger, and due to our religious culture, we are not allowed to have sex with other people outside of marriage, if we do it we will be in sin, we become sinners, right? -both nodded- in our society, our partner and our sex, must be exclusive to our husband or our wife, only with them is it allowed.

-Yes, but if energetically we need it and we can no longer with our partner, then why are we limited in that way?

-Our sexual energies are very powerful, and they awaken our pineal gland, it is a gland located in the brain, which has very powerful abilities such as telepathy, telekinesis, clairvoyance, and allows us to reach higher states of consciousness. If you had that gland awakened you would be very powerful, you would come into contact with beings who live in other worlds and you could communicate telepathically with anyone on this planet without the need for telephones, but doesn't that suit them, guess who?

-The ruling elites.

-And the church, said Roger.

-That's right, that's why we are limited from a young age and educated in what is right and what is not, they tell us what is sin, and what things God sees with good eyes and what not, so that, if we don't obey, then we will be condemned to hell, and nobody wants to be there, right?

-I don't believe in that nonsense -said Roger- those are inventions, I don't believe I don't believe in God, everything I've done has been because of my ability to work, so I don't believe in those things, I'm not afraid of hell.

-Congratulations, that's great, keep believing like that, that's good.

-But then, Alberto, all that stuff about sin is the reason why we don't allow ourselves to live certain sexual experiences with other partners, and we end up doing it in secret?

-Yes, we hide so that they don't find out and we don't become unfaithful and sinners, because religion has taught us that the unfaithful is stoned and should be removed from our lives, and you, you don't want your wife to find out and remove you from her life, do you?

-No, of course not, that's why we keep it hidden.

-That's right - Roger added - nobody really wants to end their relationship, just to have sex with someone else, that man or woman would be stupid. In reality, what we only want is to satisfy our desires or needs, not to end our families.

-That's true, but then, would you allow your wife to be with another man?

-I wouldn't -Roger said quickly- I would tell her to go to hell immediately.

-And you're not religious, where did you learn that?

-Where did I learn it, well... -he hesitated- that's how it should be, isn't it? -he turned to see his friend looking for his support.

-Yes of course -Richard confirmed.

-No sirs, we learned that from the church.

-But I've never been to a church.

-Yes Roger, but you are part of a society educated by the church and in that society, the conversations with your friends, the movies you see, all the past lives you've lived, in this or another society, tell you how you should treat women and they tell you about fidelity, so that's where you learned that.

-Are you talking about our past lives? Alberto, you're going overboard.

- Cheers friends - said Alberto raising his glass - that's another topic, but believe it or not, this is not your first life, maybe it's number one hundred or two hundred, and in each one of them you have lived the religious teachings, so you don't need to go to church in this life, maybe in your past lives you have been a priest, or a very religious man, or perhaps a woman, and those teachings remain in us.

- Ok, I understand, so let's go step by step - said Richard - first, sex is energetic, and we get saturated with energy and we no longer want sex with our partners. Second, we don't allow ourselves to live certain experiences because we believe that they are sin, and sinners must be stoned and removed from our lives.

- Yes, but if you have a true and honest love, then you have an unconditional love.

- Unconditional, meaning without conditions.

-Yes, Roger, this love is the one that gives itself unconditionally, it is the love that loves despite anything, and it is the one that understands that your partner is not your property, that she or he has the right to live their life, and that she does not belong to you. The church tells us that once married, we are handcuffed -he brought the wrists of both arms closer together simulating police handcuffs- so that she belongs to you and you to her, right? Is that what they tell us when we get married?

-Yes, yes, it's true, said Roger, they say that when a man is single, he is incomplete, and when he is married, he is finished.

Ha, ha, ha, ha, they laughed out loud.

-Sad, but true, ha, ha, ha, ha.

-But then, what should I do? This is very important.

-First, you have to understand that your wife loves you, and that she rejects you not because she doesn't like you anymore, but because she is energetically more saturated with your energy, and she doesn't need sex as much as you do. Second, you have to remember the love you feel for her, remember how you met, the early days of your marriage, all the beautiful moments you've lived together, focus your mind on the beautiful things about her. Then, you will decide if you want to continue with the other woman or not. But the important thing is that you do that, then Richard, you have to learn to give honest and true love.

-You're telling me that I should let her have sex with someone else.

-That's very difficult - added Roger, leaning back in his chair and taking his glass with both hands - I don't know if I could do that.

-I know that it is not easy, but it is due to our sexist culture in the first place, secondly, because of the type of love we give, and thirdly, because I only see her as the physical body, and not as what she truly is, an energetic-spiritual being living in the physical body she has.

-Seeing her as what she truly is, an energetic-spiritual body - Roger repeated as if hypnotized.

-Well yes, if I see things from that point of view, of course I can.

-allowing to have sex with someone else - said Richard.

-Look at things this way, you have been having sex with another woman, has that changed you physically? Is your penis different? Or has something physical in you changed with that sex?

-No, of course not, everything remains the same, it is just the emotions.

-That's right, nothing changes for them either, their vagina will remain the same, their body too, it is only the energies that are exchanged in a sexual act, and these change a little at the end of the encounter, but it is something that we do not see, it is spiritual.

-Well yes, it is true, if anything what hurts us the most is our machismo, how could my wife be with others!, or not Roger.

-Yes brother, it's true, I'm thinking about it and it's true, in fact, it's so true, that my ex had been with who knows how many without me realizing it, I didn't notice anything, until someone told me, and then, well, it's another story, but ultimately, nothing physical changes them, or us.

-Excuse me, gentlemen, we're going to close, we're offering you something else.

-Not me now, said Alberto.

-Thank you, the bill please -said Roger.

-Allow me to pay friends -said Alberto.

-Not at all, I'll pay, what you've taught us is worth a lot, thank you Alberto, really, at my age, you've come to give me hope, I can make important changes in my way of thinking and being.

-And to me, Alberto, I believe, without a doubt, that you're saving my marriage.

-You and Ellen have something very beautiful, and that kind of love is something that must be cultivated until it is a mature and very beautiful love.

They stood up after paying the bill and went out to the street.

-Alberto, would you give us your cell phone number, I would like us to be friends and for you to meet Ellen.

-Wow, I love hearing you say that you are going to get back together with her.

-Yes, you have made me see the beautiful things we have, besides our children, but the most important thing is that you have made me understand that she loves me and that I love her. Thank you.

She hugged him affectionately and they parted.

-Thank you, Alberto, it has been a fantastic night.

-It has been a pleasure meeting you -said Roger- I hope we continue being friends. We will send you a message so that you can register our numbers.

-Sure, we will keep in touch.

Alberto turned around and walked away.

-Alberto wait, we will take you.

-Thank you, but I live two blocks away and I love to walk, we will keep in touch.

Both friends got into their car.

-Do you want me to take you home?

-No Roger, take me to the office to pick up my car, it's on the way, I have to do something before I get home.

-Are you going with Larisa?

-No, it's something else.

Roger drove his vehicle in silence and very thoughtful.

-Don't you find all this incredible? If this information was taught to us from a young age, there wouldn't be so many divorces and marital breakups

with so much anger and hate.

-Yes, Richard, but this doesn't suit religions, as far as we know, or the elites.

-It's true, we have no choice but to learn on our own and pass on the teachings.

-We have to meet this man again, this thing about past lives really caught my attention.

-Yes, in short, we have to meet again. We're ready, have a good night.

Richard got into his car, put the key in the switch and the engine started silently, he thought for a moment and turned the wheel.

-Give me those white roses, please.

The flower market was open twenty-four hours. They wrapped the flowers in transparent cellophane paper and put a red bow on the bottom. He took out his wallet and paid, he smelled the scent of the flowers as he brought the bouquet close to his face.

On the way home, he remembered the first day they met, his face lit up with a smile, remembering her standing, ordering his cappuccino, he smiled more when he remembered when she spat out her coffee because of the joke about the lame horse.

-It's true, he said out loud and with his eyes full of tears, we have something so magical, I have to solve it.

He arrived home, entered his bedroom quietly, and turned on the lamp on the bedside table next to his wife, she was sleeping, feeling The light came on, he woke up, he knelt on the floor hugging the bouquet of roses, and said to her.

-Ellen, forgive me, forgive me for everything I've done to

you, I've been a fool.

His tears flowed, without being able to stop them.

-I was a fool, I didn't realize what you and I have, I was wrong.

She sat on the edge of the bed, holding on to the edge with both hands, her tears began to flow when she saw him kneeling with the roses on his chest, she approached him, took the roses and tenderly caressed his hair.

-My love, I love you so much.

He, kneeling, approached her and they hugged each other tightly, they cried their pain.

-Forgive me Ellen, forgive me, I didn't realize, I thought you didn't love me anymore.

-But my love, no, forgive me, I didn't realize how much I was moving away, and how much I was moving you away. When I realized it was too late, and you... -she couldn't say anything else, she just hugged his neck tightly and cried- I only know that I don't want to lose you, my love, you and I have this beautiful thing, I don't want you to leave my side.

-Forgive me my love, I don't want to leave your side, I love you too much, I want us to love each other again like before, we can get back everything we have, do you want to do it? Do you forgive me?

-Of course, my love, of course I do, I forgive you! I love you!

Their lips met giving each other the love that united them from the first day and that grew with their marriage, come my love, lie down next to me.

She lay down and moved aside, he took off his shoes and lay down with his clothes on. He looked her straight in the eyes with his arm resting on the pillow while he caressed her hair and forehead.

-I love you so much Ellen, I love you so much, forgive me I was a fool - his tears were deeply honest.

Their lips gave themselves to love, their tongues began to caress each other tenderly, then they hugged each other and cried.

-Me too my love, I love you so much too.

She caressed his face, and came closer to kiss him again. That night the reunion of love was magical, their energies were happily dancing holding hands and hugging each other, they loved each other so much, at the maximum moment of love, together with the orgasm, they merged, their souls danced happily and ecstatically, both fell asleep, while their energies remained united, fused in a single love.

The alarm clock rang at six in the morning, he turned it off, turned to see his wife, who gave him a beautiful smile, caressed her hair, got on top of her and they loved each other again, she hugged him intensely while he showed her how much he loved her.

-You know what my love, I'm going to call Roger and tell him that I'll be late for work, I want us to go have breakfast somewhere special, okay? Do you have time?

-Yes, I don't really have to get there early, I just have to send a message.

-Then we'll do that.

The children were boarding the school bus, while their parents watched them hugging each other from the front door, they took their seats and said goodbye through the bus windows.

-You know sister, it's been a long time since I saw my parents so loving, I already missed that.

-Right brother, I'm happy, I feel happy to see them like that.

III An old memory

Richard opened the car door for her.

-Come in my queen.

Ellen turned to see him and hugged him, throwing her arms around his neck, and kissed him beautifully, then she settled into her seat, he closed the door and walked around the front of the vehicle, while she watched him from her place and remembered that first day. How many times had I stopped seeing him, admiring him? Custom blinds us to the virtue that exists. We lose sight of the small details by taking them for granted, by thinking that this is normal in our relationships, and we miss continuing to admire our partner, and continuing to enjoy the details.

-Come on, you look especially beautiful today.

-Where are you taking me?

-It's a surprise.

They arrived at the old cafeteria, the one where their love was born seventeen and a half years ago. As soon as Ellen saw the place, her eyes filled with tears.

-Oh my love…

They both hugged each other.

-Don't cry my love, he said, wiping her tears with his fingers. Come on, wait for me to open the door. He reached her door, opened it, shook her hand and said.

-Come in, beautiful lady.

She got out of the vehicle, hugged him again and they kissed.

They entered the place, which was very crowded.

-Look, our table is the only one that is free.

When love is so beautiful, the universe conspires to make it last despite adversity.

-I'm going to order, the usual, right?

-Yes, my love - she said caressing his hand, he stood in line, ordered drinks and some ham sandwiches, and returned with the food on a tray.

-Today will be a special breakfast for the most beautiful love - he said leaving the tray on the table and handing out the things, she smiled. He returned the tray to its place and returned with two small spoons.

-Ready beautiful, now enjoy.

-You know my love, I'm so happy, I feel like that time we

met.

-Ellen my love… - he said with his eyes full of tears, trying to contain himself, she took his hands.

-I feel very sorry for you, for everything I did and everything I made you feel, please forgive me. I want you to know that I love you, that I truly love you, and that what I had with this woman, is not going to continue, do you want me to tell you?

-Of course, please, we have to talk about it and clarify it well, in order to move forward.

-Ok, last night I went with Roger to a bar, I had to talk to someone about all this and you know he is my best friend, almost my brother. So, we went to this bar, we started talking and suddenly a man showed up, he asked us if he could sit with us, because he had accidentally been listening to the conversation, and he wanted to share some things with us, so he sat with us and told us that sex is a

question of energy.

She opened her eyes.

-What is that man's name?

-Alberto, I don't remember his last name.

-It's not possible, it's just that...

-Do you even know him?

-Yes, the day you told me you were in love, I didn't know what to do, I met with Karla and Erika, we went to a restaurant, and Karla told me: "There is a man I met at a dinner, I think you need to hear him, I'm going to call him to see if he can see us." Of course, I said no, I didn't want to air my private life with a stranger, but he insisted so much that I ended up accepting, well, we went to his house, by the way, he has a very beautiful apartment, and we started...

-To talk about energies - Richard interrupted her.

-Yes exactly, but then, is it the same man?

-He is thin, tall, gray hair on the sides, like he is fifty-five years old.

-Well yes, actually he told us he was sixty, but yes, he looks younger, and he is very nice.

-Yes, we definitely met the same man.

-Wow my love, don't you think it's a big coincidence.

-Yes, my love, definitely, someone up there -he said pointing to the sky- wants us together.

-But of course, they do, my love -both held hands and caressed them.

-But go on, what happened afterwards?

-With what he told us last night, he made me understand that in reality you hadn't stopped loving me.

He reached out his hand and tenderly caressed her face.

-I was very angry and distant, you wouldn't let me get close and I just thought that I didn't satisfy you anymore, I needed to have sex, so well...

-Now I know my love, now I understand -she held her hand to his face, to extend the caress- that energetically we don't need as much sex between us anymore, like at the beginning, but that we have a very special and beautiful love, and that's what matters, not so much sex, which of course is still something very beautiful, last night was very special, -he said, his eyes filling with tears, and kissing the palm of her hand- I promise to do more of my part so that we are okay.

-I understood it too, beautiful, Alberto made me know that he doesn't You had stopped loving, but you were saturated with my energy, but we had not learned to give an honest and true love, that's what he called it, he also said it was called unconditional, that when we learn to give it, the love that is given without conditions, then we will have an honest relationship. I understood that your life does not belong to me, and that you have the right to live the spiritual or energetic experiences that you want.

-Do you mean that I can have sex with another man?

-Yes, that's what Alberto said, that physically we did not change at all with sex, but that energetically our spirits were enriched and that in this way we grew in love, that our physical body when it dies will stay on earth, but our energy and our spirit will continue to live, that we will only take the experiences and energies that we have lived and experienced in our life. What do you think?

-Yes, he told us a lot about this, but he did not go into depth about sex and letting our partners experience sex with someone else.

-You should have seen Roger, when she asked him if he would let his partner have sex with someone else, he went crazy, and said no way, that he would send her to hell quickly.

-Well, that's what we know and have learned - said Ellen.

-Exactly, he told us that we had learned that from the church, the movies and our social laws, that we were not allowed to freely live our sexuality, because it is not convenient for the church and the ruling elites, since we would awaken certain powers through sex.

-You're telling me that the more sex we have, the more powerful we become, come on, let's go now - she took him by the hand and made the gesture of getting up from the table - ha, ha, ha, ha. Now it turns out that we were denying ourselves power, ha, ha, ha.

They both laughed out loud.

-Oh, my queen, I missed your laugh.

-Oh, my love - she said caressing his hand.

She stood up and walked over to his side, sitting on his lap.

-I love you Richard Cisneros, I missed all this too - they kissed tenderly.

-Young men - an older lady was standing next to their table - congratulations, you are a very beautiful couple, you remind me of my relationship, but my husband is no longer here, he left his body a year ago, we will be together soon, I know it.

-Thank you, madam, you are very kind.

The lady turned around and walked to the door leaning on a cane.

-You see miss, you and I are a very beautiful couple.

She hugged him tightly.

-I love you my love, I love you.

-And I love you Ellen, and you don't know how much.

She stood up and went back to her chair.

-Well, this coffee is already cold.

-So, he told you that sex gives us power.

-Yes, he talked about a gland..., what did he say?, ah yes, pineal, the pineal gland, the thing is that sex awakens this gland, and with it many mental powers, which is why they didn't teach us to use our sexuality and that they had taught us not to live it freely, because they really didn't want us to awaken that power.

-Wow, that makes a lot of sense, of course, mentally powerful people can't be easily manipulated.

-It's true, on the other hand, he made us understand that if we didn't let our partners live their lives, including their sexuality, it was because we didn't understand about energies, and that we didn't understand that that was the way our spirits are nourished, that they are nourished by the energies of others.

-Well, he told us about our energetic bodies, but he didn't mention spirits.

-Yes, he told us that the energetic body and the spirit are the same, that our spirit feeds on the energies of others, that these mixes when you meet someone and when you have sex.

-Yes, he did tell us that.

-Well, he also told us that we had to learn to see our partners not only as a physical body, but as spiritual beings, living an earthly life, in a physical body, that our spirits feed on the experiences that our physical bodies live, and that not letting the other person experience their life would be selfish, well he didn't tell us that, that came from my soul.

-But if you think about it you're right, it's that we are selfish, because we are taught that when you are married, or even if you are not, when we are dating, your partner belongs to you, and that he can no longer look at anyone, he said this last thing thinking.

Jorge was a very attractive man, he was forty-nine years old, single and looking for an apartment. That day she was on call.

He walked through the door, his gray eyes turned to look at her and his smile showed a perfect row of white teeth.

-Excuse me, miss, can you help me?

-At your service, I extend my hand to greet you, I am Ellen Santibáñez, how can I help you?

-I just arrived in the city and I am looking for an apartment. I would like to see if you have anything I might like.

They both felt very attracted to each other. While they were looking at the list of properties on the computer, he stood next to her and put his hand on her shoulder. She perceived the intention and had to distance herself. She was married and did not allow herself to think about certain things, although she felt attracted. She had to see him on several occasions and he even invited her to eat, which she accepted. The meal was very nice, he was very attentive, at one point during the conversation he took her hand and kissed her palm, that awakened a sexual desire in Ellen, but her beliefs did not allow her to release her desires.

-Jorge, forgive me, I think you are confusing me, I like you very much, in fact, if I am honest with you, I like you, but I can't go beyond this, I am a married woman and I love my husband, so we better leave it here, I have already shown you many properties, we have been going out to see apartments for more than a week and I think you have not decided because your intentions are other, so, if you do not decide now which apartment you like, I will not be able to continue serving you, I will tell my boss to assign you to one of our colleagues.

-My love, Ellen, are you feeling well?

-Forgive me my love, I remembered something, but it is not important.

-Ok, then what do you think? What do you think?

-Yes, I think that this belief that we are the property of our partners does not allow us to live our lives freely.

-But do you think you are capable of changing it? I mean, would you be willing to let me have sex with other women?

-Others, how many?

-Well, that doesn't matter, even if it's one or more, would you be willing?

-Oh, my love, I don't know, of course I am willing to forget and forgive all this, because I understand that we both have responsibility, and it's not about who is guilty and who is innocent, but about recognizing our responsibilities, that will allow us to stay together, but... do you think you need another woman to satisfy you?

He remained silent thinking.

-Well my queen, it's not, if you and I are fine, if you accept me and want to continue having sex, of course I don't need anyone else, but what will happen tomorrow when our energetic or spiritual bodies become saturated again and lead us to need other energies. Don't tell me you haven't had the desire to be with another man, you are extremely attractive, so...

-Yes, my love, to be honest, yes, I have had the desire and the imagination, but I have never allowed myself to, I love you and I only want to be with you.

-Yes, my queen, I understand that, but you had stopped wanting me to do it to you, I got to the point where I thought you were with someone else.

-No, of course not -he said quickly- I just abstained from sex, I got to the point where I thought I could live without it, I don't know why I thought that.

They both remained silent thinking, while they took a sip of coffee and a bite of their sandwich.

-You know what Richard, my love, I think we need to talk more about this, do you remember that a few years ago you suggested I go to a swinger club and I didn't want to, did you go to one?

-Not really, since you didn't accept I dismissed the possibility, it was something that caught my attention, but I wanted us to go together, then I dismissed it, do you think that would be a solution?

-I would have to think about it, I don't know.

They continued eating and drinking coffee while they thought.

-Well my queen, you know what, I'll tell you something, now I don't even want to see her anymore, you know.

Richard never wanted to tell his wife the name of the other woman, he didn't want to get the office in trouble, so he hid it.

-I want to dedicate myself to you, and to build an honest and true relationship, I want to learn to express unconditional love, love without conditions.

A beautiful smile appeared on Ellen's face.

-My love, you make me so happy, I want that too, I want us to love each other as always and even more, as when we met, time will tell us what happens, don't you think?

-Definitely yes my queen, cheers to our beautiful love.

They both raised their cups and clinked them together, he reached over and kissed her on the lips, a tender and sweet kiss that said: I love you.

Ellen's cell phone vibrated, she picked it up, read the name and answered.

-Sorry, I won't be long - she said looking at her husband.

-Okay, I'll take the opportunity to give some instructions in the office, I want us to eat together with the children.

-Oh yes, they're going to love that.

-Hi friend, how are you - she said in a cheerful voice.

-Well, I was worried about you, I wanted to know

how you felt, but I hear you very happy, what did I miss?

-Nothing beautiful -she said looking at her husband, who smiled at her- everything is fine, but right now I can't talk, I'll call you later.

-From your voice I think everything is already fixed with Richard, right?

-Yes friend, everything is fine, I'll talk to you later.

-Of course, of course, I won't distract you, enjoy it, are you with him?

-Yes, that's right, I have to hang up, bye.

The three of them hung up the phone.

-Done beautiful, I just had to give them some instructions in the office for the progress of the building project, and tell them that I wasn't going to go to the office today, I'll take the whole day with you.

-My love, your words make me so happy, we really miss spending time together, like before.

-Certainly love, the habit and the responsibilities have increased.

-Yes, but it's not just that, we've stopped putting ourselves as a couple as a priority, everything else is always more important, and you and I leave ourselves for last, I have to change that, I'm going to be more aware of ourselves and your needs.

-Thank you, my queen, me too, I'm going to tell Roger not to do the meetings so late anymore, because I stop coming home early and that doesn't leave us time to talk, and it's been a while since I've seen the kids, I'm very distant from them.

-Yes, they miss you and always ask about you, and well, I always tell them it's because of work.

-I know, dads don't take the time to be with our children, I'm going to change that, you know, I'm going to do what I would have liked my dad to do with me and that he never did, because now I realize that I'm doing exactly what he did with me, I'm repeating the patterns, my dad dedicated himself to work to give us a good life, but he didn't have time for us, I'm going to change that too. What do you want to do today? I'm all yours, my lady.

He reached out and took her hands.

-I was thinking Ellen, that we should eat with the children and then go to the movies, or at least that you prefer that you and I be alone all day, from here we can go to the art museum that you like so much and then eat and then go to the movies, and who knows what can happen if it gets too dark in there.

His tone was mischievous, with a sensual touch.

-I don't know, you make it difficult for me, on the one hand, I know that the children would love for us to be together, but I think about you and me, it's been so long that we haven't spent a full day alone, I'm always thinking about the children and when you propose to do something for us alone, I always told you why don't we involve them, and in the end you accepted.

-Yes, and the truth is, not very willingly, that also distanced me, it seemed that you didn't want to be alone with me.

-I'm sorry, my love, I didn't mean to make you think that, I never imagined that you would think that way or that I was causing you those thoughts.

You know what, no, today, I will be all yours, no children, just you and me, I will send them a message telling them that we will arrive very late, that they should eat, there is food in the fridge and that they should have dinner.

-Oh, my love, I love that.

-I told you that I was going to put the two of us as a priority, so that's what I will do.

He stood up to kiss her. She caressed his face.

-I'm going to the bathroom.

-I'm going to call the kids. What time is it?

He walked towards the bathroom and she began to text the message on her cell phone.

-Well... what's up Erika?

-Hey Karla, are you busy?

-No, friend, what's up?

-You know, I've been thinking about everything that Alberto explained to us and I would like to know more about it. I've been thinking about my relationships and why, after a while I don't want to have sex with them anymore, and it doesn't take long for me to start feeling that way, but I do want to have sex with someone else, I think I have something, but I don't know what it could be.

-Oh, friend, for me it's because you're very horny and you quickly get saturated with your partner's energies.

-Do you think that's it? Because well yes, I recognize myself as very hot, but why do I look for other men, if I have mine and I love him?

-I don't know, why don't you call Alberto and ask him.

-I've thought about it, but I don't want to seem stupid and be falling on him, when did he say we would see each other?

-He said Saturday, but I don't know if I need to confirm it, I'll call him and let you know, on the other hand Erika, you have a very stupid personality, you don't give much importance to many things and you just look for distraction, could it be that you're afraid of taking your love with your partners to another level of commitment, of surrender, and you only stay on the superficial, you fall in love, you seduce them, you make them go live with you, because you're very pretty, but since you have them, you try to get rid of them, and you start to stop having sex with them and think about other men?

-Oh, friend, it's just that... you tell me this and something stirs inside me, I think you're right, I'm... afraid... of taking my love... to another level. Oh no, I need to talk to him, give me his number, please.

-Sure, I'll send it to you, let me know if she gives you an appointment and you invite me, or if she's going to make the dinner she said, hey by the way I just talked to Ellen, you can hear she is very happy, she says that everything is already fixed with Richard.

-Oh yes, yes, I knew they would work it out, they love each other, but oh well…

-Well, talk.

-A man who is unfaithful once, is unfaithful many times.

-Oh friend, don't be negative, that's why you don't take your relationships to another level, because of your beliefs. I'm going to leave you, I have something to do, let me know what Alberto says.

Erika was pensive, sitting in the living room of her apartment, she looked at her house and remembered: "The environment impregnates our energetic bodies with its vibes and vice versa." She went to the pile of dirty dishes and began to wash them. Four hours later, she let herself fall into the chair, turned to look at her house and it looked very different and beautiful, she thought a little more, went to the cupboard and took out a pink candle that she had bought for no reason, took it out, looked for the matches in the drawer and went to the coffee table in her small living room. She lit the candle, put her hands together, closed her eyes and said:

-Lord, I know I don't talk to you very often, I know I've been far from you, forgive me for that, I want to thank you for my health and for my house, I ask you to help me change, I want to love myself more, because I know that I am not my priority, I always look for things to do or to distract myself with, but that are outside of me, help me love myself, fill my house with your love and teach me, or rather take away my fear of taking my relationships to the next level of love, whatever this means, help me change. She leaned back on the couch and looked at her house.

-You really are beautiful -he said out loud- I'm going to love you, I'm going to make sure your vibe is beautiful so that you impregnate my energetic body with those beautiful vibes.

Her cell phone rang and brought her out of her thoughts, unknown number.

-Well, she answered hesitantly.

-I have the pleasure with Erika.

-At your service.

-Hello Erika, I'm Alberto.

God had answered.

On the way to his house, Roger was very thoughtful. He opened the main door and turned on the light, his house was a very beautiful residence, he had designed and decorated it to his liking, a very elegant and expensive taste. He reached his bedroom and remembered his ex-girlfriend, began to undress, went to the bathroom to clean himself. She was a very attractive and elegant woman, that had fascinated him from the first moment he saw her, she was forty-seven years old when he met her, he was fifty-five, they had had a very beautiful romance, they fell deeply in love, but after five years they lost the spark of love, and they began to distance themselves, he was with other women and she had a secret lover, of whom he continued without knowing. He thought about everything that Alberto had explained to them and why we lose interest in sex, but we are not taught to base our relationships on love, on honest and unconditional love.

-That was what happened to us - he said out loud - we really loved each other very much, but we had built a big gap between us and that led us to end our relationship. He lay reclining on the bed, stretched out and turned off the night light, he fell asleep remembering Rouse. In the morning, when he woke up, his memories continued, when he came home from work, anything was a reason to argue, if there was something out of place, or any little thing, it was the sparks of the great fire that they both started.

He was tired of that, he tried to be affectionate and she rejected him and when she was affectionate, he did the same, they began to play the game of revenge, to see who hurts who more. She also loved him, but she couldn't find a way to get closer, she tried to talk to him, but they both ended up burned, and stopped talking to each other, until the relationship became unbearable.

-You know Rouse, I've been thinking about us, and the truth is that I can't find a way to solve it anymore, I love you, I love you very much and I would like us to continue, but I feel like we can't do it, we don't want each other sexually anymore, we hardly talk to each other, we fall asleep at night without saying a word and the next day we barely exchange words, I think it's time to define what we want to do.

-So, what, now you're going to blame me for all this.

-Well, the one who started to reject me sexually was you, I looked for you many nights and days, and as soon as you felt my caresses, you ran away.

-Poor you, and you're surely innocent.

-But, what should I do? You see, we're already starting to argue again.

Rouse remained silent, it was true, she began to reject him, she no longer wanted as much sex as he needed, he was insatiable from her point of view, and she was already tired of arguing, she no longer wanted to fight, so she lay down on the couch, rested her head and remained silent. He sat next to her and took her hand.

-I love you Rouse, you and I have something very beautiful, but if we stay together, we're going to end up hating each other and I don't want to hate you, I love you, but I feel like we can't live together anymore. A tear rolled down her cheek.

She knew it was true. He took out his handkerchief and gave it to her.

-You're right Roger, I love you too, I've thought a lot about what we're living and the truth is that this is not life, not like this, fighting, not talking to each other, not wanting to get home, that's not life. I love you too, he caressed her face lovingly, but we're not happy and I think it's true, we're starting to hate each other, there's no point in waiting until we hate each other in such a way that we can't see each other again with love, there's no way I want that, if we break up, I want to keep loving you, we've had a very beautiful love and I don't want it to be lost either, I'll go to my apartment.

He hugged her and cried, they both cried.

-I'm sorry Rouse, I'm so sorry, I don't want this to happen, but I don't want you to hate me and I don't want to hate you.

-I know darling, I know.

They kissed tenderly, she got up and went to her bedroom, he stayed seated on the couch watching her walk away.

He took two suitcases out of the closet and began to put away his clothes, he dried his tears with the tissue. He left the bedroom, he didn't want her to leave, but his words couldn't tell her that.

-Let me help you, he got up and took her suitcases, they walked to the door. They put the suitcases in her car, and he closed the trunk.

-Rouse, I love you, really, I'm so sorry, I don't know how to solve it.

-Me too Roger, I'm sorry too, thanks for everything, I love you too.

They both hugged each other while tears wet the other's shoulder. He stood watching her walk away, five years of a loving relationship were leaving him.

-Say hello.

-Hello Rouse.

-Yes, who's looking for her?

-Hi beautiful, I'm Roger, I changed my cell phone, I'm sure you don't have this number.

-Nice to meet you Roger, it's been a long time since we talked, how are you?

-Good beautiful, I'm fine, are you busy?

-I'm doing some things at the office, you know work never ends, there's always things to do here.

-It's good that you're busy, so you won't have bad thoughts.

-Well, it's not that bad, there's time for everything, ha, ha, ha.

-I'm very happy to hear your laugh, I missed it. Hey Rouse, I was thinking, I'd like to invite you to dinner, do you have time, today or tomorrow? I mean if your boyfriend lets you.

-Well, he doesn't object, I'm a businesswoman, so he's used to it.

He felt his heart crumple.

-But yes, I have time, do you want today or tomorrow?

-Today itself, that would be great, I'll pick you up at eight, where to go?

-Better tell me where I'll meet you and I'll get there, I'll take my car, and then I'll get to my house without bothering you.

-It's not bothering you, let me pick you up and later I'll take you to wherever you left your car.

-No, send me the location of where it would be and we'll meet there at eight, okay.

-Excellent, that's how we'll do it.

He arrived at the restaurant fifteen minutes before eight, they assigned him a table and he went in, he ordered a whiskey on the rocks and a strawberry margarita. A tall woman entered the restaurant, she was elegantly dressed, her clothes were very fine and her jewelry made her look very beautiful, her hair was short, very short, pixie style, which made her look very young; she walked towards him with a beautiful smile. When he saw her coming he got excited.

-Wow Rouse, but how beautiful you look, that new haircut looks incredible on you.

-Thank you dear, she said approaching to give him a kiss on the cheek, you look very handsome too, those gray hairs look very good on you, I still like you… -and she thought a lot to herself.

He indicated the chair, his side and pulled it out for her to sit down, then he did the same.

-And what a miracle Roger, who died?

She said while placing both elbows on the table, interlacing the fingers of her hands and putting her face on top of the fingers, a beautiful smile dazzled him.

-You look so beautiful Rouse.

-Yes, I know, thank you for saying it.

That was a quality that he had loved, she was an extremely self-confident woman, owner of her own company and with a lot of character, sweet and tender when she needed to be, or tough and energetic if the moment required it, she knew how to get her employees to do what was needed and it was not through fear, but through leadership, she was an avid reader and knew how to guide her team.

-Nobody has died, by the way.

The waiter arrived with the drinks.

-And this?

She said surprised when the waiter placed the glass with the strawberry margarita in front of her.

-I allowed myself to order your favorite drink, is it still that one, right?

-I'm flattered that you remember, yes, it's still my favorite. Let's say cheers for the pleasure of seeing you.

They both raised their glasses and clinked them.

-For the pleasure of seeing you Rouse.

-And tell me, what is the honor due to, it's been so long since we spoke that well I had already gotten used to it.

-Excuse me for that, I wanted to call you many times, but I didn't dare, I was very stupid, I'm sorry, but from close sources I knew you were fine, they would let me know occasionally, don't think I was spying on you.

-Look at those gossipy people, but the truth is that I did the same, I always asked about you, I knew if you were sick or not, but I didn't want to call you, our relationship was over and now it's part of our story.

-Unfortunately, yes, it's true, it's over. You know Rouse, I've been thinking a lot about you, but do you have a boyfriend?

-Cheers, she said without answering, what were you thinking about?

-I don't have anyone, I've been alone for a while, nothing serious, I've gone out with friends, but nothing serious

-How strange, you're very handsome, what's the reason for this abstinence.

The waiter showed up, they ordered their food and he left.

-No one has reached my heart, I think it's still occupied.

-Yes, and who is the lucky one who occupies that heart?

-You Rouse, I haven't stopped loving you, I've tried, but I can't.

She smiled, she hadn't forgotten him either. After her relationship ended, she also ended it with her lover, certainly this friend and her felt something very nice, one for the other, the sex was intense and playful, that turned her on; he was younger than her and had a high sexual energy, so when she needed to balance her energies she looked for him, his presence made it easier for her to end their relationship, because she felt accompanied, they always met at his apartment, so they had made a nest of sexual love very suitable for her needs; but when she ended her relationship with Roger she began to distance herself, she did not give herself the time and ended up being alone, she still loved her ex. When she received his call, she was extremely happy, but she was not willing to make it easy for him.

-Well, try harder, look at me, I could do it.

She smiled while stretching her arms in triumph. His chest hurt.

-Well, it must be that... -he thought about it carefully and said- it's that I'm very bad at forgetting you.

-Well, don't worry, I know you can.

-But I don't want to, Rouse.

She reached out and took his hand.

-I don't want to get you out of me, I still love you.

-But... -he remained silent.

-I know, I know you have someone else, I only ask you to give me the opportunity to see each other more often, I have changed, I have understood many things and why our relationship cooled down, now I understand and I know why.

-Oh, yes, and why did we cool down?

She began to tell him what Alberto had explained to them about the energetic body and energies. They brought them their dishes and they ate while he explained and resolved their doubts.

-But then Roger, everything that happened to us was because we were saturated, with our energies and sex was no longer so necessary?

-Yes, that's right.

-And that's why you were seeing other women, to balance your energies?

-But how, did you know?

-Well, those perfumes are not the ones you wear, of course I realized, that's why I didn't want to be with you anymore, that pushed me away even more.

-I'm sorry, I'm sorry for having done that, and I'm sorry for having hurt you.

-Don't worry, the truth is that I was also balancing my energies.

-What! so you...

-Yes, I have to be honest, I also had my needs and you didn't want to be with me anymore, you also rejected me.

-Well, darling, it's true, -he said thinking things over- we both have energetic needs and we did what we could at that moment.

-It's true, looking at it carefully, it's true.

-A friend told me something that seems very important to me, he said: "If you don't allow your partner to live their life and their experiences it's for three reasons, first, your love is not an honest and true love, second, you don't understand about energies and energetic bodies, and. Third, you only see your partner as a physical body and not as what he truly is, an energetic and spiritual body, living experiences in a physical body," he said that at the end of time, when the body dies, the energetic and spiritual body would continue to live. He spoke to us about reincarnation, but only named it.

-Wow, what an interesting way of seeing ourselves, as energetic and spiritual beings, living experiences within a physical body. Wow, that is interesting. I do believe in reincarnation, I have read some books about death, and life after death, and it has everything to do with what he explained to you.

-You will have to lend me one of those books, I was very intrigued.

-Sure, it's not a problem, I will bring you a couple of them. But then, our problem would have been solved if we had been more honest.

-Partly yes, but at that time I would not have allowed you to be with another man, I was a little jealous, now it is different, because I understand energies and I understand that our energies are

-Yes, of course, I understand you. If you had told me that you needed to have sex with other women, I would have allowed it.

-But I wouldn't allow you, and that would bring us problems, because according to the energies, you would continue to have needs and I wouldn't allow it, you would end up doing it secretly and that would bring us problems.

-And now, if we go back, would you leave me?

He leaned back in his chair and took his glass with both hands while he thought. The waiter picked up the plates and left.

-You know what, yes.

-I don't believe you, I think you're just saying that so we can go back.

Well, Rouse, I can't deny that at sixty years old it's hard for me to think about seeing you in the arms of another, but if I see you as an energetic spiritual being, of course I can allow you to do it. I just have to tell myself many times what you really are and what I really am, that way we can create a relationship based on honest love. I understand! -he said raising his voice.

-What? -she asked smiling at his raised voice.

-I didn't understand what Alberto meant when he talked about honest and unconditional love. He means this, seeing each other as what we truly are, and allowing each other to live our lives, loving each other unconditionally, loving each other despite anything, if we managed to create a relationship like that it would be wonderful, don't you think?

-An honest relationship, like a swinger, well, I had never thought about it.

-Well, I hadn't thought about being a swinger, but seeing us this way, I think it could be possible.

They both thought about whether they would really like to live a relationship like that.

-I have a friend, who is married, and they are a swinger couple, and they get along really well, she says that from then on, they are very happy, but that they only do it when they are together, she says that it is more fun that way.

-If I have heard about that, it is just that for me it didn't seem fun, you know me, I am a little jealous, well I was jealous, now I am not.

-A little, ha, ha, ha, cheers, because you're not jealous anymore.

They both raised their glasses and clinked them, he looked for the waiter and made a sign for them to bring them other drinks.

-But anyway, she said, don't think we're going back, I'm not... - he remained silent and lowered his gaze. Inside he was happy, but his face didn't express it.

-Come on beautiful, just give me the chance to see you again, let's go out to eat or if you want, let's go on a weekend together.

-Are you suggesting that we be lovers?

-Yes, that's right - he said with complete confidence, leaning back in his chair in the position of a great lord. She laughed.

-I don't know, I've never...

He narrowed his eyes and frowned as he watched her.

-Ha, ha, ha, ha, let me think about it, I'm just not sure.

He straightened up in his chair and put himself seriously in the position of a great lady. He laughed, straightened up and moved closer to kiss her, at the last moment she put her cheek to him.

-Okay sir, be still, what if someone watches us.

The waiter returned with the glasses.

-Let's say cheers, for lovers, they both raised their glasses and laughed.

The dinner dragged on and the drinks were taking effect.

-I'm leaving, it's very late and they're waiting for me.

They left the restaurant, the valet parking brought their vehicles, he accompanied her to hers and before she realized it he hugged her and kissed her on the lips, she let him kiss her, but she didn't hug him.

-Sir, if I have problems because of you, you'll see.

-I don't care, my house is waiting for you and I..., I miss you.

She caressed his face while smiling.

-Thank you for dinner, we'll say hello later.

He closed the door and waited for her to leave. They both smiled happily.

Richard and Ellen enjoyed painting, they were both art lovers, he as an Architect liked to draw, his style was watercolor, and she had learned to admire painting, he had taught her.

The museum was a little empty, they walked hand in hand, admired a painting, made comments and kissed, sometimes more or less passionately.

-Oh, my love, I'm so happy, I really feel like this is our second wind.

-I'm very..., he turned his gaze to his crotch and a bulge was visible in his pants.

-Sir, but what's happening to you, -he said as he lowered his hand and caressed that bulge, while he turned to see if no one saw them.

-Wait my queen, there are security cameras here and I don't want us to be on social networks later.

-Let me go, let's see if we become famous.

-No, he said, separating from her and walking away, while turning his face to smile at her. He stopped in front of a watercolor painting.

Later they went to a restaurant located in the center of a very beautiful park, the tall trees moved gently in the fresh wind, and the flowers that lined the paths released their aromas, they walked arm in arm.

-Do you remember this place?

-And of course, my love, it was one of our first outings, I loved it.

-Well, after how many? fifteen, sixteen years it is still operating, the owner died recently, I came to eat with Roger and a coworker from the office.

They sat down at a small table with two chairs, ordered their food, and enjoyed the fun conversation that characterized them. After eating they decided to go to the movies.

-He was driving, Ellen released her shoulder from the seat belt and approached to kiss him on the cheek and began to caress his lower belly and thighs.

-Ma'am, what are you doing?

-Nothing, I just want to turn my man on.

She caressed the bulge that was growing in his crotch.

-Oh Ellen -he said, half-closing his eyes a little, to increase his sensations.

-My love, she said, wouldn't you like, instead of going to the movies, to go to a motel? You and I, without any clothes and just enjoying all this, he was putting his hand inside his pants.

-Then it's this way.

He turned the wheel, and while driving he began to caress his wife's beautiful thighs, she separated her legs a little, allowing him to go deeper in his search, when he finally reached the desired place, she moaned.

-Oh, my love -she said, closing her eyes and squeezing the legs that imprisoned his hand.

-I love feeling you, beautiful, and I love how you caress me.

Their energies were at their maximum, they embraced each other, loving each other and dancing, they came out from all sides of the vehicle, it seemed to shine, if someone had the ability to see energies, they would know what was happening there. They arrived at the motel that they both frequented when they were dating and entered. A voice coming out of a speaker, indicated them to room number seven. He found number seven and entered the garage, got out, closed the gate, and opened the door for his wife, she got out, and they kissed, she continued caressing him, he took her hand and they ran up the stairs, they closed the door and the energy dance began.

They were both lying down, tired, hugging each other, he caressed her back and she was lying on his chest, she could hear his heart, while she caressed his torso. Their energies were recovering, they slowly returned to cover their physical bodies, after having merged and mixed.

-My love, I'm happy, but I don't want to spend the night here. Tomorrow I have to go to the office, it's better if we go home.

-You're right, my queen. It's already after one in the morning.

They both got dressed and continued to show each other loving, non-sexual caresses throughout the entire journey back home.

Richard took his cell phone, he was sitting at his desk in his office, looking at some plans, he saw the name on the screen and greeted me happily.

-Alberto hello, nice to meet you.

-Hi Richard, I hear a lot of joy in your voice, I deduce that everything is better, right?

-It definitely is and I owe it to you.

-That's great friend, hey, I'm calling you because I want to organize, well, I'm organizing a dinner at my house next Saturday, I hope it's not too late and that you already have a commitment.

-Well, I was thinking of proposing to Ellen that we go away alone for the weekend, it's been a long time since we did it and we need it.

-I suggest, if you allow me, come to the dinner, then you can make that trip and believe me, it will be different.

-Okay friend, it will be a pleasure.

-Please extend the invitation to Roger and his girlfriend.

-He is not in the office now, he has not shown up since I arrived, you know the good thing about being a boss, but you can count on it, I don't know if he has a girlfriend, but I will tell him to bring someone, he will be very happy.

-Great, I sent you my address, I'll see you on Saturday starting at eight thirty.

-Of course, we'll say hello there, thanks for calling.

IV An Angel on Earth

-Karla, you won't believe it, you won't believe what happened to me.

-What happened to you, friend?

Erika told her all the changes she had been making, about the candle and her prayer.

-Don't you think it's a coincidence that Alberto called me, right after I finished saying my prayer.

-Well, it's not strange, God answered you, friend, isn't that beautiful.

-Oh no, but that means only one thing, that God really wants to help me change.

-How great, friend, how great that you see it that way.

-You have to come to my house tonight, I have two bottles of wine and you have to see what I've been doing, I'm going to call Ellen.

-Don't count on her, she's with her boyfriend, they were together all day yesterday, as far as I know, and they're still celebrating, but call him to see if she's free later in the evening.

-If I'm going to call him, I'll see you tonight at whatever time you want, don't bring anything, I'll prepare dinner.

-Oh, friend, I really have to see that. I'll see you later in the evening.

-Ellen, hello friend.

-Hello Erika, what's up?

-I already heard that you two got back together.

-Yes, friend, that's right, we're happy, what Alberto explained to us has made all the difference.

-You told Richard about Alberto.

-No, he introduced himself to Roger, Alberto's boss, and him at a bar. They were at a bar and he introduced himself to them.

-Oh no, don't tell me that. Something important happened to me, you can come to my house tonight, Karla will come, I have wine and I will make dinner. I'll wait for you, go on, it's important.

-Well, I think it will be fine, Richard has something in a building and is running around, he didn't go to work yesterday, we were together all day, it was incredible.

-Friend, we have to talk about all that, I'll see you tonight ok, after seven, ok?

-Okay, see you there.

Richard took his phone and called his wife.

-Hello my love, how are you?

-Happy my love and you, how's work?

-Accumulated, you know one day you don't come and it seems like nobody does anything, but well, everything works out favorably. Hey, guess who called me.

-I have no idea, my mom.

-Ha, ha, not at all, Alberto, he called to invite us to dinner at his house this Saturday, I'm letting you know so you don't make plans.

-Excellent news, my love, that's going to be great.

-I believe it, Roger will also go, by the way, I'm late today, I have things to do to finish.

-Okay, I'm going to meet Erika and Karla for dinner at Erika's house.

-That's great, my love, have fun, I'll see you later tonight.

The phone rang, he thought about hanging up when he saw the name, but he decided to face what he should.

-Hello Larisa, how are you?

-Upset, how do you think I feel? I spend my time waiting for you to call me and nothing, days go by and not a message, what's wrong? Do you not love me anymore?

-We have to see each other, how about today? I'll stop by your apartment at nine.

-Ok, I'll wait for you.

They hung up the phones. He remained silent thinking, and Alberto's voice came to his mind: We have to learn to develop an unconditional love, an honest love. He dialed the phone.

-My love, hello again.

-What's wrong, my love?

-I want to tell you something... I feel sorry, but you have to know.

-What's wrong, my love? You scare me. Is everything okay?

-Yes, of course. She called me, and I'm going to see her today at her apartment at nine. I'm going to finish that matter. I just wanted you to know that I'm trying to create an honest relationship and that means telling each other everything.

He remained silent, waiting for her answer. She took a while to answer. She was thinking about what the correct position was. At another time she would have been upset, but now she understood.

-You know, my love. I don't hold any grudge against her. Now I'm seeing you as what you truly are, a being of energy and spirituality, who lives experiences and what you've lived has enriched you spiritually, so I don't have to hold any grudge against her. And it seems to me that yes, you have to face her and speak honestly to her, tell her what you want, and if... -she remained silent, thinking. What she was going to say was very delicate- and yes...

-Yes, what? -he encouraged her.

-If you don't want to break up with her and you want to keep seeing her, because you think you need her, go ahead, from today on I'm going to love you unconditionally, and how, yes madam, I have a very special love and it's the one I've given you all these years that we've been together, and I must admit that you helped me since I met you, you helped me to let that love come out from within my being, no one before knew how to get it out, only you, that's why I loved you since I saw you and I love you more now after all these years.

He remained silent, his eyes filled with tears, the words disappeared, it was one of those magical moments when only love exists and words are not necessary.

-My love, she said, you're there.

-Yes, my queen, it's just that your words...

She felt how he began to cry, and he couldn't speak, she was crying too. She remained silent giving him time.

-Thank you, my queen, thank you for this beautiful love that you have always given me, forgive me, because I lost sight of it, but now that I can see and feel it, I can only thank you. Thank you for being so understanding... but no, definitely, I don't need it, now you and I are reuniting, I don't need anyone else to fill me or satisfy me, I have the most beautiful love at my side, I don't need anything else.

She smiled as she wiped her eyes with a tissue she had taken out of her bag.

-I love you Ellen, my queen, I'll see you at night.

-Thank you, my love, for talking to me and being honest, I appreciate it, I appreciate your sincerity.

They both hung up.

The building was very elegant, she got out of the elevator and walked the wide hallways with beige porcelain floors with gold veins, she rang the bell, waited a few seconds, Larisa opened the door.

-Hello my love, welcome.

-Hi Larisa

She wanted to kiss him on the lips, but he pulled back and kissed her on the cheek.

-Wow, why so cold? What's wrong?

-Can we sit down?

She pointed to the living room.

-Do you want something to drink?

-No thanks, I'm fine.

He sat down on the single chair, which was very strange, and she had no choice but to sit on the long chair.

-Larisa, I came because I want you to know something, I'm back with my wife and we've sorted things out, so, I'm sorry, but what we had has to end.

-Well, I'm not really surprised.

He was surprised by her peaceful attitude, she had a very capricious personality, she was the only daughter of a millionaire, used to everyone doing what she wanted, and therefore, getting her way.

-Since you've been away for weeks, I imagined something like that. I'm going to pour myself a drink, are you sure you don't want something?

-No thanks, I'm fine.

-I'll tell you something, last week I was sitting in the golf club restaurant, I had agreed to meet a friend, but she called me and said she couldn't make it, so I had breakfast alone, I was looking at the green grass and a man stopped in front of me, preventing me from looking outside. -Miss -he said- I want to tell you that you are the most beautiful woman I have seen in a long time, may I accompany you? He had a charming smile and for some reason I could not refuse, so I accepted and he accompanied me. He was a very nice man, his last name was Rojas, I did not hear his name because a noise did not let me, but well, it was a very pleasant conversation, but I do not know why he said to me: Did you know Larisa, that when two people meet it is because their energies attract each other? -Richard raised his eyebrows upon hearing her words and looked at her intrigued. She continued- and that in reality we are not the physical body we inhabit, but rather we are spiritual and energetic beings, that we were only living experiences on this earth, that any experience is actually an exchange of energies, and that personal relationships were to free us from karmas from past lives. I had read a very interesting book about past lives and agreements, have you heard of that?

-Well, about past lives yes, but not about agreements.

-Ok, I'm not going to explain it to you because it's very complex, but what I had read and what this man explained to me was that you and I had a pending relationship that came from one of our past lives, which is why we met again. I remember the day I saw you, that morning in your office, in the meeting room, the moment I noticed you, you seemed very familiar, as if I had known you for a long time, I don't know if the same thing happened to you.

-No, actually I liked you, you're very beautiful, but I didn't feel that.

-Well I did, later, with time, I started flirting with you because I liked you a lot, but you stayed away, you talked to me about your relationship with Ellen, and the truth is that I liked that you had that special love, I thought that you and I could have something like that, if I could get you to fall in love with me, and then, well, you gave in to my charms and finally we fell in love.

-Yes, I admit that it is true, I came to feel something very special for you, in fact, I still do.

-Well, deep down, I didn't want your marriage to end, I've heard of many stories of women who steal another woman's husband and in the end, after keeping him, they also lose him, because another woman is going to steal him again, so I didn't want that, but the most important thing is that this man made me understand that when we stay in life doing something that we know is not right, in reality what we do is keep ourselves tied to karma, and that in the end, when our body dies, we will not take anything of all the wealth that we have achieved, not a cent, nothing, we will only take our karmas and our ties, which we would then have to reincarnate to relive those experiences, which we could not or did not want to stop doing. I understood that you and I had already had a relationship in past lives, that's why I felt like I knew you the first time I saw you, and that in one of these lives I stole you from your wife's side, and that now I was repeating that, but that if I did it again, I wouldn't end the karma, but I would have to come back again and again, until I had overcome that matter of stealing husbands; therefore, I don't want us to continue either, I want you to go back to your wife and be very happy, I don't lack suitors, so... cheers - she said raising her glass with whiskey and ice. - Cheers - he said with his fingers interlaced, and thoughtful - I am speechless, I have just met a man who spoke to me about energies, he made me understand that my wife had not stopped loving me, as I thought, but that energetically she was saturated with my energy, and that I, spiritually, had joined you, because our energies had liked each other, and now that you tell me, in reality it is not just that our energies liked each other, but that they knew each other, that is why our encounters were so special.

-Yes, I felt that from our first intimate relationship, that was very special.

-But it was that special, because our spirits knew each other, and perhaps, in our past lives we also had something beautiful.

-Yes, perhaps I stole you from your wife.

As soon as he said this, they both felt it was true, he let himself fall back on the back of the chair, leaning his head.

-Wow Richard, it's true! I don't know how, but I feel it, I feel that it was true.

Her eyes filled with tears, her spirit was happy, both spirits danced together holding hands, bathing in violet light, transmuting and removing karma from each other.

-Wow, it's incredible, we have met again to solve this, I don't mean this moment, but this whole relationship, from the first day we met, we met again under the pretext of the house, but in reality, it was because we had to free ourselves from our bondage.

-Oh Larisa, it's incredible, all this about karmas, reincarnation, past lives, our meeting, everything, wow, how incredible.

-That's right, it's incredible.

He stood up and stood in front of her, he extended his hands to her, she took them and stood up, he hugged her affectionately.

-Thank you, darling, thank you for having lived with me this and all the adventures in our past lives, if I offended you, if I humiliated you, if I hurt you, in any way, Larisa, I ask for your forgiveness, I'm sorry, it was not my intention.

The violet light of transmutation enveloped their physical and energetic-spiritual bodies, freeing them definitively. She shed tears, but not from pain, but from something that was lifted from her.

Richard -she repeated instinctively, releasing him from the hug and taking his hands, both looking directly into each other's eyes- if I, in any way, offended you, hurt you, stole your wife or your family from you, please forgive me, I'm sorry, that wasn't my intention either.

-Thank you, darling -the violet flame enveloped them as their souls embraced each other feeling freed from karmas.

-I have to go, thank you Larisa, really, thank you, I want us to continue being friends, good friends, we're not going to have sex again, but I want us to be friends, what do you say, do you accept?

-Of course, Richard, we'll be very good friends, one day you'll invite me to your house and I'll be friends with Ellen, we'll see.

-We'll see, it would be nice, we'll see.

They hugged again and kissed each other on the cheek. She walked him to the door and he left.

-Hey Larisa, this man, what was he like?

-He's about fifty-five years old, thin, with gray hair on the sides, very nice.

-It's not possible -he said, turning around.

She was a little disconcerted, closed the door and leaned against it, she was happy, liberated and happy.

-Hi girls.

Ellen entered Erika's house, and when she saw her condition she was surprised, everything was clean and shiny. On the coffee table a pink scented candle was burning, which filled the room with a very soft and pleasant fragrance.

-Wow friend, what happened here? What happened to you?

She was also very changed, she looked thinner and her clothes made her look very pretty, she had discreetly put makeup on her face.

-You're not beautiful -said Karla, getting up from the individual chair.

-But of course, you are, you look incredible and your house is not, well, we've known each other for many years and I've never seen it like this, it feels a very different vibe, more spiritual.

-That's great Ellen, I'm glad you like it, come in, sit down, leave your bag and jacket here, she pointed to a new coat rack that was next to the main entrance.

-No, well, what happened to you? Tell me.

-Wait, do you want some wine? We already opened the first bottle and Karla brought two more.

-I have another one in my bag, please take it out.

Erika brought the bottle, the glasses, some plates with snacks, olives and square cheese to the coffee table, and the three of them sat on the floor leaning on the chairs, it was their custom.

-Ready, now we are complete. First let's say cheers to my new life.

The three childhood friends raised their glasses and clinked them.

-To our new lives, said Ellen.

-To our new lives, chorused Karla.

-Okay, friends - Erika said - I'll tell you. Well no, first Ellen, yours is more important, tell us, what happened?

-Oh no, friends.

Her eyes filled with tears wanting to come out, she waved her hand to dry her eyes.

-Oh no, you scare me, Karla said, didn't you say you had made up?

-She didn't cry from sadness, but from joy, I can't hold back. I'm so happy.

She couldn't hold back her tears, her friends came over to hug her and she cried from happiness.

-Oh beautiful, how nice, Erika said, starting to shed some tears.

-Tell us, go on, you have me on tenterhooks.

-It's just that I'm so happy. The night we met Alberto I came home, Richard was asleep and I didn't want to bother him, the next morning I asked him to talk, he said maybe we could have lunch together, but that he would call me, he didn't, so I called him, he refused, he had a lot of work, I cried all day, I didn't want to lose him and I felt like he was leaving my life. I fell asleep alone, he wasn't going to come home early, he came back around four in the morning, or something like that, he woke me up when he turned on the light of my night lamp, he knelt down, he was carrying some white roses, and he asked me for forgiveness,

-Oh yes, I knew it -Karla wiped her tears with the napkin- you love each other, go on, and then? -He told me that he loved me, that he had been a fool, I couldn't stop crying, I hugged him so much, then we made love.

Everyone was crying, Erika had brought a box of tissues and handed them out, everyone was wiping their faces.

-I thought I would lose him, that I had rejected him so much that I had already lost him, but no, it wasn't like that, we met again and we spent the whole next day together, we went to

114

have breakfast at the cafeteria where we met and curiously, the whole place was full and the only empty table was ours, the one where we talked for the first time.

-Oh friend, how beautiful, it's just that...

Erika cried with a lot of feeling.

-His love is so beautiful and I cry thinking that I have left such a beautiful love, because I was stupid, because I was stupid I got rid of a good man who loved me, all because I didn't know this about energies, if I had known he and I would still be together.

Karla caressed her back and said.

-We have all lost loves because of ignorance, but the important thing is that now we know and our next relationships will be honest. Don't worry Erika. Go on Ellen, what else?

-The next morning, while we were having breakfast, Richard told me that he went to a bar with his boss and that a man introduced himself to them.

-Alberto, shouted Erika pointing at Ellen.

-Yes.

-It's not possible, that must be an angel, there are already too many coincidences.

-Yes, but wait, he taught him about energy saturation with sex, and how our sexual desire decreases when we are saturated, that made him understand that I really did love him, but that spiritually I could no longer have as much sex as he needed. He told me that we had never been taught to have an honest, true and unconditional love, because the church and the ruling elite do not like it, that sex awakens various powers, and that with those powers they could not manipulate us.

-Alberto did not explain that to us -said Erika.

-Well, friend, it was too much information.

-Yes, but then, my love told me that if we wanted to have a lasting love, we should learn to express an honest and unconditional love, that is, without conditions, that means, loving our partners no matter what. Then I said to him: Would you be willing to let me have sex with other men?

-What did he answer you?, Karla asked, opening her eyes.

-Alberto says that, if we do not accept that our partners live the experiences that they have to live, it is for three reasons, wait, let me remember... yes, the first, because we do not understand what we truly are, energetic-spiritual beings, living experiences in a physical body, because at the end of life, he says, when we have died, we will not take anything with us, except the energies of the relationships that we have lived, whether sexual or friendship, and the karmas; second, because our love is not an honest and unconditional love and third..., -she thought a little- ah yes, because of our culture and religious ideas, which tell us that it is a sin.

-But of course -said Erika- we have always been told in the church how to live and what is good or not, what is sin or not, and how we should treat the infidel, right? In fact, we see it in the movies.

-Exactly, that's what Richard said, that religion didn't want us to wake up.

our power and that's why we had been taught that sex was outside of marriage...

-It's a sin, -Karla confirmed- of course, my grandmother and my mother always told me that. That's why we hold back the desire, because I have had desire, and how, I have met some guys who well... but I have always had to hold back the desire, for fear of sin, and that's even though I'm not very religious.

-Think about it, Ellen said, we don't need to be very religious, our teachings have always told us so, our teachers at school, your aunts, uncles, all women and all men believe in that, so we don't need to be religious, it's enough to live in a society.

-And that's all over the world, Karla confirmed, I've seen films from India, from Russia, and they all treat the unfaithful the same.

-But of course, the dominance of religion is all over the world, now I understand - said Erika very thoughtfully.

-What are you thinking about, Erika? You stayed silent.

-I just think about all this and that it's true, we think that sex with other people is a sin, when in reality, it's not, on the contrary, it's something energetic and spiritual, wow, this is revolutionary.

They all kept silent thinking, Ellen ended the silence.

-Cheers friends, let's toast to the awakening of our consciences.

The three of them raised their glasses and clinked them smiling.

-But then, what's the deal with you and Richard, are you going to give yourselves permission to have sex with other people?

-We don't know yet, we have to talk a lot about this, we have to get used to seeing ourselves as what we truly are, energetic-spiritual beings, and become aware that sex doesn't harm us, but rather enriches us spiritually, in fact, we think that would be like being a swinger, and we're talking about it, we don't know yet.

-My friend Laura, I don't think you knew her, she was a coworker, she and her partner did that and according to what she told me, they got along very well, but they ended up separating.

-Why, I don't understand, they didn't get along very well?

-It turns out that one night at a party she met a guy, with whom she had sex, but she and her partner were always at these parties, and they had agreed to do it, as long as they were together, never alone; but this guy invited her to be alone with him, so she went to a hotel secretly from her husband and he found out, she told him and he got furious, he almost hit her, she says that she had never seen him so jealous, that he was jealous, but not that much, from that day on he became insufferable and she ended up telling him to go to hell, they separated.

-It's true, I've heard of many divorces of this type of people.

-I don't understand, said Ellen, sex like this is supposed to be more fun, who knows why that is? The important thing is that now my Richard and I are so in love and what do you think, the cherry on the cake.

-Tell me, tell me.

Both friends looked at her intrigued while they ate cheese squares.

-He called me a while ago and said he was going to see this lady, his lover.

-Oh no, that's not true, said Erika, but then...

-No, it's not that, wait, he said he was going to see her in her apartment, but that he was going to end their relationship, that he wanted us to have an honest, true and unconditional relationship, so he had to be honest with me, that's why he told me.

-And what did you say to him?, questioned Erika.

-I thought about it carefully and said. My love, I love you, now I understand that your life does not belong to me, that we are energetic-spiritual beings, if you need to continue maintaining that relationship, it's okay, do it.

Both friends opened their eyes, unable to believe it.

-If you think you need that energy, go ahead, I'll understand you.

-And what did he answer you?

Ellen's eyes filled with tears again.

-He told me no, that he loved me so much, that he didn't need anyone, that with me he had the best sex he'd ever had, since the first time we did it, that he only wanted to give himself to me and that he loved me.

-Oh Ellen.

The two friends approached and hugged her.

-Congratulations, beautiful, you two really have something so strong and special. How happy it makes us to hear you.

-Thank you, friends, thank you.

They all wiped their eyes.

-Let's toast, to honest, true and unconditional love - the three of them raised their glasses and clinked them.

-Now Erika, said Karla, tell us, what happened to you? What caused this change?

-Wait, I'm going for another bottle.

-I'm going -Ellen said, getting up- you tell us, I'll listen to you.

-Well, it turns out that the other day I spoke with Karla, and she told me that I was actually afraid of taking my love to the next level, because every time I had a boyfriend who was worth it, I took it upon myself to dump him, to push him away, rather.

-Well, that's true -Ellen confirmed- we had both talked about this before, I think we told you this on some occasion, but you didn't believe us.

-Well, I hadn't understood it, but Alberto made me understand it, when he explained to us about energy and how we get saturated with our partner's energy, I think I get saturated very quickly, because shortly after living together, I feel like I don't want sex with him anymore and I start to want to meet another man, this made me think. I also heard Alberto's words in my mind: "Our environment impregnates us with its energies, if it is dirty, that impregnates our energetic body," I looked at my house, and I think that for the first time I realized how neglected my life was, so I began to clean my environment, I washed everything, dusted and well, you should see my room.

-Come on, show us.

The three of them headed down the hall and arrived at the room, it was impeccably clean, it no longer had the posters of their rock groups stuck to the wall, they were clear, a picture of a very beautiful landscape adorned the headboard of the bed, and some smaller pictures adorned the sides. There was a new bedspread and everything was in order. Some roses placed in a small vase placed on the nightstand finished off the decorations.

-Ellen turned to her friend and hugged her, Karla also joined the hug, Erika cried with joy, they all cried.

-We are so proud of you Erika, of the beautiful woman you really are and the beautiful way you are loving yourself.

-Yes, I had not realized that he did not love me, that is why I had my house in those conditions, I did not pay attention to it, because I was not important, now I understand, now I understand that I am a being of energy and that I must take care of the energies of my environment.

-It is incredible Erika, this change alone has made you lose weight, you look thinner, it is incredible.

-It is true Erika, you look beautiful, said Ellen caressing her face.

-Oh friends, you are making me cry.

-And you make us cry -smiled Karla- let's go to the living room, come on, let's continue.

They poured themselves more wine and settled in.

-And then what happened.

-Well, since I finished, I went to the cupboard and took out a candle that I had stored away, I lit it here and said a prayer, I asked God to help me, that I really wanted to take my love to the next level, that I needed his help, after I finished my prayer, I saw my house, and I told him that I was going to love it, that I would fill it with my love, so that it would fill my energetic body.

-Oh Erika -said Ellen- that is so beautiful, I think I am going to do the same, it has been a while since I have taken care of my house, my environment is very neglected, I leave everything to the lady who cleans, but the love, I definitely have to give it to her.

-I am going to do that too, you will see how I leave that palace -said Karla smiling, you will see.

-Well, it turns out that I was looking at my house, when the phone rang. Well, I answered hesitantly because I did not have the number registered.

-But I had sent it to you.

-Yes, but I hadn't registered it, so I didn't know who it was.

-And who was it? -said Ellen intrigued.

-Alberto.

-What, Alberto called you after you said the prayer asking God for help?

-Yes -Erika's eyes filled with tears again- isn't it incredible. God, my daddy, answered me -she said this and her tears overflowed.

Everyone cried with emotion.

-Oh beautiful -Ellen hugged her- it's incredible, now I realize, he has been behind all of us, helping us, and his messenger is Alberto.

-He must be an angel -said Karla wiping away her tears- there are too many coincidences, don't you think?

-He has to be an angel, hey, have you seen the time, I work tomorrow, it's really late -Ellen looked at her wristwatch.

-It's been a great night, thank you for coming beautiful, I love that you are the first to see my transformation.

-We are always here for you Erika - Karla hugged her affectionately and Ellen joined in the hug.

-Hey, but what did Alberto want, why did he call you?

-True, I forgot, he said he was expecting us on Saturday, after eight thirty at his house for dinner, that I should bring my boyfriend, but I don't have a boyfriend - she said with a sad face.

-It's true, Richard just told me the same thing about dinner.

-Well, - Karla added - then we'll see each other on Saturday, let's not talk about it anymore.

-I love you very much, friends.

It was already very late, the time with her friends had passed too quickly. She entered her children's bedroom and kissed them, made sure to cover them well and closed the doors. Richard was sleeping peacefully, the lamp on his bedside table was on, he had left it like that.

-My love, I'm here, -she sat down next to him and caressed him, he opened his eyes and smiled at her.

-How did it go, my love?

-Amazing, you don't know what a beautiful night I've had with the girls, but it's already late and you've slept little these days, tomorrow you have to go to the gym.

-Well, I can't go and I'll stay for breakfast with you and we'll talk, I also have something important to tell you.

-Ok excellent, sleep then, I'm going to change, rest.

She leaned towards him and kissed him tenderly on the lips, looked him straight in the eyes, ran her hands through his hair, and his eyes clouded over.

-Do you have something? he said a little worried.

-It's just that I'm so grateful to my father, God, for all this that, well, I'm very sensitive, we've been crying.

-Ok, my queen, rest, we'll talk tomorrow, it's late.

She got up, went into the bathroom and did her routine, looked into her eyes in the mirror and said: Thank you father, thank you for always being with me! You're welcome -she heard the voice in her mind, but she thought she imagined it- she smiled.

The children looked very happy, breakfast was already ready, the maid always prepared it for them. Their parents prepared a sandwich for them that Ellen placed in a plastic sandwich maker, along with yogurt.

-Here is your lunch.

-Kids, I want us to have dinner together today, do you want to do it here at home or do you want to go to a restaurant?

-And that miracle, dad?

-Well, daughter, I want to spend time with you, lately I have been overwhelmed by work and I have not dedicated anything of my life to you, and you are growing up very fast.

She caressed her daughter's hair and then her son's. They accepted the caress, Brandon stood up, walked around the bar and hugged him, he turned around and hugged him lovingly.

-Oh daddy, I thought that... -he said with his eyes full of tears- I thought that you didn't love us.

-No my love, don't think that, don't believe that, not at all, it's just that I got lost, I stopped valuing what really matters in my life, which is you, and I focused on other things, forgive me.

The lady who helped them with the housework, watched the scene standing, leaning on the sink, and wiped away her tears, she had been with them for many years, and they loved her very much.

His little girl also stood up and hugged him along with his brother, He extended his arms and loved them, a tear rolled down his cheek. Ellen watched them and wiped away her tears. After hugging her father, they went to her mother and did the same. Finally they returned to their benches.

-So, my loves, -he continued- what do you say, do we eat or have dinner, well no, better have dinner, but at home or in a restaurant?

The young people turned to look at each other and smiled.

-At the restaurant, dad, it's been a long time since we went out together.

-It's done, I pat the bar, so be it, I'll come for you at seven, be ready, I'll make a reservation, and hurry up, the bus won't be long.

They got up and ran to brush their teeth. They came back, grabbed their backpacks and the

plastic sandwich box, and left escorted by their parents, who watched them from the door, hugging each other.

-Our children will soon fly the nest.

-That's right, my love, but there's still a long way to go, Ellen turned to look at him and they kissed.

-Come, let's sit in the dining room. Mrs. Mary, help me carry the plates to the table, please.

-Of course, sir, how nice that you're having breakfast here, we miss you, the house misses him.

-Thank you, Mrs. Mary, it's true, I have left aside the most important thing, I have left aside everything I have worked so hard for, my family and my house, aren't we human beings stupid? We work all our lives to have a house and for our family to be well, and we forget to love our house and to dedicate time to it, as well as our children and our partner, isn't that being stupid?

-Yes sir, you are right, we are stupid.

-Yes, my love, you are absolutely right, we are stupid.

Mrs. Mary returned to the kitchen to continue her work. They sat down and continued eating breakfast. He took a sip from his cup of coffee and said.

-How did it go last night my love? Tell me about the girls, you came very excited.

-Oh no, that was beautiful, but no, first you, tell me how it went.

-You don't know, it was super interesting.

-Interesting, how is that? What happened?

-I arrived at Larisa's house.

-The owner of the house they were building?

-Yes, my love… forgive me, I never told you so as not to make you feel bad, forgive me.

-No, my love, we are learning to have a relationship of true and unconditional love, say whatever you say, I will not stop loving you, so do not be afraid to tell me everything, I have no problem, after all, you are only energy living in this beautiful body, she caressed his face while looking at him.

-I love you honey, that makes me feel very good, I also want you to know, that whatever you tell me, I will continue to love you, unconditionally.

-Thank you love, you continue to have me intrigued.

-I arrived at his house, and as always, he greeted me... well, I will skip the details.

-Oh no, we agreed unconditionally.

-Ok, she wanted to kiss me, but I didn't let her, we just greeted each other with a kiss on the cheek, we sat down, and she told me that she met a man at the golf club, who made her understand that our relationship was because we had unfinished karma.

-Oh no, what do you mean a man told her that?

An inevitable smile appeared on his face.

-Wait, let me continue, so well, she had already read books about reincarnation and agreements, so what this man told her made her understand, she says, that since we met, she felt like she already knew me, it was like seeing me again after a long time, I didn't feel that, of course, the first time I saw her, of course I liked her, she's very attractive, but nothing more, I always kept myself away.

-But then, when you met her, you liked her, and you started dating, that was almost a year ago and more, right?

-No, it wasn't like that, we met, I liked her, but nothing happened, she always made advances on me, but I stayed out of it, we just became good friends, I didn't want to jeopardize our relationship, for me the most important thing has always been you, my family and then work, so I stayed out of it despite her flirtations, I knew that if you found out about us it would end and of course I didn't want that, but also that if I did that I could put the project and the office at risk, so no, I held back, but then...

-Go on my love, don't be ashamed, this will help us understand.

-Then you started to reject me and not want me to touch you, sex was becoming less and less common, we only made love when I asked you and then you accepted, but I didn't feel satisfied, I didn't feel your commitment, I didn't feel your love, it was just sex and I didn't like that, I felt like you did it out of obligation, so I felt very dissatisfied, all day at work I was in a bad mood, I couldn't concentrate; on one occasion, Roger said to me: Richard, have you been very irritable, are you okay, is everything okay at home? Yes, I answered him, but inside I was burning up.

-Oh, my love, I didn't know that this was affecting you so much, I didn't know why, but I just stopped wanting to have sex, I loved you, but my libido is gone, forgive me honey.

-No, my love, there is nothing to forgive, yesterday I understood, let me explain. Larisa kept telling me that she didn't really want you and I to break up, that we had fallen in love, but that she knew of the love I have for you and that she didn't want to steal you from me, because in reality she and I had a karma, that in another life, she stole me from my wife's side, and that karma kept us tied, that it wasn't a coincidence that I was the head of the project for her house, that when she saw me for the first time she felt like she had known me for a long time, do you understand, are you understanding?

-Yes, of course, now I understand. You had to meet, so that she could steal you from your wife again, because that was something she had already done in a past life, I understand, go on, go on.

-Yes, and that, if she did it again, then she would remain tied to that experience, that her karma would not disappear, and that she would have to reincarnate again to repeat the experience, until she stopped doing it.

-Wow, so her house was just the pretext to meet you again, and for us to stop wanting to have sex, it was so that you could go with her and accept her, to repeat the experience of her stealing a husband, me, to live the experience of losing a husband, and you the experience of losing and leaving your family.

Both opened their eyes, surprised by their discovery.

-Oh love, this is incredible, it's as if it were a theater set up on purpose to live certain experiences.

-Oh Ellen, you have a way of analyzing and seeing things, that is not good, you are clarifying the situation even more for me.

-Ok, but go on, and what else.

-Then I understood everything, I stood up, I took her by the hands, we were both standing, and I said to her: Larisa, thank you, thank you for having lived this experience with me, thank you for having lived with me the experiences of our past lives, forgive me, if I offended you, if I humiliated you, if in some way I hurt you, I want to ask for your forgiveness, I'm sorry, it was not my intention, we hugged each other and she cried, we were feeling something, I don't know what it was, but it was as if something was being lifted off us, we felt liberated, we gave each other a kiss on the cheek, and we let go, and I told her that I wanted us to be friends, good friends, that we would not have sex again, but that I wanted us to continue seeing each other as good friends.

-Oh, my love, that was so beautiful. Ellen took her hand and caressed it. And what did she say to you?

-Yes, we would be good friends, and maybe later you and she would be good friends.

Ellen smiled.

-But of course, I would love to meet her.

-Well, we'll see later, she's sure to invite us to the opening of her new residence, that house is turning out beautiful.

Ellen leaned back on the chair and took her cup of coffee with both hands, taking small sips.

-Oh, my love, this is incredible, I don't believe it, it's all a plan made by someone, so that we live these experiences, because they give us the opportunity to free ourselves from karma, if we repeat them we remain tied and if we stop doing them we free ourselves, wow honey, how incredible - she turned her face to look him in the eyes, straightened up and gave him a beautiful kiss.

-My love, remember dinner with Alberto, this Saturday.

-What wonderful news, it will be an incredible evening.

-Hey love, and if we take the children, the baby will soon be seventeen, and sexual awakening is imminent, you see how beautiful she is, and the suitors are already hanging around her.

-The flies it will be, I'm going to have to buy my spray poison against the flies, ha, ha, ha, ha, I can already see myself spraying the spray in the faces of her suitors -she raised her arm pretending to press a button- yes, I will do that, ha, ha, ha, ha. Hey, you haven't told me about the girls.

She turned to look at her wristwatch, oh no, we're already late, I have things to do. I'll tell you later, I'll see you at seven. The kids thing isn't a bad idea, talk to Alberto and ask him, maybe he wants it to be just adult talk, you know, there will be a lot of talk about sex and all that.

-That's precisely why I think about the children, they have to learn about all of that before they start experiencing it without knowing anything, like us.

-Well, yes, you're right, call him and see what he says.

-Thank you, Mrs. Mary, breakfast was delicious, I already missed it, let's see if next time you'll spoil me with some chilaquiles.

-Of course, sir, with great pleasure, have a good time.

The lovers gave each other a beautiful kiss and he left the house.

-Oh lady, you don't know how happy it makes me to see you so in love, I already missed that.

-Yes Mary, it's true I missed that too. I'm going to change, because I have to go out.

-And now boss, why are you so happy?

Roger arrived at his office and hugged his secretary.

-It's a beautiful day, isn't it?

-Yes, of course.

He turned his back smiling and went to his friend's office. Richard was reviewing some plans on the drawing board. Roger approached him and patted him on the back - Happy Friday friend, today is a great day.

Richard turned to look at him, it was very strange that he was so friendly, normally he was more serious.

- And now Roger, why are you so happy?

- You don't know friend, I'm changing, I began to be aware of my environment, I came home and I think that for a long time I had not taken it into account, so I looked at it closely, and I realized how beautiful it is, Alberto's words echoed in my head: Your environment impregnates you with its energy and you with it; So I started to change my vibes, I started to feel a lot of affection for my house, I appreciated it and I felt it, I think that for the first time I really felt it, when I was walking to my bedroom, I felt the texture of the chair, I saw everything that decorated it and I don't know, something beautiful lit up in me, but there is also something else.

-What was it?

-I saw Rouse.

-Rouse, and that? You had told me that after breaking up you hadn't talked to her again.

-Yes, it was, I was very sad after we broke up and I missed her, but I never dared to call her, after our talk with Alberto I realized the special relationship that she and I had, so I called her and you know what? I'm going to win her back.

-Seriously Roger, wow, I thought that was serious about

living alone for the rest of your life.

-That's what I thought, but I realized the beautiful love that we have; After Laura, it was hard for me to find someone with whom I connected so beautifully, until Rouse came along, with her I did connect, and after knowing the reasons why we broke up, I realized that we could get back together, I think our love is still alive, I felt it when I saw her.

-Well, what excellent news brother, I'm very happy for you. By the way, Alberto spoke to me.

-How nice, I was thinking about calling him and inviting him to dinner, I want Rouse to meet him.

-Well, it won't be necessary, he's inviting us to dinner at his house on Saturday after eight thirty.

-Fantastic, everything is lining up perfectly, I'll tell my beautiful one.

-Are you back together?

-Mmm, no, she has someone, that's what she told me, but I asked her to let me see her more often and I'm thinking about inviting her to dinner today, I suggested that we be lovers, well, she actually said it.

-No, well, that's very strange...

They both thought about that.

-You know, Richard, I'm thinking that a person who is in love with someone, if he or she were to find someone who falls in love with him or her, would eventually have another lover, right?

-Yes, Roger, that's what I thought too, those people are

always looking for lovers, but let's remember that this happens because of the saturation of our energetic bodies, and that what it's about is having an honest and unconditional love, understanding the needs of our partner, if you and she are honest and love each other unconditionally, you can allow yourselves to live your experiences without having to let each other down or hurt each other with concealments and lies.

-Yes, it's true, in fact, I've been looking at myself in the mirror and I say to myself: Remember Roger that you are an energy being living in this body; That has given me another vision of things and of my dealings with others. Now I began to see people as they truly are, beings of energy, and if I continue doing this, I will be able to see Rouse that way, and my mind will know that at the end of her life, as with mine, we will only take our energies and the energies that we have been spiritually enriched with.

-Yes, I am also doing that, and it feels different, I am more tolerant with everyone, I like that. By the way, brother, I have already fixed everything with Ellen and ended things with Larisa.

-Congratulations, brother, how nice, you have something very special, let me tell you that, in matters of love, you and she are my teachers, you don't know how much I have learned from you by seeing you together.

-Are you serious?

-Yes, when Alberto said it, I immediately thought of you, and I realized that it was true, I have learned from you to show love.

-Well, I am glad to be a good example.

-How did it go with Larisa?

-That was incredible, you don't know, it was just wow.

-That big, really?

-Yes, but I'll talk to you later, I have to go to the building and I need to finish these plans.

-Yes, okay, I also have things to do, I'll see you later so you can talk to me. Today I'm going to have dinner with Rouse, well, I'm going to talk to her, but I'm sure she'll accept.

-I'm also going to have dinner with my children, we'll go to a restaurant, I already made the reservations.

-Hey, what if the six of us get together?

-I was thinking of telling them what happened to their mother and me.

-Are you going to tell them about your lover?!

-Yes, because they have to know everything else and what happened to me with Larisa.

-No, friend, we have to hear that, Rouse is going to love it too, come on, she'll learn a lot too.

-Let me talk to Ellen about it and I'll let you know, okay.

-Excellent, but call her now because I'm going to talk to Rouse so she doesn't make plans. Let me know as soon as possible.

Roger left the office and Richard picked up the cell phone from the stretcher.

-Hello love.

-Hello sweetheart, how's your day going?

-Good, with plans to resolve, but good, hey, I was thinking about dinner and I want to ask you something, if we are going to develop a relationship of true and unconditional love, we need our children to know the truth of our love, I want to tell them everything we've been going through and about Larisa and karma, I think it will enrich them a lot.

-I was also thinking about that precisely, so yes, I agree, let's do it.

-But, also, you won't believe it, Roger and Rouse want to get back together.

-Seriously, wow, love, what good news, they loved each other so much.

-Yes, and he asks me to invite them to dinner today with the children, he wants to hear what happened with Larisa and for Rouse to hear it too, he thinks it will help them understand everything.

-Of course, it will help them, go ahead and invite them.

-Excellent love, I'll see you at seven. I love you beautiful.

-And I send you lots of kisses, put them where you like.

-Mmm what delicious kisses.

They both laughed and hung up.

-Roger, yes, at seven thirty at the Madison, -Richard said

from the door frame of the office.

Roger was sitting in his high-backed chair, talking on the phone, he raised his thumb in acceptance, he continued talking.

-So beautiful, how is your day going?

-Good, my day is going very well.

-Hey darling, I want to invite you to dinner tonight, we're going to go to the Madison, Richard, Ellen and her children, there are very interesting things that I think can help us, it has to do with everything we've talked about.

-I don't know, wait, let me see my calendar.

He took his cell phone away from his ear and searched for the digital calendar with the keyboard.

-Ok, Roger, I'm very interested in hearing that and I'm free.

-Excellent -he said enthusiastically- I'll pick you up at seven, okay, and don't take your car, let me pamper you.

-Well, fine, but don't get your hopes up too much, I'm going because I want to hear about it.

He said this smiling slightly.

-So, you're not going for me, but for gossip, fine, I don't care as long as you're with me. I'll see you at seven, at your house or at your office?

-At my house, oh no... -he remained silent smiling.

-Will he be at your house?

-No, fine, come to my house for me.

-Sure, I won't get you into trouble? I don't want to be the cause of your separation.

-No Roger, I'm not really with anyone, I'm still single.

-Really? Yes, he said euphoric, sorry, he became serious, I'm sorry to hear that, no, it's not true, I'm not sorry, darling, I'll pick you up at seven at your house, kisses. He hung up the phone, got up from the executive chair and danced enthusiastically making circles with his hips and hands together, looking like a teenager on his first date.

V A magical dinner

The restaurant was quite busy, Richard and his family were sitting at the round table assigned to them, two seats were still empty.

-Gentlemen, good evening -the waiter greeted them- welcome, can we offer you something to drink before taking your order.

Ellen ordered a glass of white wine, her children ordered soft drinks, and Richard ordered a rum and cola drink.

-Well, my loves.

He said, putting his hand on his wife's thigh. She was wearing a very beautiful dress that fitted her entire body.

-Do you like the place, children?

-Yes, mom, it's very nice, isn't it, brother.

-Yes, I like it a lot. I like these elegant places a lot. I've always thought that only wealthy people come here, because they surely won't be cheap, right, dad?

-Hello, good night.

Roger and Rouse were standing at one side of the table, both smiling.

-Rouse -said Ellen, getting up- nice to see you again.

-Likewise, Ellen, you look beautiful.

-And you look incredible, you're still very beautiful.

They hugged each other and kissed each other on the cheek, they had become friends during the time she and Roger were together, and they continued to see each other occasionally afterwards, always greeting each other with great affection.

Richard hugged Roger and then her.

-Rouse, you look beautiful, it's nice to see you again.

The children stood up and shook their hands, she kissed them on the cheek.

-Wow, children, sorry, young people, how you've grown.

-I think we only notice how time passes when we see other people's children after a while of not seeing each other.

-That's right, beautiful, haven't you grown? Come sit next to me.

Ellen pointed to the chair next to her, Roger sat next to her.

-It's nice to see you children, said Roger, you've really grown.

The young people smiled and turned to look at each other in

complicity. The waiter returned with the drinks and the newcomers ordered theirs. The waiter left the menu cards on the table and left.

-It's so nice to see you together - said Richard, looking at his friends - you look great together and you Rouse look spectacular.

-Yes, brother, she looks incredible. You should have seen my face when I saw her leave her house in this beautiful dress. My heart wanted to jump out of my chest.

-Well, with good reason, said Ellen, you look beautiful, friend.

-Yes, said Brandon, you look very pretty.

-Yes, said Susan, when I grow up I'm going to be like you, always elegant and very well dressed.

-Oh, my loves, how sweet, thank you for your words, you've already made my night. You

are also getting very handsome, Brandon, every day you look more like your dad, but you're going to be much more handsome, you have your mom's eyes and she is beautiful, and you Susan, how beautiful you have become, how old you are, eighteen.

-Oh no, said Ellen, he's sixteen, he's almost seventeen, and he's fifteen.

Susan felt very flattered and smiled widely, turning to look at her brother.

-Well, imagine -said Rouse- if you're barely sixteen, I don't want to see when you turn twenty, wow, this beauty needs to be taken care of, I'm going to give you some good advice.

-Thank you, yes, I would love to -she answered enthusiastically.

After a while of chatting and having ordered their dishes, Richard said.

-Well, children, friends, we have invited you because we want you to know something important.

-Oh no, don't tell me we're going to have a little brother, said Susan.

-No, of course not -said her mother quickly- the factory closed after Brandon -Ellen smiled looking at her child.

-No -Richard resumed- children, we want to share with you something that has happened to us recently and well, now we have the pleasure of sharing the table with our friends, so you're going to find out too -he took a breath and said- I had a lover!

Both children opened their eyes in surprise, Rouse did the same, she was about to take a sip from her glass and the liquid slipped from her lips, she had to wipe it with the napkin.

-But dad, -said Susan- why?!

-Wait children, don't jump to conclusions, let us tell you what happened to us, so you understand why things happen to us.

-But mom, did you know? - questioned Brandon.

-Your dad confessed it to me.

-That's why you were so distant, Brandon and I knew

something wasn't right, you were always very affectionate and suddenly everything cooled down, my dad wasn't home anymore and you were always quiet and distant, you didn't look happy. We talked, and we knew something was wrong.

I used to ask you, but you always said they were fine -her eyes were beginning to fill with tears.

-No, my love, don't cry, -said her father, drying her eyes with the cloth napkin- wait, this is very interesting, breathe, go on, smile.

She controlled herself and smiled forcibly, her tears stopped.

-Well, let me tell you, your mother and I have been married for seventeen years, we have always loved each other very much, and today more than ever -he said taking his wife's hand smiling at her, Ellen smiled at him and then turned to see her daughter winking at her- but it turns out that, with time, sexual relations...

-Oh dad, don't tell us that -said Brandon.

-On the contrary, son, soon you two are going to begin to live your sexuality, and you will have a girlfriend and a boyfriend, so you better understand what happens in relationships.

-Well yes, you're right, sorry.

-Don't worry, then, well, when you meet someone and fall in love, over time sexual desire is born and when the time comes we start having intimate relations, I fell deeply in love with your mom the moment I saw her, in that cafeteria, and after only six months I asked her to be my wife, that was very fast, but I was madly in love with her and I knew that she was the woman with whom I wanted to spend the rest of my life, so I proposed that she be only mine and she accepted, then the children came, and with time and years, routine, work, obligations, and many things led us to a distance, I spent a lot of time at work and I didn't dedicate the time they required, after seventeen years together our sexuality was fading. In the beginning of every relationship, sex is something that you want to be having all the time, but over time, that sexual desire begins to diminish. -I stopped wanting to have sex - Ellen said - and I began, without realizing it, to reject him, to reject his father, so he got angry with me and complained, he asked me why I didn't want him, why didn't he satisfy me anymore? I answered that it wasn't that he didn't satisfy me or that I didn't love him anymore, but that I had simply stopped wanting to have sex.

-That's right, after some long months of distance, and of sexual absence, I met a very attractive woman, but I didn't become his lover immediately, because I didn't want his mother to find out, that would end our relationship and I didn't want that.

-That happens with all couples - Rouse intervened - when one of the two finds out about the other's infidelity, the relationship ends, that's why we all do that secretly.

-But then, you two also had secret lovers?

Roger and Rouse turned to look at each other.

-Yes - they both said at the same time looking at their children - we both had secret lovers.

-But then mom, that's going to happen to us too when we get married, many of my classmates' fathers have divorced because of infidelity - said Susan.

-Yes, in my class too, there are many children of divorced fathers.

-Well, children, let's say that's the main reason for divorces, but wait, you have to know more.

The waiter arrived with the plates and distributed them, once everyone had their food in front of them, they continued.

-Eat, I hope you enjoy the food.

-Wait, do you mind if we say a prayer - said Ellen looking at Roger and Rouse, they nodded, they all held hands and she said - Father, bless this table and this food, thank you for the love, among all of us, and for helping us understand the magic of life, help us continue learning to give honest and unconditional love, amen.

-Mom, what is unconditional love? -Susan asked.

-It is the love that is given without conditions.

-You see children -interrupted Richard- we met a friend, who spoke to us about energies, he told us that our physical bodies also had an energy body, if you look around all of us, there is a light that surrounds us, can you see it in me? -he pointed around his head.

-Yes, I see it -said Brandon- wow, is that white thing the energy body? It is true, everyone has it,

look at that man, it is bigger, everyone turned to where he was pointing.

-True said Rouse, how big it is.

-I don't see anything -said Susan a little disappointed.

-Don't despair love, little by little just keep trying.

-Well, then, that energy body is also our spiritual body, when we die, that body leaves the physical body and we continue living somewhere.

-Dad - said Susan excitedly - a friend recommended a movie to me, it's called Our Home, and it talks about death and what When we die we go to live in the City of Light, that's what it's called, and that's where we meet with those who had already died, it also talks about hell, -he said shuddering.

-Our home, Rouse had taken out his cell phone and written the name. Yes, here it is, we have to see it.

-Hey Richard, isn't this the movie that Alberto recommended to us?

-You're right Roger, I had forgotten, look how small the world is, well, it's good that you've already seen it, daughter, can I continue?

-Yes, yes.

-This energetic body, when you meet someone, meets with the energetic body of that person, and if the energies like each other, then they can get together a little, exchanging some of their energy, but if they don't like each other, then they reject each other, that has surely happened to you, when you meet someone you like a lot, it's because their energy is very similar to that of that person. And when we don't like someone, it's because we don't like their energy.

-How interesting -said Rouse- but it's real, we are all energy - she was a great reader and knew something about the subject.

-When your mom and I saw each other, our energies fell in

love with each other, we couldn't stop thinking about each other. It turns out that when you have sex, the energetic-spiritual bodies merge during orgasm -Richard put his palms together and interlaced his fingers- so that a single energy is formed, after a while, the energies separate and surround each other's physical body again, but they already bring the other's energy with them.

-Ok, I understand, said Brandon, we see that in the movies, I mean... -he was a little embarrassed.

-No son, don't be embarrassed, don't be embarrassed, speak freely, express your doubts, it's time to talk about this freely, without prejudice, your mom and I want you to learn this, because it's very important.

-Congratulations -said Rouse, looking at them both- how nice that as parents you express this to your children, and children, consider yourselves lucky to have these parents, not all are so sincere.

-Thanks friend -said Ellen, taking his hand.

-So, -continued Brandon- after the sex scene, they stay lying down, recovering, is that really because their energy bodies are returning to their physical bodies? Is that it?

-But, in addition, do they already bring the energy of the other? -intervened his sister.

-Exactly, that's right, that's what happens.

-Well, I didn't know about energy bodies, but Roger explained it to me and the truth is that it is extremely interesting.

-It really is Rouse…

-Continue dad, and then?

-It turns out that our energy bodies become saturated, and there comes a time when they can no longer receive so much energy from the other, and since we only have sex with our partners, because that's how we've been taught, then there comes a time when you can no longer receive energy from your wife or husband, but you still need sex, because if not, that energy, which is the Kundalini energy, saturates your chakras and you go crazy, you're not happy, and nothing satisfies you, not work or anything, in fact, you're always in a bad mood.

-That too -Rouse intervened- happens to us women, we need to have sex, maybe not as much as men, but it's something important in our lives.

-Is that why they were always angry? Because they didn't have sex anymore, and that put them in a bad mood? - Susan raised her eyebrows questioning them.

-Yes, my love, but we didn't know that -Ellen answered- we didn't know anything about energy bodies, so we just got angry and distanced ourselves.

-But then, should we get divorced when that happens, because if not, we would have to have a secret lover and that would bring us problems?

-No - answered her father - what we have to do is learn to give unconditional love, that is, without conditions; it is the love that loves, despite anything, for example, children, that love is the one that your mother or I give you, if you do something bad like steal or kill someone, it will hurt us a lot, but we will continue to love you forever. In marriages, we only love if the other person is faithful to us, or if they give us money, or if they do what the other person tells them to do. If the man is jealous, he will ask his partner not to go out, not to have friends, not to wear sexy clothes, and in that way, he will continue to love her. That is a selfish love, that is not an unconditional love but a conditional one.

-But then, in reality, were we taught to give a selfish love, because we only love if we meet a lot of conditions?

-That's right, Rouse -said Roger- I now have to learn to give you an honest and unconditional love.

-She smiled- Don't get your hopes up, I still haven't given you the yes. What do you want?

It costs you work, this doll is worth it - he quickly approached and kissed her on the cheek - Okay sir, be calm - he said waving him in the air, everyone laughed.

- Well, then children, are you understanding?

- Yes, yes, then we have to learn to love unconditionally.

- That's right, but then, what happened to us is that I needed sex and her mother... well.

- I didn't want it, say it love, without shame, that's the truth.

- Ok, her mother didn't want it and I needed it, that happened, then I met a woman whose energy liked mine, and in that way our energetic-spiritual bodies were enriched, because when our energies mix with someone else's, our spiritual bodies are enriched. Right here, sitting, our energetic bodies are enriched, by rubbing against other people's energies.

- Ok, I understand - said Brandon - that's why we look for

friends.

-That's right, son. Later, it turned out that I fell in love and was thinking about leaving his mother.

-Oh no, dad, don't tell us that.

-No, daughter, wait, let me continue. His mother and I were already very distant, we barely spoke to each other and well, I did a lot of stupid things; but then we met Alberto, and he explained all this to us and made me understand that his mother hadn't really stopped loving me, but had just moved away...

-Because she couldn't receive your energy anymore - said Susan.

-Exactly, that's it.

Rouse turned to see Roger and smiled, he returned a tender look.

-If we had known all this, darling, we would still be together.

-Definitely yes - she said.

-And then, dad, continue - Brandon hurried on.

-So, I understood all this, and I realized the beautiful and special love that his mommy and I have, and that I had to make it last forever, so I went back home and asked for forgiveness, she and I met again, our love was reunited and here we are.

-Did you forgive him, mom? How great.

-No, daughter, it's not about forgiving, it's about understanding, we both had responsibility, I rejected him and he had needs, so I almost threw him into the arms of the other lady, so we both have responsibility in this, but what I did know was that I didn't want to lose him, that I loved him like no one else and I wanted us to stay together.

-But wait, it gets better, then I went to see the other lady, who is now my friend.

-What? -Rouse opened her eyes- what do you mean, your friend Richard?

-Yes, -Ellen said- now she will be my friend too.

-Oh no, this has gotten out of hand -said Rouse, amazed.

-Mom, what do you mean you're going to be friends with my dad's lover? That's crazy - Susan took her glass and took a sip.

-Let me continue, I went to see her and she told me that she met a man who spoke to her about karma and made her understand that she and I had...

-Stop - Roger intervened - what do you mean she met a man? Don't tell me that...

-Richard just smiled - This man told her that she and I had a karma debt from some past life, and that we had come together because our energies knew each other and that it was really to heal that karma.

-What is Karma? Dad.

-When you do something bad to someone, like stealing a pen, or lying and cheating, or hurting and abusing them, when you bully another child, abusing your strength and size, or hurt someone, then you create karma, it is a debt between you and that person, that debt must be paid in this life or in the next, and only until you pay that karma, you are free from the experience, if you don't pay it, you will repeat the experience again and again, again and again, again and again, until you stop doing that.

-But how do you pay karma? -Roger asked.

-Stopping doing that which is not right, anything that you know is not right, gives us the opportunity to stop doing that and end the karma.

-Ok, I understand, please continue, and what happened?

-She told me that she had understood, that when we met, she saw me and felt that she already knew me, it was as if we had already seen each other in some past life, so our meeting in the office, was actually what gave us the opportunity to meet again, then we fell in love because our energies already knew each other and we felt very good, but that in reality she did not want Ellen and I to end because of her, that we had a very beautiful love and that she understood that in another life, she stole me from my wife's side, and that if she did it again, we would continue to be tied to that experience over and over again until she stopped doing that, that that was her karma and mine, then I understood everything, I took her hands looking into her eyes and I said to her: "Thank you, thank you for having lived this and any other experience in past lives, if I offended you, humiliated you, hurt you in any way, please forgive me, it was not my intention"; she began to cry and we hugged each other, I felt that something was lifted from me, I do not know what it was, but I am sure that something was lifted from me, then she asked me for forgiveness, because in a past life she had stolen me from my wife's side. We kissed on the cheek and she said to me:

152

"Thank you, Richard, thank you"; then I said to her: "I want us to be friends, good friends, if we have already spent some lives together, I want us to be friends, we are not going to have sex again, but I want us to be good friends, what do you say, do you accept?" "Sure -she answered- and you know, someday I would like to meet Ellen, and I think we will be good friends", "maybe, maybe I said." And so, I said goodbye, but before leaving I asked him, "Hey, what was this man like?" "Tall, thin, about fifty-five years old, with gray hair on the sides."

-It's not possible, it was Alberto -Roger said, opening his eyes- I knew it, he's the one who introduced himself to us at the bar.

-Yes, that's right -Richard confirmed.

-And he's the same man I met the day Richard confessed to me about his lover -Ellen said.

-What, did you already know him, Ellen?

-Listen, those are too many coincidences, don't you think -Rouse observed- This man has helped you solve very important things, he has helped us all, -she pointed to everyone present with his index finger.

-Of course, he is, those are too many coincidences,

-I can't believe it -Roger agreed, bringing his whiskey to his mouth.

-To Alberto -Richard raised his glass, and everyone did the same, clinking them together.

-To Alberto -they all said.

-By the way, tomorrow Saturday he invited us all to dinner at his house, okay, we agreed to be there after eight thirty.

-Us too dad?

-Too son, today I called him and he seemed very happy, he said he would love to meet you, we are going to talk a lot about sex, but you already understand and you should learn well.

-That will be great - said Brandon giving his sister a slight nudge.

-I sure do.

-But then, let's get this straight, said Ellen, it turns out that I began to reject your father when I stopped wanting to have sex with him, that led him over time to accept this woman even though he really didn't want to, because he didn't want to damage our relationship, so finally, after she insisted a lot and he needed to have sex, he accepted her, and finally they fell in love, so we could all live, again, the experience of her stealing him from me.

-But mom, what do you mean everyone?

-Of course baby, think about it, if your dad had left home, you, you -I pointed at both of them- would have lost your father, and that would have hurt you a lot, so, in some way, I don't know how, you are also in this whole performance, that's how I see it, think about it, it's like a big theater, put together by someone so that we all could live this experience, and surely it's something we've already lived in other lives, so all of us are tied to a... Karma... my love.

-My love -they both said at the same time turning to see each other- that means that you and I have also lived this experience of separating before, and there's a karma between you and me, so come on, Richard moved his chair away and faced his wife, she turned around bringing her knees together, and they held hands. My beautiful queen, Ellen smiled and her eyes began to cloud over, thank you, thank you for having lived with me this and all the experiences in past lives, if I offended you, if I humiliated you, if I hurt you in any way, I ask for your forgiveness, please forgive me, I'm sorry, I love you, he approached her and they kissed tenderly - the violet flame of transmutation surrounded them setting them on fire and burning all their karmas related to this experience, their energetic-spiritual bodies danced embraced, subtly merging in their love, while they were transmuted; they shone, without realizing it, some diners at their sides, remained silent observing them discreetly, when they finally separated, everyone at their side began to applaud, the diners around them applauded excitedly. They hadn't realized they were being listened to and watched, so the applause took them by surprise. They turned to look at the people around them, and some women dried their tears with the white cloth napkin. They smiled and thanked them and went back to their seats.

-Congratulations, Ellen -Rouse approached to hug her- I don't know what it was, but I can swear that something was lifted off you. I don't know how, but I'm sure I saw it. I can't believe it.

-Thank you, Rouse, thank you.

-Children -Richard turned to see his children- thank you my loves, thank you for having lived this and all the experiences like this in our past lives, if I or your mother offended you, humiliated you or hurt you in any way, we ask for your forgiveness. -Richard had stood up and hugged his little girl-

155

my beautiful girl, forgive me my love, forgive me if I hurt you in this or in past lives, if I humiliated you or did something to make you feel bad, forgive me.

-Yes daddy, yes, I love you, yes, I love you.

Brandon got up from his chair and walked around the table until he reached mommy's arms, she took him in her arms and hugged him, both of them were crying- forgive me my child, if in this or in any past life I hurt you, or offended you, forgive me, I am so sorry.

-Yes, mommy, yes, I love you very much - the crying healed their souls while the energetic bodies of all of them embraced each other in their love and subtly merged, the violet flame transmuted their karmas from past lives and freed them.

Rouse wiped her tears with the napkin, Roger turned to look at her, moved his chair and took her hands.

-My love, Rouse, if in this or in past lives, which I know I have done, I humiliated you, hurt you, or failed you in some way, please forgive me, thank you for having lived with me all the experiences we have lived, thank you for having been by my side all these years, I love you.

-I love you too Roger, thank you for everything - she threw herself at his neck and hugged him, he took her by the waist, both of them cried with their faces hidden in the other's shoulder. The violet flame transmuted their energetic bodies while they embraced each other and subtly merged, being freed from their karmas.

Some couples at the nearby tables began to do the same, asking for forgiveness, just by giving thanks for the experiences in the present life or in past lives, the violet flame cleansed and transmuted their karmas without them knowing it; love and violet light filled the room and went out to the outside like a beautiful light, touching and filling the energetic bodies of those who passed by, and in a subtle way, also cleansing their karmas.

Ellen was cleaning the face of her child, who with a childish face was sobbing. Richard came up to him and touched his shoulder.

-Hello my love - the child immediately hugged his daddy and cried - I love you my beautiful, forgive me if in this or in past lives I hurt you, forgive me.

-Yes daddy, yes, I love you, I love you very much.

-And I love you my love and I love you.

Ellen was already hugging her little girl.

-Forgive me, my girl -he said while caressing her hair- forgive me if I have hurt you in this or in past lives, if I humiliated you or did something that hurt you, forgive me.

-Yes, mommy, yes, forgive me too, forgive me, she wanted to say more things, but she couldn't, her crying wouldn't let her.

Roger had stood up and went up to Richard.

-Brother -and said, hugging him- thank you, and forgive me, if in this life or in past lives I humiliated you, offended you, abused you, stole from you or did something that hurt you, forgive me, I'm so sorry.

Both friends hugged each other.

-Thank you, brother, forgive me too, forgive me if I did something bad to you, I'm sorry, thank you for having lived this life and others with me.

They both separated, holding each other by the forearms and smiled.

When they were finally able to sit down, and had finished cleaning their faces, they smiled.

-Cheers -said Richard, raising his glass.

Everyone stood up.

Cheers, said everyone in the room, the diners had stood up and were toasting with them. They clinked their glasses, took a sip of their drink and sat down.

-How do you feel, love? -Richard turned to see his beloved and sought her lips. She caressed his face while she gave him her love in that kiss.

-Happy my love, I am happy.

-How do you feel, children?

-I feel light, dad, I don't know why, but I feel light and happy.

-Me too, I am happy.

-Isn't it interesting to discover that everything we live is actually a theater to be able to experience emotions and feelings that are tied to a debt from previous lives.

-It definitely is Ellen, why aren't we taught this? -Rouse asked intrigued.

-My love, Alberto, told us it was because the ruling elites and the church did not want us to know.

-But why the church? asked Susan, I don't understand.

-The church doesn't want us to think outside the box in the first place, they tell us because if we do we will be considered heretics and sinners, right?

-Yes, it is true -said Rouse

-Secondly, they do not want us to use our sexuality freely, that is why they teach us that it is a sin to have sex with someone else besides your partner; and they teach us that we would be unfaithful and sinners, and that you cannot live with a sinner or an unfaithful person, that is why there are so many divorces.

-But then -said Susan- if our energy bodies are saturated with the energy of our partners and we no longer want to have sex with them, but we still need sex, why do they tell us that we are sinners, if sex is the need we have for someone else's energy?

-That is the trap they have put us in, that is what they have made us believe -answered Roger.

-But then, does that mean that I can have sex with someone else, even if I am married?

-Yes, and your partner too, son -said his father, looking him in the eyes.

-But dad, would you let my mom have sex with another man? -Brandon opened his eyes wide, waiting for the answer.

-Of course son, now I understand, because now I know that we are actually beings of energy, that we are energetic-spiritual bodies -he said pointing with his index finger at the energy around his head- and now I know that sex is the way our spirits are nourished, now I understand that when your mom dies, the only thing she will take from this world will be her energy and all the beautiful experiences she has lived, what kind of husband would I be, if I didn't let her live her life and all the experiences she has to live, what kind of love would I be giving her if I didn't let her be herself.

-Wow Richard -said Rouse- what a nice way of explaining it, it's true, what you say is totally true, when I die the only thing I will take with me are my energies, my experiences and all my karmas.

-Exactly! -Roger said- our karmas, that's it, we're only going to take our karmas, and in reality, our experiences are what give us the opportunity to feel emotions again, to transmute... our karmas.

-Listen, but then it's not about having sex with anyone -said Rouse- because then we would remain tied to karma, that encounter would actually be the opportunity to free ourselves from karma, to stop doing that, and ask for forgiveness.

-Of course, Rouse -Roger took her hand- that's it... that's true, it's not about sleeping with anyone, but about clearing our karmas.

-Now it makes sense, Alberto told us that they hadn't taught us, pay close attention, he said taught, that they hadn't taught us to have an honest and true, unconditional love, but to have a selfish and conditioned love.

-But of course -Ellen confirmed- if we have a selfish love, we don't allow our partner to live his/her life, so we stay together forever, but angry. Because we don't want to have so much sex with our partner anymore, but we still need it, so we end up doing it secretly and that brings anger in couples.

-Or we end up repressing ourselves so as not to sin.

-And when the couple finds out about the infidelity, divorces arise -Rouse added, Roger raised his eyebrows and said.

-But also, they don't want to get divorced because it's a sin, so they stay together, angry and hating each other for life; at least that's what our grandparents and parents did, they stayed together hating each other. I always told my mom: Hey mom, but if you don't love each other anymore, what are you doing together? Your crazy son -she answered me- ours is for life, that's how God wanted it, he blessed us when we got married. That's the trap, do you realize children? We get married for life, but we stay angry and lie, in order to satisfy ourselves sexually.

-Or repressing ourselves, holding back the desire to have sex with someone else, to avoid becoming unfaithful and sinful - said Rouse.

The young people tried to assimilate all the information, their minds were being revolutionized.

-Excuse me, gentlemen, do you want to order something else, we have to close now.

Ellen turned to look at her watch.

-Gosh, you saw the time, it's already one in the morning, let's go, it's already late and you have school.

-Tomorrow is Saturday, mom, well today is already Saturday.

-True, sorry, I rushed it - everyone smiled.

-The bill please - said Roger.

The waiter left taking the dirty cutlery.

-No Roger, don't make things up, I'll pay, don't start with your things.

-Shut up, I'll pay. How long has it been since I invited the family to dinner?

Besides, today is a night of special celebration, he said with a beautiful smile and taking his beloved's hand, she smiled back, accepting it.

-Ok, said Richard, ok, fine, we will let ourselves be pampered.

-Well, what interesting discoveries -Rouse commented.

-Hey dad, I can also have sex with whoever I want, even if I'm married or have a boyfriend.

-According to all this, you should ask yourself, do I have any pending karma with this man? If you feel that I don't, maybe it's good for you to live that experience, but if you feel that there is a karma, you should free yourself from it.

-Giving thanks and asking for forgiveness?

-That's right daughter, it's correct.

-That's called transmuting -said Rouse- by asking for forgiveness you transmute your karmas, I read it in some book, but I didn't give it much importance, now I understand.

The waiter brought the bill, gave it to Roger, and paid the bill.

-Well family, a final toast -he raised his glass and everyone did the same- for love, for honest love, so that we all learn to give unconditional love, so that we live in love, for life, and not by force.

-Well said my love, cheers.

Cheers they all said and clinked their glasses.

Some diners came over to say goodbye and exchanged cards.

-Thank you - a gentleman and his wife, both very elegant, approached the table and greeted them- we couldn't help but listen to them, but the truth is, this was incredible, they also helped us, thank you, we would like to be friends, this is my card -said the gentleman stretching out his arm with the small piece of cardboard in his hand- call me, we will invite you to our house.

-It will be a pleasure -said Richard keeping the card, and handing her his- I will call you.

-Madam he said looking at Ellen, congratulations, you have a beautiful family.

-Congratulations, dear -his wife greeted- you and your husband make a beautiful couple, and you have beautiful children -she said, turning to look at the young people.

-Thank you both, I'll make sure I call you.

-Excellent, good night everyone.

-Well, family, let's go.

Roger and Rouse were aboard the convertible.

-Beautiful, you want to go to my house, go on, she misses you, you should see how beautiful she is now.

-And why is that?

-I learned that the environment impregnates our energies and that we impregnate our environment, so I have been impregnating my house with my love, she misses you and she told me: Go for Rouse and bring her, do not return if she does not come with you; so, if you do not want me to sleep in the car, you will have to accompany me.

-Yes, my love, of course, it will be a pleasure to see your house, she lowered her seat belt leaving her shoulder free and approached him, caressing his face she leaned on his shoulder, a tear fell down her cheek and disappeared into his shirt.

-Why are you crying?

-I was thinking about the beautiful time we lived together and how sad it was to leave each other.

-I love you Rouse, and I want to give you a true and unconditional love, I know my love is very beautiful and I want to give it to you. I know I made many mistakes, but it was because I was unaware of all this about energies, if we had known, I think we would still be together.

-And I accept it Roger, I accept your love, and you are right, I think that with all this that we now know we can have an honest relationship that lasts a lifetime -They both kissed softly.

-I would love that, I think that if we all knew this, as a society we would be very different, I have come to think that many of the social problems have to do with our sexual dissatisfaction. When you can't have sex, you are not complete or happy.

-It's not that you are not complete, but that you are not in harmony, you said it, we are all angry and nervous, that happens to me too, just like you, I need sex, sometimes much less than you men, but we definitely need it.

-But let's see, clarify something for me Rouse, why do some women say that they can live without sex?

-I think that, in reality, it is not that we can live without sex, I think that we have been educated to resist sin more than men, they have made us feel like sinners and the cause of men's misfortune, you see, Eve gave the apple to poor Adam.

-Oh yes, poor thing, ha, ha, ha - both laughed out loud.

-For the same reason, many women do not allow themselves to live their sexuality more freely, and even less if they are married. They prefer to repress themselves, and when they are older, they will want less sex, even if they want it, don't you think?

-Yes, women definitely repress themselves more than men, but we both have the need, I think that is why there are more women in prostitution, because there are more men looking to have sex than women. Ready, beautiful, we have arrived.

-Thank you, dads, for this incredible dinner and for speaking to us so openly about your experience.

-Yes, baby -Ellen answered- it was important, I think there shouldn't be secrets between us, especially if we are honest, I think that normally we don't want something to be known, because in some way it embarrasses us, or because we think, deep down, that it's not right.

-Yes, mom, it's true.

-Children -Richard said- I want you to know that you can count on us, if you have questions or doubts about something, about sex, drugs, or whatever, you will always have our unconditional love, so don't be afraid to tell us whatever you want.

-Are you sure, dad?

-Of course, my love.

-Well then -said Susan- you should know that I already had my first sexual relationship.

Richard was driving and opened his eyes in surprise, but he didn't say anything, then,

calmly he asked:

-And how did you feel, did you enjoy it?

-Oh no, dad, I'm joking.

-Silly, I was going to hit you, ha, ha, ha, - said his brother.

-Wow, said Richard, here we have a clear example of our religious education, and you don't go to mass.

-What example? - Ellen questioned.

-Brandon said: Silly girl, I was going to hit you. That reaction shows that, for him, her having sex without being married is a sin or that it's wrong, that's why he was going to hit her.

-But I said it as a joke, Dad.

-I know, love, it's not about that, but about the teachings, deep down, you know that it's a sin to have sex without being married.

-Ok, ok, I understand, it's just that my grandmother told us that, that sex before being married is not correct, that it is frowned upon by God.

-Ah, I understand now -said Ellen.

-But it's not true dad, the truth is that I've been close, but I think only until I'm married, although my friends tell me that I'm stupid, that it's not fashionable anymore, most of them already did it at fifteen, but me, as my grandmother said, until I get married.

-No my love, said his mother, not until you get married, until you're sure; I had my first encounter with my boyfriend at seventeen, but we didn't last, and it was only until I met his father that I felt that special thing that sex leaves when energies are very similar, and then we fell deeply in love and got married, then you came along and you were always wanted and loved children - Brandon smiled holding the back of his father's seat and sitting on the edge of his so he could hear better.

-But then mom, you had sex long before you got married, because you got married, at what age?

-At twenty-three and I at twenty-five - answered his father.

-That's right Brandon, I had other boyfriends and other experiences, but in reality, I only felt that special with your dad, and here I am, learning what unconditional love is.

-But what my grandmother told me, that only until I got married, isn't that right?

-Of course, it's not right, Susan -replied his brother- didn't you hear that it's a trap so that you don't use your sexuality freely.

-Well said son, your grandmother is an older woman and she was taught many things in the church, you don't go to church because we haven't instilled it in you, and now you are understanding this, older men and women faithfully believe what the priest tells them, but it's part of the trap.

-And the priests will know that that is a trap? -questioned Brandon.

-Well, if I think about it carefully -said his father- I don't think they know, they have been indoctrinated to believe what the religious leaders have told them said by generations through their books, their doctrines and dogmas.

-What is a dogma, dad?

-It is an idea that cannot be judged or reasoned, it can and must only be accepted.

-So, I cannot doubt that idea?

-Exactly, that is how the priests accepted those ideas and do not judge them, they only accept them as correct and true, and teach them.

-Wow, how interesting -said Susan- so my grandmother's

beliefs are actually a trap and she believes in that trap.

-Yes, my love -said her mother- in fact, we have all believed those traps for hundreds of generations, since religion was created, start to find out, when was religion invented and why? They immediately sat back in their seats and took their cell phones.

-We are arriving home.

-Richard got out of the car and turned around to open the door for his beloved, he gave her his hand and she got out, they stood, looking into each other's eyes and he approached to kiss her, a passionate and loving kiss that ignited her Kundalini energy. His son continued with his eyes glued to his cell phone watching something. Susan watched them tenderly through the closed window.

-Someday, I will have a man like dad -she thought to herself.

-Excuse me young man, I am looking for a book about energies and the spirit, do you have something like that?

-Of course, miss, come with me - he guided her to a shelf full of various titles, the piece of furniture reached her eyes, she bent down to pick up a book that was on the lower shelf, she took the book with red letters that had wedding rings on the cover. -"Relationships and sex," she said out loud, reading the title. "Wow, that sounds interesting," she stood up.

-What a surprise," said a man's voice, breaking her concentration. "Hello Erika, how strange to find you."

-Carlos, hello, what are you doing here?

They had stopped seeing each other two and a half years ago, they ended their relationship upset by her lack of interest in everything, including him. After him, she had gone out with some men, and had crazy nights, as they said when they went out for a drink and met someone with whom they had one-night stands.

-I'm looking for a book that can help me," she answered.

-That's strange, do you read books yet?

-Yes, I've been making some changes.

-I can see them, you look beautiful, you're thinner.

She was wearing jeans that made her look very sexy, that's what her friends would say, chubby, she had always had a beautiful figure, but she didn't value herself, she didn't pay attention to herself and she wore clothes that were always loose on her.

-Thank you - she said putting the book on her face to cover it a little.

-Oh, you're going to love that book, I've already read it, it's great!

-Really? - she said turning it over to read the back.

-He turned around the piece of furniture and approached her to read and point out something the author said. Their energies joined and they hugged each other recognizing each other, both perceived this energetic encounter - Look here: "Build your relationship, from true love."

-Yes, yes, this is definitely the book I need - Erika turned to look at him, they were very close, and she couldn't help but look at his lips - and you, have you found what you were looking for? - she said a little upset.

-Yes, I do - she picked up one that had a luxury truck on the cover and huge buildings behind it, Erika read out loud - "Beliefs, how to change them to transform my life." Wow, I want this one too.

-Wait, there's this other one too, in case you ever decide you want to be a mom - She leaned over to pick up a copy and handed it to her - "Awakening your potential, a guide to being better parents and raising happy and powerful children" oh, but if it's by the same author, wow, I think so, I'll take it too.

-Okay, here you go.

-Well, thank you, I already have what I was looking for, so I'm going now.

-Erika, are you in a hurry? Wouldn't you like to have a coffee? It's been a long time since we've seen each other.

-Actually, I'm not in a hurry, come on, it's okay. They got to the checkout, he paid for all the books.

-No Carlos, I...

-Nothing, nothing, it's my gift for you.

-Well, if you insist.

They were walking very happy about the reunion.

-Hey Carlos, wouldn't you like to go to my house to have that coffee? I mean, if your girlfriend doesn't scold you.

-I don't have a girlfriend -he said quickly- it's been half a year since I broke up with the last one.

-The last one, well, how many have there been?

-Well, you know, I believe in love, but the woman who... wait, hasn't arrived, she took the red-lettered book out of her bag and read: "We're looking for someone to share our sunrises with and fill our sunsets with love," I believe in love, so I'm still looking.

She smiled, remembering what happened to them, they really loved each other, but she took it upon herself to push him away, back then he was completely devoted to her, but he couldn't take it anymore, he didn't feel appreciated.

-I understand you, I think the same thing has happened to me, I've had some boyfriends, but they don't last, no one has fulfilled me.

-Did I not fulfill you either?

-It wasn't you, actually, it was me -he opened his eyes in amazement- I realized that when I started to have a beautiful love, I was afraid of commitment and I always pushed you away, like I did with you, in fact, you have always been the most special, my friends know it, they remember you and they always scold me, why did you let him go, he loved you?

-That was true -he said, shaking his head in agreement.

-I know and I screwed up, but come on, come to my house, I want to show you something, we'll have coffee there.

-Sure, let's go -they walked happily, their house was not far away, and the day was very nice.

They went up to the apartment and as soon as they entered, he perceived a very pleasant aroma, the house looked beautiful and clean.

-What happened here? Erika, how beautiful it looks, is it the same house we lived in? It looks so different.

-It's love.

-But you don't say you don't have a boyfriend.

-Not anyone else's love, it's my love, I've learned to love myself and my house, I've filled it with my love and it fills my energetic body with love.

-Is that why you look so different? I love the way you look - he said, admiring her from top to bottom, seeing her silhouette wrapped in those tight jeans, and that white button-down blouse that let him see the birth of her beautiful breasts, made him desire her and caress her again, his energy went towards her, they recognized each other and danced holding hands, turning, merging slightly, remembering their love, both energies had something of the other, and they loved each other. She felt his energy coming towards her and how he hugged her, that awakened her Kundalini energy, but she didn't want to speed things up, she had always let herself be carried away by her sexual impulses and she didn't want that anymore, she had decided to only have sex with someone whose energy enriched her, and not just because she liked someone a lot, that kind of sex left her empty, and many times not even satisfied.

-Let me prepare the coffee, or do you want wine? I have an open bottle from the other day.

-Wine, please, I'm craving it more.

She brought the bottle and two glasses into the living room, poured each one, handed one to him and took the other.

-Cheers, Carlos, for the pleasure of seeing you again - she gave him a beautiful smile.

-Cheers Erika, for this miraculous encounter.

They both raised their glasses and clinked them gently, he rubbed his glass against hers and in a gentle movement he slid it to the bottom of the glass, it was a game they played together, it meant the collision of their bellies, and that he would end up under her, if she slid her glass to the bottom of his, it meant that she would end up sexually that way, they both smiled.

-Tell me Carlos, how have you been? Are you still in the office?

-No, I became independent, I started my own firm, they stressed me out too much, they kept demanding and threatening to kick us out if we lost a case, now I'm my own boss, I work the same, but I earn more, and now I'm the yeller, ha, ha.

The conversation continued pleasantly, she stayed close, but without provoking him, he wanted to get closer, but he didn't want to speed things up either, so he didn't insist too much.

-Pretty, I have to go.

-Yes, but first I want to show you something.

She took him by the hand and led him to the bedroom.

-Okay, he said, seeing how different everything looked, wow Erika, what an incredible change.

-Do you like it?

-But of course, I love it.

-Well, what you see now is my love - she said, moving away from him and opening her arms.

-I have no doubt, you have a very beautiful love, I always knew it, that's why I fell in love with you, and how - he smiled and continued to admire everything - but what was the reason for the change?

-I realized that didn't really love me, that's why he didn't give importance to many things, including my house.

-But it's not just your house, you too, you look thinner.

-Well, yes, to everything actually, to everything in my life I'm giving my love, my house, my furniture, my clothes, my body, everything. My friends made me see that I was actually afraid of commitment and taking my love to the next level, so when I had a beautiful love like yours, I started to want to get rid of it, my indifference and lack of importance made you move away, and finally, you got tired of living that way.

-It's true, I felt undervalued, and well... you know, I love your change, but did that just make you lose weight?

-It seems incredible, but yes, I began to feel appreciated by myself, I started to wear tighter clothes, and even though I haven't lost much weight, I feel very different, now I take better care of my meals and what I put in my mouth, every night I have a light dinner, something I didn't do before thinking that not eating would make me lose weight, when it was totally the opposite, did you know that a light dinner is better than going to bed with an empty stomach? And that not eating at your hours and not eating, makes you fat, did you know that?

-No, I didn't really know that, well, I don't go on diets, but I do exercise.

-I realize, you look very good. Well, come on, go on, she took him by the hand and they went out into the living room again.

-So, let's see if I understand, your love fills the atmosphere of your house, and this in turn fills you, that's why when you started to love yourself everything changed. -Exactly, that was it, we met an incredible man, he spoke to us about energies and taught us this and many other things.

-Well, I would never have thought of that, I'm into laws and legal issues.

-Yes, but you have to consider that you are not this physical body, that we are actually beings of energy living lives in these bodies, that was what he taught us, so your environment also permeates your spiritual energetic body.

-So, I can change the vibes in my office, because you know? lately when I arrive, I feel very... I don't know how to describe it, but I feel a bad vibe, I have hired two lawyers recently, and they have a special vibe, in fact, when I met them at the first interview, they seemed familiar to me, but it turned out that no, we had never met, they are very good lawyers, but there is something about them that I don't quite like.

-Sure, they are their personal energies, these are impregnated, and who knows how they live in their houses, but one thing is certain, they impregnate their energies in their environment, and now your office is their environment, they spend a lot of the day there.

-But, how to do it? Should I clean them with branches? -he made the gesture of hitting something with his hand, ha, ha, ha, ha, they both laughed

-What I did here was light a candle and say a prayer, then I started to fix everything, but I also began to feel things, the armchairs, the curtains, my dining room, my bed, I caressed it for the first time, and I began to feel a very beautiful affection for all this that you see, in that way I impregnated it with my love.

-But Erika, how do you think I'm going to spend my time caressing the desks and all that.

-Why not, everything is made of energy, didn't you tell me that?

-Look, you remember it well.

-You were a great teacher.

-Well, yes, if I see it that way it's true, everything is energy.

-So, impregnate everything with the energy of your love, why don't you light some candles when you're alone and go around the whole apartment, with the candle and bless everything. You still believe in God, right?

-Yeah, sure, although I haven't really been very close to him.

-Well, he loves you anyway, he helped me make this change, I asked him to teach me and help me and look at you, now you're here -she raised her eyebrows and smiled, realizing that it was true, God had responded to her desire to take her love to another level.

-So, I'm here in response to your prayer.

-Well, it's a possibility, I don't know, but he responds, he responds.

-Ok, you know what, yes, I'm going to do that, I'm going to light some candles at night when no one is around, and I'll do a cleansing, I'll tell you how it went.

-Wait -she stood up and went to the cupboard, she took out a pink candle- here, this one is special, it has my love, so use it.

-Yes, but I'll use that one in my house and you'll see how I fill it with this beautiful love -she said holding the candle with both hands, he finished her glass of wine and said- I have to go -she got up and went to the door, she took the bag from the coat rack, with the purchases she had made- Erika, it was great to see you again, would you like to have dinner together another day?

-Well, on Saturday I have a dinner, why don't you come as my date, it's at a friend's house, I'm not telling you to dress well, because you always know how to dress, it'll be at his house, it's a luxurious apartment, he has very good taste.

-I'd love to, what time?

-At eight thirty, I'll see you here at eight.

-Excellent, beautiful, I'll see you here on Saturday - he took her by the waist with one arm and gave her a tender kiss on the cheek, she returned the kiss on his cheek.

VI A question of agreements

-Hey love, I was thinking, why don't you invite Larisa to dinner, so we get to know her and well, Alberto is single, maybe they like each other, they would make a nice couple don't you think?

-I hadn't thought about it, it could be, let me call her to see if she's not already engaged.

It was Saturday morning, they had just had breakfast and they were alone, their children were going out, so they were getting ready, he took his cell phone and called, the ringing was heard and he said.

-Hi Larisa, how are you?

-Hi Richard, I'm fine, how's everything at home?

-Everything's great, thanks, in fact, I'm here with Ellen.

-Wow, that's a surprise, I'm glad it's like that. What happened, tell me?

-Today we're going to have dinner at a friend's house and we want to introduce you to him, he's very nice, I think you already know him.

-Oh, yes, who is he?

-Well, I'm not sure you know him, maybe, but well, you're going to like him a lot, do you want to come with us? I'm going with my children too, and some other friends.

-Ok, fine, I don't have any commitments, I was just about to call some friends, I didn't want to stay locked up at home.

-Well, great, do you want us to pick you up?

-No, no, give me the address and I'll get there, what time is the appointment and what do I need to bring?

-From eight thirty onwards and you don't have to bring anything.

-Ok, then I'll see you there, do you hear the dress code is very formal?

-Well, smart casual.

-Well, then we'll say hello there, say hello to Ellen, I'd love to meet her, we have a lot in common.

-I will, see you later - he smiled.

-And that smile?

-She says hello, she told me she'd be delighted to meet you, that you both had a lot in common.

-And it's true - he said caressing her face and giving her a kiss on the cheek.

The elevator opened, her children and Ellen went out into the hallway, Alberto was waiting for them with the door open.

-Hello, family, welcome, well, well, so you're the Cisneros family - he said looking at Ellen and Richard - how small the world is, don't you think?

-It really is, I didn't know that Ellen already knew you, I found out the day after you and I met.

-When someone has a very beautiful love, the universe -he said pointing up with his index finger- conspires to keep it together despite the adversities, but come in please.

-This is my baby Susan.

-Susan, you are very beautiful, for being only sixteen, you look a little older -she smiled flattered, she loved to hear that, she stretched out her hand to him, he shook it and they came closer to kiss each other on the cheek.

-And he is my beautiful Brandon.

-Brandon, how tall and how handsome, you look like your dad, but you have your mother's eyes, come in -the young man stretched out his hand to him and he shook it- welcome son, come in. Hello Ellen, wow, you look beautiful, congratulations, she smiled widely and hugged him with much love.

- Alberto, how nice to see you, you don't know how grateful I am to you, - she approached his ear and said - I owe you my marriage, -he winked at her- nothing, it is their love that must prevail. Come in, Richard, welcome brother, how good you look, you look radiant.

-Thank you, we are delighted to be here.

Alberto closed the door, a young waiter collected their coats and bags.

-We brought two bottles of wine.

-Excellent Richard -he took them and looked at the label- mmm what a good wine, a Cabernet Sauvignon and a Malbec, excellent varieties- he handed them to the waiter.

The doorbell rang and he headed for the door.

-Hello Erika, welcome, wow you look good, you're amazing -

he hugged her and they kissed each other on the cheek.

-Alberto, this is Carlos, my..., my friend -he said remembering his position.

-Nice to meet you Carlos, welcome, make yourself at home.

-Thank you, Alberto, I've heard a lot about you, and I wanted to meet you.

The elevator opened and a very attractive woman got off it, turned to look at the open door.

-I can't believe it, hello, do you live here?

-Hello Larisa! That's right, welcome, this is your house, I'm also surprised to find you here, in fact, it's a very nice surprise, how nice to see you again.

-She's our guest -Richard approached the door followed by Ellen- I told you about her,

-But of course, it's a nice surprise, it's nice to see you again, we met at the golf club, right?

-Yes, that's right, I brought a little dessert to share.

The waiter approached to get the dessert.

-You shouldn't have bothered Larisa, what a nice gesture - Alberto hugged her affectionately and they kissed each other on the cheek.

-Larisa, welcome -said Richard, he hugged her too and said- she's my wife Ellen, the owner of my dreams.

-Hello Larisa, welcome, I've been wanting to meet you.

-Thank you, Ellen, me too - they both hugged each other

affectionately, and kissed - how pretty you are Larisa, now I understand -he winked at her, she blushed a little.

-We have to talk, okay? -they both smiled.

-Of course, it will be a pleasure -Ellen hugged her again affectionately and closed her eyes, then they separated, Larisa was feeling something- you know Ellen, I feel like I already know you.

- Me too, it's funny, but yes, I feel that too.

- Come in, come in, welcome Larisa, you're at home - he was going to close the door when the elevator opened again, Roger and Rouse approached the door.

- Roger, friend, welcome -Alberto shook her hand and they hugged - she must be the lucky owner of your love, right?

- That's right, she's Rouse.

- Hello, welcome, how beautiful you are.

- Thank you - she was carrying a box in her arms, she handed it to the host - carefully it's a cake.

Alberto handed it to the waiter and he took it away.

- Wow, I turn to look at Roger, what a lucky man, congratulations you make a very nice couple.

They felt flattered.

-Please come in, this is your house.

They were still at the door and Karla was standing behind them, wearing a short, fitted dress that made her look spectacular.

-Wow Karla, how nice to see you, welcome, you look so beautiful.

-She smiled and hugged him affectionately, thanks Alberto, you look very handsome too - they both gave each other beautiful smiles.

-Come in, welcome.

He closed the door behind him and followed her, admiring her walk.

Everyone greeted each other and introduced themselves, the waiter standing, waiting for everyone to finish greeting each other.

Friends, said Alberto, you are all welcome. He made a sign to the waiter, who began to offer the drinks he had prepared in advance.

-If anyone wants something else, please there is everything at the bar, we have prepared clericot to start, but if you prefer the wine alone, just say so, ok.

-It's perfect, thank you, they all said.

The young men looked at their mother, she smiled at them and they took a drink.

When everyone had their drinks, Alberto raised his.

-Friends, a toast, for a great night, thank you all for coming, cheers. They all raised their glasses and began to clink them; the room was quite large and the armchairs quite large, the waiter brought a few chairs from the dining room and everyone sat comfortably, on the coffee table there were trays with different cheeses, olives and snacks.

-How beautiful your house is, said Roger, you have very good taste.

-That's right, several confirmed.

-Thank you, friends, I owe a lot of this to my wife.

-Are you married -asked Larisa, who had been observing him closely, she felt attracted, since she met him at the club he seemed like a very attractive man, and after talking she knew he was very smart, they had agreed to meet later, both were members of the club.

-No, actually, I'm a widower, my wife Carmen left her body four years ago, but she's alive, so well, we communicate from time to time.

-We're very sorry - they said almost in chorus.

-Don't be sorry, she's better than all of us, we should feel bad for those of us who stayed, we are really bad, ha, ha, ha.

-Alberto, I don't know if it's time to get serious, but why do you say that she's alive, not that she left her body?

-Do you remember our energetic-spiritual bodies?

-Yes, of course.

-Well, when the physical body dies, we leave in the form of our energetic bodies and we continue living, in the City of Light.

-And where is that City of Light?

-Alberto pointed with his thumb towards the sky- above the clouds, they are cities like ours, but made of etheric energy, they are real, you can touch them, and they are solid like ours, but you can only touch them with our primordial bodies, let me explain a little, I just don't want you to get too serious, we came to have fun ok.

-Yes, of course.

Wow Alberto, what a beautiful view your apartment has, Larisa was standing at the window, he approached the glass door and walked around it revealing a fairly large balcony with a glass railing, they went outside, followed by some others, they breathed the fresh air and the smell of pine trees.

-I'm glad you like it, this park is very special, it has an energy that fills everything, but also the fact that it is right at the end of our land makes it even more special.

They chatted happily and then went back inside.

-Cheers Alberto, thanks for inviting us, we are delighted to be here.

-A pleasure friends, thanks for coming.

-Well, tell us about the body -said Larisa.

-Of course, our physical body has an energetic-spiritual body.

-You have it quite big, said Brandon, I can see it clearly.

-Wow champion, that's great, keep developing that ability, you're doing very well, then you'll be able to see its colors - Brandon turned to look at his sister and raised his eyebrows, she winked at him-. Well this energetic body has a name, it's called primordial, and we also have a body made of a more subtle energy, that is, lighter, called the body of light.

-Are those bodies inside our physical body? -asked Karla.

-Inside and outside, they fill us -she pointed to her aura with her hand- and they can also completely leave us, they are made of energy. Let me tell you a story so we can understand it a little bit, a friend's father passed away eight years ago, recently, a neighbor told him that she had seen her father, whom she had not seen for a long time, but that on Palm Sunday during Holy Week, she was in a procession and he approached her and said: Hello neighbor, Rogelio, how are you? Nice to meet you, she answered, and they went talking until they reached the park near her house, where he said goodbye and walked away.

-But is that true? questioned Susan.

-Yes, the primordial body exists and is real, it can leave you without you realizing it and go live a life on this same planet, without you knowing, that happens when the person does not love themselves, and they spend their time angry or in bad vibes all the time, if that is so, the primordial body will leave the physical body and will go away, so that person will live many experiences in their physical body, but these will not be recorded, because their primordial body is not there, nor will they be recorded in their light body.

-But then, are all our experiences recorded in our primordial bodies and in the light body?

-That's right, Ellen, that's why I told you that when we die, we will only take our energies and the experiences we have lived, you cannot

take any of the wealth you have accumulated, nothing material, except the energetic wealth you have lived and absorbed spiritually.

-Wow, how interesting - Ellen replied - So our karmas are

recorded in our primordial body and in our light body?

-No, they are only recorded in our light body, but they have to pass through the primordial body, as well as the Dharmas; a Dharma is created when you do good to a person or an animal, if you help someone you create a Dharma, it is a blessing that will come to you in different ways, in this or in a future life.

-That's why it's better to do good, because if you do bad, you create Karma - said Karla.

-Alberto - Ellen sought her husband's approval and he nodded - we want to tell you something we discovered with our present experience. Not everyone knows, but... Ríchard had a lover.

-I -Larisa, raised her hand smiling, she was a very self-confident woman.

-How... you?... -said her friends astonished- but...

-Wait, don't get ahead of yourself, this is getting good -Ellen leaned over to put her glass on the coffee table.

Her children smiled at Larisa and raised their glass in greeting, she felt embarrassed, but smiled at them and bowed her head in gratitude; Her mother told them that if they had gotten rid of their karma, then they didn't have to hold a grudge against her, on the contrary, they had to thank her, because she allowed them to live their experience and free themselves from their debt. They understood and that's why they smiled at her. They had already agreed between the two of them on how they would act when they met her. Her mother told them that she would be at dinner.

-We discovered, Ellen continued, that it was all a plan, a plan for us to live this experience and to be able to free ourselves from our Karma.

-Sorry -said Carlos- I don't understand.

-What do you mean, a plan? -seconded Karla- shuffle it more slowly.

-Yes, -said Larisa- when I met Richard at his architectural office, I had asked them to build my residence, so he was the chief architect of the project. When Roger introduced him to me, as soon as I saw him, I felt as if I had known him for a long time. I wasn't sure, but I even thought that it was from some past life, and of course I liked him a lot. Later, while we were working on the project, he told me a lot about his family. I began to try to seduce him, but he rejected me. He said that he loved his wife and his family and that he didn't want to put all that at risk, so he kept doing only the work. But a few months later...

-I began to reject him -interrupted Ellen. Everyone turned to look at her- yes, I began to not want to have sex with him. I didn't know that my energy body was saturated with his energy and that was why I didn't want to have sex anymore, so little by little we distanced ourselves, and without knowing it, I threw him into Larisa's arms.

-Then he accepted me and we fell in love, but it turns out that our energies knew each other, that's why we felt so comfortable.

-That was when I confessed to Ellen that I was in love.

-Afterwards -continued Larisa- by the work of fate, I met this gentleman in the golf club-she pointed with her head to Alberto and made a slight bow, he did the same and smiled at her- he made me aware of energies and karma, I understood that what I had with Richard was a karma from past lives, that I should not steal anyone else's husband, because if I did, he, would later find another woman who would steal him from me, and if I did, I would remain tied to karma, and I would have to return to earth to live the same experience again, until I stopped stealing the husband from some woman; So I talked to Richard and I made him see this, he understood and we asked for forgiveness, we hugged each other and felt something beautiful, something was lifted off us, I don't know what it was, but I felt it, I think it was karma.

-You see, said Ellen, everything was planned by someone so that all of us would live this experience, I would live the loss of my husband, my children, the loss of my father, Richard, leaving his family for another woman, and Larisa, stealing another woman's husband.

-How crazy, but it's true -said Karla- everything makes sense, it's like a play.

-Exactly Karla, that was it, a great play, -said Ellen.

-Bravo, friends, congratulations, you found out, I'm proud of all of you, congratulations, cheers to that -said Alberto raising his glass, everyone did the same, some were silent weighing all the information-. To understand a little more, let me tell you about the agreements.

-Sir, dinner, do you want us to serve it?

-Yes, the children said, we are already hungry.

-Please do it.

The service ladies began to bring the dishes and everyone

went to the dining room; the table was very long, it had four chairs on each side and one at each head. Alberto assigned the seats and he sat at one head, Larisa at his right side which made her feel flattered, he smiled at her in a special way, then Carlos, Erika, Karla, Roger at the head, Rouse, Brandon, Susan, Richard and Ellen.

-Let's toast to the delicious food -once all the dishes were served, Ellen intervened.

-Sorry Alberto, I am so happy for this night that I would like to say a prayer if you allow me.

-Of course, Ellen, it is your house, please do it.

They all held hands and bowed their heads, Alberto lifted them up.

-Beautiful Father, I want to thank you for being present, tonight and throughout our lives, thank you for the presence of Alberto, who has brought light and understanding to our minds, and joy and love to our hearts, bless him, bless all those present so that we continue to grow, learn and transmute our karmas, to free ourselves, and so that one day when you decide, we can return to your side -a tear rolled down her cheeks, many of them also felt that- amen; they took the cloth napkin and wiped away their tears.

-What a beautiful prayer, thank you Ellen -he took her hand and squeezed it.

-Thank you, Alberto, thank you.

-I want to share something, said Erika, I can't hold myself back, I want Alberto to find out.

-I can see it Erika, I can see it, but tell us, what happened?

-Well, after you instructed us about our energetic bodies and how the environment impregnates us with its energies, I looked at my house and realized how much I had abandoned it, and how it had abandoned me, she said putting her hand on her chest, then, my friend Karla told me that I was afraid of taking my love to the next level of commitment, that's why I always took it upon myself to chase away the men who loved me, especially this gentleman, Carlos and I live together and we loved each other very much, but I took it upon myself to chase him away.

-No beautiful, we both had responsibility, Carlos held her hand.

-Well, thank you, darling. After realizing this, I started to change my whole house. I cleaned, threw away a lot of things and left it beautiful. Afterwards, I lit a candle and asked God to help me, to help me change, that I was willing to take my love to the next level. After finishing praying, the phone rang and guess who it was? It was Alberto. You were God's answer to my prayer. You have helped me incredibly and you continue to do so.

-Thank you, Erika. -He smiled beautifully. -What a beautiful transformation. In fact, you look thinner and very beautiful.

-That's right. -Carlos said without letting go of her hand. She squeezed it while wiping her eyes with the napkin.

-That's right, friend. You look beautiful. Ellen smiled at him and raised her glass. Karla at her side held his hand.

-There is no doubt, said Alberto, that love is the key to change this planet, but we have to learn to show honest, true and unconditional love - everyone nodded as they savored their dishes.

-Dinner is delicious - said Roger - can I have some wine? - the waiter approached with the bottle wrapped in a white napkin and began to serve the glasses - but go on Alberto, you have me intrigued, what is this about agreements?

-Is that all Erika, or do you want to add something else?

-Not really, I just wanted you to know the change I have made.

-But that is not all, he has started reading books, in fact, we met again in a bookstore.

-Wow Erika, that is a great advance.

-Yes Ellen, in fact, I have already finished the first book, which by the way I recommend, it is incredible, it is called: "Relationships and Sex" and it deals precisely with true love, it is great.

-I recommended it to him -said Carlos- it has helped me a lot, I also recommend it to you. Before reading that book I was very, well, you know we were always looking for someone to have sex with, and we went out to bars to see if we found someone, but after reading the book, I understood that it is not only about sex, but about energy.

-Here it is, - interrupted Brandon, holding up his cell phone showing a photograph of the book cover with red letters and wedding rings.

-These young people today, how great, it didn't take them long to find it, isn't it incredible, in my time I would have had to go to a bookstore to look for it, now you can buy everything online.

-That's how new technologies are - said Larisa smiling.

-Are you enjoying dinner? - Alberto placed his hand on top of hers and smiled.

-It's delicious, thank you -he replied, squeezing her hand and returning the caress, both smiled, Ellen and Richard, looked at them and turned to look at each other in complicity, and smiled.

-Tell us -said Rouse- what is this about agreements?

-Yes, go on, tell us -said Susan, while cutting the meat.

-Carlos, I'm glad you understood that, later we will go deeper into that subject, it is very important, but let's go step by step; it turns out that when a person dies, he goes to the City of Light in his primordial body of light, there he meets his family and friends, who left their bodies before him.

- Are my grandparents and my uncles there?

- Yes, that's right Brandon, all of them are alive, they are not really dead, the only thing that dies is the physical body, but they are all still alive in these cities.

- It's the city that appears in the movie Our Home, by a certain... Xico Xavier? if I remember correctly - said Susan.

- Yes, you've already seen it, how nice, did you like it?

- I loved it, it explains very well what happens in death, I've already seen it twice.

- We have to see it, love - said Ellen looking at her husband.

- How many of these cities exist?

- Four, on the entire planet, we can't see them, because they are made of energy...

- Etheric - answered Larisa quickly.

- Well said, darling. There, people take time to recover if they are sick or have some damage.

- How, does the primordial body get sick?

-Yes, if a person gets cancer, his or her primordial body also gets sick and has to be healed.

-How incredible, I would never have imagined -said Roger- so the energy also gets sick?

-Of course, yes, the energy is filled with certain vibrations, if it is a bad vibe, it is felt in the environment, let's say it is a sick environment, if the energy is charged with love and beauty, this is felt in the environment, right?

-Yes, of course, I live it every day in my house and in my person, in fact, I have become very sensitive to energies.

-Exactly Erika, energies are perceived because they are charged with vibrations, so if your body is sick your energetic body also gets sick, if you want to heal your physical body from an illness you have to fill it with love, fill the sick organ with love and it will vibrate in love and will be charged with that energy, healing itself.

- Can all diseases be cured, including cancer or diabetes? - Roger asked- you see, the doctors say that they are not cured, that they are for life.

- All, absolutely all diseases can be cured, if you only see yourself as a physical body, you will not believe that you can cure yourself, but if you see yourself as what you truly are, an energetic-spiritual body, and that you are made of energy, then you can cure yourself, you just have to fill the sick organ with love and it will heal. For example, you are starting to develop cysts in a breast, you just have to put your hand on it and caress it, give it your love, love it, think of this organ as if God were putting his hand on it, feel that beautiful love and let it fill you with love, feel that love, vibrate that love, stop thinking that your organ is sick, stop talking about illness, stop telling your friends or family that you are sick, tell them how healthy you are and how you are loving yourself, look at yourself in the mirror and decree: I am perfect health, love fills my organs and they smile healthily; I am God's health, here and now; I am an energetic-spiritual being and my body vibrates in love; if you keep decreeing this, your vibrations will change and health will come to you, produced by yourself.

-How interesting Alberto, that is wonderful, we can cure ourselves of anything, how wonderful.

-That's right Roger, we can do it.

-Now I understand more why you were telling me about the environment and its vibes, in fact Erika, I did the thing with the candles in the office and wow, how different everything feels.

-Did you clean your office Carlos? Alberto asked.

-Yes, I was telling Erika that I just hired two people who have a very special vibe that I don't like, so everything there was filled with those bad vibes and I didn't feel comfortable.

-Well, you have to talk to these people and explain this about energies, recommend them to do what Erika told you, because if they don't, I suggest you fire them, it's preferable, because their energies will infect you, unless you infect them, but whatever, it's necessary for them to make the change, if not, it's better to get rid of those bad vibes, fill your office with only love vibes and everything else will be fantastic, you'll see how more clients and more money come to you, money likes places with good vibes.

-Thanks Alberto, I'll do that.

Roger took his cell phone and said into the microphone: -Buy candles to clean the office, done bro, -turning to look at Richard- you have to do that and you know, if you don't change your bad vibes you know, ha, ha, ha, ha. Let's see if it's not me who gets fired, ha, ha, ha, for being bad-vibe, ha, ha, ha. -Everyone laughed.

-Back to the agreements, can we continue or do you have any doubts?, -everyone was thinking about this, he raised his glass and turned to Larisa- cheers, for the For the pleasure of having you in my house, I never imagined, in fact, in the club we didn't even exchange phone numbers, after I left I said: But why didn't you ask for her number? You're so stupid.

-I thought you had a girlfriend, and that's why you hadn't asked me, I wished you had.

-Well, I won't lose sight of you now, cheers - she raised her glass, clinked his and brought it to her beautiful red lips, which he watched as he took a sip of his glass and the fresh red wine went down his throat.

-Alberto, why aren't we taught all this?

-It's part of the work that a person must do Rouse, each one must discover all this to free themselves from life on this planet,

-Free ourselves from the planet? How is that? -Karla questioned.

-The planet is a school of advanced spiritual development. We all come from higher worlds, from some higher dimension, and we came to learn about love and many things. We were volunteers, nobody forced us to come, each one of us agreed to come to live the experience, and we got stuck, tied to the planet by karmas. Our real objective is to free ourselves, not to make wealth.

-Are you telling us that we come from higher worlds?

-That's right, Roger, but when we enter to live the experience on this planet, we forget where we come from, our memory is erased, just as we don't remember our agreements, or with whom we made them, like you -he pointed to Richard and Larisa- you had forgotten the agreements you made and what you had done to pay a karma and free yourselves; to free ourselves is what we all want in this world. Our challenge is to discover karma and finish with our debts, that way we do not have to reincarnate again, as long as you have karmas, you will continue to reincarnate, that is to say that you will continue to be tied to this planet, when you finish with your karmas, you will be able to return to your original home.

-What is our original home? -Susan asked.

-There are different ones, we do not all come from the same place, some come from worlds of the sixth dimension, the fifth, etc., there are many dimensions and millions of inhabited planets.

-Wow Alberto, these issues get complicated.

-That's right Roger, that's why I don't want to go into more issues, perhaps on another occasion we can meet again and analyze them, for now I invite you to watch videos on the internet about the universe and extraterrestrial life, surely some or all of us have seen videos of spaceships from other worlds.

-Yes, yes, I have seen many and there are some incredible ships.

-That's right Brandon, now there is a lot of information that can no longer be hidden or denied, thanks to the internet. But well, investigate it, in the meantime, let's continue with our topic of agreements.

-Yes, yes, go ahead - some chanted.

-The important thing to understand is that each one of us comes from a higher world, and that we are here in this world living plays, I will continue to clarify this point ok. The information about all this exists, it has always existed, but it is a little hidden, and each one must discover it to free themselves, have you heard the saying: When the student is ready, the teacher appears!

-Yes, of course.

- Well, when someone seeks wisdom, it always comes, it is no coincidence that Erika found that book, it appeared before her when she was ready to receive her information.

-Wow, what a beautiful way you have of explaining things to us, everything is understood very easily, said Rouse, isn't that right children?

-Yes, of course - they both said.

-Thanks Rouse -Alberto gave him a smile.

-But then, we are not taught because it is our job to discover it! -said Carlos.

-Hey Alberto, sorry Carlos for interrupting you, it's just that all this seems like a big game, think about it: We all come from higher worlds to live experiences, they dress us with a physical body, because in reality we are beings of energy, they make us lose our memory, we experience life and we are filled with karmas, we live sex, hate, anger, the same that if we do not forgive them, they tie us to the wheel of reincarnation, then we die and we go to live in the City of Light, am I doing well? -asked Richard looking at Alberto.

-Excellent, continue.

-Afterwards, we are reborn, but our memory is erased and we relive the hatred, the anger, the loss of our wife, etc., etc., to try to free ourselves and end the game, but to do so we need to end our karmas, only then can we finish the game and go home.

-That's true brother -Roger was excited- wow, that's true, this seems like a great game.

-It really is, friends, - Alberto confirmed - that's why I was telling you that we're in a big theater, life is a big theater! If I continue, you'll understand a little more - everyone had finished dinner - do you want us to stay here or do you prefer to go to the living room? - they turned to look at each other looking for the answer.

-Let's go to the living room -Roger said- do you agree beautiful? -he said looking at Rouse.

-Sure, no problem -everyone stood up, chatting happily.

Ellen approached Larisa -Alberto was pulling out her chair to allow her to get up.

-Larisa, can I have a minute? -everyone walked into the living room and they stood one in front of the other- beautiful - said Ellen taking her hands, she was pleasantly surprised by the detail- I want to thank you, thank you for helping me live this experience of losing my husband, and thank you for helping me understand this karma, if in some way -her eyes began to cloud- in this life or in the past, I offended you, humiliated you, or hurt you in any way -tears began to run down her cheeks- I ask for your forgiveness, please forgive me, I'm sorry sister, I'm sorry, thank you.

-Beautiful Ellen, thank you -the tears slowly ran down her cheeks- if in this life or in the past I humiliated you, hurt you, stole your husband, or hurt you in any way, I ask for your forgiveness, please forgive me, I'm sorry, I love you sister, thank you.

They both hugged each other, and beautiful tears relieved their hearts, their energetic bodies they danced embraced being cleansed and transmuted by the violet flame filling them with this beautiful color, then they separated to return to their physical bodies, full of this transmuting energy; both felt that something was being removed from them and they smiled, they let go and kissed each other, I want us to be friends, do you agree?

-We will be like sisters Ellen, it will be a pleasure.

They both wiped their tears with the napkins, and then walked to the living room with their glasses in hand, Richard watched them.

-Come sister, let's do it -Brandon and Susan came to Larisa.

-Larisa, we can talk to you.

-Of course, beautiful.

-We want to thank you, for helping us live this experience, if in past lives we hurt you, please forgive us, we want to take our karmas off with you, thank you.

-Thank you, Larisa, Brandon said, not knowing what else to say.

-Thank you, my loves, -she hugged them affectionately, tears of healing fell on her cheeks- you see what you're doing, you're making me cry- she said, separating herself and trying to clean her face. Alberto handed her his handkerchief, she brought it close to her eyes, and she smelled the scent of the citrus wood perfume- thank you children, thank you, I also ask for your forgiveness, if in this or in past lives I hurt you, or wounded you, forgive me, I'm sorry. The violet light embraced the three of them, and their karmas disappeared from their energetic bodies and their Akashic records.

-How do you feel? - Alberto asked.

-I don't know, I feel lighter, I don't know why.

-Me too brother, I feel the same.

-It's the karmas, said Alberto, they are disappearing from our energetic bodies, mainly from the light body, that's where all our karmas are stored, that's why they feel lighter.

-Take it Alberto, thank you -Larisa returned the handkerchief to him.

-Please keep it, so you can take a souvenir of this night.

-Ok, thank you.

-Well, you haven't reached the agreements, ha, ha, something else always comes up -said Rouse.

-Yes, you still have me on tenterhooks, ha, ha, -Roger laughed.

-Ok let's continue, what did I leave off? Ah, yes, in the City of Light,

-Sorry Alberto, I have a question, you told us that we must have an honest love with our partners, and that means understanding that we are an energetic-spiritual body that feeds on the energy of others, and that if we understand this we should allow our partners to live the experiences they need, right? -everyone nodded- but then it's like being a swinger, is that what we have to do?

-It's good that you bring up this topic because it's important. Swingers, I explain it for the young people here, are couples who allow themselves to have sex with other people, so that in their sexual life, they live the variety, but the problem with this is that the vast majority of couples only allow themselves to live these experiences if they are together, never alone, because they are afraid that their partner will find someone better than him or her, and that he or she will leave, and they will lose him or her; in other words, despite allowing themselves to have sex with others, they continue to be jealous and try to control when and with whom they can have sex, everything is born From their lack of true and honest love, and from the lack of their personal love; let me explain a little more, when a person does not love themselves honestly and truly, they will always be afraid of losing their partner, and of being left alone and empty. We mistakenly believe that our partners fill us, that our lives are complete only because someone loves me, and if I have no one, I feel empty. When a person loves themselves, they understand that they themselves are the most beautiful love that exists in the universe, so they are not afraid that their partner will leave, or move away, because if that were to happen, first, they will not end up hating each other, as it normally happens, and second, they could give their honest love to another woman or man with whom they will want to walk the next leg of the road, do you understand me?

-Yes, clearly, said Ellen. -True love is not about sleeping with every woman you like, or with every attractive man you meet, no, it is about understanding the needs of our partners and ourselves, so that when someone comes along, with whom you feel that special attraction, you must first transmute your past lives with him or her, to make sure that there is no karma between the two of you. If there is karma, most likely, when you transmute the relationship, the sexual desire will disappear; if the sexual desire persists even after the relationship is transmuted, that means that this encounter could be good spiritually for both of you, and it will definitely be an encounter that will enrich you. -But Alberto, if you get to know someone with whom you have already transmuted everything, and you still feel sexual desire, and you have that encounter, and you like him a lot, it is certain that we will want to continue having relations with him, and that can lead us to fall in love,

-That's right, but that's where intelligence comes in, before doing this you must ask yourself: What am I looking for with this encounter? Am I looking for a lover to satisfy me? Am I looking to enrich myself spiritually? Or am I looking for someone to replace my husband or wife? Let me tell you about my personal case, my wife Carmen and I had a magical and very special relationship, we loved each other enormously, but we both had, occasionally, intimate encounters with an acquaintance, the other was always aware, -some of those who listened, raised their eyebrows in astonishment, but remained silent- there were no secrets between us, when I returned from having that encounter, she would say to me: My love, hug me, and share with me that love, that energy.

-That love, that is, that they fell in love.

-No, it meant that spiritually we accepted the other's love and that enriched us, so my wife and I hugged each other and raised our energies, sharing them in that energetic embrace, my energy, which now brought the energy of the other woman, and vice versa, I asked her the same when she returned.

-Wow, said Roger, that is really out of this world.

-I understand you Roger, to think that your wife was with another man and ask her to share her energy, it is difficult for many men, but remember that the main energy is that of your wife, that of the other gentleman only enriched her energy and made her more beautiful, that is what you have to think about, on the other hand, always remember, if you only see yourself as a physical body, you will only see the limitations, but if you see yourself as what you truly are, energetic-spiritual beings, living in a physical body, you will be able to enjoy your experiences and share your energies with the person you love.

-Well, it's true, it all depends on how we see ourselves and our partners.

-That's right Richard, but well, it happened to us, that we met some woman or man with whom the encounters were magical and special, we both told each other about our experiences, but before having an encounter with anyone we told them that our partner knew, that we weren't looking to fall in love with anyone and that we didn't want anyone to fall in love with us, that made the encounter more honest, nobody expected anything from the other, that's how we lived our experiences, and when he or she began to fall in love with my wife or me, we ended the encounters, we knew that more than three encounters could bring us problems of falling in love, so we thanked each other, we transmuted those encounters, and we ended that relationship, in this way, my wife and I were our priority, no one else, with the others we were excellent friends, we all knew each other and we went to dinner together, but that didn't mean having sex every time we got together, or that we participated in orgies. When a person has too much sex, their energy becomes sick and decomposes, you have seen someone who is addicted to sex.

-Yes -said Karla- a classmate of mine.

-And what did he look like?

-He looked very grey, and he had a very strange smell, he left that mood wherever he stood.

-That's because his energy body was sick, and that smell because somehow, it's like it's starting to break down.

-I -Erika said... and she stayed silent.

-Go ahead love, don't be ashamed we can be honest -said Carlos, she smiled.

-I had a friend who had that smell, and he always wanted us to do it, I threw him away because he was already tired of me, I didn't want to have so much sex.

-That's right, so it's not about mixing your energies with anyone, it has to be someone whose energy is beautiful, if not, what's the point? Those kinds of encounters with energies that are discordant to yours leave you more empty than anything, in an orgy, your energies mix with anyone and that, in the end, ends up making you sick, and if you become addicted to those parties your energetic body gets sick, on the other hand, remember that sex is one of the main causes of karma, which ties us to the earth, and that each experience is actually an opportunity to free ourselves from karma by stopping doing that; On many occasions, after having group sex or with someone whose energies leave you with a bad feeling, you think: Wow, it would have been better not to do any of this. Has that happened to anyone?

Several raised their hands in confirmation.

-These types of relationships also teach us something. How do you know something is good if you haven't tried anything bad?

-That's true, -said Carlos- thanks to those bad experiences we can recognize one that is worth it.

-Ok, I understand, said Roger, so it's not about sleeping with anyone, or really being a Swinger, because that only affects our energies.

-That's right, it's about being honest and staying in love with our partners, knowing that I am the most beautiful love that exists and that I am giving that love to her; and that she is the most beautiful love that exists in the universe and that she is giving it to me.

-But what if you really fell in love with someone else? said Larisa.

-If that were to happen, you can let your partner go live with the other person, so that he or she can live his or her experience, his or her life does not belong to you, you know that he or she has the right to live this new experience. We are spiritual energetic beings, living, learning and transmuting karmas, what if this new relationship is the way your partner has to continue learning and paying his or her karmas, think about it a little, maybe with you, he or she has already learned everything that you had to teach him or her and now he or she needs another teacher, someone who teaches him or her other things and helps him or her transmute his or her karmas with these new experiences. Let me tell you the story of my two friends Monica and Efrén, they loved each other, they learned to give an honest love, he was a gentleman and a very special love, but she fell in love with another man, and knowing all this they let each other go, and each one continued with their life, she left and made her new relationship, it turns out that, over time, the guy began to mistreat her and humiliate her.

-Oh no, but how -said Karla- opening her eyes, she had a beautiful love, and she left with a jerk?

-Wait, now you'll understand. She, knowing all this, realized the karmas she had pending and transmuted them, freeing herself, at the same time she taught her new partner this and both were freed, if Monica had stayed with Efrén, she would never have been able to transmute the karmas of this type, because Efrén would never have humiliated her, so she found the right teacher who would help her live those experiences to make her understand her karmas and be able to free herself.

-So -said Karla- if someone humiliates you or hits you, it's because you have a karma, and he or she is not really hurting you, but is helping you live that experience to free yourself from karma.

-That's right. Now, the important thing about giving true love is that, if your partner falls in love and wants to go live that new relationship, you will let it go in honest love, you will thank each other, you will transmute your relationship and you will continue loving each other, without clinging to each other. The love between you will last a lifetime; and who knows, maybe you will get back together later. Maybe the other relationship was just a short experience that enriched you and helped you free yourself from karma; and if not and it turns out to be a very positive and enriching experience and you stay in that relationship, you will be able to find someone else to give your honest love to. That happened to Efrén, she ended her new relationship, and went back to her husband, both of you are still together and very close.

-Wow Alberto, that sounds fantastic, I hope I become an honest love and learn to think that way.

-You will Larisa, you will. Any questions? -Everyone was pensive, Richard turned to see Ellen and approached to kiss her, he pressed his lips strongly to hers, a deep kiss, full of love. She caressed his cheek.

-No, said Carlos, it's very clear, isn't it beautiful? -Erika smiled at him.

-Yes, beautiful, that's right.

-So -continued Alberto- we arrived at the City of Light, there We stay to live with our families and friends, then we meet with our guides, who help us analyze what our past life was like, we see where we made mistakes and we keep the karmas instead of transmuting them, we see and discover what new karmas and dharmas we did, and based on this, we decide if we want to take another body to be born again or not; if we decide yes, then we begin to plan what we want to live and where, and with whom; so we begin to make agreements with those who will help us live those experiences.

-That's why I felt like I knew Richard, because in reality he and I had made an agreement.

-That's right, but you also made an agreement with Ellen, she asked you, help me lose my husband, I will love him very much, but I need you to take him away from me -they opened their eyes wide- then, Larisa, you agreed with Richard and he asked you, make me fall in love with you and steal my wife from me, I want to live that experience, I am going to experience abandoning my family for another woman, because I have not been able to stop doing it, so I hope this time I can stop doing it to free myself from karma, excellent you said: I have already stolen husbands in past lives and I need to stop doing it to free my karma, I will gladly help you; Your children asked you two, we want you to be our parents, and for you, dad, to abandon us, we want to experience the abandonment and loss of dad's love, this will awaken a lot of anger in us and sadness, if we do not manage to let go of the anger and sadness and we stay hating you or hating the other woman, then we will continue to be tied to karma, we have to stop hating and being angry to free ourselves, hopefully now we can free ourselves, already in many previous lives we have experienced the loss of dad or mom because of a third party, even, we have been those third parties -the children turned to look at each other astonished by all this- this is how agreements are established.

-So, Rouse and I, established agreements to help us live everything we have lived.

-That's right, each emotion experienced is the gift that you have given each other to be able to free yourselves from karma.

-Let's see, I didn't understand that.

-Yes Roger, if you felt very angry with the breakup of the relationship, and for example, you were so angry that you never spoke to each other again, and you hated each other, those emotions kept you tied to karma, you were not able to free yourself from the emotions, so you will repeat the same experience again, either as a man or as a woman, to feel anger and hatred again, to see if this next time you manage to free yourself from the emotion.

-So, it is true that everything is a big play, where each person plays a role, so that the other feels the emotion, feels the hatred, the fear, the resentment and so that you can free yourself from karma?

-Exactly Roger, well explained.

-But how do I know if I have karma when I get angry or feel resentment? - Rouse asked.

-The way to know if there is karma in something, is to know that in this life, there are no injustices, nor accidents, I repeat: In this life, there are no injustices or accidents; perhaps in a past life, you did the same thing to another person, so now you asked, I repeat: you asked that they do it to you, to pay your karma, they would make you angry so you would feel that emotion again.

-So -said Brandon- if someone bullies me at school, it's because I did that in a past life with someone else.

-That's right Brandon.

-So, Erika and I asked each other, well I asked you: Help me feel like I don't matter, so that I feel undervalued and unloved, and I could leave you, that seriously damaged me, you know, it was hard for me to believe in my personal value again, I felt like I wasn't enough, despite being successful in my career, but in love, since we broke up, I felt like that, of little worth, not anymore, I have worked hard with my personal value.

-I'm sorry, beautiful, I didn't know; but then, I asked you: Make me fall in love and help me, because I need to take my love and my commitment to the next level, I have always gotten rid of my loves and I need to stop doing it, if not, I will continue tied to karma, if I don't manage to change, then you will leave me.

-And you will not credit the subject -added Alberto- love is a subject, in fact it is the main subject on this planet, we come to learn about love; Hate teaches you about love, humiliation teaches you about your lack of self-love, the loss of your father or mother teaches you about love, your partner leaving you teaches you about love, helping another teaches you about love, everything teaches you something about love, love is the key to change, but honest and true love, not conditional and manipulative love.

-How does hate teach you about love?

-Light and darkness, Susan, are opposites, love and hate are opposites, heat and cold are opposites, to know one you have to know the other. When you hate you learn, when you love you learn, you need to know what darkness is, to know what light is. Just as hate is the absence of love. Did I explain myself? -Susan looked like she didn't understand.

-Yes, daughter -intervened Richard- when you hate someone,

you are experiencing the lack of love towards that person, that is learning about love, okay?

-Yes, I understand, now it is clear to me.

-So, everything we live -said Karla- is a plan to pass a subject, and that subject is love?

-That's right.

-But also -added Ellen- to help another to live an experience, and for them to help us, and in that way pay a karma or try to pay a karma, is that so, right?

-Exactly, that's right

-So -Larisa looked him in the eyes- that you and I met at the club, it wasn't a coincidence, but a plan, that you talked to me about this was because I asked you: Help me understand karma to free myself, -she was surprised- but of course I did, I asked you that! Now I remember.

-How do you remember Larisa? -Erika questioned.

-Yes, I'm seeing the image, we're sitting with some people, and you and I -she assured looking at Alberto with her gaze lost in memory- are making our agreements.

-Wow, Larisa, you're having a memory, how incredible.

-Alberto, that you introduced us at the bar wasn't

a coincidence either, but an agreement between the three of us, we ask you: Help us understand to free ourselves from our karmas.

-And the fact that we three went to your house and you told us about all this, it wasn't a miracle, it's not that you're an angel, but that we asked you to help us, right?

Alberto smiled.

-Excuse me sir -said the waiter- that I'm here, listening to you, is because I asked you, help me understand about my karmas to free myself.

-That's right Fabricio, nothing in our lives is a coincidence or accident, everything is an agreement.

-That someone -said Karla- steals from you or sexually attacks you when you're still a child, is that an agreement? I mean... that I asked him, help me feel... -she remained silent, her eyes, Rouse's and others' eyes filled with tears.

-That bastard, I hope he rots in jail!

-He will, they've sentenced him to a hundred years, nobody lives that long in those places.

The girl was four years old, he was a good friend of her father, very cheerful and affectionate, and the children in particular followed him a lot, he made them laugh and played with them.

-Hilario, my wife and I are having dinner,

could you take care of my daughter, she loves you very much.

-Of course, Luis, it will be a pleasure, my wife will love it.

From that night on, the girl's behavior changed, she became a little withdrawn and quiet.

-What's wrong Karlita? -her mother noticed the change- did

something happen to you my love?

-No mommy, -the girl continued playing with her doll, in silence.

When the parents were going out, she cried, asking them not to go, but the father thought they were just tantrums, so they forced her to stay at her friends' house.

One day, while her mother was putting her in the bath, the girl complained that it hurt when she sat down.

-What happened to you my love? You fell.

She just kept silent, her mother examined her and noticed that her anus was not normal, her eyes immediately filled with tears, remembering her youth, she hugged her tenderly.

-My girl, my girl, what have they done to you, what have we done to you, Luis, run, come! -she shouted desperately.

-Luis came running- What happened? You scare me, what's happening? -He entered the bathroom and his wife hugged the girl.

-They raped her, they raped our girl -he said with a heartbreaking cry.

-What? What are you saying?!

-Yes, look, she took off her childish buttocks and horrified observed the damage.

The police arrested her neighbors, they were tried and sentenced. From that day on the girl's childhood changed, they had She had to move to another city, because everyone in town knew about the trial. Her mother became paranoid, taking excessive care of her, to prevent her from being harmed again, two years later her parents divorced, and she never saw her father again, her mother became half alcoholic, and she grew up in fear, she was very angry with her mother for the excessive care she had of her, she could not go to parties, or go out alone with friends, or have sleepovers, she could not come home late after school, because her mother would strongly scold her, when she turned seventeen she left home, met Oscar, a dentist ten years older than her and they went to live together, he was addicted to anal sex and she, despite her childhood trauma, enjoyed it.

VII Finding out hurts a lot

The ladies in the kitchen listened with the door open and wiped away their tears remembering the beatings and humiliations in their childhood and even as adults. -I -Karla thought out loud- asked my parents, help me live this experience, because... because... -her tears overflowed- because I have to pay for a karma! Oh no, it's not possible, no... -Ellen arrived quickly and hugged her.

-Why Ellen, why did I do that? Why...? Why...?

-It's not possible..., said Carlos.

-Damn brat, wait until you get home.

The boy came home from school, ran up the stairs to his bedroom, entered, threw his backpack on the floor and threw himself on the bed, the door hit hard against the wall when it was pushed, and he, startled, raised his head.

-Damn boy, you're finally here, his mother was standing at the door with the iron cable tangled in her right hand and a meter of the cord hanging threateningly.

-But mom, what did I do? I haven't done anything.

-You think I'm your maid, I went to work and you left the dirty dishes on the table, you think I'm your maid, she approached him and began to hit him on any part of his small body, he was seven years old.

-Mom no, no, I didn't want to, no, his tears flowed and bathed his small face, full of horror, he saw his mother raising her arm, the cable hit his legs and his back, he tried to protect himself, finally he huddled up covering his head and face, she got tired of hitting him.

-That will teach you that there are no maids here, ungrateful brat, I work myself to death to take care of you, I should give you up for adoption. She left the bedroom and slammed the door on her way out. Carlos slowly got up and saw himself in front of the mirror, a red welt crossed his forehead, he took off his shirt and his small body was covered in lashes,

old marks from previous spankings could still be seen on his chest and back, the

punishments were excessive for his small childhood, he could only cry, there was no one to defend him, his father abandoned them three years ago and his mother worked all day trying to survive. He fell to his knees crying and rubbing his arms.

-Why? he cried to heaven, why? I'm not bad, why does my mother treat me like this? God, why? Neither his crying nor his words were heard, a lonely child, who felt abandoned.

At school he always tried to hide the marks of the blows, he knew that if his teacher called his mother, the punishment would be worse, so he was careful not to be seen, he was a quiet child, he had few friends, but he did not seek to get into trouble, he feared punishment. Despite his childhood of abuse and mistreatment, he was a good student, one of his teachers recognized his intelligence and became his mentor; Carlos was already sixteen years old and the teacher knew how to become the paternal image that the young man needed; his mother stopped abusing him many years ago, and even though their relationship was not very good, he, being an only child, loved her and tried to take care of her; his mentor guided him to a love for books and made him read many topics of personal development, he was able to finish his law degree thanks to a scholarship.

-So... -the tears did not let him speak clearly, his face had become that of the child, he lowered his voice until it was almost a whisper- I asked my mother, mistreat me so I could feel the hatred, and to free myself from it, from resentment, and from karma, no! Why? Why would I want to do something like that? I was a child - Erika hugged him lovingly, and he cried his pain with his face on her shoulder.

-My love, I'm sorry...

-Why Erika, why would we want to do or ask for something like that? -her crying showed her pain.

Meanwhile, Karla calmed down, hugged by Ellen, Fabricio brought more boxes with disposable tissues to the center of the table, Ellen took some and passed them to Karla.

Alberto remained silent and waited, discovering this hurt a

lot and they began to understand. When he thought it was convenient he continued.

-When we are in the City of Light, Carlos, there is no ego, so we make plans, many of them very painful, finally discovering this hurts a lot, it is something very difficult. But once you understand it, when you understand that everything was an agreement between that person and you, you can free yourself from karma, you can ask for forgiveness, because most likely, what they did to you, you also did it in a past life, I repeat, what they did to you, you did in past lives, and you have chosen to have it done to you in this one, to pay for your karma.

-But then, he said a little calmer and wiping away his tears, maybe in another life, I humiliated and mistreated my mother and that's why I asked you, now you humiliate me and mistreat me, but if I hate her and I stay angry, the karma remains and I don't free myself, and what it's all about is freeing yourself? Ok, ok... I understand.

-So I did the same to someone else... no, no, no... - his crying was deep, Karla covered her face with her hands, feeling the shame and pain of just thinking that she could have abused a child, Ellen hugged her lovingly without saying anything, she also cried.

Everyone cried when they saw them and also understood their own life stories.

Alberto waited a little, everyone was moved, each one had something in their past that embarrassed them, and it hurt, and now they were beginning to see it and understand it, that hurt a lot. When he thought it was appropriate, he continued.

-Discovering this hurts a lot, friends, but it is not to hurt you, but to understand, to ask for forgiveness, even to thank, and to free yourself from karma.

-We understand - said Richard - wow - he brought the glass of wine to his mouth and took a big gulp, trying to undo the lump in his throat.

-Yes, you understand - continued Alberto - then tell me, if a teacher helps you live an experience and gives you the opportunity to feel that emotion again, what should you feel for that teacher? Should you hate him or bless him? Should you stay angry with him or thank him? Should you hate him or love him?

-Of course, we should love him and thank him, if what he is doing is helping us, he is not harming us, on the contrary.

-That's right Richard, that's right - Alberto lifted his glass from the coffee table and took a sip. Everyone was very thoughtful.

-That time when a guy came with a gun and took my jewelry and my purse, did I ask him to do that to me? To pay my karma, because in a past life I did the same to someone else? Wow, so the fear I felt and then the hate, keep me tied to karma?

-That's right Larisa, as long as you don't thank your attacker or your abuser -she said turning to look at Karla, Rouse and Brandon- and ask for forgiveness, for having hurt someone else in that same way, in your past lives, you won't be freed from karma, and perhaps, in this life or the next, you'll have to live the experience again -she remained silent, brought her glass to her lips and took a sip, then continued- Can I continue? -Alberto looked at them all waiting for the answer.

It took them a while to respond and finally they said.

-Yes, yes, please.

-Discovering that someone did something to you because you asked them to in order to pay for karma can be very painful, especially if it is someone very dear to you, and you have continued to hate or reject that person. But we have to understand that we did it, in order to mutually help each other not to continue doing that, because that other person also has karma. After someone does something to me, I must say, thank you, thank you, if in this life or in past lives, I did the same to you, or to someone in your family, or to anyone, I ask for your forgiveness, please forgive me, I accept this act as the payment I must make for my past karmas; in this way you will be free, and the violet flame will remove from your body of light and from your Akashic records, the karma related to that experience; so you will never suffer it again, and if you do suffer it again, it is because there is still karma that must be paid, so be thankful for that again, remember, you planned it to be that way, no one is forcing you to live the experience again.

-Oh Alberto, this is incredible, we have remained, how many lives, twenty, fifty? tied to karma, repeating experiences over and over again by ignoring all this.

-I know that the maximum number of reincarnations of a person is five hundred lives on this planet.

-Wow, that's a lot of lives five hundred lives! -everyone turned to look at each other, their eyes wide.

-But why aren't we taught this so we can work on it and free ourselves? I mean, I understand what you told us: that that was our job; because it's about living the emotions to give thanks and not get stuck in anger or negative emotions.

-Yes, and once you understand this -continued Alberto- we could free ourselves and we wouldn't be afraid of dying, nor would we fear God, nor would we need religions, and that's what they don't want to happen, that's why they hide the truth from us.

-But then -said Karla- if everything is an agreement, the wars, the assaults, the rapes and abuses, our losses, any bad thing that happens to us, it's not because God wants it that way, but because we planned it that way, wow, and the church has made us believe that it's because God wanted it that way, that it's divine will.

-That's right Karla, because that way they take away your power and give it all to God, and they make us believe that he decides our lives, when in reality, it is and has been our decision. Do you remember Free Will? That was God's gift to all of us, on this planet and in the entire universe, we would all decide what we want to live and experience, and yes, there is karma, deciding how to pay for it.

-That's why the church - Roger said - doesn't want us to know this, because they would lose their power.

-Yes, but the most interesting thing is that even the church leaders themselves do not realize that they also live tied to karma and reincarnation, and that their life is their own planning, they really believe that it is God's will, and God is nothing more than the observer of everything, in fact, he is not only the observer, he is the one who is living all the dramas and all the "ugly" or "bad" things, as well as the good ones, each one of us is God - he remained silent waiting for the phrase to penetrate deep into their minds.

-We are God?! - said Brandon.

-Each one of us is God, - repeated Carlos as if hypnotized.

-Our mind, - continued Alberto - is a creative mind, right Roger, Richard, is it not with your mind that you create all these buildings and houses?

-Of course, first we imagine it in our heads, then we make the plans and finally we carry out the works.

- Exactly, your mind, our mind, the mind of every single inhabitant of this planet and on any planet or dimension in the universe, is the creative mind of God. God, as we call him/her, has no gender, he/she is actually the creative mind of the universe, he/she. God, the creative mind, made the constellations, the galaxies, the dimensions, the planets, the beautiful universe that we see now through telescopes or special cameras, all of that was made by him/her, the Creative Mind, and we, each one of us, have his/her creative mind; we are the Creative Mind of God living in these physical bodies. We created this world as it is now, over the years and centuries, with all its buildings, its beaches full of hotels, the small or large cities, each and every one of us has participated in this creation, in the present or in the past, in this and through all our past lives. Think about it, how many lives have you been reincarnated in? And in each one of them you have participated in the creation. Think about it, and you will see that it is true. As the Creative Minds, we have designed our lives, what experiences we were going to live, and with which of them we were going to pay some karma. So, is your life not your own creation? Who brought you to live where you live? Who chose the partner you have? Everything is your creation, or do you still think that it is God's will? Well, in fact it is, but not the God who is out there somewhere, watching you to see if he punishes you for not following his rules. No, the God that you are, the Creative Mind that you are.

-Wow, -said Roger- this is incredible.

-Of course, -said Rouse, bringing his glass to his lips- there is so much to think about.

-I believe it is -replied Ellen.

Karla, sitting next to him on the edge of the chair, raised the glass of wine to her lips, her gaze lost in the past.

-The most important thing, friends, is that you do not punish yourselves thinking that you were unfortunate or cursed for having hurt someone, even if it was a child or someone else. It is not about abusing yourself emotionally. I know that discovering that hurts, but smile, because now you can free yourselves from those experiences. Besides, they asked us to help them live that. And one more thing, what it is about once you know that you are God, the creative mind, is to decide: What kind of God do I want to be? And what will my creation be from now on? I am going to be a God of love and blessings, and I am going to create a world of peace, harmony, respect for others, and of the world of peace and harmony.

with each other, or what kind of God am I going to be?

-Thanks Alberto, you're right, -said Carlos smiling- you're absolutely right.

-Well, and finally, there's something that each of you have to do at home, it's an exercise that I call "The Cup of Personal Love", are you ready?

-Yes, yes, go ahead.

-Pay attention. You have to lock yourselves in your bedroom, you will have to undress completely and you must sit in front of a full-length mirror preferably, then, you are going to get close enough to the mirror with your knees, sitting on a chair, you are going to look into your own eyes, you have to endure the gaze, you cannot look away, at first it will be difficult for you, some more than others, but it is necessary that you can sustain the gaze, you have to look inside the iris, the dark area in the center of the eye, it is not about seeing your face, or around the eye, it is about looking directly into your eyes, your eyes are the gateway to your soul, once you have achieved this, you are going to begin to talk to yourselves saying: Richard, you, each one, say your name, of course; Richard, now I see you, now I see you and I want you to know, everything that has hurt me since we were little, let your mind open and cry, cry everything that is kept in that cup, the abuse you were a victim of, the pain of abandonment, the blows, the humiliations, the sexual abuse, everything, everything that hurt you since you were little, tell that person what you felt and what hurt you, talk to them about the fear you felt, tell them you were just a little girl or boy, complain to them, don't keep anything to yourself, it's important to get out as much as you can, don't think it was an agreement, put yourself at that age and speak from there, how old were you, three, five, fifteen? -all the men and women wiped their tears and tried to hold back- you will have to cry all that; after you have cried, which will take a long time, many of you will have things that you don't remember, but you will feel it, it will be as if you know there is something, but you don't know what it is, but it hurts you, so if that happens to you, ask for help, just say out loud: Father, help me, put your beautiful hand on me and open my mind, help me get out this that hurts me so much, free me, free me, help me please - the tears of many came out like the river that begins to overflow the floodgates that contain it - try to get out as much as you can, many times in a single session, we cannot finish getting out everything that we keep inside, much of it is very hidden, that is why you need to ask our father for help and do the exercise again, a week after you do it for the first time. When you feel that you have cried everything you have and you are calmer, you will look at yourself in the mirror again and you will begin to love yourself, rub your hands and begin to caress your face, you have to love yourself, I repeat, you have to "l-o-v-e-r-e-s, so, you're going to caress your whole body giving it love like you've probably never done before, thank your face for your beauty, your eyes for allowing you to see life, your ears for listening to life and what it has to say to you, caress your hair and thank it, and each and every part of your body, let nothing be left unloved, not a nail, not a single phalanx, nothing, everything has to be caressed and loved by you, your penis and vagina, everything, don't do sexual caresses, only love, true and honest love for yourself, the anus is also important, put your hand on it and love it, ask for forgiveness if you have abused this organ, if you are used to having anal sex, I recommend that you don't do it anymore, there is a karma tied to it, the anus was not made for sex, it is an organ that has many nerve endings and because it is in the root chakra, it has a lot to do with sex, but it was not made for that, respect it, love it and leave that activity, later, on another occasion, I will teach you how to make love, to achieve sublime states of energy without even needing penetration.

-Is that possible? -Roger asked.

-Of course, I will teach you all later, okay, but first, do this. When you have finished loving each other all over your body, you are going to do something very special, this is very special, pay attention, sitting in the chair, you are going to look into your eyes again and say: Your name, I see you now, I want you to know that I love you, that I am proud of you, of the lovely man that you are, of the beautiful love that you express to everyone who knows you, of the special love that you have for Ellen and your children, I love you, talk to yourself and tell yourself beautiful things, many, say many beautiful things about yourself to yourself, then hug yourself again, when you have stopped crying and are full of love for yourself, you will look into your eyes again and now, comes a magical part, are you ready? Pay close attention: Inside you, there are three or four beings - everyone opened their eyes full of expectation - four beautiful beings, who are your selves, from your childhood, there is a boy or girl, who from they must be three or four years old, I don't know, each one is unique, another must be six or seven, another fifteen maybe, and the other I don't know, mine is twenty-three years old.

- Are they our internal children? - Ellen asked.

- Yes, and now, are you going to tell them: My loves, I know they are inside, please, come out of me, and wait, you will see what happens. After that, start loving them, love your children and continue loving each other. What we have done with this exercise is to fill our cup with our Personal Love, which is the most beautiful love that exists in the universe. Believe me when I tell you, each one of you has within you the most beautiful love that exists in the universe, so start giving your true and honest love to everyone and everything around you; tell me how you feel.

Larisa threw herself into his arms and cried, she couldn't hold it in any longer, everyone was crying, there was not a soul that hadn't been touched by those words, the ladies in the kitchen hugged each other, they were friends from a long time ago, Fabricio at the bar wiped his eyes with a napkin, trying to contain the lump that formed in his throat. Ellen had stood up and was crying in her husband's arms, her children covered their faces with a napkin and tried to contain themselves. All hearts longed to leave to do the exercise.

-Thank you, Alberto, thank you -Larisa told him hugging him leaning on his shoulder- thank you, you have touched me in a way that... -she could not continue, he hugged her tenderly, containing her, after she calmed down, he gave her a tender kiss on the cheek and wiped her tears with the handkerchief she had.

-I am very happy that all these serves, beautiful, so that this beautiful love, vibrates greatly and blesses everyone around you, you have the most beautiful love that exists in the universe.

-She stood on her toes and gave him a kiss on the cheek- Thank you, thank you.

-Friends -said Roger- I propose a toast -he raised his glass, forcing himself to smile so as not to cry- for the most beautiful love in the universe.

- Cheers, - they all said with their glasses in hand, and took a sip of the delicious fruity wine, which undid the lump in their throats.

- Friends, you saw the time, it's almost three thirty in the morning.

- Wow, we didn't realize - said Carlos.

- But it's been worth every minute, this is changing our lives - said Erika.

- Ellen approached Alberto and smiling hugged him - thank you friend, thank you for helping us - she separated from him and they held hands - I want to ask for your forgiveness, if in any life I humiliated you, offended you or hurt you in any way, please forgive me, I'm sorry, thank you for fulfilling our agreement.

- Thank you, Ellen, also forgive me, if in any way I offended you, in this or in past lives, I'm sorry, and it was a pleasure to fulfill our agreement.

Everyone began to hug each other, the violet flame was present throughout the apartment, setting fire to the energetic-spiritual bodies of all those present, the souls danced embraced and being illuminated by the violet light, little by little, they returned to their respective physical bodies, full of life-giving light, healing light, violet light, and love, the creative mind was pleased, seeing itself in all of them.

After saying goodbye to the last of her visitors, only Larisa remained, she had waited until the end.

-Ladies, Fabricio, please leave everything like this, on Monday you will fix it, now it is time to rest, thank you for everything, congratulations ladies, as always you stood out, thank you for your love.

-Sir -said the waiter- I am going to go to rest, may I give you a hug.

-Of course, please - they hugged each other, Fabricio had to contain himself from crying.

On the roof of the building there were two bedrooms that he used for his domestic service.

-We would also like to hug him, would you allow us?

-Please, but of course, it will be a pleasure - she said approaching each of them, and hugged them affectionately, they could not hold back their tears.

-Thank you, Mr. Alberto, thank you, today we have learned so many things...

-That's great, beauties, rest and do the exercise.

They were finally alone, and sat on the main chair, each with a drink in hand.

-Larisa, I had planned to ask you to stay with me tonight, but this has been very intense -she smiled- and I think it would be a very good time for you to go home and do this exercise comfortably, in your bedroom, unless you prefer to stay, I have a bedroom alone that you can use, it is isolated, it is the one I use to sing when I feel like taking the roosters out for a walk, ha, ha, ha.

-Wow, you are a real box of charms.

-Yes, there are many things you don't know about me, but if you give me the opportunity I would like you to know them. Once you finish doing the exercise, you will sleep in my bedroom and I will sleep in the study, tomorrow I can take you to breakfast if you want, and we can spend the day together, but what about your children?

-They are with their father and his family, so I have no problems.

-Excellent, what do you want to do?

-I want to stay, if you allow me.

-It will be a pleasure, when you are ready tell me ok, let me prepare the room - he walked to the hallway, entered the study, on the wall there was a full-length mirror, he took out the hidden bed inside the sofa and arranged it, took out some clean sheets and spread them on the mattress, making sure there were no wrinkles, she was standing, leaning on the door frame, with the glass in her hand watching him.

-You scared me, you evil one, you didn't make a sound.

-I wanted to surprise you, and I did it - he said with a beautiful and flirtatious smile.

Finally, he moved one of the chairs to the mirror, and a new box of disposable tissues that he placed on top of a small nightstand.

-Ready, darling.

-What's the bed for? I'm going to be sitting.

-Don't believe it, you're going to need it, you'll see. You have to get completely naked, okay, enjoy it, I'll be in my bedroom at the end of the hall, when you're ready, if you want, let me know, so I can change rooms. I'm not offering you mine because this one is more soundproof, so you can scream freely and believe me, you can't hear anything out there, so don't be afraid, the window is double-glazed, so the neighbors won't hear you either. Scream everything you have to scream, remember, don't stop looking into each other's eyes.

-Ok, I think I remember everything I have to do.

He approached her, held her by the shoulders and searched for her lips, she accepted it and they gave each other a tender and long kiss, without passion, but, even so, her Kundalini energy awakened. -Remember, no sexual caresses, just love, wait, I'll bring you something else. He came back and brought with him a very beautiful silk nightgown and a robe, I bought these a little while ago, a cautious man is worth two, you have to wear them for the first time, use them to sleep when you're done. I'll leave you, beautiful, enjoy it - he left the room and closed the door.

After a while, he heard Larisa's very distant crying, he put on the shorts he used to sleep, lay down and fell asleep.

Larisa cried, releasing all her childhood pain, her abandonment, her parents divorced when she was very young and her father left her all day in charge of the servants, one of them had sexually abused her, and from that point on she became withdrawn and quiet, her entire childhood she felt abandoned and unworthy of dad's love, he had managed to make a fortune and she was his only heir, but she always stayed away from him. As an adult, when he wanted to be with her, she didn't have time or was traveling, so she stayed away and angry with dad, punishing him for abandoning her; he never saw his mother again and that also hurt his soul, he never understood how a mother could do that to her children, until he discovered that his father pushed her away and threatened her, that if she went back to look for the girl he would put her in jail, and since he was a powerful man, his mother moved away and he never saw her again. His mother made her life and had other children, but Larisa never heard from her mother again. Later, she met her husband, with whom she experienced abandonment again, he would be absent under the pretext of work and would not return to sleep, then she found out that he had another family and divorced him, she kept her children away from him using her lawyers, but she realized that she was harming the children more than him and changed, she allowed him to see them, that helped the children a lot. Larisa cried deeply taking out so many things she had kept, things she didn't know she had, after a long time, cleaning her pains, she began to love herself deeply and truly, as she had never done before, she did everything Alberto had told her, even anal sex, that was something she enjoyed, although lately it was not so pleasurable anymore, because it hurt her, and she no longer felt comfortable practicing it, so she promised herself never to do it again; she loved every part of her body, feeling the explosion of a very beautiful energy, tears of joy overwhelmed her, tears of joy and pain mixed, for all the abandonment in which she had herself, because she had never caressed herself, much less loved like this; Then she looked into her eyes again and spoke to herself, she recognized herself, her skin looked different, she looked younger and more beautiful, her hair shone, she looked into her eyes and said: Larissa, my beautiful love -her tears began to come out again- forgive me my love, forgive me for all the abandonment I have had you in, I want you to know that from now on I will love you, I will take care of you, you will be my priority and the most important thing in my life; you have always been very brave, you were a very strong girl, you learned many things, I love you for your courage, for your beautiful smile, I love it when you laugh, you are very intelligent, hard-working, you are very good at business, and from now on I know that you will be a very loving mother, I

love you, my beautiful love, -she hugged herself lovingly
rubbing her arms and caressing her face, later, she looked
into her eyes again and magic came, she said out loud- My
loves, beautiful ones, my girls, I know you are in here, please
come out from inside me, suddenly, from her chest, they
began to come out, first a beautiful three-year-old girl, with
her black hair and beautiful bangs falling down the side of
her face; Oh no, no, how…, she said astonished, immediately
after a seven year old girl came out, beautiful and thin, then a
beautiful fifteen year old girl and finally a twenty-two year old
adult- It's not true no, but how…, she covered her face, the
crying was uncontrollable, there was so much pain in her
soul, that she couldn't even lift her face, she felt the hands of
her girls caressing her hair, the baby caressed her face, while
she pouted, and began to cry, she lifted her off the ground
and hugged her, they all hugged her, they all gave her their
love, she cried with joy and sadness, mixed feelings
overwhelmed her- But how my loves? Forgive me, I didn't
know, how come you were in here? But why…, why didn't
anyone tell me before this, my beautiful…? how is it possible
that I abandoned you without even speaking to you? I didn't
know. My love - said the older one hugging her along with
her younger girls, she heard her voice for the first time and
broke into a deeper cry. -My love… forgive me, forgive me, I
didn't know that you, that you were here, forgive me my
loves, I didn't know - they all consoled her hugging her for
the first time after almost thirty-five years - my beautiful ones
forgive me, please forgive me, I didn't know that you were
alive inside me, forgive me I'm so sorry - when she was able
to calm down a little she told them - come my beautiful ones,
come, let's go to bed, I want to hug you - she lay down and
hugged the two youngest to her chest, the other two placed
themselves one on each side hugging her, while she hugged
the little ones, they all cried, she asked for forgiveness and

they caressed her giving her their love, little by little they calmed down, and she began to thank each one of them for their dedication to living through those hard experiences, the girls cried their pain, because they had been humiliated, abandoned, abused, each one of them lived a stage of their life and hid inside, with all their pain and humiliation, to give way to the next one, who would live the following experiences and the following pains and joys, thus, each one was crying and healing, she loved them and recognized them, she explained the agreements to them and they cried understanding all that, understanding that no one had hurt them, and that they had not hurt anyone, they began to understand and forgive, they cleared their karmas, the violet flame was present setting them all on fire, transmuting their past experiences, and erasing their karmas from their Akashic records. The sun began to rise and illuminated the edge of the curtain that Alberto had closed, finally, and after a long time, they fell asleep…

Alberto woke up early as was his custom, even if he had slept a few hours he did not like to waste his mornings in bed and preferred to go to the club to do some activity, it was seven in the morning, he got up and walked down the hall, he reached the closed door of the studio and knocked softly, when he received no answer, he opened it and looked out. - Hi, hi - she was lying on the bed covered with the sheet, her hair looked shiny and she looked younger, she opened her eyes and gave him a very beautiful smile, she stretched, getting rid of her laziness, and revealed her beautiful pink breasts, her nipples were erect.

-Wow - he said admiring her - you look incredible, have you seen yourself in the mirror?

-No - he answered - what do I have? - he caressed her face - I'm sure my eyes are swollen, I've cried like I've never cried before, it's just that this is... - her crying wanted to reappear, he sat on the edge of the bed and caressed her face softly and tenderly to calm her down.

-I know, this exercise is very intense -he wiped a tear that was slipping from his eye- you are so beautiful- he bent down very slowly, slowly he approached her lips, and kissed them subtly, then he stuck to them more tightly and she hugged him, their naked torsos made contact and their tongues tasted each other sweetly, her Kundalini energy began to rise up his legs causing an erection.

-Are you ready for this, beautiful? -in response she pulled him again and kissed him, forcing him to lie down next to her, both began to caress each other, looking into each other's eyes- Do I want to show you something, will you allow me?

-How to make love without penetration? I'm not sure I want to learn that you know, ha, ha, ha.

-You're going to love it. First, repeat after me: Beloved Mother Gea, give me your Kundalini energy. Gea is the name of our planet, -she repeated each word- now, breathe through your nose or through your mouth. Which of these two do you feel the energy through more when you inhale? -She didn't answer, her energies were very active, and filled her with new sensations- slowly and deeply, feel and imagine how this energy goes up your legs to your root chakra -He removed the sheet from her and left her entire beautiful body uncovered- now, breathe- he placed his hand on her shin, and began to slide it upwards- breathe slowly and feel- he went up inside her thighs, without reaching the maximum point of her pleasure, he lowered his hand again along the inside of her thighs, then raised his hand again and stopped just before touching her magic part, she separated her legs a little and finally, very slowly, placed the palm of her hand on top of her vulva- feel- she arched her back increasing her sensations, a discharge of beautiful energy enveloped her- repeat: Let my root chakra activate!, here feel- he massaged her clitoris a little, increasing the activation of the chakra- imagine how the energy spins activating your chakra- she bent again lifting her belly from the ground bed, I was about to have an orgasm- wait he said stopping, breathe, slowly, and order: Activate my navel chakra! -he placed his hand in this place and began to make circles, she breathed holding back- repeat: Activate my solar plexus chakra! -she said each word and her energy forced her to contain herself even more, she breathed again and he raised his hand, placed it on this chakra and began to make the turns- breathe and feel the energy, now say: Activate my heart chakra! -she repeated the words, and an electric shock ran through her spine, he raised his hand to his chest and rotated his energy- breathe. -No, it's just that, no...

-Try not to cum, darling, but if you can't, it's okay, do it - she couldn't contain herself any longer, she was extremely excited, he placed his hand on top of the root chakra again, caressing the clitoris, and she exploded in an orgasm, he raised his hand along her belly, her solar plexus, her throat, and each one of her chakras, he passed his hand over her face caressing it, until he reached her crown chakra and kept his hand there, putting his fingers in her hair, he got closer to her as much as he could and began to raise his own energy with his breathing, he began to feel her orgasm and it became his own orgasm, she kept coming, again and again, her body was turning on, her energy was at its maximum, he held her close to her, with his leg between hers and feeling her as much as possible, raising her breathing, activating her chakras and raising her energy, their energetic bodies were completely fused, their souls They danced together forming a single flame of blue and pink energy, which mixed to form a beautiful color, their energies were loving each other completely wrapped in an energetic orgasm, the energy they caused was so great that it illuminated the entire building, the neighbors felt it, the most sensitive were forced to close their eyes feeling a wave of beautiful pleasure, the most unconscious did not notice anything; They continued dancing energetically and physically the dance of love, little by little she was recovering, long minutes passed feeling her orgasm, he knew he had to give her time for her energetic bodies to return to their physical bodies to recover, little by little, she let go and relaxed, she could not open her eyes, she could not articulate words, she could not move- now, I want you to raise your energy again with your breathing, draw air in through your mouth, do it quickly, now! Breathe, inhale and raise your energy again, -he did the same and she hugged him again while the air entered through her mouth, she arched feeling another new orgasm, one just as beautiful and intense as the previous one- breathe beautiful, raise your energy again, inhale, go, like this, like this beautiful, like this, all the way up -he placed his hand on her crown chakra and she hugged him, he began to pull her hair gently to cover her face and rubbed it, she felt herself floating, the sensation of her hair on her face was new and this elevated her even more, for a moment, she stopped being there, she only saw a beautiful blue light, and pink tones emerging from somewhere, he approached to kiss her lips covered by her hair while she remained dispersed everywhere, without having a body, little by little, she returned to her body, when she was finally able to move, she hugged him tightly, she

238

remained silent without being able to articulate words, beautiful tears flowed without being able to contain them, she continued to feel the energy throughout her body, and when she was finally able to speak she said:

- Wow, what was that? wow, it's just that... -he began to gently and tenderly remove her hair from her face, her tears burst forth again and she hugged him crying- it's just that... -she couldn't express herself, it was one of those moments when words aren't necessary- it's just that... oh Alberto, what was that? it's just that... -He remained silent, allowing her to feel, then, he wiped her tears.

-What was that? -she hugged him and hid face in his shoulder.

-That was an energetic orgasm, without the need for penetration -he moved and lay down beside her caressing her hair, she looked at him in love and totally ecstatic.

-It's just that I've never felt anything like that, it's just that... this was... incredible, I can't believe it.

-Now, let me show you the difference - he had an erection, he placed himself between her legs and they started the dance of love again, raising their energies, she tried to contain herself, but she couldn't, when she felt him inside her, she had a beautiful orgasm again, breathe, darling, raise your energy, both embraced each other in an energetic and spiritual orgasm, which took them to the encounter of their souls, and their spiritual bodies.

They were both lying down, hugging each other, the sheet covered them, she was lying on his chest and he was caressing her hair. For a long time, they were silent, their energies were being restored. When he believed that it was the right moment, he asked.

-Tell me Larisa, how did it go? What did you think of the exercise of the cup of personal love?

-Oh Alberto, this has been incredible..., at first it was hard for me to look into my eyes, you don't know, I think he had never really looked at me before, when I finally did, the crying clouded my vision and I couldn't stop crying, his eyes became cloudy again and he remained silent.

-What you're feeling is normal, if you need to cry, don't be ashamed, let it out, it's important that it keeps flowing, don't try to stop it.

-It's just that..., -he reached over and grabbed the box of tissues and handed her one, she took it and wiped her eyes that were beginning to wet her chest.

-It's just that... I've cried so much, I didn't know I was in so much pain, so many humiliations, -she lay down on her back, next to him, and dried her tears- I never imagined that I would be so angry with my father, that I would feel so abandoned, I grew up being an only child and he was dedicated to his business, he's a very rich man, so I grew up alone, I was abused and humiliated in many ways, but... I asked him for that..., her face transformed again into that of a little girl, I asked him to do that to me, her crying was reborn with force, that has hurt me very much Alberto, very much.

-Yes beautiful, finding out that hurts a lot.

-Afterwards -she said sobbing- I was able to forgive him and thank him, and for the first time I loved him...for the first time I loved my father -the tears overflowed again- can you believe it, for the first time I loved him... -she fell silent to calm down- afterwards, I thanked him and I freed myself from that pain, but it was not only with him, with everyone with whom I had something, there were so many things. When I felt that I had no more tears, I began to love myself, she stretched out her right arm and caressed it with her hand left, never, never had he loved me like this, that was so beautiful, my face changed, I could see it, -his tears diminished at times, but did not stop.

-But of course, he did, you look younger and your skin has another tone, you look incredible.

-That was wow, my body felt so... loved -while saying this he caressed his face tenderly and softly- After..., -his crying became a little more intense- for the first time I spoke to myself, and I told myself beautiful things, I felt so beautiful and so loved by myself, that I could not stop crying with joy, and a little sadness, for having abandoned me so many years, for not having loved me before, but I promised myself that I would not abandon myself again, that I would love myself and always speak well of myself.

-That's good, darling, to have an honest and true love, we must love ourselves first, even before loving our children; If you don't love yourself first, if you are not the most important thing for yourself, then your love for others will not be honest.

-Ok, I understand, that's why we can't truly love others, I mean, we've always been told: "Love your neighbor as yourself," but how can I love them if I don't love myself?

-Exactly, that's why your love, you must give it first to yourself, and then give it to everyone and everything else, to your family, your house, your employees, to everything, in this way your love will truly bless your life.

-How incredible, I had no idea of the importance of loving yourself; I confess that my ex always told me that I didn't love him because I only loved myself, and I always thought that was true, that I was actually very capricious and selfish, because I was always the most important, but now I realize that no, that didn't really love me, she was angry with me, and with everyone, even... -she was silent for a moment, what she was going to say still hurt her- with my children -her eyes again released some tears- those beautiful little ones, I have been abandoning them, I have never given them an honest love, I had been doing with them what my parents did with me, abandoning me, now I have been abandoning them.

-That's your karma and theirs.

-What do you mean, our karma?

-Yes, if you think about it a little, as adults they will abandon their children and in that way the patterns are repeated and the karmas are maintained, that's why you made your agreements together

-What, I don't understand?

-You asked your mom and dad to abandon me, help me feel alone, I want to learn from abandonment, to stop doing it, because in past lives I have abandoned those I love, and I have to stop doing it; your children told you: We want to be your children, and for you to abandon us, because in past lives we have abandoned our loved ones and we have to stop doing it; it is a chain, do you realize?, all of you are linked to the karma of abandonment.

-So that is why my mom left when I was a child and I have

not seen her again? I have always been very angry with her, but I understand that she did it because I asked her to do it, to feel abandoned again, and to feel the anger and rage, but in reality it was to not stay angry, but to give thanks for the abandonment and end my karma; but it turns out, because I have stayed angry, I do not free myself from karma; even with my dad; You don't know, I don't even want to see him, I never have time for him, when he asks me to see him, I always tell him I can't, it takes me months to see him; but then, since I stay angry, I do the same with my children and they will hate me and when they are adults, they will abandon their children, and we will all continue to be tied to karma, oh Alberto, this is so complicated.

-It's a game, see things like this, it's a theater put together by you, agreements made with your parents, your children and your husband, to repeat a lesson, ABANDONMENT, and to be able to pay for karma.

-So, we could say that anger, resentment, hatred, fear, are lessons that we plan to feel again, to actually free ourselves from a karma.

-That's right, that's why I told you that emotions are the gift; an experience always leaves us with an emotion and that is the gift. For example, imagine that, in front of a person, a child is shot and killed, and the murderer runs away.

-Oh no, that must be terrible.

-Of course, it is, it brings out very strong emotions…

-Anger, hate, desire for revenge, sadness, a lot of sadness and very deep depression, she said this imagining that she was the one who was living that event.

-That's right, those emotions are the gift, think about it: The murderer is someone who the mother asked: Help me, I want you to kill my son, because I need to feel hate and fear and all that, in my past life I killed a lady's son and I want to pay my karma; the one who will be her son in this life told her: I will be your son, I will help you, and I want you to help me get out of my body when I am seventeen, by then, I will have finished what I had to do, and in that way I will help you to live again what you need; once the theater is set up, and already in this life, having forgotten the agreements and why they were made, one Sunday with the family, the murderer shows up and the tragedy occurs, the mother becomes depressed, hates, remains in the desire for revenge, and after a few years she dies, returns to the City of Light, meets her "dead" son again, and the murderer, who had died murdered by someone else, and then, she realizes that she did not pass the test.

-So, are you still tied to karma?

-Yes, and you will have to live the experience again in the next life, or the one after that, until they are released. You, in many past lives, have remained angry with those who abandoned you, and that ties you to karma. Every time you return to the City of Light, you realize that you did not pass the test, and you have to repeat it again.

-Wow, I have to solve all this.

-Keep talking to me, darling, and then what happened?

-Oh no... -her eyes immediately clouded over just by remembering it- oh, it's not that... I spoke to my inner girls and asked them to come out and they came out, Alberto, they are real, they came out, how is it possible? And why aren't they here?

-They are inside you, they sleep there, inside you, you just have to tell them to come out of you when they want to, and that they can come in whenever they want.

-Do you want to meet them?

-Of course, I would love to, but wait, it's just that this reunion is so special, that it's better for you to be alone, there are still things that they have to heal and talk to you, ask them to tell you everything that hurts them, hug them and then, tell them how beautiful and brave they were to live through all that, that you are proud of them, make them feel very special, do you understand me?

-Yes, of course, this is magical, you know Alberto, I'm thinking..., I would love to spend the whole day with you, but I think it's more important that I finish with certain karmas, I'll go see my dad, then my children and my ex, I have to take advantage of all this that is so fresh.

-Of course, we have a lot of time ahead of us, we'll meet later. Wait, I want to meet your girls, let me put on my shorts. Ready, do it.

-My beautiful girls, come out from inside me.

They were coming out, materializing.

-Hello beauties, the three little girls approached Larisa hugging her, the older one stood in front of Alberto, her beautiful eyes analyzing him. My beauties, I would like to introduce you to my friend Alberto, say hello.

-Hello Alberto, said the oldest one holding out her hand.

He greeted her.

-Hello Larisa, you are so beautiful, how old are you?

-Twenty-two years old.

-Ok, wait, I want you to meet my children, my beautiful loves, please come out, her little ones began to materialize coming out of her chest, as if the physical body was a tent that kept them inside. My beauties, how are you?

-Hello my love, said the oldest, Alberto, my oldest boy, is twenty-three years old, I want to introduce you to Larisa and her girls, boys say hello to Larisa and her girls.

Alberto's boys were more extroverted than the girls. They were more accustomed to going out, little by little the girls approached them and after a few moments they were all talking and the little ones were playing.

Now that we get home, children, it is important that we all do the exercise.

-I'm sleepy, dad, said Brandon, can I do it tomorrow? I can't stand it anymore.

-Me too, dad.

-Yes, said Ellen, my love, this has been very tiring, I think it will be better if we do it tomorrow, more rested don't you think?

-Ok, my queen, you're right, it's very late, tomorrow with a more rested mind, we can do it.

VIII Transmuting Karmas

-Dad, hello - said Larisa starting to cry.

-Daughter, what's wrong, are you okay? You scare me.

-Dad, I want to see you, are you home?

-Yes, my love, of course, come here, I'll wait for you, are you okay?

-Yes, yes, I just want to see you.

-Of course, love, come -They hung up the phones.

-Who was love? You look worried.

-It was Larisa, she wants to see me, she was crying and that's very strange, I'm going to get ready a little.

Her dad was waiting for her standing in the hall of the residence, when she saw him, she ran and threw herself into his arms crying.

-Dad, forgive me, please, forgive me.

-What, my love, I have nothing to forgive you for.

-Yes, because I've been angry with you all these years, and... - she cried deeply, she couldn't explain anything to him, he just hugged her, he missed his little girl, now that he was older, he realized the abandonment he had always had her in, and it hurt him to have done it, he knew she didn't want to see him in revenge for her abandonment.

-It's that dad - she said separating from him and taking his hands, she looked him straight in the eyes and said with tears in them- I want to ask for your forgiveness, if in past lives or in this one, I humiliated you, hurt you, abandoned you, please forgive me, I'm sorry - her eyes shed tears, it was hard for him to speak out loud, he began to feel that something was being taken away from him, he felt it too. - Daughter - he said instinctively - if in past lives I humiliated you, hurt you, harmed you, in any way, if I abandoned you... I ask for your forgiveness, please forgive me - he pulled her towards him and wrapped her in his arms, she caressed his back, the violet flame surrounded them setting their energetic-spiritual bodies on fire, their souls danced embraced, loving each other, being bathed by the violet light, their karmas were erased from their Akashic records; little by little their energetic bodies returned to their physical bodies and they positioned themselves wrapped in violet light, both smiling.

- What happened, daughter? Tell me, what happened? - She felt that someone was behind her father, his wife, a young woman, who according to her had pushed her father away from her, looked at them wiping away her tears. Larisa walked up to her and hugged her- Valgarma, forgive me, please forgive me, both of them were crying, she separated a little from her, took her hands and transmuted their karmas.

-Thank you, Larisa, thank you for telling me this, you too, forgive me if I hurt you, it was never my intention, but...

-Yes, I know, I stayed angry, blaming you.

Her father approached and hugged them, then said:

-Come, let's sit down - they walked to the living room and settled on the big couch, while her stepmother sat on the individual couch. She began to tell them all about her experience and what she had learned, she insisted that they also do the exercise of the cup of personal love, she told them how and accompanied them to their bedrooms, each one alone did the exercise.

Her cell phone vibrated, she took it out of her pocket, saw the name on the screen and hesitated to answer, finally she did.

-Well - he seemed a bit cold, their relationship had not ended on good terms, there had been a lot of anger, legal disputes and revenge, so that's why he didn't want to get too close to her, only what was necessary to pick up his children and be able to spend the weekends with them.

-Hi Axel, she said in a very cheerful tone, how are you? - she didn't want to ask him about the children, because she wanted to resolve her karma with him first.

-Well, what's going on, is something wrong?

-Everything's fine, hey, are you at home, can I go see you? I'd like to talk to you.

-Yes, of course, but Martha is here, I don't want any problems.

-No, of course not, don't worry, I'll be there in a little while.

-Ok, I'll wait for you.

While her father and Valgarma were doing the exercise of filling her personal cup of love, she entered the bedroom that her father had told her was for her, but that she rarely got to occupy, she entered, and for the first time admired how big and beautiful it was, she walked touching the furniture, her vision of things changed, she felt completely different, everything surprised her and amazed her; she lay down on the bed and said.

-My loves, beautiful ones, please come out of me - her girls came out of her chest, and lay down, the older ones next to her, and the smaller ones on her chest. She hugged the smaller ones who cried pouting and hugged her, feeling her, they had been inside for many years, hidden, unseen, except by their beautiful older ones, in the evenings all of them tried to communicate with Larisa saying: My love, we are here, do you hear us? She did not listen to them, and every night the little ones slept hugged and alone. Now, she dedicated herself to talking to them and hugging them, her inner girls felt truly loved, their abandonment was being healed, she made them feel very special and valued, she found out that the youngest hid when she turned three, she was a beautiful baby. The other little girl went to kindergarten and hid when she started primary school. She must have been six years old. She was sexually abused when she was five and became quiet and withdrawn, so Larisa paid special attention to her, letting her express herself by saying:

-Come on, my love, tell me what you felt - the girl cried, hugging her neck.

-Yes, yes, I was very scared, yes, I didn't want to, because he... - her crying didn't let them continue and she buried her face in Larisa's chest. Both hugged each other trying to heal their pain.

-Yes, my love, I know that he scared us a lot and that he hurt us.

-Yes, yes, it's that he... - she couldn't continue expressing herself.

-Yes my beautiful, I know, cry my beautiful, cry, cry all that hurts you my brave girl, cry, -The girl hugged her tighter and she pressed her to her chest, little by little the crying subsided, the girl finally managed to stop crying and sobbed sighing and gasping for air- my love, now, now I know that we asked him to do that to us. -Yes, yes, but... -her child's mind could not reason that completely, but Larisa continued- yes my love, I know that this hurts you, but that happened because we asked him to, he only helped us pay a debt that we had from a past life -the violet flame lit up hugging them- now we have to..., we have to ask for forgiveness -she said this and the crying sprang forth again with force- sorry, sorry, because I did that with some other girl or boy, forgive me, sorry, God, forgive me, forgive me, I did not want to hurt anyone, I am good, I did not want to hurt, forgive me, father, forgive me... -The violet flame shone brightly cleansing their bodies and burning the karmas accumulated in all previous lives, that was an experience that they had already repeated on many occasions, she had been abused and had been an abuser- sorry, forgive me all of you to whom I did that, sorry, I am a good person, forgive me -her crying was a river without end, her soul needed to be healed, and the crying did that while she hugged her girls, finally calm invaded them, they felt at peace and liberated.

The next girl was fifteen years old, she had lived through elementary and high school, she was one of the prettiest girls in school and she abused the less attractive ones a lot, she humiliated and insulted them in many ways, she was angry with dad and with men, so she looked for a way to get her anger out by abusing the weaker ones; using her beauty she managed to get her classmates in higher grades to protect her and help her maintain her power, mistreating anyone she considered inferior. Larisa hugged her and she cried remembering everything she lived through, her pain and everything she did to the other girls.

-They asked us for it my love, it was all an agreement, they needed to live that and you helped them, you are not bad my beautiful girl.

-But yes, because I hurt them, and I made them cry, they begged me to leave them alone, but I…

-Yes, my love, but it was because they asked us to, you are good, my beautiful, you are good - The girl cried, Larisa's words could not calm her, her soul asked for forgiveness, little by little her girl understood and managed to calm down hugging her, Larisa rubbed her back and caressed her hair, the violet flame did not leave them alone, it was always present cleaning her soul and her records.

The oldest of her girls was twenty-two years old, she had lived through high school and college, she hid when she became pregnant for the first time while she was studying, when she knew she was pregnant she entered inside Larisa and gave way to the adult. Larisa didn't want to have the baby, so she had an abortion with the help of an older friend. Her father didn't find out. She pretended to be going on a weekend trip and since her father was never home, she didn't have any problems. She was too young to have a child.

-My beautiful girl - she said, hugging her older daughter. I love you, beautiful.

-Yes, yes - she cried - I love you too, my love. But then… everything we lived through was an agreement between us and them, with everyone?

-Yes, my love, everything was an agreement.

We have to ask for forgiveness, okay?

-Yes -her little girl's crying became more intense as she said-forgive me, forgive me, I didn't want to hurt you, forgive me, please forgive me -her soul began to heal- sorry, sorry.

-Of course, you are good my love, you are a very good woman, because you helped them all to live their experiences, you are good, yes -although she understood, the little girl felt great pain, and cried seeking forgiveness, it took her long minutes to find a little peace, Larisa hugged her and loved her, the violet flame gave light and peace to her soul, it cleansed her, and she calmed down. For long hours she loved them all and received the love of all of them, she finally told them.

-My loves, from now on, you can come and go in me whenever you want, okay, you are free, I want you to enjoy your life and have fun together, from now on I will love and take care of you, we will go to the park and we will be very happy.

-Yes, yes - they all said hugging each other.

Her father and his wife were hugging each other standing at the main entrance of their house, happy, joyful and rejuvenated, Larisa got into her car; it had been almost four hours since she arrived.

Larisa arrived at her ex-husband's house, when he opened the door, he was surprised to see her, she looked radiant and younger, her skin was a different tone, she was not serious, nor sullen, as was her custom, her energy was completely different.

-Hello Axel.

-What happened to you? You look... radiant.

-Thank you, Axel, wait, I want..., she took his hands and said: My dear Axel, my love.

He opened his eyes in surprise, it was too strange for her to be affectionate.

-I want to ask for your forgiveness, -the forgiveness request came from the bottom of his heart and the tears were proof of it- if in this life or in past lives, I humiliated you, hurt you, wounded you, took your children from you, or failed you in some way, please forgive me, I am so sorry, I love you.

He listened to her attentively, and her words broke down the walls of indifference and anger, knocking them down. He began to caress the thin fingers of the hands of the woman he fell in love with. After years, he had her in front of him again, and that beautiful love they had re-emerged, but it was no longer passionate love, but that of the understanding and loving couple they were during the first years of their relationship. And without being able to avoid it, while she spoke, his eyes began to shed tears, tears that healed his soul and his life, and freed him, instinctively, he said. -Larisa, if I, in some way, in this life or in past lives, humiliated you, hurt you, offended you, took your children from you, please forgive me, I'm sorry, it was not my intention to hurt you, I love you precious, I have never stopped loving you - he hugged her, and both felt their love again, a love that should never have disappeared, that should have remained uniting them, even if they no longer lived together.

His new wife watched them and her tears were also present.

The children who had been playing in the garden, entered the house, and saw their parents hugging each other at the main entrance, both ran, mom, mom, they shouted happily and ran towards her, Larisa upon hearing them separated from Axel and knelt down to hug her children.

-My beautiful loves, forgive me -her tears flowed without stopping- please forgive me, I never wanted to hurt you, I didn't know what I was doing, forgive me, please forgive me, -they cried, for the first time they felt mom's love in a true and honest way, thus embraced, she transmuted their karmas and asked for forgiveness, the violet flame did its work and their souls danced happily hugging each other, releasing their Akashic records; when she was finally able to get up, she saw Axel's wife, and walked towards her. -Lisa, forgive me -he hugged her affectionately- forgive me- Lisa looked at her husband over Larisa's shoulder and he smiled at her- forgive me, I know I haven't been a good person to you, it's not your fault, but I was angry and I treated you very badly, forgive me- he separated from her and took her hands- yes in this life or some past life I hurt you, humiliated you, or harmed you in some way, please forgive me, I'm sorry, I want to ask you to be good friends, I would really love that.

Lisa didn't cry, but she felt deeply the sincerity of Larisa.

-You too Larisa, forgive me, if in any past life I hurt you in any way, whatever it was, I ask for your forgiveness, I'm sorry, and yes, I would love for us to be friends, - she hugged her and both were transmuted by the violet flame.

Her children came closer to hug mom's legs, they longed to

feel that hug again, they were thirsty for that beautiful love. Larisa separated from Lisa and knelt down to hug her children again, they cried feeling mommy and her beautiful love, her true and unconditional love.

-Come into the living room Larisa, sit down.

Axel was behind her, seeing that love, it was the first time he saw her express her affection to her children, even as babies she was not very expressive, the nannies took care of most of the children's things, she stopped breastfeeding them very early, because she did not want her breasts to become deformed. They reached the living room and she sat on the long chair with each child at her side, hugging them and kissing their faces whenever she could, they hugged her, feeling her.

"I thought you didn't love me," her oldest child told her with his eyes full of tears.

-Forgive me my love, I didn't realize, I'm sorry, you are my oldest child and now I see you, and I want you to know that I feel very proud of what you are, how affectionate you are with your little brother and that you take care of him so much -for the first time the oldest felt truly appreciated and hugged his mother tightly crying, she caressed his hair, took his face with both hands and looking him in the eyes said- I love you my beautiful boy, I love you very much, after kissing him -she turned to see the little one who with his childish face looked at her, he was mommy's baby, she hugged him and said- my beautiful boy, now I see you, forgive me my love, if I made you believe that I did not love you or that you were not important to me, I want you to know that you are important, that you are my baby and that I love you very much, -she took his tear-stained face and kissed him, then she turned to the oldest and hugged both little ones- my loves, from now on you two will be my Spoiled ones, I love you both very much, and you will be my priority, I promise you.

Axel was sitting in one of the individual armchairs and Lisa in the other, he could not contain himself and went over to hug the three of them, they were all crying, his wife saw them, but she was not jealous, she knew that he loved his children, and she understood that they felt a great affection. He kissed each of his children and he loved them too.

-Do you want to drink something Larisa?

-Thanks Lisa, I'm fine, well better yes, plain water please, -she stood up and went to the kitchen.

-Larisa, I don't want to be indiscreet, but can I ask you, what happened to you? what is the reason for this change? which by the way I love, thanks for what you have done, I think we really needed it.

-Yes Axel, it's true, we needed to resolve this.

Lisa came back with the glass of water and handed it to her, she drank almost all of it without breathing, she was thirsty.

-Well, I'll tell you...

She told them about her experience, she spoke to them about the karma of abandonment, and she did the same thing she did with her parents.

-If you want to do that right now, I'll take the children so you can be alone, they agreed.

-Yes mommy, yes, take us with you - the children said in

chorus.

She put the children in the back of the vehicle, fastened the seat belts and gave each one a kiss, the children were happy.

-Larisa, thank you, Axel told her, gently pulling her to give her a hug, she closed her eyes and let herself be loved, her beautiful love allowed her to feel him now. They hugged each other affectionately.

-Thank you, Axel, for this beautiful gift - she said bending down a little and looking at the children through the glass - what you and I lived was beautiful, the rest, well, was our karmas and our agreements.

-Now I understand, thanks for coming, hey, do you think you can introduce us to your friend? We'd love to meet him.

-Of course, I'm going to have dinner, my house is coming soon, I think next month, so I'll have a small meeting with my closest ones and he'll be there.

-Yes Larisa, let us know - intervened Lisa, who approached to give her a kiss - we'll keep in touch.

She entered the vehicle, her ex-husband closed the door, she turned to look at her children, and her eyes clouded over, she stretched out her right hand to caress them, I love you my loves, they cried smiling at her.

They arrived at their house wrapped in a white, pink and violet light.

-Roger, my love, tonight has been incredible, I never imagined that our life was actually a play, that what we are living was actually an act, and that we chose that role to pay for our karmas.

-Definitely yes, it has been extremely enlightening, this Alberto, he really knows how to explain things, everything is so easy to understand, but do you know what makes me the happiest?

-No, what is it?

-That you and I have a very beautiful love, and that we have the ability to create an honest relationship, without lies, without hiding, because now I know that we can allow ourselves to live the experiences that we need spiritually, that will allow us to live for the rest of our lives loving each other and not putting up with each other or supporting each other, as my parents did; because yes Rouse -the traffic light was red, there was little traffic and I turned to see her- I want Rouse, if you want of course, to create a relationship where we accompany each other and love each other in our old age, I would like to take care of you for the rest of my life, would you like to do that with me?

-Of course, my love, I would love it, I also dream of that, to be with someone who loves me in my old age, not that they put up with me, or that they are satisfied with not being alone, but that they really love me.

She smiled at him, and came closer to kiss him, their lips met in a kiss full of hope and love.

-Go my love, the light has already turned green -he lifted his foot off the brake and stepped on the accelerator- you know my love, I was thinking that I would like to spend the rest of the night at my house, I want to do this exercise and I think I need to be there, there are things I have to clean.

-Of course, darling, of course, I also think it's a good idea, tomorrow we'll meet and we'll tell each other how it went.

Rouse lived alone, she never had children, she was married for seven years, until she found out that her husband had another family and children, she had been with this woman for almost five years, so when she found out she felt extremely deceived, and betrayed, because it was not just an affair, she had been deceived during the last five years of her marriage, and there were children, something that she could not give him, that hurt her a lot, so without hesitation she divorced, she went into a depression that lasted for years, she had to take psychological therapy to solve it, because she could not be happy by herself, and it was difficult for her to allow a man to approach her for a relationship, after three years of her divorce she met Alex, she fell in love with him and after six months of dating, she found out that he was dating a coworker, so from that relationship she decided not to have a boyfriend again, she only lived occasional sexual encounters, until she met Roger, he was an older and very attractive man, possessor of a great personality, she loved his security and his sense of humor, he tried to win her over as soon as he met her, but she pushed him away, so he resigned himself to being just a friend to her, but after two months of dating, she finally accepted him, she opened up completely to him and they fell in love, they decided to live together and their relationship lasted five years, they had a very intense relationship, full of sex and fun, neither of them had children, so they complemented each other very well. She entered her bedroom, turned on the light, and began to undress. She had a full-length mirror next to the entrance to the dressing room. She pulled up a chair, took off her bra and panties, and looked at herself in the mirror completely naked. She was still a very attractive woman. She smiled to herself and went over to look herself in the eyes. She tried to hold her gaze, but her eyes filled with tears, and she had to look away. "But why? What's wrong with me?" She tried to look herself in the eyes again. She brought her face as close to the mirror as she could, but again she couldn't really see herself. She heard Alberto's voice: "You have to look yourself straight in the eyes. It's the gateway to your soul." She tried again and succeeded. Her eyes released their tears, but she could see herself and said. -Rouse, now... -her crying broke the walls- now I see you, and I want you to know everything that has hurt me -the first thing that came to her mind was a memory of her childhood, she was playing in her father's office and he scolded her for making noise with her toys, her father got upset easily, and he yelled at her as if she were not his daughter, she ran scared, and left the office- why dad?, why?, I was a baby -that memory tied her to the rejection of men, then, she remembered when she was five years old and while she stayed at home with the nanny, she touched her and caressed her private parts- why, why, I did not want that, why, her crying was very deep, many painful memories were pouring out of her cup of love, they were hidden there, she did not remember any of that and suddenly the trunk of painful memories It opened, they came out one by one and she cried for them all, memories that had been buried because of how humiliating they were; After much crying, she felt that there was something else, but she did not know what it was, her chest hurt, in a moment of clarity she said:

- God, father, help me, help me, take out this that I have

saved, help me see it, I do not want to save anything anymore, I do not want to hide anything from my life, please, help me… - her mind opened, the images and the saved pain were seen, she cried, almost screamed, from the pain that all this caused her, she had abused a girl, daughter of her neighbor, but she had forgotten it- sorry, please, father forgive me, forgive me I did not want to hurt her, forgive me… -her crying was unstoppable, the tears healed her aching soul, she continued cleaning her cup, later, when she could feel a little peace, she began to ask for forgiveness for everything she did, and to thank for everything they did to her, she spoke with her abuser and forgave him, she spoke with everyone with whom she had something pending and forgave them, and she asked for forgiveness- To all those with whom I have created karma, please forgive me, I am truly sorry, I did not want to hurt you…, now I understand that it was our agreements, that we did not hurt each other - the crying did not stop, each word freed the aching soul, the violet flame set her on fire and burned her Akashic records, transmuting her debts, freeing her; Little by little she was able to look at herself in the mirror, she wiped her tears and her nose, when she felt more at peace, she could look directly into her eyes, and she said- Rouse, beautiful…, forgive me - the crying returned- forgive me my love, because I didn't see you, because I have had you so abandoned, forgive me, I want you to know, that I am very proud of you, that you are a great woman, that despite not having children, you have known how to be happy, now I know that this is how we planned it, that this was part of our life agreements, I want you to know that from now on I will see you and I will love you, she rubbed her hands and began to love herself, she caressed her face while saying beautiful things to herself, her face smiled, and the tone of her skin lightened, she caressed every part of her face and loved herself, then she caressed her hair, she thanked him, for accompanying her and making her look very beautiful, in this way she continued loving every part of her body, when she reached her breasts, she caressed them giving them all her love, put her hands on them and said- Father, be your hand that caresses them, - she was filled with even more love, in her youth they had detected some calcifications in her left breast, which were still there, she gave them her love and asked for forgiveness, she felt the energy that flowed from their hands and it filled her with a beautiful warmth, the internal tissue of her breasts received the energy and it enveloped the unnatural parts and dissolved them, she felt at peace and loved, her love grew with each caress, after a long time caressing herself, and after having traveled all over her body, without missing a single nail or phalanx of her feet, she looked into her eyes again, her face looked rejuvenated- how is it possible? - she said astonished- I look younger, how is it possible? -Indeed, she looked ten years younger, her hair shone and her eyes had a sparkle I had never seen before, she felt at peace, light and very loved, she looked herself straight in the eyes and said- I know that inside me are my inner girls, please beauties, come out - she kept silent and waited, a beautiful little girl of three years came out of her chest, as if it were opening, she first took her face out and then moved forward until she was completely outside.

-What! But it's not pos... -her crying immediately returned, another beautiful little girl of seven years came out of her chest, then another one of fifteen and finally the oldest of twenty-three years, she covered her mouth with both hands while she looked at them, and finally she lowered her face covering it with her hands, her crying didn't let her see anything- How is it possible, my beauties? How is it possible? Yes my love -said the eldest, and the moment she heard his voice, she broke into a heartbreaking cry, her girls came to her to comfort her and caressed her, she could not lift her face she felt their little hands caressing her hair, slowly she was able to lift her face bathed in tears, and hugged her two little ones, the little one surrounded her neck with her little arms and the other hugged them both, all of them were crying, a feeling of pain for having had them inside so many years, without knowing that they were there, it hurt her soul.

-I did not know my loves, I did not know, forgive me, I did not know that they were here inside, forgive me -the pain of having abandoned them without knowing was very strong- I did not know my loves, forgive me, forgive me.

-Yes, my love, we talked to you trying to get you to listen to us, but no, you didn't listen to us, every so often, we tried again, when you looked in the mirror, we took the opportunity to talk to you, but you didn't see us or hear us, we just hugged each other, the little ones cried, and I tried to comfort them, but now... now we are here - her girls hugged her tightly.

- Forgive me my beauties, forgive me, I didn't know anything about this, please forgive me, I didn't know... -The eldest hugged her and kissed her head.

-Forgive me, forgive me beautiful, I did not know... -Little by little her abandonment was healing, she hugged them and loved them, she began to talk with each one and they told her when it was that they got inside her, then she understood that they were important events that marked the end of a youthful stage, to continue growing, she recognized each one in their stages of life, she thanked them for having lived everything they lived, for being brave, she spoke to them of the agreements and helped them to heal, and to ask for forgiveness, she transmuted their karmas into violet, long hours passed, the crying stopped flowing, peace embraced them, the violet flame was still with them and their bodies and souls were healed and freed, after a long time talking, sleep was overcoming them, first the babies and then the older ones, in a moment of silence she said. -Thank you, beautiful daddy, thank you for this gift, forgive me all my sins, free me, I love you - she cried a little more and finally fell asleep hugging her beautiful ones. Rouse woke up, she was alone, covered with the blanket, she expected to see her girls, but they were not there, she got out of bed and went to the mirror, wow, she said looking at her face, but what is it..., she caressed her face, it looked beautiful and young, her body was a little thinner, she looked very beautiful, she looked directly into her eyes again, and she could do it, without feeling pain, she felt at peace, smiling she said- My beautiful girls, please, come out from inside me -again each one of them made herself present, and she hugged them, her fifteen year old girl was the most sensitive, she cried every time she hugged her, and she felt that she was the one who needed her love the most, she had lived through a very difficult stage, elementary school and high school, even though each stage had its pains, there were some that were more intense than others, so she had to heal her girls, loving them and helping them understand their agreements- my beautiful girls, I want you to know that from now on I will be with you, and I will be with you. Now, I will always see you, I will always be with you and I want you to be with me, I want you to come out of me when you decide to, you will see how much fun we will have, I will make sure that you are very happy.

-Oh, my love, -said the eldest- I love you so much, you are so beautiful.

-I owe it all to you, my beautiful ones, thanks to the fact that each one was brave and lived her stage in the best way, that is why now I am this beautiful, intelligent and powerful woman, because yes, now we are very strong and very beautiful.

Each of the dinner attendees did the exercise, and brought out from within their glasses all the pain, a pain that did not let them be completely happy, a pain that wanted to come out to be seen, but they refused to see it because it hurt too much, so they just hid it, a pain that at night or in the solitude of their rooms screamed at them, "look at me, we are here, free us," but they just fell asleep, or turned on the television or the radio so as not to hear them and to be distracted, a pain that kept true love hidden, their personal love; Each one looked at their pains in the mirror, forgave themselves and asked for forgiveness, loved themselves deeply, and then, freed their inner children, who were hidden beneath all those pains, each and every one felt the same, sadness, for the abandonment and then a very deep and intense love, they felt complete, now they had at their side the most beautiful love that exists in the universe, the love of their inner children, they could now love each stage of their lives, they no longer felt shame, nor resentment, nor anger, nor sadness, on the contrary, now they could thank, love and want those who had caused them some pain in their lives, and they could love themselves, without feeling shame or pain, for what they had done, peace filled their souls and they danced happily and liberated.

Richard came out of the guest room where he did his exercise, Ellen was opening the door to her bedroom at that moment, located at the end of the hall, as soon as they looked into each other's eyes they hugged each other and began to cry, they felt ecstatic.

-My love, Ellen, I love you so much beautiful, I love you so much - they could not stop crying, Richard had taken off ten years of age, his face looked rejuvenated and had a lighter skin tone, he separated from her to see her and gave her a smile.

-Richard, my love, but it's just that... you look so young, how is it possible?

-You too my love -he said wiping her tears with the thumbs of his hands- you look so beautiful -he took her face with both hands and brought her closer to kiss her. True love had been released and was reunited with each other, their souls freed from so many karmas and debts embraced and danced, merging in their love, they shone with a different light, blue, pink and violet colors gave beautiful pastel tones, their souls loved each other like never before. When they finally separated, she, with eyes full of tears, said to him.

-My love, this has been the most beautiful thing that has ever happened to me, I have cried so much, I never imagined having so many things kept, I never thought that..., that I could have so many hidden feelings, there were things that..., well there is no point in remembering them anymore, I am happy to know that I have already forgiven them.

-Me too my love, I have cried so much that I am almost dry of tears, I got out so many things and I feel so light, wow, this has been incredible, and you look so beautiful Ellen, it seems that you have rejuvenated, well, it doesn't seem like it, you rejuvenated, it seems as if ten years have been taken off you, you look incredible.

-I feel incredible my love -The door to his child's bedroom opened and he went out into the hallway, when he saw them he ran towards them and hugged them, both of them put their arms around him.

-Parents, forgive me, forgive me, I've been a fool, I didn't realize, forgive me.

-My love, said Richard, it was our agreement, forgive me, if I mistreated you or made you feel bad, I'm sorry my love, I love you, I've always loved you.

-My beautiful baby, -Ellen gave him a kiss on the cheek, the young man was beginning to surpass her in height- forgive me too son, if I hurt you in any way, please forgive me, I love you so much my baby.

The door to Susan's room opened and she went out into the hallway, her face looked beautiful, with a beautiful smile, she ran to her family and hugged them, tears once again burst forth from all hearts.

-Parents, forgive me, please, forgive me, I have been a fool, please, forgive me, also your little brother, forgive me, if I have hurt you, please I am sorry, now I understand everything, forgive me.

-My beautiful girl, there is nothing to forgive each other, they were our agreements, we only fulfilled what you asked of us, and that made you what you needed to fulfill your agreements with others, so there is nothing to forgive, on the contrary, I have to thank you and thank you both for the opportunity you gave me by choosing me as your father, I think I have not done so bad, by helping you fulfill your agreements, thank you for giving me the opportunity to be your father.

-My beautiful girl, -Ellen caressed her hair- I have always felt very proud of the woman you have become, if I have hurt you with my way of being I ask for your forgiveness, it was not my intention to hurt you, you asked me to do it that way, thank you both for having asked me to be your mother, I free you both from any karma between us so that we can all be free and happy. -True love was reunited, their souls danced embraced, their karmas as a family were being transmuted.

The doorbell of her house surprised her.

-Madam, Mr. Roger is looking for you.

-Tell him to come in -she ran to her bedroom, looked at herself in the mirror, straightened her clothes and saw herself very beautiful, took the lip gloss from the dresser and put some on, rubbed both lips, fixed her hair and looking into each other's eyes she blew a kiss- You look beautiful Rouse, I love you!

The maid opened the door for her.

-Sir, come in, but what happened to you? You look so young, what did you do?

-Love, Mrs. Guille, is love - she was carrying a bouquet of very beautiful red roses, wrapped in transparent cellophane paper.

-I believe it, now that you see the girl, you will see how beautiful she has become, she already told me what I have to do, but I have not done it.

-What do you mean, but that is very important, you have to do it today, without excuses, promise me that you will do it today.

-Yes sir, okay, I promise.

Rouse left the hallway and entered the living room.

-Hello handsome..., wow Roger, but you look...

-My love, you are incredible.

Roger had put the roses on the coffee table and was about to sit down when Rouse appeared, he immediately approached her and took her hands. -I can't believe it, beautiful -he lifted her hands and made her spin around, she turned on her feet and smiled at him, unable to resist he hugged her, his eyes clouded over, she also hugged him feeling and giving her true love.

Mrs. Guille watched them from a distance and wiped away her tears.

-Rouse, I love you, I love you so much - he separated and took her hands - let me give you this beautiful love, I want it to be just for you.

-I love you too, Roger, and yes, I accept your beautiful love, I also have my beautiful love and I want it to be for you. You know love, I'm so happy, all my life I have struggled to find true love, but I was always betrayed, I didn't know that was my karma, now I know, and I've freed myself, I'm not afraid that you'll abandon me, if that were to happen what I know is that I'll love you for the rest of my life.

-My beautiful queen -the tears came from his eyes- I love you Rouse and no, I'll never abandon you, that's not going to happen, I know I'll love you and take care of you for the rest of my life, I love you! -He pulled her to his chest and they joined their lips, their tongues loving each other softly, when they finally separated, he turned to look at the flowers and picked them up, he put them in front of his chest and said- these flowers represent the love I feel for you, accept it -she grabbed them, brought them to her face, and breathed in his perfume.

-Your love smells very beautiful -she stood up on the tips of her sneakers and kissed him.

-Hello sir, what a miracle!

-Hello darling, how are you? You see, I'm here, working miracles on earth, I was a little far away, you know I was in the clouds doing miracles, but now I fell and here I am, ha, ha, ha.

-I thought you didn't want to see me anymore.

-And why didn't you call me?

-Well, I'm old-fashioned, I like it when the man takes the initiative.

-You're right darling, the truth is that I didn't call you, because I wanted to give you a little space so you could live your whole process alone, but don't think it was easy for me, I haven't been able to stop thinking about you, I fall asleep thinking about you and the phone burns in my hands, I see your name and I put my finger on the call button, but the little angels always stopped me, and I heard them: "Not yet Alberto, wait a little." So, well, I can't resist any longer. Can I see you? Do you want to go to dinner with me? It's Friday and my body knows it. What do you say?

-I don't know, let me see my schedule -he said, putting on an air of importance- okay, -he answered immediately- yes, I do want to, ha, ha.

-Excellent, darling, I'll make the reservation. I'll pick you up at seven thirty, okay.

-It's not too early.

-Yes, but we'll do something before dinner.

-Ok, I'll see you at seven thirty.

-Great, see you, darling.

Larisa got ready well in advance, she was very punctual, so she didn't like to be kept waiting either, she knew that Alberto would take her to a very elegant restaurant and she chose a short black dress that was very tight to her slender figure, she had one shoulder uncovered and the other was covered by the single strap, from behind, the dress left her back completely exposed up to the base of her waist, she gathered her hair into a bun, she applied a light make-up, her natural beauty didn't need so much make-up, a little pink blush, to give light to her cheeks, she took the lipstick from the nightstand, pulled out the tip by twisting the base and painted her lips cherry red.

-Madam, a Mr. Alberto is looking for you.

-Please, Claudia, let him in and offer him a whiskey - she turned to look at her gold wristwatch, it was barely seven fifteen, she smiled. He sat on the edge of the bed and put on his black slippers with only two straps, which beautifully adorned his feet and highlighted his beautiful legs. He stood up, looked at himself in the full-length mirror and, looking into his eyes, said to himself: Larisa, I love you, beautiful, you look incredible, go on, go and be very happy, you deserve it.

Alberto was sitting in the single chair at the end of the room, his legs were crossed and he was holding the whiskey with both hands while he made it wobble.

-Hello sir! - the beautiful lady, leaned against the wall with her left arm extended, her legs were crossed elegantly, and her right hand was on her waist, she looked like a model from a fashion magazine.

-Wow, wow, and more wow - he stood up, left the glass on the coffee table and walked over to her - Wow Larisa, but it's just that... you look incredible, no, well, if you have me crazy enough, now I'm going to lose my mind.

-I'm glad you like it so much, I got ready just for you. -He took her by the waist and slowly approached her lips, barely touching them so as not to run her perfect makeup.

-Kiss me my love, this lipstick doesn't leave marks -she smiled flirtatiously, and approached him again, a passionate kiss lit the flame, her Kundalini energy was present activating her root chakra, they breathed raising their energies and hugged each other, feeling the activation of their energetic bodies.

-How beautiful you look Larisa, there is no doubt that you have been loving each other, it shows. The children came to them.

-Hello, they both said standing and smiling at him.

-Alberto, let me introduce you to my loves -she had placed herself behind the youngest and took him by the shoulders-he is Luigi, the youngest, and my favorite.

-Hello Luigi, how nice to meet you, you are quite a gentleman -the boy smiled and extended his hand, Alberto leaned down and shook it.

-This other handsome boy is Daniel, -Larisa stood behind him and gave him a kiss on the cheek- my oldest son and my favorite.

-Hello, Alberto, mom has already told us about you, we are glad to meet you.

-Likewise, Daniel, Luigi, I hope we are good friends, do you like going to the movies?

-Yes, said the youngest quickly, I like it a lot.

-Excellent, I am going to invite you, the four of us will go to the movies, would you like that?

-Yes, said the oldest, we would like that very much.

-My loves, we are going out, go to the kitchen to have dinner, and then go to your bedroom to sleep, but brush your teeth first okay.

-Yes mommy, sure -the children ran to the kitchen.

-Sit down Alberto, I see you are already having something to drink.

-Yes darling, but we are running late, we have a reservation, so we better go, if you agree.

-Sure, let's go, let me, children come and say goodbye -the little ones ran out and threw themselves to hug their mommy, she knelt down and gave each one a kiss, she stood up, they shook Alberto's hand and ran away.

-How beautiful your children Larisa, I am pleasantly surprised by how attentive and polite they are.

-Yes, thanks to you everything is changing -he gave her a smile, grabbed his bag from the entrance table and left the house.

IX Discovering Luz Bella

The restaurant was very elegant, they were guided to their table and sat down, the waiter took their food and drink order, and left.

-Alberto, I have a question, how did you come to know all this?

-Well, actually it's been many years, I think that since I was young I have been interested in many topics about life and death, I have read many books about reincarnation, UFOs, space and the universe, and many topics, I have participated in different religions, my father was a very intelligent man and he instilled in me an open mind, he taught me not to close myself to new ideas but to open myself to possibilities, so well, I have been able to learn from all of them and discover the truth of religions, so little by little I have been discovering the truth of things.

-But then you say that religions are bad, I mean, they have lied to us and kept us oppressed.

-It's true that they have done that, but think about it carefully, if everything is an agreement, then did they hurt you?

-Well, no, of course not, I asked them to show me this.

-Exactly, religions are good, do you know how many marriages have been saved from divorce? Or how many have been able to stay away from alcohol or drugs? People who were drunks and beat their families, and thanks to religion they stopped being so; because religions awaken the spiritual part of people, so ultimately, they do not hurt, on the contrary, remember that our job was to discover the truth and free ourselves, it is not to change religions or fight with them, but to understand why they were made, to thank them, and not to let them continue to dominate us.

-Ok, I understand, you're right, I thought they were the devil's work.

-Ha, ha, ha, poor Luz Bella, everyone blames her.

-Who is Luz Bella?

-Lucifer, the Devil, his real name is Luz Bella.

-Are you serious?

-Of course, he was God's favorite son, but he did something he shouldn't have done and was condemned to live in Limbo or hell, from then on, they called him Lucifer, I don't like to call him that name, it seems unfair to me.

-You really believe in hell and those things of the Devil.

-You said it, you thought that the bad things were the Devil's fault, so you do believe in him, right?

-Well yes, it's that we all believe in that.

-That's another story created by religion, to blame someone for everything bad that happened in the world, that way the bad things that happened to you weren't your responsibility, think about it, everything good that happens to you is God's fault, he's responsible, and the bad things are the Devil's fault, so what are you? A holy dove, someone who has no control over his life.

-Well, yes, because if everything good is because God wanted it that way and it is bad is the devil's thing, then yes, I am... an innocent dove, ha, ha, - they laughed.

- That's what they want you to believe, because in that way, only if you obey the rules of God, dictated by the church, then God will reward you by sending you to heaven, but if you don't comply with the rules, then God sends you to hell with Satan.

- Wow Alberto, so all those ideas that they have put in our heads are for us to be obedient to them.

- Exactly, that's why the commandments and all the rules were created, and who made those rules? The leaders of the religions.

- I had never thought about it, how interesting to know all this.

- Everything in this world, darling, is a play, a great play put together from the origins of humanity, so that everyone who came to this planet could experience domination, fear, hatred, resentment, and a huge number of etcetera.

-And so that we could discover the truth and free ourselves from karmas.

-Exactly, very well said, you understood, congratulations. Many people, however, have not discovered the whole truth of the theater, but they have developed their spirituality, they have understood the karmas, and they have freed themselves from resentment and from all those things that kept them tied, those people have already freed themselves from the wheel of reincarnation and as soon as they have left their body, they have returned to their homes of origin.

-Wow Alberto, it's just that all this is so incredible. Hey, can I ask you something very personal?

-Yes of course.

-Do you think your wife freed herself from reincarnation?

-Yes, definitely yes, she worked hard on her karmas and always sought to create Dharmas, so yes, she is already in her home of origin.

-And do you think they will meet again someday, I mean, I know you are still a long way from meeting, but do you think they will meet again?

-Yes, I do, but while I'm on earth I plan to give my beautiful love to the beautiful lady who decides to walk the next part of the road with me, and I don't think about Carmen, even though I still love her.

-How can you love a new woman and still love your deceased wife? This said with love and respect.

-I understand you, darling, I'm glad you asked that. When you love yourself truly and honestly, you know that your love is not anyone's property, just as the love of the person who is with you is not your property either, everyone is free to give that love to whoever they decide for as long as they decide, but if you truly love yourself and you are giving your personal love honestly, you cannot and should not try to prevent your partner's love from blessing someone else, because remember, love becomes more beautiful the more it is given, so if your partner loves someone else like an ex, that love will make your partner's love become more beautiful, do you understand?

-Yes, of course, it's just that we are educated to have the exclusivity of our partner, and that your partner loves another is not something simple.

-Yes, but exclusivity comes from conditioned and selfish love, we have to learn to give an honest, true and unconditional love.

-It's true, and to see ourselves as what we truly are, energetic-spiritual beings living in physical bodies.

-Well said, darling, cheers to that -they both raised their glasses and clinked them.

-But, what about your partner loving another?

-Remember what we talked about at dinner, that it wasn't about sleeping with all the men or women you liked.

-Well yes, that means we have to learn to give your honest love, without fear of falling in love, or that your partner falls in love with someone else.

-Exactly, you shouldn't be afraid of your partner falling in love, because you have the most beautiful love that exists in the universe, so your partner is very lucky to have it, don't you think?

-Yes, definitely yes, but... what if I don't believe that I am love... you know.

-That means that you are not truly loving yourself, and that is why you are afraid that your partner will find someone better than you. If you don't love yourself you will be afraid. If you truly love yourself you would not be afraid, and if that were to happen...

-I could give my love to someone else who would value it.

-Exactly, that's right. But it's not that your partner doesn't value you, it's that your partner spiritually needs to live this new relationship, it has nothing to do with the value of your love, do you understand? -She just nodded her head while taking a sip of wine- you know that you have a very exclusive and special love. I, for example, will always continue to love my wife, even when she is not physically here, because her love remains in me, and that makes my love more beautiful, so you should not be jealous of her, on the contrary, love her and thank her for everything she taught me, because now it is your turn to enjoy this love, which is love most beautiful thing that exists in the universe.

-And I love it -she said, stretching out her hand to caress his- receiving your love, I love it.

-Jealousy is born from insecurity, from a lack of self-love, from not loving yourself. That doesn't mean that you don't feel it, all of us as humans can feel it, but staying with that feeling and letting yourself be carried away by jealousy, that's the problem.

-Ok, I understand, you're right, jealousy is self-insecurity.

-It's fear, fear that your partner will find someone better, think about it. I wish that you continue to love your ex-husband, because he helped you make your love very beautiful now, with all the sweet and not so sweet things that you have experienced, you should be grateful for everything and feel proud of having fulfilled your agreements.

-You're right, now that I saw him, I felt that beautiful love for the man I fell in love with, that reunion was very special.

-That is the love that must remain in you, that does not mean that you have to come back or that you need to have sex, unless that is what you truly want.

-No, definitely not, coming back or having sex is not something I want, it is only the beautiful love that brought us together.

-And that unites you, because that love must remain, do you realize? Now you can not only be friends, but be lovers, do you understand the difference?

-Yes, I am understanding it, but it is so difficult.

-It is the programming that you have, and that we all have, it is conditioned love, that is why it is important that you continue loving yourself all the time and repeat to yourself what you truly are, that will help you keep your mind focused on what unconditional love is.

-Wow Alberto, seeing relationships from true love is so fantastic. Another question, are you going to let me have sex with other men?

-No, of course not, you are only mine -he approached to kiss her tenderly.

-I love that you tell me that.

-No, my love, you'll see, as long as we stay in love and are reciprocated, we won't need anyone else, when that happens, we'll see, the important thing is that from today to that day we manage to create a relationship, honest, full of true and unconditional love.

-Well, that's clear, let's toast, for your love, thank you for sharing it with me.

-For your love, beautiful -both raised their glasses and toasted- life is magical, Larisa, it's an enormous theater put together by the Creative mind, so that she could experience life in each physical body, because don't forget, you are God, and a very beautiful God -he approached her, took her face with his hand and gave her a kiss.

-That vision Alberto, is beautiful, now I see my children as the Gods that they are, God in those beautiful little bodies, living their life.

-And the people who work in your company and in your house doing the chores, they are all God.

-True, I hadn't thought about that, everyone here is God, some serve the tables and others wash the dishes, and others eat. We are all God experiencing different acting roles, wow, cheers -she said raising his glass of white wine, they clinked them and said- To the Gods here present.

-To the Gods that we are.

The conversation continued, they drank and enjoyed delicious dishes, the waiter returned to collect the dirty dishes.

-Do the gentlemen want anything else?

-The bill please.

-Where are you going to take me?

-He reached out his hand and took hers, choose, plan A: Go dancing and release the moth, or plan B: Go to my house to follow the energy classes.

-Mmmmm, what tempting offers, but I'll stick with plan B, I think it will be more interesting.

Alberto put the key in the lock and opened the door, he stepped aside so Larisa could enter.

-Come in, darling, this is your house. He turned on the lights and the large room lit up. Would you like something to drink?

-You have white wine, I'd love it.

He went to the bar, took out a couple of glasses and a bottle from the wine cooler, and poured the two glasses. Larisa had sat down on one of the high stools at the bar and smiled flirtatiously at him.

-Cheers, darling, for the pleasure of being together again. They both kissed and clinked their glasses. Come on, let's go to the couch. He took her hand and they headed to the living room.

-Better take me to your bedroom, let's see if I'm a good student -he winked at her.

-Well, let's see if you learned.

They entered the bedroom, she took a sip from her glass and left it on the dresser, he did the same, as soon as he put the glass on the surface, Larisa threw herself into his arms, kissed him passionately, their tongues lit the fire, she began to take off his jacket desperately, he took off his tie, she was very excited and her passion seemed out of control.

-Wait beautiful, let's not run, let's make this worth a lot.

-Okay -he said separating himself a little- he began to lower the dress from her shoulder.

-No, wait, let me do it - he approached slowly, took her face with both hands and kissed her, their lips caressed each other and their tongues played softly, the Kundalini energy began to fill his root chakra, he separated, went for his glass and gave her his wine, a few drops fell down the corners of her mouth, he kissed her chin and sipped the wine, introduced his tongue and the kiss continued, he knelt down, caressed both legs from her ankles - now beautiful, let us ask our mother earth to give us her Kundalini energy - they both said - Beloved mother Gea, give me your Kundalini energy, now, breathe and feel this beautiful energy - he began to raise his hands caressing her beautiful and shapely legs, he reached the bottom of her dress and continued putting his hands under it, caressing the outside of her thighs, she breathed and felt her energy increasing, when his hands entered under her dress, she closed her eyes and continued raising her energy, she bowed She raised her head to look at him and caressed his hair, her root chakra was spinning, activating more strongly, he reached the base of her buttocks and she moaned- like that beautiful, like that, raise your energy -he put both hands behind her buttocks and under her panties, she moaned, her energy was increasing.

-Yes, yes, like that, like that.

-Raise your energy, feel this -he massaged her buttocks gently, without hurry, covering them as much as he could with both hands- raise your energy, activate your other chakras, she began to do it, and with each breath her Kundalini moved upwards, he did the same, at the same time, and activated each of her chakras, he put his hands even further and lowered her panties, she raised her feet and he removed them, he stood up, kissed her again and began to raise her dress to take it off. He admired her beautiful naked body, she wasn't wearing a bra and her beautiful breasts gave him a wonderful view, he began to unbutton the cuffs of his shirt while she unbuttoned it, she continued to unbutton his belt, and he unbuttoned his pants, when they were completely naked, they hugged and kissed, pressing their bodies together, he caressed her entire body from bottom to top, she understood the game and increased her energy with each inhalation, she was extremely excited, he caressed her crotch and put his hand completely covering her vulva.

-Yes, my love, yes - she searched for his face and kissed him passionately.

-Don't come, when you feel that you are about to, tell me and I will stop, breathe - she did it and when she was about to.

-Now, now, wait…

-Raise your energy, up to here - he slid his hand across her belly to her crown chakra, placed his hand on her head, she could not contain herself any longer, she exploded in an orgasm, he kept his other hand on her wet vulva and raised his own energy, her orgasm became his, both closed their eyes, their energetic bodies embraced each other and rose above their physical bodies, to mix and merge into one energy, he did not wait until their energetic bodies returned, he picked her up in his arms and took her to the bed, their dance of love continued...

-Now darling, this energy is very powerful, you have to use it for something you want to bless, if you have a business or a company, your house, your children, the planet itself, send your energy to that special place during the orgasm, and ask it to fill and bless that which you desire.

The dance of love lasted all night, when he was about to come, he breathed and pulled his energy into her belly, avoiding ejaculation, and conserving his energy, finally and when he decided to, they both came in a mutual and extremely powerful orgasm.

-My energy -he said mentally- please go and bless everything and everyone on this planet, -his body energy expanded like the wave of a nuclear explosion, but without any violence, his energy covered everything it touched, it filled the forests while he watched her with his eyes closed, it filled the oceans, he saw the whales and dolphins swimming inside this energy, it filled the deserts and enveloped the entire planet, he watched her surrounding everything with her beautiful love, and at the same time, he and she were blessed by their energies.

Little by little their energetic bodies were returning to their physical bodies. They were lying down, she on top of him, they couldn't talk or move. Their energetic bodies had to reconnect, but they didn't come back the same. They came back very enriched by the other's energy.

Carlos was sitting in front of the mirror, completely naked. After several attempts to look into each other's eyes, he was able to do so and said crying:

-Carlos, now I see you, and I want to tell you everything that has hurt me. - The first image that came to his mind was being in the hospital in the incubator. He felt abandoned. He was in incubation for a month, and his mother didn't come to see him very often. When she found out she was pregnant, she didn't want the baby, so she had to have it by force of her husband. - No! -he screamed- no mom, why did you leave me there - the baby of now thirty-five years old cried, he never knew why he could not stand closed spaces and when as a child they put him in a car, he began to cry, this very old memory hurt him a lot, then he remembered when his mother and father left him alone all day, he felt undervalued and unloved; the fights and blows between the parents filled him with terror, one day his father came home drunk and began to caress him, that image of him as a small child tore his soul apart- why dad, why? I was a baby, why did you do that? -From that day on he became unsociable and withdrawn, later when he was four, his father left home and he never heard from him again, he always blamed himself for that and was angry with himself, his mother began to insult him and blame him for her loneliness, the physical abuse was not long in appearing, the memory showed itself in his mind and he felt the blows on his small body- Why mom, why? I didn't want to be treated like that, why did you mess with me? I was a child, I was a good child - His crying would not stop, he could no longer look himself in the eyes, he covered his face feeling the pain, he looked up again and managed to see himself to cry more profusely-

287

Why Carlitos, you were just a child, why? -The memories continued to flow, the hidden chest inside his cup of love had been opened, and he began to see things he didn't remember, things that were done to him and that he did, each image brought pain and healing, his soul cried tears that must have come out a long time ago, but being a man he never allowed it, he always kept the tears and shame to himself, he had kept so many things that it took him more than two hours to heal most of them, when he could feel a little calmer, he began to talk to himself asking for forgiveness for having made those agreements- I didn't know that this was going to hurt us so much, I didn't know, forgive me Carlitos, forgive me beautiful - he said looking into his eyes, then he spoke to his mom and dad as if they were there, he told them about the agreements and asked for forgiveness, he transmuted his karmas and freed himself, the violet flame became present and began to set fire to all his memories and his Akashic records. With red eyes from crying she could see his face, she felt a little more at peace, and she said- Carlitos - the mere mention of his name hurt her and made the tears flow intensely- forgive me, forgive me, now I know that everything that happened to us was because of our agreements, they were planned by ourselves to pay for our karmas, forgive me, forgive me, forgive me too for having abandoned you, I love you Carlos, I want you to know that I am proud of you and of the man you are today, that despite your difficult past you are neither violent nor vengeful, on the contrary, you are a very good person, from now on I will love you -he rubbed his hands and began to caress himself, he loved every part of his body, he asked for forgiveness for the abuse and he loved himself honestly.

Carlos was lying down, hugging his four children, he had already cried and healed his abandonment and his pain, now he felt complete.

On the screen of her cell phone she read Larisa, Richard was in the office, sitting in front of his drawing board, reviewing some plans, he pressed the green button on the screen and answered.

-Hi darling, how are you? I'm glad you called me.

-Hi Richard, I'm doing very well, thanks for asking, how are you?

-Happy, I'm happy, and Ellen just asked me last night if you hadn't called me, I told her no, and she said she would call you.

-I'll be happy to greet her, and I'm glad you're so happy, with all this we've been through wow, there's no way not to be.

-That's right, I'm happy Larisa, happy, I think I couldn't be happier, everyone at home has already filled our cups of personal love, and you don't know the change... -her eyes clouded with emotion as she remembered it, she had to keep quiet so as not to cry, she had become very sensitive, she felt her emotion- now everything is so different, I have been freeing myself from so much pain and karmas, that I can't help but go down the street smiling, to everyone I am telling you this and I suggest you do it.

-I am also happy, I have freed myself from so many things, I never imagined having so much pain stored away, and you don't know the beautiful relationship I have now with my children, now I take them and go to school for them, I love them in a way, well, you can imagine, we are happy, I have freed them from our karmas and it is magical, I want to be with them, we have a lot of fun together, before I only looked for excuses not to be, now I don't, now I am giving them my honest and unconditional love.

-How nice Larisa, I am so happy to hear you, I had already realized that you really didn't like being with your children, but I never said anything to you out of respect.

-Now I understand Richard, and I have already changed all that, also with my father and his wife, now we see each other more often and he has become the most loving grandfather you can imagine, because they have also done the exercise.

-Seriously, wow, what good news.

-Yes, that same day I went to see them and told them how to do it, so the change was magical, you don't know how he treats his grandchildren, he comes to pick them up and takes them to eat on the street or to the movies, my dad doing that... you can't believe it, he's so loving, and with me, well, it's just that... -her crying became present- I have wasted so many years of my life immersed in anger and resentment, pushing him away from me, that hurts me so much, it's just that what Alberto taught us is so incredible, it's been such a change.

-I'm so happy for you and for them, darling, I'm glad that they're loving each other now, and well, don't complain about all the years that have passed, be happy for all the ones you have ahead of you, and with that true and beautiful love that you have now, well, your life will be very special and beautiful, and have your children, already done the exercise?

-No Richard, I think they're too young, do you think they

should do it?

-Of course, you have to guide them, so that they look in the mirror and talk about what has hurt them, if you don't know how, ask for help from our father, God, the Creative Mind, I'm sure he will help you, then, teach them to love themselves, tell them how to caress themselves, they will know how to do it, I think it would be something very good for them, maybe a very small child can't do many things, but we can teach them to love themselves through their own caresses, on the other hand, your children already understand very well, they are very intelligent.

-Ok, I understand, I'm going to do it today in the afternoon before going to sleep. And how did it go with your inner children?

-Oh no Larisa, it's just that, well, to tell you that they are here right now, playing with their toys, and my oldest, who is twenty-three years old, is hugging me, he is so loving.

-Oh Richard, this is so incredible, my girls too, they come out of me whenever they want, especially when I'm alone, they're so beautiful, look, right now they're starting to come out, - she was in her office, standing, looking through the window, her beautiful ones came out and hugged her, she picked up the smallest one and rested her little head on her shoulder, while the baby put her little arms around her neck, they all hugged her and loved her- Richard, changing the subject a bit, do you remember the book that Carlos recommended to us, "Relationships and Sex."

-Yes of course, we've already read it, it's incredible, in fact, I also highly recommend it, especially because it describes the exercise of the cup of personal love, and it's incredible.

-Yes, that's exactly what I was going to tell you, I also recommend it for that reason, but also, the way it explains relationships and marriage, is exactly what Alberto explained to us. -I totally agree, Roger also read it, he's super changed, he looks younger, in fact, he looks younger every day, he's making love using his energy, so are we, in fact, and wow, what moments.

-What orgasms, I'd say, ha, ha, ha.

-Yes, it's true, hey, we have to meet to talk about this, it's been a little over a week and a half since dinner, make arrangements with Ellen, she wants to say hello to you.

-Ok, I'll do that, I was very pleased to greet you, by the way, when are you finishing my house? My decorator already has the furniture ready, I just need you to give me the green light to start furnishing it.

-We're very advanced, they're just detailing, my supervisor told me yesterday that they were painting and detailing, today I'm going to go see how the work is going and I'll call you later to tell you if you can already bring the furniture in, I don't want it to get stained with paint.

- Excellent, then I'll wait for your call. I was very pleased to meet you. We'll keep in touch.

They both hung up the phones.

Hey beautiful, I want to make another dinner so we can all share our experiences, what do you think? Larisa was lying down, with her head resting on Alberto's leg, the club had few people, it was around eleven in the morning, they had agreed to exercise together and then have breakfast, the grass was very well trimmed and they were on a towel that the club provided them.

-Well love, I love the idea, but why don't we do it at my house, they are already furnishing it, and it will be ready for next week, we can do the inauguration, we will invite everyone, what do you say?

-Ok, I think it's sensational, invite your ex-husband and his wife.

-You really don't mind?

-Of course not, I'd love to meet them and your dad too.

-Ok, let's not talk about it anymore, we'll schedule it from this Saturday to the next one so that everything is ready, okay?

-Of course, beautiful, count on me - he leaned in and their lips met.

X The Grand Opening

The residence was located in a very exclusive condominium, the land was three thousand square meters each, the area was wooded and the weather felt cool, but pleasant.

-Wow love, what a beautiful place, and this house is gorgeous, did you design it?

-Yes, my queen, the main design is mine, but you know,

everything is done as a team.

-Hey dad, would it be possible for us to live in a place like this? The car was driving on the main street, and the houses were small mansions.

-Well son, these lands are worth a lot of money, but also well, I don't think I'd like a house that big, you'll leave later and your mommy and I will be left alone, so I don't think I'd like a house that big.

- Well, Dad, that's no problem, we can get married and come live with you and our partners.

-Hey sister, that's a very good idea, that way we'll stay together and well if you have three children and I have four, then there will always be people in that house, what a good idea, ha, ha, ha, ha. Everyone laughed at the joke.

-No, my loves, there's no need for that, your father and I live very happily in our house and it's the ideal size, we'll spend our fortune on trips when we're retired, right my love?

-That's right my love, that's right, we'll dedicate ourselves to traveling.

Larisa's house was on the right side of the road, a large iron gate opened the way for them, she stopped the car in front of it and pressed the intercom button.

-Yes, please?

-Good afternoon, I'm Architect Cisneros.

-Come in, the lady is waiting for you.

The gate opened and the car started up. A wide, tree-lined path on both sides led them to the main entrance. There was a parking space on the right side. The driver greeted them in the car, they all got out and he parked it.

-Wow, dad, what a beautiful house. I would really like a house that big.

-Well done, son. If it's your wish, I really think you can achieve it. You are very careful with your money. You have very good savings, so if you know how to invest that money, you can surely achieve it later. Just don't lose sight of your dream.

Larisa opened the two leaves of the main door with beveled glass and welcomed them.

-Hello, welcome. Nice to see you, Ellen. You look beautiful. Welcome. He hugged her and they kissed each other. And you guys, wow, Susan. Look at yourself. How beautiful. He hugged her and kissed her.

-You too, Larisa. You look gorgeous.

-And this handsome gentleman, who is he? -Brandon was wearing a grey suit and a dark grey tie with wine-colored details. He had asked his dad that he wanted to dress like that, and his dad gladly taught him how to tie a tie. -Wow Brandon, you look so handsome. I congratulate you. You have such good taste. -She approached him and hugged him, giving him a kiss on the cheek- Hey Richard, this young man has a great future. -He felt very flattered. Larisa was a very attractive woman, and he had dressed like that to get her attention. He smiled, satisfied that he had achieved it.

-He definitely has it. He just told me that he wants to live in a house like yours, so yes, I think my son has a great future. -He approached her and hugged her, giving her a kiss on the cheek.

-Please come in. You're at his house.

Larisa, what a beautiful residence - the entrance hall was three meters wide, and had an oval-shaped table in the center, with a large floral arrangement, the hall led them to the main room where some guests were already.

-Thank you, I'm glad you like it Ellen, everything was designed by your husband, you know the good taste he has. ¡Dad, Valgarma! please come, I want to introduce you to the architect responsible for making this house, Richard Cisneros, his beautiful wife Ellen, and their children, Susan and Brandon -they all shook hands and hugged each other.

-Congratulations Architect, you have done an exquisite job, congratulations.

-It was a pleasure sir, we only did what your daughter told us, she has very good taste, madam, a pleasure to meet you.

Alberto appeared at the entrance with Karla, they arrived at the same time, she was wearing a white dress with straps, fitted at the waist and bust, with a wide skirt that fell to the shin, her salmon-colored sneakers that perfectly matched her handbag, she looked like a model.

-Karla, how nice, but how beautiful you look, I love your combination, dad, this is my friend Karla, and this is Valgarma, my dad's wife.

-It's a pleasure to meet you - they shook hands.

-And this handsome gentleman is Alberto - she said approaching him and putting her arms around his neck, while she kissed him and caressed the back of his neck.

-Hello beautiful, I brought you something - he took a bouquet of roses from behind him.

-Oh, my love, they are beautiful -he took them with both hands and brought them to his face to perceive their perfume, then he said- come, let me introduce you to my dad and his wife, Valgarma.

-Sir, it's nice to meet you, your daughter has already told me a lot about you, ma'am, it's a pleasure, he shook their hands and they greeted each other cordially.

-Me too, my daughter has told me a lot about you, I love that she's so happy, congratulations, but don't call me sir, just Robert, okay?

-It's a pleasure to meet you Robert -Larisa was standing next to him and he took her by the waist- your daughter drives me crazy -he said smiling.

Little by little all the guests arrived.

-Alberto, come, I want you to meet Axel and Lisa.

-Hello Axel, it's nice to meet you -she said shaking his hand affectionately- Larisa has already told me about you, only good things, by the way.

-Hello Alberto, it's nice, we were really looking forward to meeting you, you've changed our lives, thank you. Lisa also approached to greet him, she gave him a hug and a loving kiss on the cheek.

- Nice to meet you Lisa, and how beautiful, congratulations, you make a very nice couple.

- Dad, dad, the children came running to greet him,

he bent down, hugged them and gave them a kiss, they were happy.

- My loves, how are you, you already know Alberto, right? Say hello, and everyone else.

Alberto leaned down to shake their hands and hug them affectionately.

- I love your children Axel, it really shows that you made them with a lot of love - the children were happy with the comment.

- Yes, that's right, they were made with a lot of love, said Larisa, smiling and winking at Lisa - she responded kneeling down and giving each child a kiss - But come in, welcome.

- Erika and Carlos, were at the entrance with Roger and Rouse, finishing greeting each other, Larisa approached and welcomed them.

Larisa had not invited many people, because she wanted the conversation to be more intimate, so almost all the guests were present, two waiters were handing out glasses of white and red wine on golden trays.

-Larisa, your house is so beautiful - Rouse said - I love the furniture, such good taste.

- Congratulate the culprits - she pointed with her open hand and palm up at Roger and Richard who were together admiring their finished work - I want them to please come into the garden - Larisa pressed a button on her cell phone and the windows began to fold, a very pleasant stream of fresh air flooded the room.

- Wow - some exclaimed, surprised.

- Oh yes, this house has the best of the best - Richard indicated.

-That's right, my daughter deserves it - she turned to see her father and blew a kiss on the palm of his outstretched hand. Everyone began to move outside. It was still early and dusk was beginning to set in. The garden was brightly lit, it looked beautiful. The pool in the center adorned the space and the reflection of the sunset light on the water invited everyone to take a dip. The children were happy, greeting Brandon and Susan.

-Someday we're going to invite them to come swim, they said excitedly.

-Thank you, Susan replied, we'd love to, the pool is beautiful.

-Definitely sister, I'm going to have a house like that, I was born to be rich, I love it here.

-Of course, little brother, are you going to invite me?

-I don't know, let's see how you behave, ha, ha, ha, it's not true, of course you will, you will have a bedroom all to yourself - she declared smiling at him.

The hostess gave them a tour of the entire house, Richard received many compliments for the design of all the areas and how well all the details were taken care of, there were no dead spaces unused, and the gentlemen noticed that a lot, and Larisa for her good taste in decoration and furniture, then, she invited them to meet in the living room.

It was after seven in the evening, she had invited them early because she knew that the meeting would be long, once most of them were seated in the armchairs and chairs that the waiters had brought, Larisa took the floor.

-Friends, your attention please, he hit the glass of white wine with his ring and the sharp sound made them all turn around, I want to officially welcome you to my new home, which of course is also yours.

-Dad, I'm going to get my clothes - Brandon said jokingly, ha, ha, ha, everyone laughed.

-Me too - Karla seconded - it's my house, right?

-Of course, it is, this is your house - everyone relaxed and laughed, his dad took the floor.

-Friends, I want to make a toast, you should know that when my little girl was born, I was very excited, I was fascinated by the idea of being a father and when I had her in my arms, I fell in love with her, and today, well... -he had to keep silent, a lump in his throat was forming, Larisa, watching and listening to her father, wiped her eyes with a napkin and made an effort not to cry- I have had the opportunity to correct my mistakes while I am alive, and I want her to be happy, I have worked hard all my life, and I have left her alone for a long time, that did not make her happy and well, thanks to this gentleman -he pointed to Alberto sitting to Larisa's right- I have been able to correct all the damage I did, and this house is my wish that my daughter be very happy, that my grandchildren, whom I love very much, be happy, so cheers, because Larisa is very happy in this house and wherever she stops in this world -she raised her glass and clinked it with those who were by her side. Around them, everyone did the same.

Larisa stood up, clinked her glass with her dad and hugged him.

-Thanks daddy, I love you so much.

-Me too my love.

After the toasts, she patted her new love's leg, and he spoke.

-Friends, family, I'm happy to be reunited with everyone again, first of all, remember, it's not about being serious, okay, but about having fun, we can joke and participate freely, so let's enjoy it, to start, I want to congratulate you all, really when I saw you come in I was amazed by the physical change you have, so I want your testimonies, who wants to be first, -most of them raised their hands, but Roger was the first to speak.

-They say that it's the ladies first, but if you'll allow me, I want to be first.

-Go ahead Roger, tell us.

-Well, this has been incredible, I must confess that looking into my eyes was very difficult for me, I couldn't stand the look, I got to the point of thinking, but why are you so fat? Come on, you can do it, so I forced myself and well... - she had to pause, remembering that moment made her eyes cloud over, Larisa had already foreseen what would happen so on each table there was a beautifully decorated metal box, with disposable tissues. -That night, I cried so much, like never before in my life, well, you can see it, ha ha, I'm still crying, she wiped her tears with the napkin, but I discovered many, many things that I had kept, some very painful and others very embarrassing... but in the end I was able to look into my own eyes and love myself - she didn't want to give any more details of her experience, many of those present began to form tears when they felt it and remembered their own experience - the most important thing was to love myself, wow Alberto, this is fantastic - she said smiling and raising her glass - after loving me completely, which I didn't

301

want to stop doing, I confess, I discovered that I am something beautiful, and I didn't want to stop caressing me - she tried not to cry, but she couldn't contain herself, she hugged Rouse and cried, she comforted him, everyone did the same. When he finally calmed down, he said, "I'm sorry, friends, I've already made you cry, but I have a question for Alberto. After loving myself, I looked in the mirror and my face had rejuvenated. The wrinkles were gone. Well, not completely. I'm sixty years old now. I'm not a child. But I was amazed by the change. My pants are loose on me. I've started buying suits one size smaller. Why does this happen, Alberto? Why do we rejuvenate?

-Ok, first of all, thank you for sharing your experience with us. I love knowing that you were able to do the whole exercise, -everyone commented something between them- I can see that they all rejuvenated, which indicates to me that they emptied their cups and well the explanation of why this happens is the following, our physical body is the vehicle through which we live experiences, it is like a car, yes, a car is just a device that we use to move from one place to another, right?

-Of course, it is just that, a piece of furniture that transports us.

-Well our physical body -he stretched out his left hand and pulled his skin with the other hand- is just the vehicle, all or the vast majority of living beings in the universe, believe that they are the physical body that they occupy, when in reality they are not, they are the driver. When you have a car and you get in it, you take the controls and tell it where you want to go, that's how you drive a vehicle, well, when you decide to take a life on this planet or any other planet or dimension in the universe we do the same, we get in the vehicle and we start telling it where we want it to take us, the vehicle transports us, but it doesn't just transport us, it allows us to feel the environment, through our chakras, you remember that right?

-I don't - said Axel and Robert.

-Ok, it's true that you weren't at our last dinner, it turns out that our physical body has seven power centers or energy centers called chakras, which allow us to perceive the energies of the environment and know if something is good or not, if there are positive or negative energies wherever we are, through the chakras we perceive the world, our world is not only physical, it is energetic, it is made of energy, it is like a hologram, but I don't want to go too deep, I leave that as homework to investigate, there are many movies that talk to us about chakras and matter, look up the topic of quantum energies on the internet, there you will understand what the physical world really is and what they are for, so well, our chakras perceive the world and its energies, and through them we know if someone likes you, if you like them, if there is chemistry, if you want to have sex with them or not, it is not a question of chemistry, but of physics, of energies.

-I understand, ok - they both said.

-Well, then, our physical body has an energetic body, Brandon is very good at seeing it, right champion?

-Yes, and everyone now has it bigger than last time, or is it that I have been training more in that and I can see it more clearly?

-Both things son, we have all filled our cups with personal love and that makes us manifest a beautiful and true love towards ourselves, that is why our light is brighter, on the other hand, the fact that you are practicing has made you more sensitive, keep doing it - the young man felt flattered and took a small sip of his glass of wine.

-Ok, then, our physical body is the vehicle and we, the drivers, tell him where we want to go, if I tell him, I want to go to the bathroom, he gets up and goes to the bathroom, if I tell him, I want to go to my office, he takes me there.

-But of course, Robert affirmed, he had never seen it that way.

-That's right Robert, you're the driver, so your body will do what you tell it to, but the problem we have is that we forget, we forget that we're just the driver and we think we're the vehicle.

-Wow Alberto, this is incredible - said Lisa, who had been very quiet- so I'm not this body - she was pulling the skin on her arm - ouch, I pinched myself, ha, ha, ha, how silly, ha, ha, - everyone laughed.

-Let's see - said Susan taking her brother by the cheek and pulling it - so this is just the vehicle, ha, ha, ha.

-It hurts sister - she exclaimed rubbing her cheek.

-Exactly Brandon, our vehicle can feel pain, heat, cold, blows, love, anger, etc., and it lets us drivers know if something is good or not. Think about it, a person who doesn't feel pain doesn't know if something is good or bad, right? They will get hurt, but it won't hurt them, so for them there is no suffering. They could get hurt again indefinitely, without it causing them any problems.

-It's true, that's why it's important to feel. And that's what our vehicle does, it feels the outside world.

-Well said Ellen, that is exactly what the physical body does, it shows us the outside world, but it doesn't just show it to you, it also stores energy from the outside world, when you have sex with someone else, our energy bodies merge and mix, sharing their energies, in that way they enrich each other, if sex was just that, a quick fuck to let off steam, I apologize for the expression, our energies don't merge the same way as when you do it with someone whose energy is very similar and pleasant to you, think about it, before meeting the partner you have now, you surely had sex with many or few people, but the most significant experience, ultimately, was with the partner you have now.

-That is totally true - they affirmed.

-But our energy bodies they can only store a certain amount of energy from each other, and that's why we stop wanting to have sex with our partners - said Richard.

- Because we are already full of the energy of our partners, and that's why we must learn to base our relationships on honest and true love, right my love - added Ellen turning to see her husband.

- That's right my beautiful, you said it wisely - he approached and kissed her beautiful red lips. Everyone saw them smiling.

- That's right, our vehicle can store energies, all the pains, humiliations, and abuses that we experienced in our childhood, are energetic emotions, which are stored in our vehicles and kept in our cups of personal love, filling it with those energies.

- Wow, I'm getting it - said Axel.

- How interesting - confirmed Robert looking at Valgarma.

-So, all those energies are stored in our bodies, creating illnesses, or bad vibes, to such a degree that they can cause cancer, diabetes, hypertension, darkening of the skin, rashes, psoriasis, misshapen faces or big jets, angry or happy faces, depending on the stored energies.

-So, Alberto, do illnesses really have an energetic origin?

-Energetic-emotional, Lisa, remember that our body perceives energies as emotions, pain is an energy and an emotion, blows are an energy and an emotion, abandonment or loneliness is a lack of love energy, and an emotion, you realize, all emotions are an energy, and there are very different ones, and that is what is stored in our bodies.

-That is why you told us that all illnesses are curable.

-What, let's see, that interests me -Robert, he had been suffering from prostate and a week ago he had been diagnosed with prostate cancer, he had not told anyone.

-Think about it Robert, if our physical body stores energy, most of the energy that causes illness is negative energy, which has to do with negative experiences, or karmas from something that was done to us or that we did, nobody gets sick without their consent, I repeat. "NO ONE GETS SICK WITHOUT THEIR CONSENT", just as nobody dies without their consent.

-Are you telling me that any illness that one is suffering from is self-inflicted? -Larisa turned to look at her father, but did not say anything.

-Let's see, does the car get sick on its own or due to the driver's lack of attention?

-Due to the driver's lack of attention of course, if he does not put water, oil and perform the proper services, the car will fail, but it is not the fault of the car, but of the owner or the person in charge.

-And who is the owner or person in charge of your vehicle?

-Me... of course -she answered, realizing.

-Well, then let's see the cure, if what is causing the disease is an energy, and normally it is a bad or negative energy stored in our body, what we have to do is get it out, and that is achieved with the exercise of the personal cup of love, what all of you have been doing is getting out your bad vibes, or stored negative energies, after getting them out, you have loved each other, and you have filled yourselves with the energy of love, the most powerful energy in the universe is the energy of love, and you have done that when you have caressed each other, that is why your bodies were rejuvenated, you got rid of all those bad or negative energies, and your body was happy, it was filled with the energy of love and began to vibrate in that energetic octave, love.

-Wow, but... don't make things up Alberto, how wonderful - said Robert, everyone was talking to each other commenting on something and others were reflecting deep in their thoughts.

Alberto raised his glass and said.

- Cheers friends, for the healing of illnesses.

- Let's see Alberto - said Karla, everyone began to fall silent - but it is not only by doing the exercise of the cup of love that we are going to be cured, right?

-That's the beginning, my dear. The first thing is to get rid of bad energies, bad vibes or bad vibes from our body. All our illnesses are linked to karma. Remember that karma is when we have hurt someone, and with that act we create a debt between us and that person. That karma must be paid, either with that same person or with any other, in this life or in a future life, if we couldn't resolve it in this one. How do we pay it? Well, there are several ways. The first is by asking someone to do the same damage to us that we did to the other person. If we steal from them, they will steal from us. If we rape them, they will rape us. If we kill someone, they will kill us. If we kill someone's child, they will kill a child. If we cause "accidental death", remember that on this planet there are no accidents or coincidences, everything is our creation, it was our agreements, so we will suffer that death through an "accident."

-Oh no, Alberto, no, my brother was murdered when he was with me, I was seventeen and he was fifteen, and I have had enormous resentment and hatred for the murderer, he is in jail, and I have wished the worst for him, but then, in a past life, I murdered someone else's brother and now I asked to live that?

-That's right, and as long as you remain in resentment and hatred towards the murderer, you will not pay your karma, and in the next life you will again suffer the loss of a loved one, on the other hand, that energy of hatred and sadness will remain attached to your energetic body and in turn to the physical body, making it sick.

-But also, Lisa - added Larisa - you asked the murderer to help you by killing your brother,

-And your brother - said Erika - he proposed to leave his body at that age, that way he would help you and your parents to live the experience of losing a loved one, right

Alberto?

-Perfectly said girls, it seems that you have been thinking about that.

-Of course - affirmed Ellen - when we meet we talk about our discoveries, about the agreements we have in our lives, and when we watch a movie, we realize the agreements that exist, and the karmas that we do not resolve by staying with the hate.

-Well done girls, excellent, but then, going back to the illness, breast or prostate cancer, normally has to do with karmas, anger, or resentment related to sex and our feminine and masculine parts, if it is breast cancer, it is anger with our feminine part, a resentment with our mother, grandmother or with yourselves, because you are angry with your feminine part, you cause cancer; if it is prostate cancer, normally it has to do with something sexual, perhaps you were a sexual abuser and you feel guilty, or you are angry with your father or your grandfather or with yourself, because they abused you or you abused someone, and you continue to remain angry. Those energies are what cause the illness, and all those pains are what we release in the exercise in front of the mirror, right?

-Yes, of course, they all nodded.

-So, the first part of healing is to go in front of the mirror and open up, talk to yourself and discover all the shameful or humiliating things that we did or that were done to us, then, you can ask for forgiveness and give your forgiveness, then, you can love yourself, this part of loving yourself is the second part of healing, you have to love that part or that sick organ, if it is the liver, the prostate, a finger, whatever is sick, you have to love it, ask for forgiveness, free yourself from your karmas.

-How do I do that? How do I free myself from karmas?

-You have to say: If I, say your full name, hurt you, humiliated you, offended you, did something, anything that hurt you, please forgive me, I am truly sorry, I love you, thank you. It has to be a forgiveness from the heart, a deep and true forgiveness to free that person from karma with you, and to free yourself, just remember that whatever they did to you, you did it in a past life, there is no injustice. You can also invoke the violet flame of transmutation, this is the energy in charge of transmuting karmas, ask it to be present between you and that person, please transmute any karma that could exist between the two of you, I recommend that you transmute all your personal relationships, with your parents, siblings, friends, lovers, neighbors, with everyone you have something to do with, transmute your past lives, ask for forgiveness if you hurt or humiliated any man, woman, boy, girl or animal, in this or in a previous life, in that way you will also free yourself from karma.

-Alberto, can a person continue to hurt someone, if they transmute their karmas, and in that way not create more debts?

-Why would someone who understands that what they are doing is tied to karma want to keep doing it? Agreements are made because there is karma tied to that, we need to live an experience, but to stop doing it. Let me explain a little more, if I made an agreement to steal or kill or rape someone, I actually did it to stop doing it, by refusing to continue doing that, only then do I free myself from karma, if I keep doing it, thinking that now I am freeing myself by using the violet flame, in reality you are not doing it, the violet flame is not stupid, it knows when something is done from the head and not from the heart, if you try to transmute your debts with the violet flame, from your head and not from your heart, the violet flame will not appear, you cannot fool it, on the other hand, that would be like being a person who says: "Well, I already know how to read, from now on I will not read", a person who does that would not be stupid. -Of course -said Carlos- but that is what millions of people do, who have never read a book in their life, they know how to read, but they don't use it, they only use it for the basics in their lives.

-Unfortunately, it's true -Richard confirmed- that's why there's so much ignorance in the world.

-Your right guys, but think about it a little further. If everything in our life is our creation and our agreements, then there's failure in life? Do you think there are winners and losers? -Everyone was silent thinking.

-No Alberto, -Robert answered- there are no failures, nor losers, yes everything is an agreement, then some people decide to live their lives in ignorance, others in failure, others in success, I can't be a failure if I planned it to be that way, there's no failure.

-You're right -Erika confirmed- my whole life was my own plan, if I had needed to be a good reader, then I would have made agreements to become that.

-So, I'm not good at math, because it was my agreement? -Brandon opened his eyes in amazement.

-I'm not good at swimming, because that was my agreement? I don't like swimming, but I have to pass the classes, otherwise I'll fail physical education.

-That's right, friends, we made the plans according to what we needed to learn or not, to fulfill our agreements with others and to pay our karmas.

-Wow, how wonderful Alberto, so there are no mediocre people, because oh how that word hits me, that's why I always try harder to not seem like one, I got that from my dad -said Carlos- I remember that when I was little he told me, "you're mediocre, try harder."

-Well -Valgarma intervened-, all this sounds great, but to me, well, it makes me feel ashamed, but I don't believe in agreements, I have a hard time believing that it was all my own plan and that I asked to be raped or robbed, Larisa explained it to me, but I don't know, it's not clear to me, I refuse to believe that it's true.

-Well Valgarma, thank you for being honest, let me put it this way: In life there are only two options or two positions that you can adopt, the first, the position of the Victim, where you have no responsibility for anything, everything that happens to you is good or bad luck, it is a matter of fate, even of God or the devil, but you are only the victim of events, okay?

-Yes, I think that is how it is.

-Ok, the second position is that of the Creator, where you are the creator of the experiences you have lived, the assault, the rape, etc., everything was a plan to live an experience and be able to pay for karma, which of the two positions gives you more power?

-Well, if you put it that way, the creator's position gives me more power, because the victim leaves me defenseless, without the possibility of deciding about my life.

-Exactly, that is what it is about, you can believe what suits you best, it is your free decision, but think, which position gives you power over your life? If you choose to be the victim, you won't even have the power to change your life, because you don't know if good or bad luck will fall on you, so you are helpless; on the other hand, the creator's stance allows you to have control of your future, now you know that your entire past was your creation, that no one really hurt you and that you didn't really hurt anyone, that even if you killed someone, that person is alive in the City of Light, so there is no harm, you realize.

-Well -Robert interrupted- then you explain to us that they live, where do you say?

-The City of Light -said Susan- there is a movie that explains that very well, I'm going to share it with him, so he can see it.

-Thank you, darling.

-What do you think Lisa, are we doing well?

-Yes, excellent, I'm understanding.

-The beautiful thing about discovering this is that you can end your agreements, for example: to be bad at math, to not be good at swimming, to not read, to not be rich, to be a poor employee for the rest of your life, to not be successful in business, to continue harming or stealing, free yourself from all that you feel is holding you back, and start building the life that makes you truly happy, you don't need to make agreements to achieve something, now you know that whatever happens in the future will be your decision, and that if something "bad", in quotes, were to happen, it is because there is a karma that you have to pay, so instead of getting angry and hating, just be thankful, ask for forgiveness and free yourself.

-Alberto, that sounds great, I understand asking for forgiveness if someone steals or rapes you, but if that were to happen to us, at the time of the events we would feel a lot of terror and afterwards, anger and everything else, it would be difficult to ask for forgiveness at that moment.

-I understand that Lisa, and you're actually right, if someone came with a gun to point at my daughter in front of me, I would of course be terrified, but the important thing is what you do afterwards with all the emotions that this event provokes in you, do you stay angry and hating, or do you ask for forgiveness and be grateful.

-Madam, dinner is served -Larisa looked at the clock, it was ten o'clock at night.

-Friends, come to the dining room, please, everyone got up and went to the table, a square table with four chairs on each side welcomed them, it was perfectly set, everyone admired the dishes and sat down.

-Wow Larisa -said Ellen- what a beautiful dining room and how big, it is beautiful.

-Thank you, I'm glad you like it. -Once everyone was seated, Larisa said- may I say a prayer? -Her father turned to look at her, amazed, she was never attached to religion, she turned to look at her father and said guessing his thoughts- it's true dad, you should know that I was angry with God, many years I stopped believing in him..., -She bowed her head and wiped away the tears that were beginning to appear- many years I walked away from him angry, but after the exercise in front of the mirror, I felt his love, and he..., -Alberto hugged her- he loved me -she said this trying to contain a cry that was struggling to come out- and I loved him, so now -she crossed her fingers- beautiful father, thank you -she could not contain her tears any longer, but she forced herself to continue speaking- thank you for all the blessings you have given me, thank you for the health of my father, my children, and all my friends, thank you for this house, in which I ask you to live and be very happy, bless its walls and everything in it, thank you for the people of the world. The service that prepared these delicious meals, bless them and fill their homes with love, thank you for always being by my side, amen.

-Amen - they all said, some wiped away their tears.

-Enjoy your food.

-Cheers Larisa, what a beautiful prayer, thank you for inviting us - said Karla raising her glass, everyone did the same and clinked their glasses with those next to her.

-Okay Brandon -said Susan in a low voice- no more wine.

-Yes sister, you're right, no more, young man, give me plain water, please -the waiter approached with the jug and served him.

-Hey Alberto, I have a question, if someone embezzles another person and makes them lose a lot of money, let's say that it leaves them bankrupt, did the two of them agree to live that experience, right?

-Yes, that's right.

-But then, the one who embezzled is not creating karma, but is helping the other to live his experience by leaving him bankrupt, is that so?

-Let's see, we make agreements with three objectives in mind: first...

-I say them -intervened Carlos- the first is to live an experience, the second, to help another, and the third, to pay a karma, eh, how are you, I'm a good student -he said stretching his neck.

-Bravo my love, you are magnificent -Erika caressed his face and kissed him on the cheek.

-Ha, ha, well said Carlos, it's clear.

-Ok, let's see if I understand, the first, is to live an experience, the second, to help another and the third, to pay a karma.

-Exactly Robert, so then both people agree to live the experience, second, they are helping each other, the one who is going to embezzle has already done it in previous lives, so he plans to do it again so he doesn't do it again.

-So, he should have stopped and not committed the embezzlement?

-Exactly, if he committed it, he would still be tied to karma, you see?

-So, the real objective was not to commit that act to free himself from karma, he should have stopped so as not to commit it.

-Exactly.

-But then, if he stops, he would not help the other person to live the experience of going bankrupt and he would not be fulfilling his agreement.

-Both have a karma, and they make the plan to free themselves from their karma, so, if the one who is going to commit the embezzlement, realizes it and says, no more, I don't need to do this, this is dishonest, I don't need it, then he frees himself, otherwise he will remain tied, and if he stops, then the other friend, someone else will help him live his experience, but the first person will be freed.

-Ok, but then someone else will help the other friend live his experience?

-Yes, the other needs to experience the loss, to feel the anger, the hatred and the desire for revenge. If he manages to free himself from those feelings, if he is able to forgive and forgive himself, stopping blaming someone else, then he will free himself from karma. If he does not free himself from those feelings, and dies with them, he will repeat the experience in the next life. Of course, the latter can also end his karma without the need to experience the embezzlement and lose his fortune.

-And how does he do that, if that hasn't happened?

-Ok -said Alberto, thinking a little- we all have past lives ok, and in those lives we have done everything, we have stolen, murdered, loved, ignored, humiliated, raped, abused some boy or girl, in short, we have done any number of things, so if in this life a person decides to free themselves from their karmas without having to live those painful experiences, they should do an act of forgiveness, I suggest that each one buy a candle, and at home alone or with their family, light it, and begin to do an act of forgiveness and gratitude, we have to ask for forgiveness, if we stole, raped, lied, defrauded, took someone's money or their house, or their wife, if we killed, if we kidnapped, if we hurt in some way, we must feel and ask for forgiveness, we must invoke the violet flame and ask it to help us cleanse our karmas, but it must be an act of forgiveness from the heart, tears should flow if forgiveness is asked from the heart and not just from the head, in this way, anyone can free themselves from a karma, and from that day on, live and act in the name of love, giving your personal love in everything you do and only doing what is right and honest. If life gives you the opportunity to do something that is not honest or right, you should reject it and think that maybe that is an opportunity to free yourself from karma

-Wow, how wonderful, don't you think? - said Lisa.

-Life is a great play, written by ourselves, we write what role we are going to play, and with whom, to free ourselves from this planet.

-Well said Richard, hello friend -Alberto raised his glass.

-I want to share something, if you allow me -said Axel. When Larisa arrived at my house, she looked so changed, her face was totally different, she reminded me of the Larisa I fell in love with - his wife felt a little uncomfortable with his comment, but she didn't say anything, she took her glass a little seriously and took a small sip, Alberto noticed her expression - but then, she took my hands and asked for forgiveness, I don't know what it was, but I felt like something was lifted off me, I was very happy and pleased, then she told us about the energies and told us how to do the exercise and well, now we can see our changes.

-That's right my love, it's true, when I saw Larisa she was very changed, she hugged me, something she had never done before and she asked for forgiveness, I felt a very special affection for her, and well, then we did the exercise and everything has been different since then.

-Congratulations Axel and Lisa, it's good that you gave yourselves the opportunity to do the exercise. What you felt Axel, what was removed from you, was the negative energy and karma that you and she had tied up, remember that what we do is eliminate the bad energy or the bad vibes from our vehicle, after that, you felt the love that was between you two, your relationship is not the first, that is, it is not the first time that you live this experience of getting divorced and ending up hating each other, many times before you have died with anger and resentment, whether you have been the man or the woman.

-So, it is not the first time that Axel and I have gotten together and lived together?

-That's right Lisa, they have done it many times before to pay off their karmas and their debts.

-My dad and Larisa were lovers -said Brandon.

-How? -said everyone who did not know the story.

-It's true -said Ellen.

-Did you know that Ellen? and we are all here having dinner? -said Valgarma- what did I miss?

Larisa explained to them about karma between them and how they resolved it.

-That's why we're friends now, right Larisa? -Brandon said smiling at her.

-That's right, handsome, now there's a very nice affection between us.

-This happens -Alberto intervened- because of the following, when we are in the City of Light, we make plans with our loved ones, our own family, for example, those two characters, the one who embezzled the other and sent him bankrupt, those two are most likely best friends in the City of Light and most likely they are even brothers from the planet or dimension where they come from, only they are playing a role, an acting role, and one says to the other: Hey brother help me, I need you to be a businessman in the next life and embezzle me, one that makes me lose all my wealth, Ok, answers the friend, of course, I'll help you, it helps that I also pay my karmas, then they agree, they enter the scene, they forget who they are and why they came, they start living their lives and then they meet each other and what was planned happens. What do you think?

-So then, I felt a special affection for Larisa, when she asked me for forgiveness? Because we already knew each other from other lives and it could be that we are sisters and we don't know it -both were looking at each other and smiled, their eyes filled with tears and both got up from the table, walked until they met, hugged each other and cried- little sister, forgive me, forgive me -both were recognizing each other, their disguises had fallen off.

Everyone wiped their tears, the three childhood friends turned to see each other and smiled, they did the same, stood up and went to meet each other.

-Thank you, little sisters, thank you for being here for me, thank you for your love.

Susan and Brandon hugged each other and cried.

-Thank you, little brother, thank you for being here, I love you very much.

-Me too, Susy, thank you for always being there for me and being my older sister, I love you very much.

Love was found again.

After a while everyone went back to their places and Alberto continued.

-Now we are understanding, why it makes no sense to hate anyone, or stay angry with anyone, we are all really brothers.

-Well, Alberto, yes, I understand, I understand that I may be the brother of the one who embezzled me or robbed me or raped me, but brother to everyone? I don't know any Russians or Chinese, why would they be my brothers? There are millions with whom I will never have any interaction.

-I understand you, Robert, seen that way it is true, why would they be our brothers? But it turns out that everyone on this planet and on all the planets, in this one and in the millions of universes that exist, we come from the same source, we are all beings of energy, living different experiences, but all endowed with the creative Mind of God. Right Roger?

-That's right Alberto.

-We all have a mind with which we have created our lives and our world as it is today, you yourself Robert, have participated in the construction of this world, how many investments in real estate do you have?

-Well yes, many.

-That participation of yours in this and in all your past lives has created the world as it is now.

-Ok, I understand, wow, so we have the mind of God, and throughout our lives we have been creating the world as it is today.

-We are, Robert, we don't have, WE ARE the Creative Mind, the mind is what remains alive after the death of our vehicle, this vehicle will only live eighty, or twenty years, whatever each one has planned, and we will continue to live, whether you return to your original home or reincarnate in this world again, and who knows, maybe in the next one you will be..., what is the nationality or skin color that you hate the most?

-Nationality, well if I can't stand Arabs, and colored people, well I don't know, not that I'm racist, but...

-Ok, it doesn't matter, maybe in the next life you will be Arab and colored, that will help you get rid of the karmas associated with racism.

-I understand, that's why it makes no sense to hate anyone.

-Nor to belittle, a street sweeper comes to live that experience because there he can pay his karmas, but perhaps in his previous life he was a very rich man who looked down on poor people and servants, that is why now he chooses to be poor and live the contempt of those who have more than him, do you realize? We are all brothers; a country that goes to war with another country, it is because both live tied to karmas of debts with each other, and their leaders, lead them to live hatred and wars, both leaders are perhaps brothers living roles of enemies.

-My love, but if someone comes to want to rob me or rape me, God forbid...

-God or you, Larisa?

-True, me, of course, but if that happens to me, it is because there is a karma that I have to pay, what should I do, let them rape me, let them rob me?

-Yes, if you are aware of all this and of the karmas, do not oppose what has to happen to you, be at peace and ask for forgiveness; if someone, in the worst case, kills you, they are actually helping you get out of your vehicle, it is as if they opened the door for you so you can get out, to return to the City of Light, and perhaps, if you freed yourself from all your karmas, you can return to your original home, you realize, dying is not a punishment, it is a reward of freedom.

-But then, why are we so afraid of death? -Erika questioned.

-Because the church and religions have taught us to fear it, they have told us that, if we do not obey the laws imposed by God, then we will go to hell, and on the contrary, if we were obedient, then we will go to heaven; who among you has never committed a, wrongly called, "sin"? speaking of this, do you know the joke?

-No, tell it.

-Jesus was surrounded by a crowd and they were judging a prostitute, so he says: Let he who is without sin cast the first stone, and then a stone flies and hits him in the head. He turns to look at the person who threw the stone and says: No, mom, not you.

-Ha, ha, ha, ha - Larisa was about to spit out the wine she was drinking. Everyone laughed out loud.

-I didn't understand Susan, why?

-Jesus' mother is the Virgin Mary and she is pure and holy, she is free of sin.

-Ah, I see - he didn't laugh, he continued without understanding.

-So, -Alberto continued- there is no human being who can fulfill all the laws that the church imposes on us, even the priests themselves, nobody can, so we are afraid of dying because we don't want to go to hell. But now, we know that we are not going to hell, but to...

-The City of Light -said Susan, Alberto winked at her.

-And the church -Roger added- doesn't want people to know all this, they would lose millions of followers.

-People -Alberto intervened- would not need to go to church, because there are no sins to forgive, they were all agreements, and in reality, the only one who has to forgive us is ourselves, each one of us has to forgive himself, that is what we do when we are in front of the mirror looking into our eyes, we are forgiving ourselves, we are God, forgiving himself.

-And what about money Alberto, many of us are giving too much importance to money.

-Money is part of the agreements, a person who has a lot, did so because that is how he planned it, the one who does not have money, it was also his plan; the important thing to know is that in reality having it or not, is part of our karmas and debts. The objective of our lives is not to be the richest in the world, we think so, because we only see ourselves as if we were the vehicle, you do not see yourself as the driver, you do not realize that money is only a means to live certain experiences and you put it as your priority; No one living in this world is going to take a single cent, not even a jewel, no matter how small it is. We are only going to take our energies, and with them our Karmas or Dharmas. Our job is not to possess a lot of wealth, but to free ourselves from karmas. Think about it, Robert, how much money are you going to take with you when you die, when you abandon your vehicle?

-Nothing, Larisa will inherit everything.

-Exactly, and the only thing you are going to take with you are your karmas and your debts. On the other hand, the money that does not bless the people around you is not worth it. There are multimillionaires who die with billions of dollars in their accounts and they have not blessed anyone with that money. What good did it do them?

-You are telling me that we should give away our wealth before we die.

-I don't know, that's a decision that everyone should make, what to do with my wealth? What I think is important is that my money should bless the greatest number of people possible, what good are millions of dollars that I'm not going to spend, when there are thousands of people dying of hunger in the same city where I live?

-Alberto, we have talked about this issue -said Roger pointing to Richard- and we believe that it is not good to give money to the poor, because if they don't know how to manage it, we will hurt them.

-It's true, remember that a person who is poor, decided that way to pay their karmas, if you give them a lot of money they will surely get rid of it, after getting drunk and doing stupid things, because in their agreements is to get rid of the money to be poor, and as long as they don't break this agreement, they will continue to be poor, even if they won the lottery;

how many stories do you know of people who have won the lottery and after a couple of years are again in poverty.

-That's true, said Erika, there are many of those stories, I knew a coworker, her grandfather won the lottery and well, he became an alcoholic and lost his family, he ended up in absolute poverty, his family lost the houses he had bought with that money; but then, let's see... wait, then... he won the lottery not because of good luck, but because that way he would live out his agreements and his karmas, now I understand, wow.

-That's right, how interesting, that's why I tell you that being rich or being poor is actually an agreement to pay off a karma, now, going back to our wealth, there are many ways in which our wealth can bless people around us, for example, if you are a businessman, how about reducing personal profits, increasing salaries and benefits; or if you are a builder, helping people to obtain decent, quality housing, at a fair price, not with the goal of me as the owner getting rich, but to bless everyone, I bless myself of course, and I bless others; perhaps to make a fair distribution of profits at the end of the year; in short, each one has to find what makes him feel happier and then do it; the key to change is to fill our cup of personal love, and then, to give this love to everyone around us, to bless life itself, if we do that, we can change as a society. If any of you are an employee, think about how your love can bless the owner of the company you work for. It's not just about keeping a schedule to earn a salary. You're there because there's some karma you have pending with that type of work, or with the owner of the company itself. Finish the karmas and start giving your personal love in everything you do. Start seeing that company as if it were yours. Seek its growth.

-Well, Alberto, if we all learned to do that, our world would be different.

-That's what it's all about, friends. Creating a different world, but not fighting for the world outside to change, because the only world I can change is my personal world.

-Let's see, I got lost - said Ellen - I don't understand that. Why isn't it about fighting to change the world?

-Let's see, but first let's say cheers -he raised his glass- cheers, beautiful -he said, turning to look at Larisa and giving her a kiss.

- Cheers, handsome -everyone raised their glasses and commented on something with those around them.

- Alberto continues and what else.

-Ok, I was telling you that the only world that I can change is my personal world, let me tell you a story: Once upon a time there was an old man in the hospital bed, he was eighty years old and he was dying, his whole family was surrounding him, and he said to them: Children, I have wasted my life, when I was young I wanted to change the world to make it a better place, so I dedicated many years of my life to try to achieve it, but then I realized that I couldn't, so, I said to myself, I'm going to change my colony, I dedicated many years of my life trying to change the colony, but, I realized that nothing happened, then I said to myself, I'm going to change my family and I tried for many years, and I didn't succeed, now that I'm in bed dying, I realize that the only one I could and that I should have changed from the beginning was myself, but I didn't, and now I'm dying and I realize that I wasted my life -everyone was silent assimilating the story- Do you realize?, at the only thing we can change is ourselves. Each one of you who has already done the exercise and filled your cup with your personal love is beginning to change your personal world. Do you realize this?

-Of course, I have changed a lot -said Roger.

-And I -Robert raised his hand.

-And I -they all said.

-Exactly, our personal love is what is changing our personal world. My true love begins to affect my wife, my children, my employees, my coworkers, the people I bump into on a daily basis, maybe just with a smile, but it is not because your intention is to change them, that does not work, it is because I have changed, my love has changed me, and now I can bless my world with my love. Now I pick up the trash from the street, because I like to live in a clean world. Do you realize this? Your house has changed its energy, because your love is now present and that energy comes out through the walls and blesses those who are around your house. Let's do a mental exercise, imagine that your personal love is pink, now feel it, breathe and feel it, see the pink color with your imagination - some closed their eyes and others kept their eyes open, they saw it with their mind - good, are you seeing it?

- Yes, yes, it is beautiful.

- Excellent, now see that pink color covering your whole body, feel it, breathe slowly, raise your energy and feel the pink color surrounding your whole body. Now, make that pink color, as if it were a bubble around each one of you, expand, are you feeling it right?

- Yes, yes.

-Now make that pink color grow and encompass this whole house, wrap the house with your love, you are giving a huge blessing to Larisa for her new house -everyone smiled, Larisa was happy and a tear slipped down her cheek- good very good, let's go further, make that pink bubble grow and encompass this whole city, do it, just see how your bubble wraps this city, that's right, take it to the edges of the city, it feels good right, you are using your creative mind and your imagination, but the pink energy you are sending is real, very real in fact, now, take that bubble further, wrap the whole planet, all of us are children of the earth, of Gea, our mother earth, so love her, wrap her in your personal love, thank her for whatever reason you want -the tears were present, almost everyone had their eyes closed smiling and shedding beautiful tears of love- When our love is honest and true and very deep, it usually causes tears, and you are feeling it, and our beloved mother Gea is feeling it, she envelops us in her love and thanks us - Alberto remained silent, giving them space to increase the sensations, when he believed it appropriate he said - Good, Whenever you want, you can open your eyes and come back.

-Larisa took his hand and hugged him crying- my love, that was very beautiful, thank you, thank you.

-Thank you, Alberto, -said Valgarma- what a beautiful love I have felt, that was incredible.

-Thank you, Alberto, -they all said- that was very beautiful.

-That's how we should use our personal love, so that it blesses all around us, let's fill our house, our companies, the sports club, the restaurant where you eat, and our world, remember that love, the more it is given, the more it grows. Cheers -she said raising her glass, everyone did the same and a sound of small bells resonating in a beautiful harmony filled the space.

The conversation continued to flow, they talked among themselves commenting on their cases.

-Friends -said Larisa- if everyone has finished, I invite you to go to the living room, or if you want we can go to the garden. Alberto stood up and pulled out the chair to help her stand up.

Most of them were sitting in the room while the waiters were serving wine, filling the glasses.

-Hey Alberto, I have a question, we've been... you know - Ellen gave him a knowing smile.

-We too - added Roger looking at Rouse, we've read the book "Relationships and Sex", and the author, this man... what's his name?

-Ariel Oliver Comparán - affirmed Rouse, smiling.

-Yes, yes, he explains how to make love using energies.

-Exactly, continued Richard, that's where my question was, I want to know why we're getting younger? Because the truth is that's happening to us, and every time we do it, when we finish, we look younger.

-And boy, you can tell - said Karla - they look incredible. Ellen winked at him smiling.

-Remember friends, that our physical body is actually a vehicle, and that it is moved or kept alive by the energy that our energetic bodies transmit to it. The energetic body is where the chakras are located. When we have sex, we are increasing our Kundalini energy accumulated in the root chakra, to then release it with orgasm or ejaculation. If ejaculations are very frequent without knowing how to manage our energy, our body wears out, gets tired. Have you seen a person who is addicted to sex? What does he look like?

-Their appearance -said Erika- is sad, gloomy and they smell very strange.

-Exactly, these people have been throwing away, so to speak, their energy, and wearing out their physical and energetic body. On the other hand, a person who knows how to use their sex to raise and manage their energy, will enjoy their sexuality more and will conserve their energy, so that it will enrich them and their body will remain healthy and youthful.

-So, are we doing it right? -Roger questioned- because the truth is that yes, we enjoy it a lot now.

-Congratulations, and yes, you are doing very well. If you keep doing that, you will get to the point where you will not need to have penetration to have an orgasm, just by hugging each other and raising your energy, along with your breathing and your mind, and activating all your chakras, you will be able to have very beautiful energetic orgasms, and you can use your energy to bless anything you want. Just as we sent our pink energy to envelop the planet today, you can send your love energy to bless whatever you want during orgasm, that is called knowing how to use energy. You can order it to rejuvenate your bodies, to heal some sick organ, to bless your business or project, to envelop and protect your loved ones, use it to bless whatever you want, and in the end, you will not need to ejaculate.

-But then, we do not need to perform sexual penetration?

-It's not necessary, just by hugging and caressing each other a little you can provoke excitement and increase your energy.

-You -Robert asked pointing at Larisa and Alberto- do you do it like that? Is that why you look so young? Because well if it weren't for your gray hair, I would say you are fifty years old, no more, right?

-No, Robert, I am actually sixty years old, but my body must be thirty-five, and it is because I know how to use energy and I don't waste it.

-Don't make it up Alberto, you are joking, I am sixty-two and I look seventy -he turned to look at Valgarma.

-You look very handsome my love -she said caressing his face.

-Isn't energy wonderful? Our physical body responds to the energy we send it, and to the mental orders we give it.

-Let's see, what are these mental orders? -Carlos asked.

-We have to learn to see ourselves in the mirror as what we really are, the driver, not the vehicle. The problem is that Our eyes can only see the car, they don't see the driver, am I making myself clear?

-Yes, so our eyes can only see our bodies, and we don't see the driver, said Carlos thinking out loud.

-Exactly, and the driver is: The creative mind, that is, God; and the creative mind only knows how to do one thing and that is CREATE. It doesn't analyze if something is true or false, it will only create what the driver tells it to create.

-Let's see, let's take it easy, this is very interesting, -replied Robert- so the driver is the one who orders the creative mind what to produce?

-Exactly, we produce our world with our words and thoughts, because we only know how to do that, CREATE, let me explain a little more; every time you look in the mirror you say: "Wow, how old you are getting, your hair is getting whiter and whiter," is that true?

-Well yes, because I realize that that is happening to me.

-No, it is actually happening to you because you are ordering it, you are the creative mind, and since you turned fifty, you began to order that, to age, that is why your body has obeyed you, with your words, thoughts and feelings, you order your creative mind, do this or that. If instead of seeing yourself in the mirror every day older, you saw yourself every day younger, and you said, wow Robert, every day you are younger, your hair is turning black, your body would obey you.

-Is that what you do love?

-That's right, I look in the mirror and I order my body to stay young and healthy, with black hair, I am not interested in looking too young, but if I live a hundred years looking fifty it would be great, don't you think?

-But of course, I do, I think I'm going to start doing that - said Roger.

-But my love, I love you just the way you are, I don't like young men, I love your gray hair.

-So, Roger -Alberto suggested- just stay healthy, exercise and order your body to do what you want, or do you want it old and sickly Rouse?

-Well no, of course, I want it strong and healthy, but like this, looking this age, it looks very handsome.

-This -Valgarma added- of course applies to women too, right?

-That's right, we all have an energetic body and we are the creative mind, we don't need cosmetic surgery to improve our bodies, we need to love our bodies, and order it in the name of love, to do what you want, you want your breasts to lift up, instead of looking in the mirror and saying, "Oh no, they're sagging more and more every day, they're going to reach my belly button."

- Ha, ha, ha, don't exagerate, ha, ha, ha - they all laughed.

- I'm joking, but then, when you see them in the mirror, love them and tell them - Alberto stood up, pretended to be in front of the mirror, ran his middle finger over his tongue and then flirtatiously caressed his eyebrows, then placed his hands as if holding his breasts and said - Let's see my beautiful girls, I love you, you look incredible, now you're getting up and you look beautiful, see that star up there - he raised his hands a little - well I want you to always be looking at it, I love you very much - he tilted his head and pretended to give each one a kiss.

- Ha, ha, ha, ha - they all laughed out loud.

- Oh my love - said Larisa - you're going too far, ha, ha, ha.

- No, well, get serious now, this is a very formal matter - Alberto laughed - yes I explained myself, right?

-Loud and clear -Karla answered- we already know what we

must do -she put her hands holding her boobs to lift them- ha, ha, ha.

-No kidding, all this is true, you have to love yourself and order, in the love of your body, what you want to improve, any problem or defect can be improved, if you persevere long enough to see your wish come true, because if you spend your time doubting that it will become real, then it will not work for you, because your mind is doubting and remember, that your creative mind only knows how to do one thing and that is to create, and doubts are always stronger than certainties, until certainty occurs.

-Is this the same as healing an illness, right?

-Just the same, Robert, it is using our words, thoughts and emotions to send love to our body and heal or rejuvenate it, instead of talking to yourself or anyone else about your illness, you must talk about your health, perfection and beauty of your body and your organs, do you understand?

-Clearly - Robert answered, raising his glass of wine.

-Hey Alberto, could a person who is in a wheelchair walk again if he did this?

-Let me tell you two stories Ellen, the first is about a young man from seventeen years old, he was the quarterback of his high school team, and he was so good that his coach had already proposed him to several universities. One day, he left a party after having ingested a few beers, and crashed into a tree, as a result, he was left paralyzed from the waist down, and the doctors told him he would never walk again, so after suffering his grief and you can already imagine everything he went through, he ended up accepting his fate and in his adulthood he dedicated himself to coaching, from his wheelchair, American football teams; The other story is about a thirty-five-year-old man, who was piloting his plane and the engine stopped in mid-flight. He crashed, as a result his lungs collapsed, his trachea was fractured, his spine was broken in several places and he had fractures in his ribs and leg. The doctors saved him, but he would have to remain connected to an artificial respirator for the rest of his life, due to the damage to his lungs and trachea, and because of the broken vertebrae he was diagnosed with total paralysis from the neck down. He would never breathe on his own or walk again. When he was given the diagnosis, he listened to the doctors and, using a language he made while closing his eyelids, he told them that he would be walking by December of that year.

-And what happened? Ellen asked.

-The first young man remained in a wheelchair for the rest of his life; The second one began to use his mind and to order his body to breathe, breathe, little by little his lungs began to work again, his trachea recovered and they took him off the respirator, the doctors were amazed, then he began to order his bones to recompose themselves, to function correctly, he ordered his vertebrae to recover and be normal, the end of the year arrived and the man walked out of the hospital.

-Oh no, it's not possible, is that true?

-Did he regenerate his spine?

-Yes, both are true stories, you know what the difference was between one and the other.

-That one believed -Ríchard said- that he would not be able to walk again and he got used to living like that.

-And that the other believed that he could heal and he did - Carlos added.

-Exactly, that's it, each one believed what he wanted to believe, you see, now let's go deeper: Who was right and who was wrong?

-None, said Karla, that is, none was wrong, each one fulfilled their life agreements.

-Exactly, you see, there are no wrong or mistaken lives, the first one could have been cured if he had thought it possible, but that did not allow him to fulfill his agreements and the experience he should live, but let's go deeper, think, why would the young man choose to stay in a wheelchair for the rest of his life? -they remained silent thinking.

-Because being in a wheelchair -said Ellen- he could pay his karmas and help others live the experience, perhaps his parents or brothers or his friends.

-But of course -seconded Erika- surely, he had already been paralyzed in some previous life, but he died angry with himself, or with God, and that kept him tied to karma.

-You are absolutely right, that was it, on the other hand, the second man decided to heal himself and used his mind for it, that is the size of the power of our mind to heal our body.

-Wow Alberto, this gives us incredible power over our lives and our bodies.

-So, if you don't believe in agreements, you won't believe that you can heal yourself and you would have to ask God for a miracle to heal you, why would you think that this is a punishment from him or from bad luck? -Valgarma remained silent, thinking deeply.

-Do you also believe that children born with cerebral palsy can be healed? -Lisa asked.

-Let's see, let's think a little more deeply, do you think that a child born with this problem was an accident or bad luck?

-Of course not, it was an agreement -Brandon affirmed.

-Well said son -Alberto, raising his thumb- exactly, it was an agreement, let's see, one of you, imagine that this child is before being born, what would you ask your parents or how do you imagine that he made his agreements?

-I, I -said Erika- I would tell you, parents, I want to be born with a disease that does not allow me to move, so I will need you to take care of me and help me, I want to pay for a karma that I have, because..., well, I mistreated several sick children and I despised them, and now I want to pay for my karmas, how about that?

-Wow Erika, that was great -congratulated Ellen.

-Excellent Erika, well said, now we go deeper, if the child cannot move or speak, does that mean that the driver is sick and unable to use his mind? Or is it just the vehicle that is defective?

Everyone was thinking about the answer.

-Well -said Roger- if everything is an agreement, then the driver is intact and is an intelligent being, he is still the creative mind inside a sick vehicle, a vehicle that is serving to pay his karmas.

-Fantastic answer -said Alberto- what do you think now?

-Alberto, then there are no people with mental illnesses on

this planet, but creative minds inside cases or defective vehicles, to say it with all due respect, vehicles that help them pay their karmas, right?

-Of course, Richard, there are no deficient or sick creative minds, they are all perfectly healthy and powerful, the problem is the vehicles, but if we are understanding, everything has a reason for being, you realize.

-Those children come to help their parents live that experience? Wow -said Susan.

-That's right, that's what they come for, to help someone and pay their karmas.

-Hey, a friend's son is autistic and the child is very intelligent, but they can't control him, how can they help him?

-The problem, in all matters of children's health, is that parents and doctors don't know that the driver is intact, they don't know that inside the body of their sick or disabled child, there is the creative mind, and that it is perfectly healthy and super powerful, so since they don't know, they treat them as sick and disabled, they spend their time telling everyone that their child is special and that he should be treated in a certain way, isn't it true that the parents of a child with autism can't hug him?

-Yes, that's true, they go crazy if you touch them. -Yes, but the problem comes from when they were little, their parents instead of hugging them and containing them in love, and teaching them that they can receive love, that nobody wants to hurt them, they simply treat them as if they were sick, and they leave them alone and do not touch them, so that the child grows up with that way of being, if the parents treated them from a young age, like a normal child, I am sure that the child would develop normally, but by treating them as sick, they grow up as sick people and live as sick people.

-So, absolutely all diseases are curable, including autism.

-Of course, Erika, the parents, like the two people in the previous story, buy the doctors' diagnosis. There is a story about a father who had a son who was born without ears, that is, he was born deaf. Of course, you know what the medical diagnosis was, that he would never hear, but the father did not accept that his son would be deaf all his life, so he forced him to listen. While he was sleeping, he began to talk to him and order his mind to form a system that would allow him to hear. Years passed and the boy attended a normal school, because his father did not allow him to go to a special school. Of course, he had many challenges and tribulations, but after many years and thanks to his father's belief, the young man began to hear. Somehow his body created a system that allowed him to hear sounds. The doctors could not explain how that was possible, but it worked, all thanks to his father's belief in healing, instead of illness.

-Oh, Alberto, this is incredible. There is so much to tell in the world -Valgarma said- I know some cases of this type, and I think that if parents understood this, everything would be different.

-Yes Valgarma, but remember that everything is an agreement, the man who walked out of the hospital, had the agreement to heal his body, the other had the agreement to stay in the wheelchair, the deaf child, had the agreement with his father that he would not let him be deaf, your friend's child, had the agreement to be treated as autistic, you see, there are no mistakes, the important thing to know all this about agreements, is that now we can break them, we can end them to free ourselves from those experiences, and then end our karmas, to be able to heal physically and emotionally, but as long as a person does not end their agreements and their karmas, they will not be able to change their destiny.

-Alberto, but there are people who do not know about karma, however, they have asked for forgiveness, that is enough to end a karma.

-Yes, Karla, forgiveness from the heart automatically frees you, even if you know nothing about the violet flame.

-Alberto, if I ask for forgiveness from the heart, for something I did or something that was done to me many years ago, will that be transmuted by the violet flame?

-Yes, that's right, let me tell you a story, in a town they caught two assailants, they tied them up and beat them, the enraged townspeople brought gasoline and sprayed them, one of the young men was kneeling, saying, God, forgive me, forgive me for all my mistakes, I regret what I did, the other was angry crying and shouting, wretches, let me go, it wasn't me, let me go, damn it, they set both of them on fire, and they burned to death.

-Oh no Alberto, you're telling us and I think I'm seeing them, what a horrible thing.

-But the interesting thing, Ellen, comes now, at the moment when the first one was asking for forgiveness, the violet flame appeared and began to set him on fire, transmuting their karmas, both left their bodies, but one was free and the other was not.

-And both of them are still alive in the City of Light -said

Susan- the only thing that burned was the vehicle, but they are still alive.

-Exactly, Susan, very well said.

-Alberto, but dying like that must be terribly painful?

-No Ellen, no, there is no pain in death.

-But how could it not be Alberto? I seem to hear these young people screaming in pain as they are burned.

-It's true -said Karla- that must be terrible.

-Well no, there is no pain in death, the two-young people left their bodies seconds before they were set on fire, they were no longer there when the match was thrown at them.

-Are you serious? -Robert questioned.

-Totally serious, a person who dies in a tragic condition, most likely is no longer in his body at the time of the trauma, but the case or vehicle is alive, so it cries or laments, but it feels nothing, the driver is no longer there, he has already left it, so there is no pain at the time of death, vehicles do not feel pain, it is the energetic body that feels the pain.

-Ouch, -Brandon shouted, grabbing his arm.

-Sorry, -said Susan-I wanted to know if your vehicle felt the pain and I pinched you, he, he.

-Silly, it hurt, -said her brother smiling and rubbing his arm, ha, ha, ha, everyone laughed while she hugged him.

-Everyone is afraid of death -continued Alberto- because they think it hurts a lot, but it's not true, there is no pain, in reality it is a very beautiful process, let me tell you my story:

Years ago I had a dream, I was on the shore of the beach, when a gigantic wave came upon me, a tsunami, it dragged me, I opened my eyes and saw everything covered in dirt, for a second I thought, the good thing is that I know how to swim, so I'm going to save myself, but suddenly I was inside a parking lot, so there was no escape, I began to fight to survive, I opened my eyes frightened, and everything around me was brown, mud and boards were everywhere, suddenly, I heard a voice telling me, let go, I was struggling to get out, and the voice told me again, let go, so I stopped struggling and let go, in that instant, everything changed, everything turned a very beautiful aqua green and emerald color, I began to breathe again, but how?, I said, I'm alive, I'm breathing, then I woke up.

-Wow Alberto, how incredible, that was... wow, -Ellen said.

-That's how I learned that there is no pain in dying, I also had a very interesting experience, I really liked riding a motorcycle, so I was going down a street, it had rained, I was going about forty kilometers per hour, I wasn't very fast, but suddenly, a hole appeared in the ground in front of me and I couldn't avoid it, I fell, the interesting thing is that I wasn't in my body at the moment of the impact, I didn't feel anything, I came back to my body when I was lifting the motorcycle with the help of the police.

-What, you weren't in your body, but you were lifting the motorcycle?

-Yes, that's right, I got into my vehicle, once I was out of danger.

-Don't make things up -said Carlos- this is incredible, you're making me remember, when I was young I had a car accident, and I was trapped between the iron bars, I couldn't get out, but now that you say it it's true, at the moment of the impact I wasn't there, I came back when they were taking me out, I was very hurt, but I didn't feel anything at the moment of the impact.

-Oh, my love, you had already told me about the accident, but you hadn't told me anything about this.

-It's just that I wasn't aware, until now that Alberto tells us this.

-Wow, how wonderful.

Everyone was amazed thinking about it.

-Well, you know what, now, I'm going to steal this beautiful lady, come on darling, show me the garden. Alberto and Larisa went out to the pool area with other friends. They walked to the back of the green area, from where they admired the entire house, the upper floor was illuminated, the balconies with transparent glass railings allowed them to see all the rooms.

-Really, what a cool project they made you, beautiful.

-Yes, I'm happy, I love my new house, does the vibe feel good?

-Super good, you've filled it with your personal love and it feels amazing, hey, what about the kids?

-They're fine, they fell asleep since nine, but you know what, let me go to see them.

-Do you want me to accompany you?

-Sure, let's go.

Richard and Ellen walked through the garden, in the center of it there was a wooden pergola with a dining room and a living area with a fireplace in the center, and a very comfortable living room.

-Let's sit here, Congratulations, my love, what a beautiful project you achieved, the house turned out incredible.

-Thank you my queen, yes, we put a lot of effort into it, it's very different when the client has the economic power so that we can develop and when there are no limits, I'll tell you something here between us, Robert called me on the phone and told me not to skimp on expenses, that he wanted the best for his daughter, he said that since he was already an older man he wanted his daughter to have the best house possible, so well, we achieved this beautiful thing.

-Well, the economic power is evident.

-Hello lovebirds -Erika and Carlos approached them.

-Congratulations Richard, what a beautiful house, if I had the money I would love a house like that.

-Thanks Carlos, really? Would you like a house that big?

-Yes, I love wide spaces and the garden is beautiful.

-Me too -added Erika- I like it a lot, but maybe not so huge, something a little smaller.

-That's great, friend, have you seen how the second floor looks with that lighting?

-It's that lighting -explained Richard- is part of the beauty of a project, when you have the budget, you don't skimp on lighting for all the areas of the garden and the house, see how the walls of the garden are illuminated from below.

-Yes, of course we had noticed it.

-And changing the subject, what do you think of all this that Alberto has told us?

-I am delighted, the truth is that my life has turned upside down, I have decided to start my own business, you know, I have lived off my parents' inheritance, as I was an only child they left me quite a bit of money, but the truth is that I did not enjoy it, I felt angry with my dad because..., her eyes clouded over, well -she said out loud- it was your agreements Erika, so do not play the victim, you asked him to help you experience that, so enough, it is not his fault, you asked him, so go on, face it and smile -a beautiful smile appeared on her face and she continued- it is true, my dad helped me live through the abuse and I remained angry with him for many years, when we did the exercise in front of the mirror, I was able to free myself from those feelings, first came the arrangement of my house and finally, the reunion of this beautiful love -she said looking at Carlos, who smiled back and approached to kiss her, when they were released, she continued- now I want to open a coffee shop, I'm going to look for a good location and we'll see, I'd love to do something like that.

- Why don't you practice law Erika, you were very good, why don't you two join forces and open an office together, I think you'd make a good team.

- We've talked about it, but I'm very out of date, I haven't practiced law for years, and I don't know, when my parents died it was so sudden, that I sank into depression, I was left alone, and that hurt me a lot, but now I understand that I asked them for that to live the anger and fear of being alone again, now I understand that that was my karma, that's why I lost my loved ones again, so I thanked them and freed myself, now I want to truly enjoy my life.

- Sorry, Erika -said Richard- I didn't know that your father... well, the agreements, of course.

-We did know, but well, I won't tell you many things, you understand me, we've been friends for many years, since high school, we know everything about each other's lives.

-Do you think that all men and women have something to do with sexual abuse, at different levels? to put it in some way - Carlos questioned.

-I think so -Ellen affirmed- we've all experienced some kind of abuse, but the truth is that knowing that it was an agreement, oh no, that's so liberating, especially knowing that we, all of us, have done that in a past life, and that, if we live it in this one, that's the payment for our karma, wow, that's super liberating.

-True friend, you're right, knowing all this is so liberating.

-Hello friends -Roger and Robert approached- can we join the conversation?

-Of course, friends, welcome, sit down, we're talking about sexual abuse and how knowing that it was an agreement is so liberating.

-Hey Richard, how beautiful this space is, and that pergola with the dining room, wow, they were brilliant.

-Thanks Robert, we followed your instructions.

-And how -assured Robert.

-Getting back to the subject -Carlos pointed out- we are talking about sexual abuse, I was wondering if we all have had some experience of this type? And that knowing that if we did it with someone it is because we helped them pay for a karma, and that we should have stopped ourselves from doing it, but well, if we didn't stop, knowing now that we haven't hurt them, that is liberating, it is not something I am proud of, it was just our agreements.

-Indeed -added Roger- it is as if the agreements forced you to do what you had agreed to, and that you cannot avoid it.

-Yes, Roger -Richard added- but now we know that we can prevent an agreement from being carried out, we have to be aware of what we are about to do and recognize that if it is something that is not right, we have to stop, stop ourselves, so as not to continue doing that, and then in reality, free ourselves from karma, if we do not stop we will remain in karma, even if we try to transmute or ask for forgiveness later.

- Hi friends, can we join you? —Alberto, Valgarma and Rouse approached.

-It's good that you have arrived Alberto, please resolve a doubt for me.

-Of course, what is it about Robert.

-If you know that something you are doing is not right, but you still do it, and then ask for forgiveness, will the violet flame truly transmute your karma?

-Well, let's see, why would you want to continue violating it, if you know that it is not good?

-Because of the agreement we made.

-Yes, but you made the agreements so that you would no longer continue doing that. If you didn't know this information, I would understand that you continued making the agreement, but if you already know all this, why would you want to continue being tied to karma?

-Ok, I think I understood you,

-If you don't break the agreements you made to rape someone, or to defraud, or whatever, those agreements will remain active and will force you to rape the person with whom you made the agreement, remember that we make agreements so as not to continue doing those things, it's not just about the other person, but about yourself, so break any possible agreements you have about harming another person in any way possible.

-Now, it's clear to me - Ellen assured - I have to break all agreements about harming someone in any way possible, that way the other person with whom I had agreed that, will no longer carry out their agreement with me, but with someone else, right Alberto?

-Exactly, you free yourself from those agreements, that's what it's about.

-Hey Alberto, I have a question, I have changed many things in my life, but now I want to do something different, I would like to open a coffee shop or practice law, you don't know, but I am a lawyer, so I don't know what to do?

-You are a lawyer, what a surprise, you must be very good, but answering your question, just follow your heart, not your head, you chose the profession you have because there you could pay your karmas in a better way, if you have already transmuted those karmas, then you can change your activity, follow your heart and do what makes you truly happy.

-Ok, that's what I'll do.

-I should leave law, I haven't been happy there for a while now.

-Carlos, all our life experiences are spiritual. When our spirit no longer needs to live an experience, it sends us feelings of dissatisfaction, then unhappiness, so that we no longer do that. It's like with relationships. When we no longer have to be with someone, we start to feel dissatisfied, then we start to feel unhappy, then comes anger and boredom and finally resentment. Is that true?

-Totally true.

-To know if I have to continue living an experience or not, you must first fill your cup of personal love, then give that love to the activity you are developing. Love law and give the best of yourself. If you are doing that and, even so, you feel dissatisfaction, or even unhappiness, it is time to change your activity, but only until you have given your personal love to your career. The same goes for your home and your partner. Give your beautiful love and if you feel like I said, it will be time to change.

-Honey, have you seen the time? It's very late, it's three thirty in the morning. Let's go.

Everyone stood up and began to say goodbye.

XI Sex is a matter of energy

-Hello young lady, very good morning, how did you wake up today?

-Hello my love, good morning - Larisa gave him a beautiful smile, she was lying on the pillow and had her right hand under his ear, he was leaning on it reading a blue-covered book.

-What are you reading?

- "The Transformation of the Universe, the end of darkness and domination." It is very interesting, and very deep, but it is very easy to understand, curiously it is by the same author of the book "Couple relationships and sex."

-Ok, you can lend it to me later.

-You know Larisa, there is something I would like to do, I would like to take a trip, and I would love for you to accompany me.

-Where to?

-Greece -he remained silent.

-Oh, my love, I would love to, but the children leave for vacation until July and there is still time.

-Well, I thought we would go alone, but I know it is difficult for you.

-Well, I don't know. Now my children are so happy with my change that I'm afraid that if I leave them alone they will resent it.

-I know, love, that's why I know it's difficult.

-Well, let's do something. Let's go out with the children for the weekend. Let's go around here and spend the weekend with them. Let's see how we work. What do you say?

-Oh, my love, you don't know how happy you make me. Sometimes I've thought that my children could be a hindrance in our relationship. I still have many years left before my children fly the nest, and for you, well, it's not easy. You're at a stage in life where what you want is to travel and you don't want to have ties. And well, in some way I have not one but two ties, and the truth is that now more than ever I've been enjoying them. Do you understand?

-Of course, I understand you, and I love that you are now giving them that beautiful love and that you enjoy them so much, I see you so in love with them, how good, that is beautiful.

-But don't you think or feel that they can be a limitation between us two?

-No my love, my children are already adults and the truth is that I love being a father, the truth is and it is not to praise myself, but I am a very good father, but if we want to have a good relationship, you need to dedicate time to me and above all give me some authority with your children, because if we are going to spend a lot of time together, they have to know that I am not only a good friend to them, but that I am your partner.

-They love you very much, the truth is that you have won them over very quickly, they always talk about you and what you have taught them, I love that. But how do I have to give you authority? I don't understand.

-Well, you have to know that first of all, I will never do anything to disrespect your children, or any child, and if I see that they are doing something that is not right, I will try to correct them, and sometimes the corrections, well you know how they are, sometimes they are too loud, like a loud call to attention, I always try not to do that, but there are times when they are necessary, children are growing, and they are discovering how far they can go, they need adults to show them their limits, because if you do not set limits you can be creating a despotic child or a little tyrant, children who do not respect limits and rules, you have done an excellent job, I have observed how you treat them, they obey you, but I have also noticed when you get angry and their reactions.

-Well yes, sometimes I think we have spoiled them too much and they refuse to obey.

-That's where I come in, you need a backup, someone to help you set limits and back you up when you punish them or call them out, but for that to work, you have to give me authority, if you don't give me authority, then I can't help you.

-Ok, I understand, how do I do that?

-Let me tell you my story, when my children were little, if their mother told them something or scolded them, I always supported her and told them that their mother was right, that they had to obey her, so they obeyed her, my son sometimes got arrogant, especially in high school, but as soon as I heard him, I immediately intervened and forced him to respect his mother, and my son understood it; but it turns out that when I told them something, or called their attention, their mother remained silent and did not say anything, so they did not pay attention to me, I had to talk to my wife and tell her: My love, you are making a mistake, you are taking away my authority with the children, realize how I am always supporting you, but when it is my turn to call their attention, you do not say anything and that steals my authority over the children, if you continue doing that, I will not support you anymore and you will see how they do not obey you, have you seen those young people who almost insult their mother and the father just watches them?

-Well, that happens because neither of the parents supports each other. Now do you understand me Larisa?

-Does that mean that if you scold them I have to support you and tell them yes, you are right?

-Exactly, if you don't support me, I won't be able to support you.

-Does that mean that I authorize you to hit them if necessary?

-Hitting is never necessary, I prefer to talk, but yes, I need all your support, I won't be their father, but I can help you, you have to think it over carefully, because otherwise our relationship won't work, I'll have to see you alone without your children.

-Ok, I understand, you know I do, support me, you are a very focused man and I love the way you treat others and especially my children, I have no problem giving you authority.

-Well, then let's take that weekend trip and have fun, we'll see about Greece later - he leaned over and hugged her, placed his right leg between her thighs, and caressed her disheveled hair - you're so beautiful - their lips met.

A knock on the door took them out of their embrace.

-Mom, come on, mom, Daniel was in the hallway knocking on the door.

-I'm coming son, wait, no way, we'll continue later - she said smiling and giving him a kiss.

-Go on - she stood up, her naked body showing him her beauty as she walked to the bathroom, it took her a few seconds and she went out into the hallway with her robe on - what's up Dani, my love? - she bent down to give him a good morning kiss.

-Hi mommy, hey Luigi and I want to see if you can take us to the fair, it's Sunday,

can we?

-Hi mommy, good morning.

-Hi my love, good morning, did you sleep well? -The boy with a sleepy face answered.

-Yes mommy, yes, but we want to go to the fair.

-Yes mommy, go on take us.

-Hello kids, good morning, how did you wake up?

Alberto was standing behind Larisa.

-Alberto, we want to go to the fair, do you want to go?

-Seriously, wow, I love the idea, go on Larisa take us -he said this on purpose to show them that he was part of the team.

-Yes, yes -both children began to dance excitedly- eh, yes - Larisa turned to see Alberto and smiled at him.

-Well, that's it, let's have breakfast and we'll go to the fair.

-Hey, yes, see, I told you that Alberto would want to -both brothers headed to the kitchen.

-You're a pushover -said Larisa hugging him by the waist.

-It will be great, you'll see we'll have fun.

The four of them were having breakfast in the dining room, the service ladies were serving them.

-Excuse me, Mr. Alberto, I have a question, the day of the dinner and we apologize for having heard everything, but well…

-It's good that you were able to listen, I hope it helped you.

-Of course I did, and a lot, it's that, you know, I have a son who, since he was young, hung out with boys from a gang, we live in a poor neighborhood and there is a lot of crime there, in fact, after seven at night few people dare to go out on the street, the police sometimes don't even come in for fear of the gangs, one day they caught my son and jailed him for armed robbery, when you told us…

-You have a son in jail -Larisa asked alarmed.

-Yes madam.

-Why didn't you tell me?

-I was afraid of losing my job, my previous boss fired me when she found out, and I didn't want that to happen again, I've been with you for a year now and I feel very comfortable, don't be angry with me, please -she said with her eyes full of tears.

-No Mrs. Viki, don't worry, I'm not going to fire you, I only ask you to be honest with me, if there's something I need to know, tell me, so we can trust each other and maybe I can help you, okay.

-Yes madam, that's what we'll do.

-What doubt do you have Mrs. Viki?

-Do you really think that everything I've experienced with my son was an agreement?

-Well, what do you think?

-I thought it was God's will, that he had decided it that way, but now I don't know exactly.

-Everything that has happened to us Mrs. Viki, is an agreement, because in that way you can help another person to live an experience, and you can also pay for some karma.

-But, what karma do you think I have?

-Ok, let's see.

-How old is your son, Mrs. Viki? -Daniel questioned.

-Twenty years old, my son went to jail at eighteen.

-Ok, let's see Mrs. Viki, I will give some ideas and you will have to decide if any of them make sense to you. You asked your son that he should lose his freedom, because in a past life you had caused the imprisonment of an innocent young man, and now you should suffer that your son was in jail; or your son asked you, help me to feel abandoned, to feel that I don't matter to you, that way I will hang out with violent friends and lose my freedom, because in my past lives, I sent some friends to jail and I hid, that way I will pay for my karma; Or maybe he needed to be in jail to find his spirituality and help another friend, and help each other get out of that place by paying their karmas spiritually, there can be many options.

-But, how do you know which was the truth?

-What really matters is that you understand that everything was an agreement between your son, you, and the father of your children, to understand that they have not hurt each other, and that each one is living the experience that they planned.

-His father left when he was thirteen years old and he is my only son.

-So, it is true -said Larisa- that he felt abandoned, you work every day and only go out on Sundays, how would you feel?

-Yes, I would feel abandoned too.

-He planned that, living those experiences was his plan, and if that is true, did you hurt him? -questioned Alberto.

- No, if he planned it that way, no, I haven't hurt him, just like my parents didn't hurt me either, with all the blows and insults that I was a victim of, but now, what should I do?

-Have you already done the exercise of the cup of personal love?

-No, I don't really know anything about that, I heard him talk about it, but I don't know how to do it.

-Ok, then that's the first thing, in order to move forward you first need to do the exercise, later tonight I'll explain how to do it, because now we're going to go for a walk -she turned to look at her watch and said- kids, we're going to get dressed to go to the fair. At night I'll explain how to do it, okay? Larisa, do you have the book on couple relationships?

-Yes, on my nightstand.

-Why don't we lend it to Mrs. Viki so she can read it, she's resting today, right?

-Fantastic idea, I'll go get it.

Larisa came back quickly.

-Here you go, Mrs. Viki, read it.

-Thank you, madam, I will do that.

XII Transforming a life

Karla was in her office, organizing some documents, a forty-two-year-old gentleman, tall, in very good physical condition, wearing a dark blue suit, his hair was very well combed, everything about him showed neatness and elegance; he smiled at her from the door.

-Excuse me, I'm looking for the Psychology department, they told me it was around here, but I think I got lost.

-It's here, come in please - Karla felt how her energetic body approached him to look at him, but almost immediately she became aware and turned him back, she felt a little embarrassed - Good morning, I am psychologist Karla Vázquez, how can I help you?

Their smiles made them feel as if they knew each other, their energies at times came and went, getting closer and further away.

-Excuse me, Miss, I didn't introduce myself. I'm Engineer Oscar Ruiz Trejo -he stretched out his hand and as he shook it, an energy ran through his arms- I feel as if I already knew you, your face seems very familiar to me -he affirmed without letting go of her hand.

-Well, I'm sure we don't know each other, I'm a very good physiognomist, I don't forget a face, perhaps in some past life, but tell me, how can I help you?

-I require your professional services, although it's not really for me, I'm certainly a little crazy, but I have it under control, ha, ha -he laughed.

-Are you sure? -she said, half-closing her eyes, in a joking tone, to break the ice and allow him to get to know her- many people believe they have themselves under good control, but as soon as they open up and start talking, boom, the hidden demon jumps out.

-It's true, I agree with you, I hear you speak and I think I will also require your services personally.

-So, what has you so worried that you come to seek help? I hope, first of all, that I really can be the person who helps you solve your dilemma -he said this smiling kindly- but let's do one thing, do you think if shall we sit on the armchairs? - there were two armchairs placed one in front of the other, with a side table next to each one.

-Sure, go ahead, she took her notebook and they sat down, she crossed her beautiful legs, revealing her beautiful calves, her skirt covered her below the knees.

He sat without crossing his legs, his immaculately clean shoes caught her attention, he was a man very careful about his appearance.

- Actually, doctor, I need your service for my daughter, she is very upset lately and I can't find a way to communicate with her, I'm afraid she'll do something stupid, so I suggested that we look for help, and she finally agreed, so here we are.

Somehow, Karla felt very attracted to him, she felt the Kundalini energy rising up her legs and blushed a little, she breathed and shook her head trying to get her mind off those thoughts.

-Are you okay? Do you feel okay?

-Yes, excuse me, it's just that I had a little headache, she said trying to justify herself.

-As I was saying, my daughter is sixteen years old, she's an only child, and her mother and I have been divorced for five years, she lives with her mother, but they argue a lot, I see her on weekends, but for some time now she's been very angry and I don't know how to approach her, I try to hug her and she refuses, she just gets angry and locks herself in her bedroom without wanting to talk to anyone, so well...

-You, Mr. Ruiz, what do you do?

-I have some businesses, I own a law firm and an accounting firm, among other businesses, as you can imagine, I'm hardly ever at home, and on weekends I have many commitments with clients or friends, I try to get my daughter involved in these activities when possible, but lately she doesn't want to go anymore, she just gets angry and throws tantrums, like a little girl, I need you to help me.

-Okay, Mr. Ruiz.

-Doctor, we could speak to each other informally, just call me Oscar, I feel more comfortable.

-I don't think so, Mr. Ruiz, I prefer to maintain that formality, if you don't mind. She was attracted to him and wanted to keep her distance.

-Can I call you Karla?

-Yes, if you feel more comfortable.

-Excellent Karla, she said crossing her right leg over her left and holding both armrests, getting into a comfortable position.

-Before moving forward, I like to do an exercise with my potential clients, to see if we can work together or not, how about we do it?

Yes, of course.

-You believe in reincarnation and karmas.

-Yes, of course I believe in that.

-Well -he said standing up- please Mr. Ruiz, let me have your hands, he stood up, she took his hands and when she felt them an energy ran through them, both were very sexually attracted to each other, Mr. Oscar Ruiz Trejo, if in this life or in any past life, in some way I Karla Vasquez Rodriguez, humiliated you, if I offended you, or harmed you in any way or form, I ask for your forgiveness, I am very sorry, please forgive me.

-Karla -he declared without thinking and caressing her hands- if in this life or any other I humiliated you, offended you or harmed you in any way, I ask for your forgiveness, I am sorry, it was not my intention -the violet flame surrounded them setting their physical and energetic bodies on fire, transmuting their karmas stored in their Akashic records, something was being removed from them.

-Ok -she said feeling her body lighter- this was incredible, but then you and I already knew each other from some past life, you felt that.

-That's right Oscar -she surprised herself by saying his name, she blinked several times, feeling a little embarrassed.

-Wow, how nice, Karla, can I hug you.

-Yes, of course -she returned the hug without hesitation and her eyes clouded over, she didn't know why, but she was feeling it, his warm chest embraced her and she felt protected. He finally separated her.

-Forgive me, Oscar, I must seem like a...

-No, not at all, I think this is not a coincidence, that we met, it's not a coincidence, it's just that it's true, we already knew each other, that's why when I saw you I loved you, when I saw your eyes and your smile, I knew I knew you from somewhere.

-Well, if I'm honest, I felt like I knew you too, but now,

well... - they both sat down in their respective chairs without crossing their legs.

-Karla, I don't want to jump the gun, but I can invite you to eat, it's already lunch time, would you like to join me?

-I don't think so Oscar, I can't go out with any of my patients.

-Then I won't be your patient, just my daughter, can you treat her if you going out with me?

-I haven't said that I'm going out with you.

-I know, but we'll go out, you'll see, I just want to know if you can help my daughter? I think you'd be the right person.

-Yes, I'd like to help your daughter.

-Excellent, give me the appointment for her please, preferably in the afternoon around seven, what day do you have time? -She got up, went to her desk and looked for her cell phone, checked it and said- next Wednesday at seven at night, okay?

-Great, we'll be here, and now tell me, would you like to go to lunch with me? I won't be your patient anymore, we'll just be friends.

-Well -she checked her calendar and said- okay, I have time, my next appointment is until seven thirty.

-Great, let's go,

-Wait for me outside, I have to put my things away.

-Sure, I'll wait for you at the reception, take all the time you need.

He left the office, closed the door and she began to pack her things.

-Wow -she said to herself- I felt as if he had been my husband or someone I loved very much, that was very magical, but is it possible? -she remembered Alberto's words- "If you transmute a relationship and you still feel a sexual desire, it means that this encounter would be good for you."

She left the office, he stood up when he saw her.

-I'm ready, we're leaving.

The blue convertible Porsche was in the parking lot.

-Come in, he said opening the door for her, she sat down and put her legs in, the fitted dress with yellow and brown tones, reached a palm below her knees, allowing him to see her beautiful legs, the V-neck of the dress allowed him to see her beautiful breasts, he felt extremely attracted. He walked around the front of the vehicle and took out his phone, it took him a minute and he hung up, he opened the door and settled into his seat.

-What a beautiful car.

-I'm glad you like it, it's at your service, I've made a reservation at a very nice restaurant, you'll see, I don't like to arrive and have us waiting, it doesn't seem right to me, even less when I'm accompanied by such a beautiful lady.

-A cautious man is worth two, thanks for that, so that's what you do every time you go to eat with a beautiful woman.

-Yes, of course, I only go to eat for business or pleasure, and if that pleasure is with a beautiful woman, then it's better, don't you think?

-Oscar, you're either very cynical or you're too honest, sorry, forgive me, it wasn't my intention, you'll think I'm too trusting, please excuse me.

-Don't worry Karla, I really love your trust, I feel like I've met someone I loved very much, you know, and you treating me like that is the best. As for your question, yes, I'm very honest, I tell the truth, as long as it doesn't hurt anyone.

They arrived at the restaurant, in the parking lot there was a pergola with antique Japanese-style finishes and the main entrance was a circle of black wood, as if you were entering a tunnel, definitely a Japanese restaurant.

-What a beautiful place, do you come here often?

He brought the car to the main door, the young people from the valet parking opened the doors for them and they got out, he approached Karla putting his hand on her back to direct her towards the entrance. The hostess guided them to their table, he pulled her chair and helped her settle in, then he sat in the chair next to her.

-It's one of my favorite restaurants, their food is delicious, I really like their antique Japanese-style decoration, sometimes I've thought that I lived in ancient Japan, that I was a samurai or something like that, I really like everything related to this country in that time of history, as well as the time of ancient France, maybe I had a life in that time too.

-So, you do believe in reincarnation?

-Of course, I've read some books, I'm very interested in the subject of the afterlife, and what there is after death. And you, do you think there is life after death?

-Definitely yes, but tell me about yourself Oscar, tell me your story.

-Well, first of all, you should know, as I told you, I like to be honest, that doesn't mean I always tell the truth, you understand, people are not prepared to receive the truth, many times it offends them and they feel hurt.

-Let's see, explain that to me a little more.

-Yes, I don't like your dress, and I tell you that, I can hurt your feelings, if you knew how to receive the truth from others, that wouldn't hurt you, you would just say: "It's okay that you don't like it, the truth is that I loved it."

-Ok, I understand, and you're right, many times we are not ready or willing to receive the truth, even when that truth is only the truth the other, a friend says that there is no absolute truth, but that each person has his or her own truth according to what he or she believes.

-I totally agree with your friend, there is no absolute truth, and well, I am currently single, I got divorced five years ago, I only have one daughter whom you already know, her mother and I do not have a good relationship, it was a very painful breakup and with a lot of anger.

-And you are still angry.

-Actually, not me, she is the one who is angry, I had a lover and she found out, so well, you already know how those stories end.

-Yes, I know them well, but all of that has a good reason, do you want me to tell you about it?

-Please, I would love to.

-Well, our physical body has an energetic body...

-Mr. Marquez, I need you to be totally honest with me, tell me the truth, because if you lie to me, I will not be able to defend you, I need you to tell me everything, are you guilty or innocent. -Mr. Carlos, it's just that... I... am... guilty -he said, rubbing his hands nervously- I stole that money and blamed my partner, but I don't want to go to jail, you understand, just tell me how much it's going to cost me, don't worry about the money, I have a lot of money in an account in Switzerland, and I can use it, so tell me, how much is it going to cost me? - Carlos' partner approached him.

-Come, let's talk in private -they both left the meeting room.

-Carlos, let's charge him a million dollars, he has enough, and we can do it.

-Let me think a little -in his mind the karmas and debts sounded: "If you don't stop doing what you planned, you will continue tied to karma."- No Rubén, I can't do it.

-But what do you mean? -He said, holding his head- what are you talking about? How many of these cases have come to us and we have defended them for much less money? This is our chance to win a lot in a single trial. We can free him, you know, by paying favors. We will make the files get lost or we will delay the trial for years.

-I know everything we can do, and of course with money everything is much easier, but I am not willing to continue tied to my karmas.

-I understand that Carlos, you told me about it and it seems very interesting, but it would be a million dollars. That doesn't come every month. I am not willing to lose the opportunity.

-I understand you, Rubén, but then let's do something. Let me talk to the client and explain my reasons. If he wants to go free, after we talk, you will defend him. I do not want to be part of that, okay?

-But then, you will not accept any of the money he pays us? Are you sure about that?

-Absolutely, I won't receive a single dollar from that trial, I'll be completely out of it.

-Ok, then you'll talk to him and we'll see what happens. - Both of them went back into the meeting room.

-Well, Mr. Marquez, my partner and I have reached an agreement, I just need to tell you something before accepting your case.

-Mr. Marquez -interrupted Ruben- would you be willing to pay us a million dollars if we get you free?

-Of course, you would, I have no problem, just assure me that I will get out free and clear of all this.

-Ready, brother, it's all yours.

-Mr. Marquez, what I'm going to tell you may sound very strange to you, but it's essential to know if we're going to defend you or not, you can judge me as crazy, but it's essential, do you agree to listen with an open mind.

-Yes, what is it about?

-Good -Carlos stood on the opposite side of the window a little far from his client and said- Can you see my energy around my head and maybe around my whole body?

-Yes, I think I can see it, it's like a whitish mist, -Carlos inhaled raising his personal energy through all his chakras- now it looks clearer, yes, of course I can see it.

-Excellent, what you saw was my aura, we all have a physical body and an energetic body, when we are alive the energetic body is attached to the physical body and that is why our body is hot, have you ever touched a corpse?

-Yes, when my parents died in that accident, I had to go identify their bodies, they were very cold, it is a very special sensation.

-My condolences, I am sorry for your loss, but continuing with this, corpses are cold, because at the time of death the energetic body is released from the physical body and continues to live, in the City of Light, that is where his parents are, truly, they are still alive.

- Well, that is what I have heard, but I am not a religious person, so I do not believe much in that, for me at the moment of death everything ends and there is nothing more, that is why you have to live in the present and enjoy it to the fullest, I am aware that one day I will have to die.

- Good philosophy, but allow me to continue, when the energetic body is released from the physical body, it only takes its karmas or debts, and its Dharmas, you have surely heard of that.

- Yes, I know what that is, but what is all this about? Get to the point, lawyer.

-You see, Mr. Marquez, when a person dies, the only thing he takes with him is his karmas. In this life, everything we do is to free ourselves from our karmas. It is no coincidence that you are here. The three of us planned this before taking the body we have, to help each other live the experience we are living. But if you decide to defend yourself instead of pleading guilty, you will remain tied to your karma, and in the next life you will go through another similar case.

-Are you telling me that I should plead guilty instead of defending myself and going free? You are asking me to live the next, how many, ten, fifteen years in prison?

-Mr. Marquez, I know this sounds a bit crazy, but it is better to free yourself from karmas than to live tied to the wheel of reincarnation. How much money did your father take with him when he died? I say this with all the respect I have for you. How much money are you going to take with you the day you leave your body? How much of all the millions you own will you be able to take with you?

-Well... no, it's just that...no, nothing, I'm not going to take anything.

-Exactly, and do you know how many lives you've been repeating the same thing? The other day I was watching a TV series about a scientist. The man was trying to get out of an overturned car. He finally managed to get out safely through the back window. Inside the car was a young man in the driver's seat. His seat belt was stuck and he couldn't get out. He was yelling at him, "Get me out!" "Help me!" "Please don't leave me, get me out!" The man went back to the car and instead of helping the young man, he climbed in through the window where he had gotten out and took out his briefcase. Then he drove away and the car caught fire. You could hear the young man's howls of pain, and all the curious people in the streets were recording everything with their cell phones. After that, he lost his job, his wife left him, his children wouldn't talk to him, everyone repudiated him. How was it possible that he would have preferred to take out his briefcase than help a trapped young man? Because of all that rejection, the man became a murderer. He died later on, and went to hell. He was again trapped inside the overturned car, he was able to get out of the vehicle through the window, and the young man in the front seat was asking him to get him out, not to let him die, he came back and took out his briefcase, walked away, and saw all the people coming with their cell phones saying to him: Damn you, why didn't you help him?, bastard, no, no, he shouted at them, you don't understand, I have my research here, a second later, he was again inside the overturned car and trying to get out through the window, after managing to do so, he went back for his briefcase and as he walked away people came to him saying, damn you, bastard, why didn't you help him?, the scene was repeated over and over, over and over, over and over again he saw people saying to him damn you, selfish, why didn't you help him?, hundreds and thousands of times he saw himself being pointed at and rejected by people, and returning to the overturned vehicle, you can imagine the man saying, no not anymore, they don't understand I..., and again, and once again, can you imagine? Your guilt, Mr. Marquez, kept you in your self-created hell. - Carlos remained silent, his client had a lost look, Carlos' words had had an effect, Ruben was also very thoughtful- Every event in our lives, Mr. Marquez, is an opportunity to stop doing what is wrong, to be able to free ourselves, if we continue acting doing what is not right, we remain tied to karma, and even if you do not believe in hell, your guilt will take you there.

- But no, I do not believe in hell.

- Okay, but we all believe in our guilt, and we keep those guilt's inside us, because we know that what we did was not right.

- But then, what should I do, should I declare myself guilty?

- The first thing you must do is a very special exercise. - Carlos explained to him how to fill his cup of personal love, when he had finished he said- Mr. Marquez, I propose something to you, go home and do the exercise, talk to yourself, and after doing it, we will talk and make decisions, do you agree?

-Yes -he said very thoughtfully- yes, I will do that and then we will talk -they stood up and said goodbye.

-If you have any doubts, when you are in front of the mirror, call me, it will be a pleasure to guide you.

-It will not be necessary, I clearly understood everything that needs to be done, but that thing about the inner children, just like that, should I ask them to come out?

-Yes, ask them and wait, let's see what happens.

Mr. Marquez left. Carlos and Rubén were alone, still sitting in the meeting room.

-Wow bro, that thing about hell, wow, that was very strong, you even made me think.

-I had already told you that you have to do the exercise, if not, you will not free yourself, don't you notice me very changed?

-Of course, I do, and a lot, I love your way now, the secretaries have also noticed it, the vibes here are different now. -Okay brother, do it, don't stay tied to your karmas, hell is real, and even if you don't believe in it, it exists, besides, you don't have to do this out of fear of hell, that's not the way, you have to do it to free yourself from the pains of your childhood and to love yourself and your inner children. You know what, we're going to do something, is everyone in the office?

-Yes, everyone is here,

-Call them, I want to talk to all of them -Ruben stood up, opened the door, went out into the hallway and shouted.

-Young people, gentlemen, ladies, urgent meeting for everyone, come on, please come, leave everything, this is important.

The room began to fill up, everyone was sitting in a chair.

-Friends, I want to take a little of your time to explain something to you.

-What is it about boss?

-Do you know what karma is?

-I do -said his secretary.

-No, I don't -answered one of the lawyers.

-Ok, a karma is created when you hurt someone, when you steal, lie, cheat, kill, or do something bad to someone, and a dharma is when you help or do something good for someone, karmas are debts that must be paid... -Carlos continued explaining, once everyone understood he said- The other day I saw a television series, and a lawyer entered hell: She was sitting at the kitchen counter of her house, having breakfast with her two children and her husband, then one of her clients arrived, a very special one who was guilty, but she had freed him from jail, lying and using her intelligence to free him.

-Well, Carlos, that's what we do -said one of the lawyers- we use our knowledge to make a lie become true.

-Exactly, that's what we do, it turns out that this lawyer was having breakfast with her children when this client came in and said to her: Thank you, Christie, he took out his gun and shot her two children in the head, while she screamed, No, no, not my children! Then he shot her husband in the chest and finally her, when she was falling to the ground, a fraction of a second later she was back standing at the bar with her children and her husband, having breakfast very happily, when another different client came in with a gun in his hand and said, thank you, Christie, then he shot all three of them, to finally shoot her, when she was falling to the ground, in a fraction of a second she was back on her feet, and the scene was repeated over and over, over and over, over and over, hundreds of times, thousands of times, the pain of seeing her children die with their heads exploding from the bullet, and then her husband, was repeated thousands of times, that was hell. -Oh no -said his secretary- no, boss, why are you telling us this? That's very...

-Difficult?

-Boss, it's that we are dedicated to getting many guilty people out of jail, so what do we have to do, how do we get rid of karmas?

-From now on we will only defend those who are innocent, that way we won't be filled with karmas.

-But Carlos -said Rubén- those who pay the most are the guilty ones.

-True Rubén, but I prefer to be poor than to live full of riches and full of karmas, believe me, hell is not worth all the gold in the world, I prefer my mental and spiritual peace.

-Wow boss, so we will only defend the innocent?

-That's right, unless one of you wants to defend a guilty person and lie to get him out of jail, you can do it, but I won't participate in that.

-But will the office support us?

-I'm afraid I don't know what to do yet, so I'll give you my answer later.

-Boss, how do I free myself from my karmas?

Carlos explained to them how to do the personal love cup exercise in detail, when he had finished he continued.

-If you don't get all those pains out of your cup, you won't be happy, nothing you do will make you happy, how many people do you know who are very rich in money and yet are unhappy?

-That's true, I know many clients with a lot of money and they are so unhappy.

-They are unhappy, because in the end their cups are still full of pain and empty of their self-love; by the way, I have a gift for you, wait here - he left the meeting room, everyone was talking about this, he came back a few minutes later.

-Well - he placed a stack of books on the table - I have a gift for you, read it, it explains how to do the exercise of the cup of personal love.

His secretary read aloud.

-"Relationships and Sex, build your relationship from true love, a different way of loving, so that love lasts a lifetime", by Ariel Oliver Comparán.

-Hey boss, this sounds very interesting.

-It is, study it, don't just read it, it's worth every word that's written there, and think about hell, okay, do you have any doubts?

-Boss, we have an open case that we are already working on and he is definitely guilty, he is free on bail.

-I know, let's cite him and talk to him, let's see what happens.

-Hey Carlos, but what if they don't agree to plead guilty, what do we do? They have already given us the advances, we won't be able to return them.

-Don't worry, we will solve it, I am sure that the universe wants us to stop filling ourselves with karmas, so everything will be resolved in favor of good.

-Boss, we have three cases where our clients are innocent and they are suing the other party, what should we do?

-Let's cite them all separately and talk to them.

-Hey Carlos, are you going to become a spiritual counselor or something like that? Are you serious?

-There are no coincidences, brother. I think this was my life agreement, to help as many people as I can to teach them how to free themselves from their karmas.

One of the secretaries asked him.

-Counsel, my sister has a problem. Yesterday a lawyer showed up at her house. It turns out that she is about to lose her house. What do you recommend?

-Is the loss of her house unfair?

-Her husband is a gambler, and it turns out that he pawned the deeds and she had not told him anything. Now they have come to demand payment of the debt. He lost all the money. They are going to take away her house unless they pay, but they do not have the money.

-Ok, Patricia, in short, they have a karma with that matter. In this life, the way we agree to pay a karma is that they do to us what we did. In other words, in some past life, her sister took the house from someone. She surely lent money to someone and since she did not pay, she took her property. Now she asked, do to me the same thing that I did to feel what they felt, that way, if I recognize the damage I did I will free myself from karma, if I die angry and with all those resentments, then I will remain tied to karma.

-But then, what should she do? Should she defend herself legally or what?

-She should first do the exercise of the cup of personal love, before making any decision we should all do that exercise, then, once our cup is full of our personal love, we can decide what to do, defend ourselves or not, and let life take care of it; if she loses the house it is because it should be that way, and that, if she does not have anger or resentment, neither with her husband, nor with the creditor, then she will be paying her karma; if she does not lose the house, it will be because it does not have to be that way and then she will keep it, in some way clearing her karma will free her from the loss.

-Hey Carlos -asked Ruben- if from now on, this is going to be like this, we are going to be out of work, nobody is going to need a lawyer to defend them. If what they have to do is pay a karma by letting them sue them without defending themselves, and accept the result, where do we fit in?

-I've been thinking about it the last few days, and you know what, I think that, if we all understood the importance of paying our karmas, to be able to free ourselves from this planet, and win the return to our world of origin.

-What do you say boss, let's see again, please?

-Karma is a debt that keeps us tied to reincarnation on this planet, all those debts accumulated during many past lives, do not let us free ourselves. Freeing ourselves means being able to return home. All of us come from higher worlds, belonging to the fifth dimension, or to something much higher, and we enter this planet, to learn about love, in all its forms, during our lifetime we have hurt, lied - he raised his eyebrows and looked each one straight in the face - raped, offended, hated, and many etcetera's, those facts tie us to the planet, and do not let us return home, so if you do not resolve and pay those debts, you will not be free from this world, and therefore, you will not return home. I, personally, have decided to work to free myself from my karmas, and if that means giving up being a lawyer, I am willing to do it.

- But partner, is that serious, would you leave everything we have worked for, for a spiritual fantasy?

- It is not a spiritual fantasy, can you see my energy around my body?

- Yes boss - said one of the lawyers, and they all nodded - that energy is real, it exists, and it will leave this body when it dies, through that energy I will continue to live, and I will take another body, until I have completely freed myself from my karmas, only then will I return home. You have to understand, Ruben, that you will not take with you from this life, not one cent, no jewel, or car, you will not take with you any of the wealth that you manage to accumulate, the only thing that remains attached to you are your karmas or your Dharmas, so you must decide, do you want to continue clinging to wealth and money? Or do you want to take advantage of this life to free yourself? Choose.

-Oh boss, what you are telling us is true -said one of the lawyers- my father was a man who made a lot of money, and he took nothing, just as he was not happy, despite all the wealth.

-Read the book that we are giving you, you will understand all this better.

-Boss, are you really willing to leave your career and everything you have built?

-Totally, this life is the best opportunity I have to free myself from my karmas. I might think that I will do it in the next one, but as my friend Alberto told me: "When we enter the planet we lose our memory, and we forget everything we have lived in past lives, so we have to start trying to free ourselves again." I prefer to do it in this one when I am already conscious, and work spiritually, mentally and emotionally to free myself. I don't want to do it in the next one, I want to do it in this one.

-So, to pay for a karma, I have to stop defending myself and accept everything in peace?

-Exactly, stop defending ourselves and accept anything as payment for a karma.

-If someone comes to you with a gun in his hand and shoots your son, do you just accept it and not defend yourself? Are you serious?

-Yes, Ruben, at the moment I'm not saying that you don't get scared or that you don't feel angry, but if you understand karma, you'll know that you did that with someone else, you killed someone else's son in a past life, you understand that you asked, do this to me to pay my karma. My friend Alberto says that nobody is really dead, that everyone who has left their body is alive in the City of Light.

-I saw a movie about that -said one of the secretaries.

-Yes, that movie is called "Our Home, by Xico Xavier", watch it, it's very interesting. And so, if we understand, my son, who was shot, will not actually be dead, he will just leave his body, but he will still be alive, and if I accept the fact of his murder as payment for one of my karmas, then I am free, it is as if my son gave me the opportunity to relive the loss of a very loved one, to feel again, the rage and anger, and if I stay with those feelings, then...

-You remain tied to karma -the secretary intervened- I understand, wow, so everything is like a play, right boss, everything is just a play?

-Exactly Paty, that's right, you understood it perfectly. Do you get the idea Ruben?

-Yes, yes, -answered his partner- by explaining everything, of course I can, I can understand it. We are only living a performance, where the actors help each other to live certain experiences in order to pay for karma, if we do not forgive, or stop doing bad things, then we are not free, and the goal is to free ourselves from the planet to return home. Wow, this is really interesting.

-Well, friends, let's get back to work, think about all this. Please read the book, and do the exercise of the cup of personal love, so you can understand more and better.

-Wow, Karla, all this that you tell me is incredible, but ultimately, I feel it is completely true, when I saw you, I felt that I knew you, and ultimately, I think it is true, you and I have something very beautiful from past lives, I must confess something to you, when you took my hands, I felt a very beautiful energy, almost sexual, but as soon as you started to...

-To transmute our karmas.

-Yes, that's it, as soon as you started to transmute our karmas, and then I, I told you that, I felt like something was lifted off me and my sexual desire for you, well, not that I don't like you, because I do, I love you, but at that moment my sexual desire vanished, I feel very happy with you, but it's not a sexual desire, you know what I mean.

-I understand you perfectly, that we met was our agreement, to help us free ourselves, and it's not a coincidence that we did it days after I knew all this, if we had met three weeks ago, you and I would be having sex, that's for sure.

-Ha, ha, ha, incredible, don't you think? -both remained

silent- cheers, darling, for this beautiful reunion -both clinked their glasses-. Hey Karla, let's see, thinking about this a little, we already transmuted our karmas or debts that we might have together, that means that we are free of past debts, right?

-Yes, that's right.

-I like you a lot, do you like me?

She remained silent and brought the glass to her lips, while looking into his eyes, she took a sip very slowly.

-You're not saying anything?

-Yes, Oscar, I do like you.

-Would it be bad if I keep looking for you and we get to know each other a little more? Who knows? Maybe something good will come out between us, after all we know that what we had in the past was good and with all this knowledge, well, I don't know, what if something fantastic turns out.

-Well, she thought a little, remembering the book of marriage rings, you know I recently read a book that I loved, if you really want us to see each other again to maybe form something together, you have to read this book and you have to do the exercise of the cup of personal love, I already explained that to you.

-Yes, ok, I have no problem, I like to read, what do you say it's called, she took out her cell phone, gave him the title and looked for it, here it is, is this it?

-Yes, that's it, read it and study it, do the exercise, I'll notice if you really did it.

-How are you going to know that I did it? Are you going to spy on me? -she narrowed her eyes and smiled.

-I'm a sorceress, so I'll notice -she indicated smiling widely.

Karla opened the door to her office, and a sixteen-year-old girl walked in. She was wearing black jeans that were a bit too big, a black t-shirt with a rock band print on the front, black platform boots, black varnished nails, her hair was black with blonde streaks, she had a lip piercing, and another one in her nose, her personal style was totally dark.

-Hi, you must be Kimberly.

-Hi, yes, she said reluctantly.

-Please sit down, Karla pointed to the chairs and sat down in one. Welcome Kimberly, what a nice name, why did you choose it?

-It wasn't me, it was my mom, she loved it.

-Ok, but it wasn't your mom, it was you, but well, I'll explain a little more later.

-Okay, she sat in the chair with her legs together and holding on to her forearms. -Tell me Kim, I can call you that, I'm Dr. Karla, my friends call me Karla.

-Yes, Kim, my friends call me too.

-Tell me, how have you been, are you happy?

She remained silent and a moment later said.

-No, I'm not, you know, I've thought about committing suicide, I don't want to be here anymore.

-Why? What, specifically, don't you like about your life?

-I don't like anything, everything stinks, my house, my bedroom, my relationship with my mom, school, everything stinks, and I don't want to be here anymore - a state of fury made her open her eyes as she spoke, and then one of disappointment depressed her feeling defeated.

-Ok, but help me understand you a little more, I know you're an only child, that makes you feel like that.

-Alone, I feel alone, my mom is hardly ever home, I grew up with maids and they... - she remained silent, Karla sensed what was coming and approached her without touching her.

-Tell me whatever Kim, don't be ashamed, just trust me, nothing you say will be known to your parents unless you authorize me to tell them, but if you don't want, nothing you and I talk about will be known, okay?

-Okay.

-Will you trust me? -Karla looked at her sweetly, sending her thoughts: I love you, Kim; Don't be afraid, everything will be okay; You can trust me.

-Yes, was her answer, the truth is that I need to talk, I don't want to keep anything to myself anymore.

-Excellent, I'll be your confidant, okay? So, tell me, what happened with the domestic assistants in your house?

-Years ago, when I was a child, one of them was very old, she was about twenty years old, I was only five. She helped me bathe and touched me all over, and I liked it, but one day she told me that I shouldn't tell my parents because then she would kill them and that scared me a lot - the crying started to flow, she took a disposable tissue from the box on the side table and wiped her nose and eyes - from that day on I didn't want her to bathe me anymore, but I couldn't push her away, she was older and I couldn't tell my mom, I just told her that I didn't want her to be there anymore, that I didn't like her, but my mom didn't listen to me and I had to get used to it, later, over the years, I liked women. My dad was never home, he always came home late at night, then they divorced and I went to live with my mom, my dad kept the house, I didn't see him for many years, when I turned fourteen, I looked for him and we were able to reestablish a relationship, but for some time now I don't want to be with him, I stay at his house, but...

-Has he touched you sexually?

-No, he doesn't, but he has a friend who comes to the house when my dad's not home, and he always harasses me, he threatened me that if I told my dad he would deny it, and that would cause my dad to lose a lot of businesses that make him a lot of money, so that's why I don't want to be at his house anymore, but my mom is now living with an older man, she fell in love, and he came to live with us, he's also been harassing me, he's very affectionate and I like him a lot, he hugs me and is loving, but I feel when his hugs have another intention, so I don't want him to hug me anymore, and that's why I don't want to be at my mother's house anymore, I have nowhere to be in peace anymore, my only refuge is my room, I lock myself in and turn my music up loud, I fall asleep and wake up at night, my mom put a special sponge tube under the door so that the noise from my bedroom can't be heard. I feel alone, my friends tell me to get out of there and go to another city together, to live alone, forgetting about our families.

-And what do you think about that idea?

-I like it, but it scares me.

-Unfortunately, Kim, most of the young girls who leave home end up in prostitution, being abused by pimps, older men who beat them and use them so they can earn a lot of money, they induce them to drugs and they end up selling their body for a few coins, to be able to buy drugs. Do you want to live an experience like that? Do you think you need to live an experience like that?

-No, of course not, but I don't know what to do.

-Well, the first thing is to understand the following, this Kim, is not your first life, have you heard of reincarnation?

-Yes, I have seen some videos.

-Ok, let me show you something. He took a ring binder from the bookcase with the following message on the spine:

REINCARNATION. He placed it on the young woman's legs and began to show her photographs of some children and adults who claimed to have been reborn. He briefly told her their stories and how they turned out to be true.

-But then it's true, we've all lived past lives?

-Yes, that's true, we've all lived, not one, but hundreds of lives, some have lived up to five hundred lives on this planet.

-Five hundred lives, that's a lot.

-Yes, but the reason why we are reborn is our Karmas. Do you know what that is?

-One of my friends at school says that it's when you do something bad to someone, that karma is created.

-Exactly, that's it, when we hurt someone, when we humiliate them, when we sexually or emotionally abuse someone, when we steal, lie, take drugs or sell drugs, etc.; anything that hurts someone else creates karma for us, that is, a debt that we must pay with that person or with someone else, in this life or the next.

-Let me see if I understand you, if I sexually abuse someone, do I create karma with that person, and do I have to pay that karma?

-Yes, we must pay those karmas, and the way to pay them is for someone to do to us the same thing that we did to that person.

-No, doctor, then, that woman abused me, when I was six years old, because I did the same thing to another girl in a life past?

Karla remained silent, she just nodded her head.

-In order to change something in our life Kim, the first thing you have to do is see it, I repeat, you have to see what you have to change, if you don't see it, you won't change it. Did you understand me? If you understood me, repeat what I told you.

-Yes, I think so, in order to change something, I first have to see it, if I can't see it, I can't change it, that makes sense.

-Exactly, so now let's see what happened to us.

-Ok, ok, I understand, it's just that... -she said upset, lost in her thoughts- everything they did to me, was because I did it to someone else, and that's the way to pay for my karmas? Is that what you just said?

-Yes, that's how life works Kim, but it's not enough for someone to do it to you, for the karma to be paid, you have to give thanks,

-Do I have to thank those who have abused me? Is that it?

-Yes, you have to thank that person for having done what they did to you, but that forgiveness, you must do it from the bottom of your heart, did I explain myself?

-Yes, I understand

-Okay, now think about this a little, everything bad that happens to you is because of karma, so that you pay a debt. If that's true, all the people who have helped you live that experience, have they hurt you or have they helped you?

-Have they... helped me?

-Think about it carefully, and tell me an answer with all certainty.

Her eyes filled with tears and she said

-They have helped me, yes, they have helped me.

-And if they have helped you, what feeling should you have for them, should you hate them, should you be angry, should you hold a grudge against them? What feeling should you have for those people?

Kim, she couldn't stop crying.

-Why can't I stop crying? I don't understand.

-Because you are acknowledging that all of them didn't hurt you, that's why you cry, but you haven't answered my question, what feeling should you have for those people?

-I should thank them -her lips trembled- that's it, I should thank them.

-Well said Kimberly, well said, you have to forgive and give thanks, thank you for everything they have done to you. Now I have a task for you, there is an exercise called the cup of personal love, are you ready...

Carlos and Rubén were sitting in the meeting room, and Mr. Márquez came through the door, his face looked very rejuvenated, he looked ten years younger, his skin had a special glow, he smiled very happily.

-Mr. Márquez, welcome.

-My dear lawyer, what... -he approached Carlos and hugged him- thank you, thank you, you don't know how grateful I am, that exercise is magical, I have cried a lot, you don't know how much, look at me, I barely remember and I cry again, but not from sadness, but from joy, do you understand?

-Of course, I understand, and it's true, it's an exercise full of magic, I'm glad you did it.

-I had never cried the way I did, I took out so many things, things that had made me a very hard man, always thinking about money and material things, then I loved myself, and how..., it's just that... -his eyes betrayed the love he had given himself- no one ever loved me like I did with myself, never, and now... it's just that I feel so happy, that...

Carlos waited a little for him to calm down and then, when he believed it was the right moment, he said:

-Mr. Marquez, the reason why "bad things" appear in our lives is because we have a karma related to those things, we have done to someone the same harm that others do to us. That is the way to pay for karma. This is not the first time that you, in some life, have committed fraud, and it is not the first time that you have been freed from jail, you have done it before, that is why you repeat living the same experience.

- Are you telling me that this is not the first time I have committed this type of act, and that, on this occasion, it is presented to me to pay for karma?

- Yes, exactly, and if you refuse to live the karma as a payment, you will remain tied to that debt and will live that experience again, so that you understand me, let me explain the agreements, - Carlos began to speak, he explained the agreements, he spoke about the City of Light, the karmas and the Dharmas.

- But, then what I am experiencing is an agreement, between the other people involved and me, and between the three of us, to be able to pay our karmas?

-Yes, if I agree to defend you to get you out of jail, if you are guilty, then I remain tied to my karma, but if I refuse and thank you for the opportunity, then I am freed from karma.

-And from hell.

-Yes, I am freed, but if you do not recognize what you did and do not accept the payment that the law imposes on you, then you will remain tied to karma.

-And to hell - he repeated with his gaze lost on the surface of the desk - so, do you suggest that I declare myself guilty and accept any penalty that the law imposes on me, how do I pay for karma and that will free me from hell?

-Yes.

-And what about money, will I have to return it?

-Money is part of the trap of life, it is what leads us to commit all kinds of acts to obtain it, you should not tie yourself to money, free yourself from the love of money, at least from ill-gotten money.

-But it's not that simple, my family, my children, what are they going to say about me?

-They had all already agreed with you to live that experience.

-In the City of Light?

-That's right, so you're not harming them, you're allowing them to live their experience, and they, instead of despising you, should thank you for helping them live this.

-I feel so happy, what do you know, Attorney, yes, I'm going to plead guilty and accept the sentence imposed on me, I prefer to pay my karmas and free myself, then to follow the path to hell. Hell isn't worth all the money in the world.

Rubén was silent listening to him, he resisted doing the exercise, he thought he didn't need it.

-I sincerely congratulate you, Mr. Marquez, do you want us to represent you or do you prefer to go with other lawyers? - Rubén turned around in amazement to see Carlos.

-No, of course I want you to represent me, prepare the documents and I will sign them, I am willing to live whatever I have to live, as long as I don't get to that place.

-The best way to avoid that place is loving life, continue filling yourself with your self-love, your personal love, and give that love to everyone you meet, and make your money bless the people around you, it is not by fearing hell, but by loving life, and the good, that we truly free ourselves.

-I understand perfectly, thank you very much, lawyer.

-Wait a second, -Carlos stood up and went out into the hallway.

-Mr. Marquez, is that exercise really so powerful?

-Don't tell me, lawyer, that you haven't done it?

-No, not really, my partner tells me that it is necessary, but I don't believe in many of the things he says.

-Well, you're making a mistake, sir, a very big mistake. Look at me, I almost don't look any younger.

-Yes, definitely, you look very good.

-What you see, sir, do you think I would have achieved by going to the spa, or putting on creams? No, of course not. This is very deep. I got rid of so much pain, a pain that I had no idea was inside me, and now I'm loving myself in a way that's wow. -Carlos came back, with a book in his hands.

-Mr. Marquez, receive this gift from both of us. I hope it helps you to be happier and to live a different life. Enjoy it, study it more.

-"Relationships and Sex, build your relationship from true love...", ok, it sounds very interesting.

-It is, I'm sure you're going to love it. Do you have any questions? We will prepare the documentation and present it, we will let you know what the judge told us and we will give you the date to appear. Are you afraid, Mr. Marquez?

-No, I'm not afraid, it's just that I think about prison, it's definitely not a place I would like to go to.

-A friend taught us that, in order to make things easier to understand, we should see ourselves as what we truly are, we are God, the creative mind, living inside a vehicle, our physical body is the vehicle, and the creative mind is the driver, when the vehicle is no longer necessary it will die, but the driver will continue to live in the City of Light.

-Or in hell -he said, shaking his head negatively- lawyer, that is an extremely interesting way of seeing us, so are we really God, the creative mind?

-Living inside this vehicle? -Ruben intervened while touching his face.

-That's right, my friend made us understand that life on this planet is actually a great theater, and that each one of us was the writer of what would happen to us in this life.

-Is that what we use agreements for?

-Exactly, that's right, that's what agreements are for, to help us live what we planned.

-Thank you, Mr. Carlos, thank you very much, today I'm

going to meet with my children, they haven't seen me, you'll see the surprise I have for them.

-Have a good time, Mr. Márquez, enjoy your new life. The three of them stood up, he gave each one an affectionate hug.

-Mr. Ruben, -he said taking him by the shoulders and looking him in the eyes- you can't not do this exercise if you want to be happy; I'm leaving, with your permission. -He left the meeting room.

-Wow, partner, you still don't believe that you need to do this, there's no doubt about it, there are woods that don't take varnish, ha, ha, I'll leave you, I have things to do, by the way, have you started reading the book yet?

-No, not yet.

-I assumed so, I'll leave you.

-Good morning Mrs. Maciel, please sit down, Mr. Maciel, welcome. The clients had been summoned to help them resolve legal conflicts.

-Well, sir, why did you summon us? What's so important?

-Mrs. Maciel, I want to talk to you about something I've discovered and that's extremely important. Carlos began to explain about the energetic bodies, he spoke to them about Karma and debts, about reincarnation, and they understood.

-I have read books about this, Mr. Lawyer, so what you are telling me is not new to us. In fact, I thought about it a lot before coming to you to file the lawsuit, but I am so outraged by what they have done to me that I cannot let it go unnoticed.

-I understand your anger. I would be the same as you, but if you think about it carefully, perhaps in a previous life you did the same thing to them or to someone else, that is why you planned for them to do the same to you.

-It is true. If I look at it from the point of view of karma, it is true. I did that in past lives. But then, you recommend that I drop the lawsuit.

-It will depend on you, do you want to remain tied to karma and money or material things, or do you want to free your souls from debt? Because remember, when we leave these bodies we will not take a single cent of the millions we may have, but we will take our karmas, which will tie us to the wheel of reincarnation to live the same experience over and over again, until we can free ourselves. -The couple turned to see each other.

-It's not worth it, love, -he said- even if we think they deserve it and that we can win, I think that if we remain angry, we will actually be losing, so I say that we give up, it's not worth it.

-You're right, you know what, sir, do it, let's give up.

-Excellent decision, but there is something you have to do, you must transmute your debt, I recommend that you repeat with me but from your heart: I, say your full name, I ask for your forgiveness brother, if I stole from you, humiliated you, failed you in any way in this or in past lives, I ask for your forgiveness, I am truly sorry, forgive me - both repeated the words closing their eyes, she placed her hands on her chest, while the violet flame set them on fire transmuting their Akashic records and freeing them, the feeling that something was lifted off them was real. As soon as they finished, they opened their eyes, turned to look at each other and hugged each other.

-Wow, sir, what a special feeling, I feel as if ten kilos had been lifted off me, something special has happened.

-That is real, your karmas have been removed and that feeling of lightness is for the same reason. For the legal aspect, we will present the withdrawal before the judge, we will let you know.

-Sir, this is very special, but I'm afraid that if you do this with all your clients you will be out of a job, don't you think?

-Of course, I know, but now I understand that if I chose this career it was to free myself from my karmas, and one of them is not being honest, you understand me, I must defend the guilty or the innocent and that means lying. So now, I choose to free myself from my karmas and if that means stopping practicing law that will be fine for me, I prefer my spiritual peace, after all this life is just an act, a perfectly executed role, when I leave my body I want to make sure I don't reincarnate again and return to my home of origin.

-And what is that, sir?

-We all come from higher worlds, from worlds of fifth, seventh or higher dimensions, we enter this planet and forget who we are and why we came, then we tie ourselves to karma and debts and that forces us to reincarnate again and again.

-Wow, that is a very interesting vision, I think I am going to take it into account from now on to free myself from this world and be able to return home.

-That, Mr. Maciel, is the true meaning of life, returning home after having learned many lessons about love.

-Thank you, Mr. Carlos, you don't know the peace I feel -he said- I think this has been worth it, the rest is not important.

-Then, take charge and let us know the result.

-That's what we will do, Mrs. Maciel, sir, it was a pleasure to greet you.

-Mrs. thank you very much, Mr. Rubén, it was a pleasure to see you, although you were very quiet now.

-Everything is fine, Mrs. Maciel, sir, we will take care of it.

Kimberly was sitting in front of the mirror, her thin body naked, she didn't like it, she looked at herself with disgust, she tried to look into her eyes, but she couldn't, just trying made her want to cry, she tried again, she looked directly into her iris and she could only do it for a couple of seconds, she felt ashamed, she never imagined it would be so difficult, the doctor's voice echoed in her mind: "You have to look into your eyes, as difficult as it may seem you have to do it, your eyes are the door to the inside of your soul, so you have to do it." She tried again, and she could see herself, although her eyes were beginning to release her tears. When she was able to speak she said to herself:

-Kimberly, -the crying didn't let her continue, she had to breathe heavily- now I see you, and I want you to know, that when I was a baby I felt alone, why mom? Why did you leave me alone? I was a baby, I was very small and you didn't love me, I never mattered to you, why? -She continued talking to herself, she spoke of every pain kept inside her cup, she cried every memory, every abandonment, every abuse, many moments that had to do with sex, she cried everything she kept, she recognized that she dressed in black because she was angry with her father and that it was a way of punishing him, he always rejected her for the way she presented herself to her friends.

After crying for a long time, and taking out all her hidden pains, she looked into her eyes again, but without feeling shame, and began to caress herself. The doctor had told her: After crying, you have to look into your eyes and caress your body to love it, talking to yourself and saying beautiful things about yourself. She began to do so.

-Kim, I love you beautiful -the tears did not stop- forgive me, forgive me for having abandoned you, because I did not love you, I was very angry, and I blamed you for everything that had happened to me, please beautiful, forgive me, I love you Kim, I love you so much -she caressed her face and her hair- forgive me, I will not abandon you anymore, not anymore, all of them helped us live our debts, thank you, thank you all for helping us -she continued passing her caresses all over her body, and giving herself love, this was filling her and she felt happy with each caress, she reached her vulva and put both hands on it - forgive me beautiful, forgive me, I did not want you to be hurt, forgive me, now I will love you, I will take care of you, forgive me, I love you beautiful, I love you, -she continued giving herself caresses and filling her cup of her personal love with each one of them, she did not leave anything of her body unloved, she did not want to stop doing it, each nail and each foot They were loved...

Doctor Karla was sitting at her desk, a beautiful young woman, without any piercings on her face, perfectly dressed, with tight blue jeans and a white button-down blouse, with very clean white tennis shoes, smiling at her standing in the doorway.

-Hello doctor.

-Wow, beautiful, come in - Karla couldn't help it, she stood up and went to hug her.

-Doctor, -she said crying leaning on her chest- thank you, thank you.

-Come in Kim, come in, sit down, you look so beautiful, tell me, how did it go? How do you feel? -both of them settled into the armchairs.

-This was incredible, I did what she told me, I sat in front of the mirror naked, at first I couldn't see myself, but then, it's just that... I cried so much, -her eyes were shedding some tears again, reminding her of her pain-, I didn't know she had so many things stored, -Karla handed her the box of disposable tissues.

-Kim, tell me everything, don't hold anything back.

-It's just that, actually, I don't feel so much pain anymore, yesterday I talked to myself, and I thanked everyone for doing something for me, I felt happy to be able to do it. When I thanked, I felt a beautiful peace, yes, that was it, a beautiful peace. Then, I started to love myself and that was, wow, -she ran her hands over her arms caressing herself- that was incredible, no one had ever loved me like this, now I feel so happy -she wanted to cry again, but resisted, inhaled and sighed- it's that, every time he touched me my skin would get goosebumps, you understand, when he got to my vagina, I asked for forgiveness, for everything, I just asked for forgiveness, it's that I had abused her so much, that...

-Say it, don't be ashamed.

-She was abused because I did that to someone else.

-Yes, but what you did to someone else, it was because she asked you to, it was her agreement, there is no guilt, do you understand?

-Yes, and that makes me feel very free.

-That's what this is all about, darling, that you free yourself from everything they did to you and from what you did. How do you feel now?

-Happy, doctor, I feel happy, how do you see me?

-Beautiful, you look beautiful and liberated, now I can see the real Kimberly, the other one was just a mask, a mask you put on because you were very angry.

-Yes, yes, that's it, I was very angry and I dressed like that to keep men away and to make my dad go away too, he got very angry when he saw me dressed like that.

-I understand you, and what else.

-After so much crying and loving myself, I saw myself in the mirror again, I looked so pretty, my skin was different -she ran her hands over her face- I looked so beautiful, I couldn't believe it, after a long time, I got dressed, I put on shorts and my shirt to sleep, it was around eleven at night, when I heard the main door, my dad was coming in, I went out to the hallway and ran to the entrance, he turned to look at me, scared, because I scared him.

-Kimberly, what's happening, is something wrong? -he said to me.

-I couldn't tell him anything, I just ran up to him and hugged him, I cried a lot- thank you dad, -I said- thank you -he caressed my hair.

-Why are you thanking me darling? What happened?

-Thank you, dad, because now I understand that you haven't hurt me, that everything was our agreement and that you only did what I asked you, forgive me for being angry with you, I didn't know, I didn't know that I had asked you, -he hugged her tightly and with much love.

-Forgive me, daughter, -the tears appeared, it had been a long time since she had allowed him to hug her- forgive me Kim, I love you very much, forgive me, if I humiliated you, if I hurt you, if I offended you in any way, forgive me my love, it wasn't my intention. -Both cried hugging each other giving their love, the violet flame surrounded them transmuting their karmas and debts, freeing them.

Karla, breathing deeply to keep from crying, smiled,

-Kim, now there is another task that you have to do, let me explain. Since we are born, we all begin to live the experiences that we ourselves plan, in this way we live the abandonment of mom or dad, sexual abuse by someone, theft, abuse of all kinds, as well as we also live things of great love, like the affection of dad when he came home after a long day of work and hugged you, or with mom when she took you to the park and you were very happy, you felt loved, or with your grandparents and then, as we grow up we begin to live different experiences, some very painful and others very happy, that is how our life goes by, until we reach the present moment, but all those experiences remain stored inside us, you already realized, when you look at yourself in the mirror, right?

-And yes, I didn't think I had so many things stored.

-That's normal, many of the painful things that happen to us, we send them to the unconscious and they stay there until we see them again, we understand them, we forgive them, we free them and we free ourselves. That's what you did in front of the mirror, you entered your unconscious and it opened showing you everything you had kept.

-Yes, that was beautiful.

- True, yes, but what you have to understand is that each stage of our lives has sweet and bitter things, "good" and "bad", and inside you there are one or several Kimberly's, those little ones were the ones who lived all those pains and abuses, as well as the good things that have shaped your life. Now, being at home, you are going to sit in front of the mirror again and looking into your eyes you are going to talk to those little ones -the young girl's eyes did not stop crying- you are going to tell them beautiful things, you will recognize how brave each one of them was, how intelligent, how loving, etc., praise any quality that each one of them has, and then you are going to ask them to come out of yourself and you are going to wait, you will tell me how it went.

-Ok. I understand, I have to ask them to come out of myself. Should I get naked?

-No, it is not necessary, tell me Kim, do you feel that there is something that you have not talked about.

-No, not really, I feel very light, and very happy.

-That's good, darling, now, in front of the mirror, you need to love yourself again, every day a little more, every time you see yourself in the reflection of a glass or in a mirror, you are going to say beautiful things to yourself, you will see only the good in you, and how valuable you are, you Kim, you are the most beautiful love that exists in the universe, repeat that.

-I Kimberly, am the most beautiful love that exists in the universe.

-Again, now with more love and emotion, feel the emotion of each word.

-I -Kim closed her eyes and put her hands on her chest- am the most beautiful love that exists in the Universe! -she shouted opening her arms wide.

Karla smiled feeling her.

-Well said precious -she applauded excitedly- now, you have to give it to yourself to then give it to your parents and all your friends, do you understand me? Only if you love yourself can you truly love someone else.

-Thank you doctor, -both stood up and hugged each other- thank you very much.

-Karla released a tear of joy not only for having healed Kimberly's soul, but because she had discovered a very powerful tool that she would use from that moment on with each patient, the change had been sensational, just being able to see her dressed like that, truly being herself, a sixteen-year-old teenager, loving herself, dressing like a beautiful young woman, made all her years as a professional worthwhile.

-Hello beautiful, how are you?

-Hello my love, everything is fine, I've had a lot of things to do.

-Beautiful, I have to go on a trip, something unexpected came up.

-Ok, Alberto, will you be long?

-No, my queen, I'll be back in a few days, I don't know how many exactly, we'll keep in touch, ok. Hey Larisa, say hello to your dad, Valgarma, and your children.

-Of course, my love, I will, are you going to stop by to say goodbye?

-No, my queen, excuse me, I already have everything in the car and

the exit to the highway is close to my house, because of the traffic I would lose a lot of time going to your house, so I ask you to excuse me, I send you many kisses, put one on your forehead, another two, one for each cheek and ten more so that you can put them wherever you like.

-Mmmm my love, you are turning me on, don't say those things to me, ha, ha, ha.

-I'll leave you my queen, we'll call each other later. -They both hung up their phones.

Alberto got into his convertible car, started the vehicle, the sun was shining on the horizon, and headed towards the highway, the traffic was a little heavy, he put on classical music and relaxed, he had been driving for over an hour, he was not in a hurry so he did not exceed one hundred and twenty kilometers per hour, he wanted to take his cell phone, but it slipped from his hand and fell under his seat, he quickly bent down to take it again, and for a moment he lost sight of the road, when he looked up from the ground, in front of him was a parked truck, he could not stop and crashed headlong into the back of it. Alberto appeared walking, on the side of the road, while his car was embedded in the back of the truck, his body sitting in the driver's seat, was covered in blood.

-Hello son. -The road disappeared and next to him were his parents.

-Mom, Dad, but, how is it possible, what...?

-Hello son, we were waiting for you. -But... I don't understand, what happened? Both parents stepped aside, and Carmen walked towards him.

-Hello my love, we were waiting for you.

End

To the reunión of Love

Words to the reader

Dear reader, I hope that this novel has touched your soul, and has awakened the desire to change your life. Even though the characters are fictitious, they reflect the reality of the life that many of us have lived, so I invite you to do the exercise of the cup of personal love, in front of the mirror, to love yourself, and then, bring to the surface the most beautiful love that exists in the universe, and of which you are the owner, so that this love blesses your life and the life of those who are lucky enough to know you. Afterwards, bring out your inner children, love them, recognize them, thank them, because thanks to them you are today, this beautiful being, so make them happy with your love.

You are very special, do not allow death to find you without having awakened to that unique and beautiful love. Perhaps the reason for coming to live on this planet was to bless the world and those who live in it, so allow us to know your unique and special love.

Once you have brought this exclusive love to light, give it to everything you do and to everyone you come into contact with, together you and I can take this planet to its higher dimension, to its fifth dimension. Can I count on you?

Receive my blessings, with love.

Ariel Oliver Comparán

About the author

Ariel Oliver Comparán

Born in the city of Chihuahua, Chihuahua, on June 18, 1964. Third son of seven siblings, his father was his great teacher and his mother his teacher in love.

He graduated in Fruit Engineering from the Autonomous University of Chihuahua. He currently resides in the city of Puerto Vallarta, Jalisco, Mexico.

He inherited his passion for writing books from his father, Rogelio Oliver Hernández, who was also a recognized author in the field of Vocational Guidance.

He has currently written seven books:

"The Transformation of the Universe, the end of darkness and domination." Books 1, 2 and 3.

"Relationships and Sex, build your relationship from true love. A different way of loving, so that love lasts forever."

"Beliefs, how to change them to Transform my life."

"Awakening Your Potential, Guide to Becoming Better Parents and Raising Happy and Powerful Children!"

"I chose to be chubby, Overweight and obesity, how to solve it. A spiritual vision and a real solution,"

Author contact links

Web

www.arielolivercomparan.com

Facebook

Ariel Oliver C.

Instagram

Ariel Oliver C.

@arieloliverc.mx

YouTube Channel

Ariel Oliver C.

Email

arieloliverc@gmail.com

To the reunión of Love

Ariel Oliver Comparán

Puerto Vallarta, Jalisco, México

October 2024

To the reunión of Love

Made in the USA
Columbia, SC
01 February 2025

52422494R00250